I heard the footsteps again, finally. But they were getting louder; he was coming back.

I saw the same glove slide around the side of the door like a moray eel slithering out of its lair, and swing it open. The quick glance I got through the tiny slit was enough to see the trenchcoat, the hat, and the glasses of our old friend the wall-smasher from the mill building scarcely a mile distant. And almost instantly a change came over me; all the fear turned to anger. I remembered Mary unconscious in the mill yard. I remembered the way he'd shot at us. I didn't like the skulker in the raincoat, hat, and glasses. I didn't like him at all. . . .

Also by Rick Boyer
Published by Ivy Books:

BILLINGSGATE SHOAL

MOSCOW METAL

THE DAISY DUCKS

THE WHALE'S FOOTPRINT

THE
PENNY
FERRY

Rick Boyer

IVY BOOKS • NEW YORK

For my brothers, John and Bruce,
and my sons, Clay and Ted

Acknowledgments

The author wishes to thank the following people for their help with the manuscript: John Boyer, Phyllis Lang, Bill Tapply, and Paul Tescione. Dr. Tescione, in addition to providing technical medical information, also gave the author a name for an entirely fictitious character in this book.

The Hot Item

THAT LADY STANDING OUT THERE IN NEW YORK HARBOR has welcomed a lot of people to this country. Some, like my wife's father, made out very well here. A lot of his countrymen weren't as fortunate, and wound up working in the mills.

Two of them, a shoe trimmer who lived in Stoughton and a fish peddler from Plymouth, got an especially raw deal. But that was a long time ago, and nobody cared much anymore except the Italian community. Or so we thought . . .

Then a friend of ours came to grief up in the factory town of Lowell, and even his two attack dogs couldn't save him. Somebody still cared about those two guys. Cared enough to kill people. At first I just went along for the ride. But then I kept inching my way into the mess, bit by bit, until I was right smack in the middle of it.

1

1

Mary and I wound our way down the plush pile-carpeted stairs of Joe's Beacon Hill apartment building. The paint and carpeting of the dimly lighted stairwell smelled new. They were. Joe leaned over the banister and yelled down at us.

"Have a good time at the ball, children. And Doc, if you see Hunter Greyson there, ask him why I wasn't invited."

"Why would they think you were a Republican?" I asked. "With a name like Brindelli?"

"Are you a Republican?"

"Naw. Not much of anything. You know that."

"Yeah. But your last name is *Adams*. See what I mean?"

Mary paused on the lower landing and looked back up at me.

"I don't think I want to go to this thing, Charlie. Hell, it's only because Hunter and Kathleen insisted we go . . . Hey, Joey—if it's real snooty I'm coming back here, okay?"

"Now, Sis, it wouldn't be fair to all the Brahmins if you—"

"Shove it," she said, swinging her way around the final newel post and down into the lobby. I heard her high heels clicking and clacking on the terrazzo floor. I joined her in the lobby. The wallpaper was burgundy-colored silk with thin white stripes. The oak doors were covered with lots of

2

brass, and the windows were thick bevel-cut leaded glass that gave off a prismatic effect of rainbow hues.

"Hard to believe that a cop lives here," I said. And indeed it was, since the fourth-floor apartment had cost a pretty bundle. Joe had skylights, two terraces, and a tiny rooftop garden. This was not made possible through his salary as a state policeman; it was possible because Joe and Mary's late father had done extremely well in business. And although Hunter Greyson, senior partner in the law firm of Greyson, Morrison, and Stands, knew we were related and close to Joe, he had not extended him an invitation to the Beacon Hill fund-raising party for Joseph Critchfield, the man who was supposed to be our next governor. I wondered why.

We walked along the ancient brick sidewalk of Pinkney Street, where Joe's flat was, to Cedar Street and over to Mt. Vernon, which Henry James once said was the only civilized street in America. Typical of him. I'm partial to South State Street in Chicago myself. Mary clicked and bounced along. Her cheeks shook a tiny bit with each step, and her ample bosom jounced. She's a knockout.

"What's the matter with these creeps anyway?" she finally said. "They think every Italian's a Democrat?"

The party was being held at the Greyson home in Louisburg Square. We entered and joined the other two hundred or so guests. Sipping champagne, we ambled our way down the hall and up the stairs to the formal living room, which was huge, with a fourteen-foot molded plaster ceiling. Here there was more food and drink, and an informal receiving line where we met "the next governor of the Commonwealth of Massachusetts," Mr. Joseph Carlton Critchfield III.

He shook my hand warmly, and beamed.

"Are you of the Boston Adamses?" he inquired. I told him no, the Chicago North Shore branch. He looked momentarily confused, then complimented Mary on her beauty. She couldn't help smiling. He was pretty slick, and had Grade A credentials and a flawless record of public service to go with the poise. Joseph Critchfield III was a graduate of Choate and Harvard, and had taken a law degree from Harvard as well. He had distinguished himself in his own firm and more recently in several state offices, which he'd handled admirably. In fact, his grandfather, who was still alive, had once been the state attorney general. And Joseph Critchfield was only forty-six—younger than I. It was hard not to be impressed by him.

Mary and I walked through the line and took another champagne into the sunporch. A big hand clapped me on the shoulder from behind, and I turned to see my hunting and fishing buddy, Brady Coyne. Brady's an independent lawyer who specializes in serving the very rich. As a graduate of Yale, he's somewhat of a maverick in the town that worships the Crimson. It was Brady who recommended me to treat Hunter for a badly abscessed tooth several years back. Even the very rich and successful can get abscessed teeth. And Hunter Greyson and Joe Critchfield were classmates at Harvard and still bosom friends. So that's how it happened that Mary and I were among the invited to meet, and contribute to the campaign of, the candidate who would replace the current Democratic governor. This incumbent represented corruption, patronage, nepotism, and all the other bad things associated with the big-city machine politics Boston is infamous for.

"We need this man, Doc," said Brady. "We need him very badly if Boston is to stay competitive with the Sun Belt cities that are drawing away our high tech. I mean, Jeeez . . . who's going to put up with this kind of bullshit forever, huh?"

"I agree," I said. "People are sick of paying through the nose for the privilege of getting ripped off."

We followed the flow of guests back to the big room, where chairs were being set up. Mary looked around the room. She was going to drool any second, I thought. She gazed covetously at the oil paintings, antique Chinese porcelains, Persian rugs, and Hepplewhite furniture. And we don't live in a slum, either.

"Ladies and gentlemen," said a loud voice. "If we may have your attention for a few minutes, Joe Critchfield would like to say a few words about his platform to save the Commonwealth of Massachusetts."

There was applause and cheering, and the impeccably dressed Joe Critchfield positioned himself next to the concert-grand Steinway. Resting one hand on it, he assumed a casual yet elegant stance and gave a brief speech, in which he thanked us for our support and explained his program to bring our city and state back on course. It was good. Afterward he answered questions, and did an equally good job. Certainly, if the gubernatorial race came down to a televised debate, Critchfield's opponent would be hard pressed.

Then came a tough question. "Joe, I'd like to open by saying that your platform sounds terrific," said a middle-aged lady. She was standing in the back and had on a bright flower-print dress. "But I suppose I have one big reservation about how you're going to implement it. How do you propose to defeat the Catholic labor–ethnic coalition? How can a Republican break up the Irish-Italian bloc vote?"

A murmur of assent rippled through the crowd. Apparently the lady had hit it on the head: how indeed defeat this vast, monolithic majority?

"That's a very good question, Anne. But I'm going to answer by saying something that may shock some of you. I say this: the so-called Irish-Italian Catholic voting bloc no longer exists. Certainly the ethnic groups do. Our Irish and Italian neighborhoods are still very strong and sharply defined. I also think they're a tremendous asset to this city and to the Commonwealth. But I submit to you that as a voting bloc that's impregnable—I simply say that it's a myth. Don't forget, ten years ago we had Frank Sargent, a Republican, in the statehouse. It's been done; it can be done again. People are sick of the way the state's being run. I ask you, all of you: what issue or event could occur tomorrow that would unite them? For example, if the Sacco and Vanzetti case were tried today, would the law-abiding citizens of the North End support those two radicals? I say no, and furthermore—"

"Just a minute!" came a clear voice. It cut through the room like a tungsten ice pick. Now who would have the nerve to interrupt Joe Critchfield in the middle of his talk? Critchfield was staring at me, his mouth halfway open. No. He wasn't staring at me, he was staring at the person who'd stood up next to me. He was staring at Mary.

"Are you implying that Sacco and Vanzetti were common criminals? And if so, that they were guilty?" she demanded.

There was another murmur that rippled through the room. But this one was confused, chaotic, disgruntled.

"I, uh . . . no, that's not what I meant—or implied—I was speaking of their radical connections, that's all. But as to their guilt or innocence, surely you cannot deny that the evidence was overwhelming in favor of their having been connected—"

"If everyone will excuse me," cried another female voice, "I really think it will be most constructive, considering all we have to accomplish here, to confine the discussion to the issues at hand rather than to history."

There was applause. Loud, steady applause, directed at Anne, the lady with the flower-print dress in the back, who'd gotten Joe C. III nicely off the hook. Mary sat down, folded her arms across her chest, and glared.

After the talk was over she didn't clap. People looking at us saw that she didn't clap. I clapped a little, and she glared at me. People avoided us afterward. All except Brady, who winked at Mary and said, "Way to go, Mare!" But we both had the feeling he didn't really mean it. I thought we'd better thank Hunter and Kathleen before we left, but they seemed to be nowhere near us. Ever.

"I think it's time to fade, Toots," I said under my breath.

"Yeah. Sorry, Charlie. It was just a reaction. A conditioned reflex. I guess it reflects my childhood more than anything. Hell, I don't know if they were guilty or not—"

We filed out of the house, smiling bravely. A few people

returned the smiles, but mostly everyone looked away. We passed the small table where people were writing checks and stuffing them into envelopes. Nobody even seemed surprised when we walked right past it.

"I'm still voting for him," I said as we walked back down Mt. Vernon Street. "I think he'll do a good job."

"I think so too. But his attitude. I just—oh, forget it."

As we turned the corner I saw a gigantic Cadillac limo sweep along the street at a whisper. It swung to a slow stop in front of Louisburg Square. It was probably the original Joseph Carlton Critchfield, the candidate's granddaddy. Purportedly, he was backing young Joe financially. If this was true, then Joe would run out of gold pieces about when the rocks would melt into the sea and the lion would lie down with the lamb. It made me a little less regretful I hadn't written a check.

So we walked back to our Joe's. He greeted us at the door and asked Mary if she'd lost her glass slipper.

2

NEXT DAY I WAS JUST SITTING OUT THERE IN OUR SUNPORCH sipping on a silver bullet when I saw Joe's unmarked cruiser slide into our driveway. Here to get a free Saturday dinner. He got out of the cruiser and made a beeline for the porch steps. He moved fast and gracefully for a big man. I had been listening to James P. Johnson riffle the ivories in a stride number called "Old-Fashioned Love." The sidemen were good too: Cootie Williams on cornet and Eddie Dougherty on drums. I took another sip of ice-cold gin.

"Hi, Doc," he said as he came in. "What's for supper?"

I set the martini down on the coffee table and looked up at his dirty mask of beard stubble. He hated to shave on Saturdays. Maybe because shaving was such a big job for him—like a farmer cutting a field of wheat. On a normal person a day's growth is a faint shadow; on a Calabrian it's a death mask. I slid the glass along on the rattan, watching the trail of condensed water it left in its wake.

"Spaghettios," I said.

His face fell slack.

"Say it ain't so!"

He grabbed a cane chair and spun it around in front of him. He straddled it backward, laying his head on his big beefy hands, which rested on the top of the chair back. He tapped a Benson & Hedges out of a long pack and lit it. He studied my drink carefully, the way Itzhak Perlman would study a Strad.

"It might interest you to know, Joe, that I've been on the phone all afternoon trying to locate someone you introduced me to last year: Johnny Robinson."

"Well, Johnny's usually not too hard to track down, Doc . . . *if* you know where to look. If you're using him professionally, then what, may I ask, is Dependable Messenger Service carrying for you?"

"Remember Tom Costello? The stockbroker? Well, I've completed an anterior fixed bridge for him. That's a whole set of uppers all the way back to the canines, plus all the interior joinery. In materials alone the piece is worth maybe a grand. In terms of labor, add another grand. So I've been using Robinson and Dependable to carry these expensive pieces from the lab. Lately a lot of the mails from there have been ripped off—"

"Don't I know it. Post-office junkies looking for the gold."

"So now I've got Tom all over my back. Don't blame him, either. How can a broker peddle stocks with no mouth? The piece was due yesterday, but so far I can't raise Johnny."

"Did you call Sam at Dependable's office?"

"Yeah. Closed. Saturday."

"Of course. Well, we could go up to Lowell and hunt Johnny up if you need the thing right away. I know his hangouts pretty well. Hey, were you serious about Spaghettios for supper?"

"Could be."

His eyes returned to my frosty glass. He eyed the silver bullet wistfully.

"Nice-looking booze you got there."

"Yes, isn't it though? Mmmmmmm. Dee-*lish*."

He drummed his big fingers on the cane back irritably. He glared in my direction. Joe was about as subtle as his sister. After ten seconds the glare became pronounced. Oh, all right.

"Would you uh, care for a drink, Joe?"

"You bring it and I'll care for it."

"Don't steal mine while I'm gone. I'll get Mary and we can, uh, plan supper. To pass the time you might telephone Robinson again. Want the number?"

"Naw. Every good detective in Boston knows Johnny's number. But if he's not home I know where he is. Leave it to me."

I headed for the sideboard to make him a gin and tonic, and on my way thought about the unique career of John Robinson.

He was a black man about sixty years old. In his younger days he was a fighter, although he never made it to the big time. But he was tough and he was straight. These two qualities comprised a natural foundation for what was to become his career. John Robinson was a foot courier. With his partner, Sam Bowman, he had founded Dependable Messenger Service in Cambridge. He walked around the city carrying important papers, cash, stock certificates, jewelry, and prize lottery tickets. Much of his business centered around the wholesale jewelry houses down on Washington Street, for whom he toted pocketfuls of ice and bars of silver and gold.

With his Smith and Wessons, his rearview mirrors, his stun-gas canister, and his two German shepherds he was a human Brinks van. Only he could go through the twisty little Boston alleyways, up and down dark stairs, and in elevators and such, where a van could not go. He was routinely seen working in places and with people that most security companies want no part of.

Mostly Robinson kept his mouth shut, discretion being essential in his work. But every now and then he'd dangle a little tidbit on the grapevine. Joe had told us several stories in which he played a key part in bringing bad guys to justice. Generally he put information on the line when he sensed that somebody good or innocent was about to get hurt. Once his indiscretion almost cost him his life. He screwed up a big deal for some North End biggies and they had his legs broken. Then they had him dumped into the cold harbor water off the General Ship and Engine Works in East Boston.

Johnny couldn't swim so well anyway; with two broken pins—not to mention the pain—it was a bit tougher. But Robinson was nothing if he wasn't tough, and he somehow got out of there before he died of exposure. Later, he helped send the two thugs to Deer Island.

Mary was in her atelier firing pots. She was hovering near a brick beehive structure in the center of the large workroom, wearing old stained overalls, welder's gloves, and dark goggles. She was looking in through the kiln peephole, and a bright circle of orange light was flickering on her face. A blast-furnace roar came from the kiln, which was fired by the bottled gas in big steel tanks outside. I shook her arm and she removed the goggles.

"Baby brother's here."

"Joe's here: it must be Saturday. It's *Saturday*? Oh Jeez Charlie, and I haven't even thought about supper yet."

"Better start thinking; you know his delicate appetite."

We walked back to the porch. On the way Mary doffed her baggy overalls, which left her in jeans and a cotton blouse. The cassette deck was now playing Bessie Smith singing "Merry Christmas Blues" with James P. Johnson backing her up on the piano. No trills and frills, just solid stomping chords to accompany that legendary voice that never sang a note without bending it.

"I can't get Johnny at the Lucky Seven," said Joe.

"What's the Lucky Seven?"

"A bar up in Lowell where Johnny hangs out on weekends. He doesn't go there to drink, just to visit with the neighborhood regulars. Whenever I've gotten in touch with him before, I've reached him either at home or at the Lucky Seven."

"Well, if and when you get him ask him about my package from the lab, will you?"

A new number came over the tape: Art Tatum riffling through "Cotton Club Stomp." It was a toe-tapper. Tatum was going through the piece with that pyrotechnic, no-holds-barred style of his that put his fingers all over the keyboard.

He was everywhere at once, making all other piano players, past, present, and future, seem like they've got triple arthritis. The sound was so spellbinding that Joe stopped and listened.

"Hey that's great. Who is that guy?"

"That guy *was* Art Tatum."

"Wow! Never heard of him."

"That was the problem; not nearly enough people ever did. He died broke."

Like so many unrecognized geniuses in the arts, Tatum drank himself to death before he'd even peaked. *Sic transit gloria mundi,* as they say. "Any more thoughts on dinner?" I asked Mary.

"No. Gee I really don't feel much like cooking, Charlie. I've been firing stuff all day and I'm hot and pooped. Don't you guys think it's hot for early June?"

"Yeah," said her brother, who placed himself directly beneath the whirling blades of the ceiling fan. Mary seemed suddenly to be aware of his presence and went over and kissed him. She almost took her skin off in the process.

"Why didn't you shave? You look awful."

"Got up late. I was going to shave here." He hesitated a second before adding, "Uh . . . you know how I sometimes stay for supper?"

"Sometimes?"

He gave me a hurt look, then turned back to his sister.

"We could go out to eat, or . . . *or* . . . I could make my veal and eggplant parmigiana—"

This suggestion sent my salivary glands into a brief grand mal seizure.

"Well why didn't you say so? Care for another drink?"

"What made me think of it was thinking about finding Johnny Robinson up in Lowell. There's a great little meat market up there. Not as good as Toscana's, but still great. They slice the veal right off the carcass. Doc, if you really need that thingamajig, I'm pretty sure I could track Johnny down for you. Then we get the meat and eggplant and head back here. Mary, you can fire your pots; Doc, you can re-lax—I'll do it all.''

Well, that settled it. Mary wanted to come along, so the three of us got into Joe's cruiser and headed up Route 3 to Lowell, about twenty-five minutes away.

"And you really think we can track down Johnny? It would be great if I could get that anterior bridge for Tom this week-end," I said, watching Mary fiddle with the dials on Joe's two-way radio.

"No guarantees. But I've known and worked with Johnny for years. So have most of the other cops. His routine doesn't vary much. He's got no family and sticks pretty close to his old neighborhood where he grew up. I've got a hunch if he's up there, we'll find him.''

Lowell is not pretty; but it wasn't designed for aesthetics. Like the other towns along the Merrimack River (Lawrence, Nashua, and Manchester), it was laid out in the early part of the last century to see how many big buildings could be squeezed along the source of water power and barge traffic. Then a lot of effort was expended to see how much machin-ery each building could hold: looms, carding machines, spinning machines, and finishing machines, and how many immigrant workers—of all ages and sexes—could tend these machines for the maximum number of hours on scant wages without falling down and dying of exhaustion, hunger, dis-ease, or grievous injury.

This cruel experiment in Social Darwinism lasted roughly from the 1830s until the First World War. During its duration a few families and corporations made enormous fortunes, and many thousands of new Americans were chewed up and spit out by these gargantuan mill complexes. Then in the twentieth century, at an ever-increasing pace, the industries left for other places where they could find other people to tend the machines for less money and so do the whole ghastly thing all over again.

For all of its freedom and efficiency, capitalism can be a night stalker. A benthic fish with gaping jaws and snaggle teeth. A Jabberwock. Looking into these old buildings can be enough to turn a hardened Republican into a trade unionist. If you ever get a glimpse of these mills in action (some of them are still working in these New England towns), it's a spectacle you won't soon forget. As you leave your car, even a block from the building, you can hear the giant locomotive thump of the looms. The walls of the mills are thick masonry, the windows shut or boarded, but the sound comes through: a monstrous syncopated two-stroke thumping of the swinging loom arms and frames. It is a pulsing mechanical heart that shakes the old wooden steps as you climb inside. Then go through two or three more doors and you see the huge interior halls with rows and rows of big metal machines, with racks of bobbins twirling off thread like fishing reels. And on the far side spills out cloth, inch by inch, made in thunder. The women who work here wear ear protectors, but they're deaf anyway.

You shout and cannot hear yourself. The women walk to and fro on the old wooden floors, which are soaked with oozing oil and clotted with fibers. The machines are fuzzy-soft with grease-soaked lint. The floor shakes and trembles underfoot with the swinging metal and spinning flywheels. Sometimes even the old endless drive belts of wide leather remain overhead shrieking on the wooden drums. Perhaps the most depressing thing is that the women don't complain, don't plan to quit and move on to something else. They just serve out their time here on the gummy wooden floors, ears protected against the clank and thump, but already deaf.

And this scene makes you realize that there are two New Englands. There's the one with kids dressed in blazers and madras blouses strolling on green lawns surrounded by ivy-covered walls, and there's this one trying to prop it all up. This one made of veiny-armed, pocked-faced kids in factories, of frowzy old ladies in cotton print dresses and torn stockings worn over purplish puckery legs, tending the machines in the din.

We wended our way along the twisting streets to an area

near the river and the General Electric wire and cable plant. A little side street off Broadway was lined with two-family houses. The area was green and offered a nice view of the Merrimack River. The university was within walking distance too. This was a nice section of town; no wonder that Johnny Robinson had elected to stay here and commute into Boston and Cambridge. Joe pulled up in front of a gray house. It was sided with asbestos shingles and had white trim. It was well maintained. There was a wide stairway up to the open front porch. But Joe took us to a roofed side stairway that snaked up the far side of the house and led to a door on the second story. He rang the bell, waited, and knocked. There was no answer. We went downstairs to ask the neighbors, but nobody was home.

"The dogs weren't barking, so he's got to be out with them," said Joe, leading us around the corner.

We went over to the Lucky Seven tavern, which at five in the afternoon was filled with regulars sipping draft beers and rye and gingers and watching the Red Sox. A man behind the bar was adjusting a rack of potato-chip bags. He had a damp bar rag slung over his shoulder. Nobody had seen Johnny, so we walked back to the house.

"There's his car," said Joe, pointing to a new Olds Cutlass. "He can't be far."

"Where do we try next, the laundromat?"

"Dunno. He'll be back shortly. Listen, Doc, I just know that if Johnny did pick up that dental work for you, it's sitting right on his coffee table. Tell you what. You two wait here. Sit down on the front steps while I go get the groceries. Be back in twenty minutes."

So we sat there until he came back. Still no Johnny. Now Joe rubbed his beard stubble and looked a bit worried.

"When was he supposed to deliver the stuff to you?"

"Yesterday."

"And he didn't call or anything?"

"Nope."

Joe went back to his car, opened the trunk, and returned carrying a metal toolbox.

"Follow me," he said. And we did.

At the top of the small side stairway, just outside Robinson's door, Joe set the toolbox down and opened it. It was dark up on the landing but we could see that the box was packed with tools, most of which were strange to me. The most familiar things were two gigantic rings of keys.

"Johnny's not going to like this particularly, but it's not like him to default on a delivery and not telephone. Hmmmm. Medeco D-Eleven deadbolt . . . piece of cake. Baldwin pin tumbler mortise lock . . . Big lock's *unfastened*—he's been home . . ."

He hummed a little ditty while he burgled the door, and before very long we stepped inside the dim apartment. "Good thing I'm an honest man," he said, turning on the lights.

The living room opened right off the door. The window shades were half up and the sunlight looked bluish in contrast to the yellow-gold glow of the sun passing through them. Faded gingham curtains wafted in and out with the slight breeze from one window which was wide open. There was a love seat against the wall and two old stuffed chairs that had seen better days. Much better days. A TV sat on a small table facing the couch. Above the couch on the wall were boxing photos of Robinson in his prime; with his almost shaven head, he looked a bit like another Massachusetts fighter: Marvin Hagler of Brockton. There were some big posters too, publicizing upcoming fights.

"Oh *Christ*," said Joe in a weary voice. I followed his gaze down the short hallway and saw Robinson sprawled on the floor. He had that frozen spastic look, that almost comical appearance of the silent-movie pratfall, an embarrassing flumpy look of a pile of old clothes with a person inside.

He was dead.

Joe stayed where he was and held up his hand as a sign for us not to move.

"Tommy! Here Tommy!" he called. "Susie! Susie? Here girl!"

Silence and stillness. Mary started for the man on the floor, but her brother held her in check.

"Hold it, Mare. If Johnny's here he's got a hundred and eighty pounds of fur and fangs with him. And they can tear hell out of a *Tyrannosaurus rex* when they're mad. Here Tommy! Here Susie!"

I started down the hallway.

"Tommy and Susie are either gone or indisposed," I said, "or they'd have been on us like lightning when we first came in."

I knelt down on the worn carpet runner and looked at the late John Robinson. Handsome. Smooth, nut-brown skin that was tight and unwrinkled. A kind face with large and expressive eyes. Short salt-and-pepper hair, like mine except curly. His eyes were open a fraction. He still wore his Windbreaker jacket. His clothes were the ones he wore when working: blue gabardine uniform well tailored, almost dapper on his fine body. There wasn't a mark on him. I could see no blood anywhere. Heart attack? Sudden cerebral hemorrhage?

Joe knelt down beside me and let out a slow sigh.

"This was one nice guy, Doc. A good man who never made a crooked buck and who always helped people who needed it, even it if meant sticking his own neck out. This makes me sick."

"Could have been accidental. Look, the body's cold but not stiff. Then he's been dead for over twelve hours. He's still got his coat on; he'd probably just come home. Maybe he was walking toward the kitchen and just collapsed. An autopsy will tell us."

"Where are the doggies then? *Tommy! Susie?*"

I looked up at the old black wooden door at the far end of the short hallway. The doorknob side was cracked and splintered along its length, as if the door had been smashed open.

I opened it and looked inside at the tiny bedroom. Mary stood behind me, looking over my shoulder.

"Here they are, Joe. In here. Looks like it wasn't accidental after all."

One dog was just inside the door, lying on its back and twisted through the body as if it had died in pain. It was a female shepherd, the one Joe had called Susie. The bigger, darker one—Tommy—was frozen in front of a window that was open all the way. He was lying on his stomach, his head on his outstretched paws. His mouth was partly open and his lips curled in a frozen snarl. Both dogs were unmarked.

"How the hell were they all killed? Doc, see any signs of bludgeoning?"

"No. But that doesn't mean there wasn't any."

Joe went back to Robinson and knelt down again, pointing at the holster on his belt.

"Look here," he said to us. "Smith and Wesson model ten, a standard-issue thirty-eight. Never taken out of the holster."

"But look," said Mary, "this strap is unfastened. Don't people carry it snapped?"

"Good eye, honey; yes they do. So Robinson came home, shut the door behind him, and began walking down the hall with his jacket still on. Then something happened. Somebody jumped him and the dogs . . . or *something*. But whatever it was, it was fast. He saw it or heard it, but only had time to flick off his carrying strap."

"And he had the reflexes of a boxer, Doc. He was very fast for an older guy, and tough too. I wonder . . ."

Joe pulled up Robinson's right pantleg. There was a small holster strapped to his leg with a tiny snub-nosed revolver in place.

"His belly gun. Smith and Wesson Bodyguard Airweight. Untouched. Let's try the other leg."

Up went the left pantleg. Fastened to the left calf was a bone-handled stiletto. Finally, on his belt up under the Windbreaker was a spray canister of Mace.

"He was a walking Sherman tank," I said. "Too bad it didn't do him any good."

"This is real nasty, Doc," said Joe, glancing around nervously, "and it looks like a pro job too. Looks like some of Johnny's old enemies finally caught up with him."

"But what killed him?" asked Mary.

"A good question. No marks are visible on him or the dogs. No blood either, except in the bedroom, where Tommy tore into someone. So John Robinson, fighter, armed to the teeth and with two big attack dogs, comes home from work Friday afternoon. Now they're all dead. Doc, how would you handle a heavily armed boxer with two dogs?"

"Gas."

"Exactly."

I dropped to my hands and knees and looked around.

"There's no odor remaining," I said, "but that's to be expected. It was yesterday and windows are open. Thing is, how was it dispersed? It had to be fast—"

"To your right," said Joe. "There, next to your knee—"

I reached over and retrieved a pair of glasses with gold frames and tinted lenses. Attached to the top of the frames were two small convex mirrors, one on each side. They were the type worn by bicyclists for seeing backward. With these two mirrors out on both sides Robinson could see directly behind himself, in the manner of horses and deer. The mirrors were most useful when he walked up dark narrow alleys and stairwells, where hiding places and thieves abound.

"Now," pursued Joe as he leaned over me, "these glasses were thrown off to Johnny's right side. Let's assume he was walking down the hall as you suggested. His glasses being four feet from him means they were flung off his face, right?"

"Right. Probably when he spun around fast."

"*Real* fast, Doc. As fast as only a boxer can turn, like to avoid a punch, no?"

"Uh-huh," said Mary. "He spun his head to the right and at the same time jerked the safety strap off his gun. So there was something—like a noise—right near this table."

And on my hands and knees I was looking at it. A faint conical stain lay on the wallpaper directly under the table. It spread out as it rose like an inverted triangle. It was dark; it looked like smoke. I decided not to lean over and sniff it. Then all three of us were looking at it. There was no doubt it was a scorch mark.

"An explosion," said Joe.

"Yeah. And the explosion is what sent the gas flying all over the place instantly. Thing is, how'd they get the explosion to occur when Robinson was right nearby? And what sort of canister did they use?"

"Took it all with them. We'll be able to identify the gas, though. I'm gonna call the lab now. Don't move anything."

Joe went out to his cruiser to call the crime lab and the locals. We had some time to kill. I wandered back into the small living room and snooped. I wanted to see if my anterior bridge was anywhere around.

Snooping is something I deplore in people, like gossiping. But it's surprising how easy it is to become a snooper. Looking around at the possessions of one absent or deceased, you find yourself saying, I wonder why he had that thing? Or, why on earth did she have so many of those? I stared at stacks of old magazines. Most were back issues of *The Ring*. They went all the way back to the late sixties. Did Johnny have a girlfriend? There was no evidence of it. And when Joe came back he said he knew of no romantic interlude in Robinson's life since the death of his wife in 'fifty-eight.

"The dental work you said would be here isn't," I said.

Joe and I sat on the love seat and speculated on the murder. Mary went back toward the bedroom, saying she wouldn't touch anything. Joe said there were lots of people who had reason to hate Johnny Robinson. I was staring at the tan-and-gray carpet when Mary screamed from the bedroom. We rushed in and found her backed up against the wall, as if at attention. She was gritting her teeth and shaking all over. A trembling hand reached out and pointed at the corpse of Tommy, the dog next to the open window.

"L-look in his mouth . . ."

I leaned over and noticed something between the dog's clenched fangs. When I tried to pull the teeth apart I felt them touch me, and shuddered.

"What are they?" asked Joe.

"Fingers."

3

THE BOYS FROM THE LAB, AND THE LOCAL POLICE, WEREN'T long. Prior to their arrival Joe and I busied ourselves by trying to reconstruct the sequence of events. One of the first things we noticed was a recently bored hole the size of a pea in the broken door of the bedroom. The hole was at eye level. A peephole.

"Okay, here it is, Doc. The guy, or guys, watch the hallway with the door closed. They're here behind the closed door when Robinson and doggies come home. They watch. When he's opposite the gas bomb in the hallway they somehow fire it—"

"Yeah, but the dogs don't die right away. Maybe they're hip to something fishy a few seconds before the gas explodes around them. Maybe they smell trouble. So they charge this door and smash it open. Then the gas does its work and they die too. But not before Tommy grabs one of them—I keep thinking there's more than one—by the hand and rips off two fingers. Then the killers escape by this window here that we found ajar. See? There's a small porch roof just below it, then an easy drop to the ground, even for an injured guy."

"Won't work, Doc. If the dogs broke down the door the gas'd get the killers too."

"No, Joe. They'd be wearing masks. You can bet on it. If

22

the gas was to be at all effective, especially against two quick dogs, it'd have to be very potent. They'd have masks.''

"Then how'd they set off the charge from in here?''

"Some kind of juice; a trigger of some kind. Let's look around a little outside till the help comes.''

After discovering the human fingers in the dog's mouth, Mary had decided she'd had enough of sleuthing for the day and split for the Lucky Seven. Her brother and I found her in said joint, hiked up on a barstool with the other fellas, a shot glass full of clear liquid in front of her. She saw us come in out of the corner of her eye as she knocked back the shot and slapped the heavy glass down on the bar. She squinted at us menacingly.

"You guys wanna start sumpin'?''

"Mary, how many of those have you had?''

"That was my third. I don't like to feel fingers when they're not attached to a guy. But I'm better now. Gonna have coffee.''

"I thought you didn't like gin,'' I said.

"Don't. This is peppermint schnapps. Tastes just like a candy cane. Want one?''

"No. You stay here. We just checked out the lower apartment of the house. It's been vacant for some time.''

"It sure made it easy for them, Mare,'' said Joe in a low voice. "Hey, you didn't tell the guys at the end of the bar anything about—''

"No. I just said we couldn't find him. Listen, come pick me up here when you're through. And it better be soon.''

She pounded the thick little glass on the varnished bar. "Barkeep! Round four,'' she said.

"Hey, thought you were having coffee now, Toots.''

"Changed my mind. And don't call me Toots.''

We walked in the alley behind the little gray house that now looked ominous to me, that was too silent and cute. Too buttoned up. I was looking at the garbage cans in the alley. Then I looked at the asphalt. It was old and hard as rock. There were no impressions there. A light metallic-blue Chevy

sedan swung around into the alley toward us. Its tires crackled on the loose cinders. A man was leaning out the driver's
window, wearing a fedora. He yelled and Joe hollered back.
Then I recognized Kevin O'Hearn, Joe's detective partner.
The beefy Irishman squinted at both of us and spoke low.

"You call the lab, Joe? They're up there now. Jeez, sumpin', huh? Poor Johnny . . ."

"Hey, Kevin," I said, "can you give us a ride up the alley
a ways? We're looking for something."

"What?" asked Joe.

"If you had the remains of a gas bomb what would you
do with it? Would you carry it around in your back seat or
trunk?"

"Yeah right. Okay. Go slow, Kev," said Joe.

We rolled along through the dismal alley choked with litter
and sparkly with broken glass. I pretended I was one of the
killers as I watched the garbage cans slide by the window.
They all looked too full and too small. In the third block I
saw the angular jaw of a big dumpster and told O'Hearn to
stop. We all got out and had a go at the big metal container.
We lifted up the heavy lid and tried to rummage around
inside but it was chock-full of old plaster and lath boards.
The stuff was all tightly packed and very heavy; I hated to
guess what the whole thing weighed—probably about as
much as a destroyer. We drove on for another block and ran
out of alley. We were back on Broadway. I swore, and Joe
suggested we try a few more alleys, since the lab boys
wouldn't want us getting in their way anyhow. We cruised
around, never going more than ten blocks or so from the gray
house. Joe and I both figured they'd have dropped the evidence off fast, not wanting it in the car.

We struck pay dirt on the fourth alley. There was a dumpster there, filled with the usual trash and garbage. We grabbed
an old fence board and snaked around in the mess awhile
before we turned up a shopping bag with a canvas strap sticking out of it. I reached down and plucked out the bag by a
corner. Inside were two army-issue gas masks. Canvas and

rubber, brand-new, each in a little canvas carrying pouch. I kept rummaging with the fence board, turning over juice and booze bottles, beer cans, frozen-dinner trays, plastic garbage bags, and junk. Then I saw it.

"Look. There's your bomb, Joe."

"That can? Hey yeah. Look, Kev, it's all burnt. I see a horse on the side of it. A horse jumping over a fence."

"It's a tobacco can," I said. "Kentucky Club. A tobacco can with a pry-off top is perfect, don't you see? The lid's a friction fit, and airtight."

I drew out the scorched can carefully, holding it by the lip. It was a few minutes before we located the burnt and blown-out lid with the little metal sliding pry lever still attached. We looked at the can. A household electrical cord ran from its side right near the bottom edge. The hole had been made neatly; it was just the right size. Putty had been packed in around the cord. On the can's interior bottom the broken copper strands of the wire were fused solidly, and all around the wire ends was a white powdery ashlike deposit.

"Take that goddamn thing away from your nose, Doc, you'll croak!" yelled O'Hearn. I thanked him for reminding me.

"Wire's melted all over in here," I said. "It took a terrific amount of heat to do that. I'd say they used powdered magnesium, or flash powder. Maybe they mixed in some crude gunpowder too, for more oomph. This stuff here would be magnesium oxide."

"How come you know all about that chemistry stuff?" asked O'Hearn belligerently. "Thought you were a doctor."

"A lot of medicine is chemistry. In my work with teeth I deal a lot with metals and alloys . . . and their oxide residues come with the territory I guess."

The cord was long, about twenty feet, and terminated in a standard-issue plug. They'd used current from Robinson's apartment to set off the lethal bomb. Seven feet from the plug, the wire on one side of the cord was stripped and cut. The wire on the other side remained whole.

"See? Here's their crude knife switch," Joe said. Then, holding the wire ends about a half-inch apart by the insulation still left on the cord, he touched them together several times.

"This opens and closes the circuit just like a switch in the cord. Now the ends of the wires in the can were joined to a fuse wire—a thin wire that'd heat up really fast as soon as house current was run through it. Then this wire is covered with an explosive substance, like flash powder."

"Yeah, a rocket fuse," said O'Hearn. "But how 'bout the gas? Where does it come from?"

"Don't know. There's lots of different kinds. Phosgene—that was the favorite of the Third Reich. Cyanide is probably the most widely used. That's what they use in prison gas chambers."

"Then aren't there special military gases? Nerve gas? Paralyzing gas? Stuff like that?"

"Yeah. But if it was homemade, which it appears to be, then cyanide is the best bet. All you need, if I remember right, is ferrocyanide crystals and sulfuric acid. You can get those chemicals. It's hard but it can be done. Then when they're mixed—bingo, poison gas. Sometimes it goes by the name prussic acid. Same deal though. Instant death. Let's take this stuff back to the house for a mock-up."

The lab boys were all over the place. They had Robinson and his two dogs covered and placed on litters in the living room. The print guys were dusting windowpanes, doorknobs, chrome table legs—everything that would take a print. They blew powder all over the place, swept big soft brushes over surfaces, lifted prints off with special Scotch tape. It was absorbing to watch them, like watching bricklayers or blacksmiths.

One guy was working on the wallpaper that had been scorched in the hallway. He was delighted when we handed him the empty and burnt-out Kentucky Club can. When the can was placed against the wall under the small table the scorch mark began right above its lip and fanned out and upward. You could almost visualize the big flash the explosion had made, probably blowing the metal lid up against the table. The cord ran back under the carpet runner, under the bedroom door, and into the wall socket with some to spare. Enough cord was left for a person to stand behind the door staring through the peephole with the pieces of cut cord in his hands. When he sees Robinson come up the hall, he touches the wires together. *Boom!* Poison gas in the hall. Robinson falls, dogs charge the door in a death agony. We acted it all out. The pieces fit.

The lab man fiddled with bottled solutions and test paper. He took scrapings from the can and the wallpaper.

"Potassium cyanide," he said softly as he watched the solutions change color. "Or prussic acid; take your pick of names. Lethal within seconds."

"What do you think, Larry? Pro job?"

The man nodded and left, taking the evidence with him.

We sat at the kitchen table now that the crew was through dusting. My brother-in-law sighed.

"Nice going with the can and stuff, Doc. Gotta hand it to you. Well, the big boys got Johnny at last. A simple gas bomb, made with everyday things impossible to trace, but deadly, and built with a lot of experience. Poor guy. And I guess you're out of luck as far as the dental piece goes too."

"Good God, Joe! *Mary!* She's been in the Lucky Seven all this time. Do you think—"

We hustled downstairs and around the corner. There was quite a crowd around the bar now. It was getting on toward evening. Mary was nowhere to be seen. We asked the barkeep and he nodded in the direction of a crowded table.

The men around the table were huddle-tight. They were yelling encouragement at invisible parties. We approached and saw two arm wrestlers at the table. One was a wiry guy about my age with rolled-up sleeves and tattoos. His arms were stringy and pretty thick. He looked strong. The other combatant was Mary. She seemed to be winning.

The crowd's chatter increased. Money was changing

hands. Mary's face contorted with effort and pain as she
pushed to put the man down.

"Come on, Mare!" shouted Joe.

"Hey, you know that broad?" asked a bystander. "Man,
is she strong!"

"And mean," I added.

"Yeah?"

There were three more shot glasses near her left hand, all
empty. But then I saw a bottle snake in and out, and one of
the glasses was full. Mary reached for it with her free hand
and knocked it back. Now where the hell did she learn that?
As her head went back she saw my face and slammed the
glass down.

"Hi good-lookin'!" she called. And lost the match.

Her opponent, sensing her lack of concentration, made a
final assault and slammed her hand down on the table. Some
of the crowd booed, but I couldn't tell if it was directed at
the opponent who took advantage or at Mary's defeat. A half-
dozen guys were headed for the bar to buy Mary some more
liquid candy cane; I stepped in and snagged her.

"That's the *nicest* place!" she exclaimed as she tripped
along the cracked sidewalk between us. We helped her ne-
gotiate it now and then.

"Those guys were just trying to get you drunk, Mare.
They weren't being nice," said Joe.

"Right," I said. "They were just trying to get you drunk
so they could get in your pants, right Joe?"

"Absolutely."

Mary stopped and weaved. She stared at us, squinting in
incredulity.

"Really? *Really*, you guys? They wanted to get in my
pants?"

"Yep," I said. "That's all they wanted. They just—*hey*!"

She was heading back toward the bar. She wasn't dawdling
either. We caught her and turned her around.

"You gotta watch Sis . . . hasn't changed a bit since the
old days."

"What do you mean by that?" I asked.

"Nevermine Charlie . . . jes' never*yoouuu*mine . . ." she said.

When we rounded the corner O'Hearn was waving us over with his arm. Mary said she was tired. I parked her in Joe's car, where she stretched out on the back seat. Before I'd shut the door she was asleep. No more Lucky Seven for you, kiddo.

O'Hearn swung his car around fast with Joe in front. I hopped in the back. Joe turned and looked at me.

"Well guess what? They just found another stiff in a ruined factory off Western."

"What? What the hell is this, a Cagney flick? Joe, correct me if I'm wrong, but Lowell's not a murder town, is it?"

"Naw. It's a tank town but not a murder town. It's scruffy and rough, but not mean. Killing is pretty rare up here; that's why I think the Mob's in on this one."

"Factory we're goin' to's an old textile mill," growled O'Hearn. "Found this dude inna chimney."

"In a *chimney*? Look you guys, all I wanted to know was what happened to my dental work, and so far we haven't found out anything."

"And sad to say you probably won't now. If it's not back at Dependable's office, I can't imagine where in hell it is. The murderers might have just grabbed everything. Shit— now I'm going to have to phone Sam Bowman and tell him that his partner and friend John Robinson has been murdered. I tell ya, my job's a barrel of laughs sometimes."

"You think Johnny might have left the stuff he was carrying at his office?"

"A chance. We'll check it out tomorrow. Turn here, Kev."

We turned and saw a Lowell black-and-white parked over beyond the old factory gate, its blue lights winking. We drifted into the yard. It had all the earmarks of a hundred-year-old textile mill: huge chimney for the boilers, loading docks, sheds, long, low buildings with roofs of tar and corrugated metal, but mostly the mill itself, a huge building of dun brick with narrow, metal-frame windows, an old clock turret, and tiny street-level doorways. It had a wall around three sides. It was a brick penitentiary. It was dismal and deserted. It was a little frightening, perhaps made more so by the nature of our errand.

The chimney was huge but unattached to the boiler room, which had been torn down when the plant was converted to electric power. There was a large jagged hole in the chimney's base where the flue had entered it. All around this opening lay piles of broken bricks, the remnants of the old flue bridges, which had collapsed. Some of these were yellowish-red; others were glossy black, indicating they'd been on the inner flue wall.

A uniformed cop and a plainclothesman stood halfway up the rubble mound inside the chimney, which was about twenty feet across at its base. Their feet and pants were bright, their upper bodies dim in the darkness of the interior, and their faces invisible. We entered the old structure and began climbing the pile of bricks, mortar, and junk. Joe knew the detective and stopped for a second while O'Hearn and I went on up alone. On top of the heap was a dead man lying on his back facing straight up, his glazed eyes half-open. His mouth was drawn back as if he had died in pain. The reason for this was obvious: a giant reddish-brown stain on his shirtfront the size of an LP record.

"Stab wound," said the detective to Joe. "Opened him up real good. No I.D. or wallet, but it's not robbery."

The man was young and handsome and looked Italian. His clothing was expensive and well cut. His hair appeared to be styled, and he wore soft calfskin loafers with tassels. Dead or alive, he was surely out of his element on a rubble heap in a ruined factory chimney in Lowell, Mass.

The four of us stood on the talus cone and stared at the faded elegance at our feet. The scene was eerie, surrealistic. Far above a shaft of dying sunlight plunged across the sooty blackness of the chimney top like a theater spotlight. It struck the curved wall up near the lip, and the white patch of light lay there in a bent ellipse. From the darkness overhead came the faint squeaking of swifts, their wing flutters and echoing power dives. Now and then dark specks flitted across the shaft of light, twittering. The rubble cone rose up inside the dark circular walls like a grotesque Paleolithic altar. And the corpse on it a sacrifice, his sightless eyes staring up at the circle of light a hundred feet above. The scene could have been on the cover of a sci-fi paperback, painted by Frank Frazetta.

Behind me I heard the clinking and clacking of broken brick as Joe climbed up to join us. I wanted to leave.

"What makes you think it wasn't robbery?" asked Joe.

" 'Cause they didn't take the gold watch. Take a look, Joe—that's some clock the guy's wearing."

The watch was round, with a red onyx face and Roman numerals. The body was gold, the band lizard. Around the gold face was engraved, in bold classical letters, BULGARI-ROMA. Joe stood up and looked at the corpse.

"Yeah, I'd say it's not robbery, too. But I've got a different reason. Look here."

He took the man's other wrist and drew the arm up, exposing the hand.

It was missing two fingers.

4

We stood staring at the corpse for quite a while, not saying a word. He was the guy who'd iced Johnny, and we did not like him. Finally O'Hearn broke the silence.

"Rich," he said.

"Yeah. Rich and Italian. I bet he didn't even speak English," said Joe.

"How can you tell?" asked O'Hearn.

"He just looks it. No, wait. Maybe he was educated in some snooty English prep school. Or maybe he spent a year at Harvard. But he's rich, just like you said, Kev, and he's Italian. He's as Italian as *fettuccine al burro*."

"Mmmmm," said O'Hearn. "As Italian as linguine with clam sauce."

"Yeah. As Italian as rigatoni bolognese," I added.

"Or chicken tetrazzini."

"Veal Marsala."

Then silence for a minute.

"I'm hungry," said O'Hearn.

"Me too," I said.

We stumbled back down the rubble heap and headed for O'Hearn's car. Joe stopped to talk to the detective, who was writing in a pocket notebook. I sat in back; O'Hearn turned around and faced me, resting his pale triple chin on the seat back.

"Well Doc, nice quiet Saturday afternoon, eh? Coupla stiffs up in Lowell, Mass. Any ideas? I thought it was a straight Outfit hit until a few minutes ago. Now I'm not so sure."

"It looks like an Outfit hit, then a double-cross from inside. Do you think they fought over the loot?"

"Naw," he said. "Johnny Robinson was small time, moneywise. The Outfit would never squabble over loot that small. Frankly, I don't think it's a question of loot at all. I think Johnny did something they didn't like, like maybe blew the whistle on them. It wasn't loot."

Joe got in and we drove over to the Robinson house. Mary was still sacked out in the back of Joe's cruiser, so I got up in front with Joe. Halfway home Mary sat up and said she was going to be sick. I helped her from the car; she felt cold and clammy to the touch. She staggered over to the side of the road and got rid of all the peppermint schnapps. She groaned and retched, and tears streamed down her face.

"Doesn't taste as good coming back up, does it, hon?"

"Oh Charlie. Ohhh . . . Why do I ever drink?" she wailed.

We got her back in and covered her with Joe's sport coat. At home we woke her up and got her inside on the couch. Then Joe threw a handful of coarse cornmeal on the butcher's block, spread it deftly with a few broad sweeps of his big hand, threw the pink-gray slabs of raw meat down, and began to pound them. He hit them gently with a wooden mallet, not a steel one. Steel tears 'em up too much, he says. The meat began to flatten and spread out. He wanted them wafer-thin.

"Too bad about Johnny," he said with a slow sigh.

"Yep. Death comes to all of us."

"Mmmmm. Makes you stop and drink."

"Okay."

I had fetched two bottles of Chianti classico and we tasted it. I cut slices of eggplant a quarter-inch thick, as per Joe's instructions, then arranged them on a clean white towel. I put another towel on top, then a thick steel cookie sheet, then a heavy cast-iron skillet for weight.

"That'll squeeze them out," said Joe, "so they won't be all watery and will soak up the olive oil."

We put olive oil in a pan with a crushed garlic clove and some onion and let it work on medium heat. That is about my favorite smell in the world. If you aren't hungry when you start, you soon will be.

"Gee, I forgot to ask Kevin if he wanted to have dinner too. It was only polite. Sorry."

"Forget it. Kev went up to Wonderland to play the puppies. Guy's got a real mania for the pups. Keep it just between us, Doc, but he dropped almost six grand last year on the pups."

"Six grand? Wow. He's feeding a habit."

"I know. And don't ask me where he gets the bread either. Okay, get out some flour, some eggs, and vino bianco and two bowls. I'm going to make some calls."

He reappeared twenty minutes later, clean shaven. He said he'd called headquarters and the lab and asked them to keep him posted at our house. He'd also called Johnny's partner, Sam Bowman, who had agreed to meet us the next day at nine thirty at the Dependable Messenger Service.

Joe returned to the veal and resumed the gentle but steady thumping with the mallet. He could have been a Renaissance Florentine stonecutter. From the side his sharp and sensitive features stood out in profile. Like his sister, he had the straight brow and nose seen on Roman statues. He had the high, wide cheekbones so common in the people south of Naples. But unlike Mary's face, which terminated in a neat chin and clean jawline, Joe's face, at its lower terminus, lacked definition. The fine features were hidden in thick jowls and heavy neck. His body too was heavy, with a paunch over the belt—which he wore lower and lower in front each year—and big legs. He had a powerful upper torso, and could be mistaken for a former boxer or street brawler, except for the eyes. His eyes protruded slightly and his mouth pouted. This gave him a gentle, cocker-spaniel face. His eyes were like those of Marcello Mastroianni. They were hardly killer eyes.

Joe concentrated on his tasks. He took the pounded scalloppine and drew them through unbleached flour, then tossed them quickly back and forth from hand to hand. I refilled the glasses while he beat up a couple of eggs and added a splash of white wine, seasoning, and a little milk.

"I saw you eyeing that Bulgari watch on that guy's wrist, Doc. I know your fetish for fine watches. You almost gleeped it."

I nodded. I hate jewelry, but well-made watches are a weakness. I glanced at the one currently gracing my wrist. It had a big flat black face and band, a movable bezel, three separate dials on the face with different functions, all luminous numbers, and a bunch of buttons on the face rim. It looked great. It weighed as much as a hand grenade and with luck—with a whole lot of luck and twists of fate thrown in— I might even actually *use* it once every decade or so. Joe was staring at me staring at it. He frowned.

"So tell me, what're all those buttons and dials for?"

"Well," I explained, "it's kind of complicated. They're all for different things. Now this dial here is for high-speed aviation. Now suppose you're in a military aircraft, say an F-4 Phantom. Okay. You pull out of a dive and go into a barrel roll. There's an enemy fighter on your tail at seven o'clock, what you do is—"

"I think you and I can skip that one, Doc. How about this one, the one with the red-and-blue outlines?"

"Glad you asked. Now this is the elapsed-time bezel. It's essential for scuba diving. Okay. Say you're down over two hundred feet—that's when it's really essential—and you're running low on air. This bezel here tells you when to start back, allowing for decompression, and that's important. Now if you've got a complication, like a shark after you—"

"Yeah yeah, Doc. You can use that in Walden Pond. How about that last one?"

"Oh, simple. Auto racing. Okay. You're negotiating a turn

at, say, Watkins Glen, and you're in the middle of the pack
and go into a four-wheel drift, why all you do is—''

"Can you check the eggplant, Doc? It should be about
ready to dip. There's no apparatus on that watch for checking
eggplant? Or timing eggs?''

"Of course not. This is an expensive watch.''

"Pardon me.''

"You can make fun, but remember, I went scuba diving,
you know.''

"Wasn't it in the YMCA pool?''

"You've gotta start somewhere. And also, I thought about
taking flying lessons at Hanscom. You never know. By the
way, how come you don't even wear a watch?''

"Don't need to. Always got somebody yelling at me. To
wake up I got my clock radio. Then before I even get to
headquarters I got the dispatcher on the box: 'Brindelli, it's
eight forty-five, where are you?' Later it's 'Lieutenant, hurry
up! It's after eleven!' And so on. I always got people *telling*
me what time it is; I don't need a watch. But that Bulgari, I
bet it cost over a grand. Maybe two. What do you think?''

"Lots of bucks. And lots of class too. Look, I'm no fashion plate and neither are you. But I do notice nice things.
The guy was dressed expensively and with taste. I would
think your average Outfit hoodlum would be a tad more
flashy.''

"I agree. Double-knit suit instead of wool and silk. He'd
wear lizard-skin shoes, or something else obnoxious . . .''

The phone rang. Joe went to answer it and I kept talking.
I followed him over to the wall phone and spoke loudly.
"There's two things here. On the one hand we assume it was
a local grudge and done by the Outfit. On the other hand—''

"Hello,'' said Joe into the phone. He was getting egg
batter on the receiver.

"—there's this Italian thread,'' I continued, "if the guy in
the chimney was really Italian. Maybe one of the killers
doublecrossed the other . . .''

Joe hugged the phone closer and held up his hand for silence. I saw his eyes widen a bit.

"Really?" he said. "They just took the prints and there's no way? Uh-huh . . . uh-huh . . . *snipped off?* Like with wire cutters? Uh-huh . . ."

Well, I assumed the phone call was for him. I went in and checked on Mary. I kissed her on the cheek. She murmured to me in the manner of dying men in movies.

". . . coffee . . ."

Of course. I'd forgotten Mary's all-purpose elixir. If she ever gets seriously injured, I'll just have the attendants hang a sterile bottle of coffee over her with an IV. The Krups machine whirred and whined and seconds later I handed her a big mug, and soon she appeared in the kitchen, her chipper self.

Joe hung up the phone, looked at it, wiped it off, and looked me in the eye.

"Guess what? What is it you always say, Doc? Funnier and funnier? No . . ."

"Curiouser and curiouser?"

"Yeah. Well get this: we found two fingers in the dog's mouth, right? And a guy with two missing fingers on the rubble heap, right? Well they don't match. They compared prints and the fingers the doggie had aren't the property of the guy with the fancy clothes and watch. Tommy *did* tear off those fingers lodged in his mouth. That's certain. But the guy in the chimney, his fingers were cut off with cutters. Curiouser and curiouser."

"But there's some sense to be made of it," I said after a few seconds' thought. "It's a frame. Mr. X kills Robinson with a lethal gas bomb and in the process loses two fingers. He also kills this young Italian guy. Incidentally, we keep saying he's Italian but we don't know for sure—"

"He's Italian," said Joe firmly.

"So he kills this second guy with a knife. He probably used a knife because it was silent."

"Or . . ." said Joe, "or because he couldn't get a gun.

He couldn't get a gun *if* . . . he's just come to the States. He couldn't buy a handgun here. And he couldn't bring one with him even in his checked luggage because of the possibility of a customs search.''

"Hey Joey, that's good," said Mary.

"Go on, Doc."

"Well he's looking down at this young man he's just killed and gets an idea: if he removes the kid's fingers the police will automatically assume—at least for a while—that the kid did it. This gives him an open field for an end run."

Joe sipped his vino rosso meditatively.

"Shit!" he said, and jumped for the phone. He punched in a familiar number with lightning speed. He used his drill-sergeant tone of voice, telling headquarters to check all clinics and emergency wards in New England for treatment to amputated fingers.

"Everything from Providence to Portland," he growled, "and let me know at this number."

Still grumbling, he returned to the veal, which he dipped in the batter and then in the seasoned bread crumbs and Parmesan cheese. Then he set them on a rack to set, and helped Mary and me dip the eggplant slices in egg and flour. We began frying them.

"You're right about one thing," he said over the sizzling skillet. "The corpse with the missing fingers fooled us enough so we didn't put the hospital call out. Damn! Gonna have my ass handed to me Monday morning—"

"But Joey, it wasn't even your day to work—"

"A good cop's always on duty, Mare. Hell, if I'd just come out here and loafed around . . . Nah, we did the right thing. We just got a little tripped up by a clever ruse. Actually, it's s.o.p. to do the clinic check. Maybe somebody did it already and I wasn't told."

With the veal and the eggplant slices lightly browned in the olive oil, Joe now stacked them alternately, with thin layers of Parmesan sprinkled between each piece, in a baking dish. There were four big stacks in the dish when he was finished. He covered them with more cheese and then lots of tomato sauce. He put it in a very hot oven to bake for twenty minutes.

When it was ready we lit into it like a pack of *orcae*. We needed an extra bottle of wine because in tasting it we had killed the first one. And the second was gone in a twinkling. The third took longer. The Krups machine whirred and whined, and shot out cup after cup of cappucino. We sat in the living room sipping it and eating ice cream. After that Mary took us on a tour of her atelier, showing us all the latest pots and standing sculpture she'd made. The dogs were with us the whole time, wagging around and whining. Then the phone rang again and Joe went to answer it. He came back saying it was Tom Costello on the line for me.

"And he sounds mad. Without his teeth he also sounds like a fairy," said Joe.

Tom *was* mad. I explained I was on the track of the bridge and hoped to have it to him shortly.

"Well leth hope tho! I'm thick of thounding like a god-damn panthy . . . Would you buy thtockth or bondth from thomeone who thounded like thith?"

"No, I would not—"

"I'll *thue*!" he promised, and hung up. I joined Mary and Joe. Joe was yawning.

I stared at my watch again, this time with some newfound distrust. Joe saw me staring at it.

"Any other fancy things that watch can do?" he asked.

"Glad you asked. Actually, I forgot one of the most important things of all: the para-drop function."

"What the hell is the para-drop function? As if I can escape finding out."

"For paratroopers doing delayed-opening jumps. Let's say you're a commando ten thousand feet up in a transport plane over El Salvador. Okay. You want to pull your chute at exactly fifteen hundred, not before, to maximize speed and concealment. Okay. You set the outer ring for ten thousand . . . your rate of fall, and the altitude your chute should open at. Then when the jump light goes green, just before you leap out the door, you—"

"Goodnight, Doc. Night, Mare," he said, kissing her. He shuffled toward the stairs. "Uh, Doc? *Happy landings.*"

"Hey wait a sec, Joe. There you are, see, with all this combat gear on, and the ground's rushing up to you at a hundred forty per . . . you've got to know when . . . *Joe*?"

"He went up, Charlie."

"Oh."

She came over and sat down next to me.

"Was that watch expensive, Charlie?"

"Kind of."

She undid the black band and removed it, hefted it.

"It's really heavy. You don't really use all these things do you?"

"Well not yet. But—"

"Whatever happened to that nice Omega I bought you?"

"Upstairs in the drawer with the rest. Honey, it's a nice watch. But it doesn't have . . . you know—"

"The gadgets?"

She read the tiny words on the instrument's face.

"Blackwatch Chronograph Adventurer. *Adventurer?* Adventurer, Charlie?"

"Can I help it if that's what they call it? You've got to admit it's handsome."

"I don't know about you sometimes, Charlie. The handgun shooting, the karate lessons from Liatis Roantis . . . then there's the motorcycle. And now this."

I thought about it for a moment.

"Well, next to the other things it's pretty innocent."

"You know, for most people having a nice house, a good family and friends, a good career in medicine, plenty of money . . . is enough. Hell Charlie, it's *more* than enough. I mean, you've got *everything*."

I stared at the wall, looking at nothing, like a character in a Hemingway story.

"I know. That's my problem."

She shook her head sadly and clicked her tongue at me in a quiet scold.

"I just don't understand I guess. Why can't you be content, like Joe?"

"Like Joe! Joe's miserable half the time. The other half he's desperate. How would you like to go around nailing psychopaths? How would you like to have hardly a month go by without mopping up some poor battered teenage hooker from under a railroad bridge? That's what he did last *Christmas Day*, remember?"

She lowered her head and nodded slowly.

"And think of his previous incarnation. A priest! You've gotta be kidding—"

"He was so good at that. I don't see why—"

"He became a cop? He had to, don't you remember? He kept hitting those city punks in the kisser. He kept kicking ass, which is the only realistic way to deal with the situation, and the bishop didn't like it. Don't tell me how happy Joe is."

"I just don't see why you seem to need all these . . . adult toys, Charlie."

"I guess it's because I think we need to have adventures. When you strip off all the icing and poetry, Mary, life is a pretty grim enterprise. Grim and brief, to paraphrase Thomas Hobbes. And you better get in a few licks while you can. Otherwise you wind up spending your life reading *The New Yorker*, listening to your stereo, and worrying about the IRS. And then you're in the ground for keeps."

We turned the lights out and went upstairs with our arms around each other.

How could I explain to her the desperate ache in the breasts of middle-aged men? Our fanatical devotion to the world of sports and our adoration of its heroes? Is it the heroes or their lives? The license for violence, the strength and endurance, danger and courage . . . all the elemental things so sadly missing in a world filled with glass-and-steel buildings, air conditioning, and Muzak? Why do we secretly yearn to follow the guy with the mustache and cowboy hat who spends his life roping mustangs, chasing horses that charge through clouds of red range dust? The guy we all want to be but can't, and so we smoke his cigarette or drink his beer instead?

How to explain this longing?

"I just think we need to have adventures," I repeated.

She sighed.

"Well the last adventure you had almost got you killed. You weren't the same for months afterward."

"Still not. But I'm not sorry it happened."

In the bedroom I stared at the watch in my hand, then put it into the bureau drawer. I picked up the Omega. Octagonal face, Roman numerals, gold case—it was almost as handsome as the watch worn by the murder victim. A perfect watch for a successful suburbanite. A bit *boring* perhaps, but we mustn't quibble . . .

Mary had disappeared momentarily. She reappeared at my elbow.

"Found it, Charlie. In Jack's room. Here, this is more your speed."

She grabbed my wrist and fastened it on.

"Aw Mary. It's such a comedown after my Chronograph Adventurer. And a red plastic band too."

"It's the real you, dear."

"Thanks a lot. Gee, I bet his arms get tired. How come he's wearing white gloves?"

"They always wear white gloves. See the little bird that flies around the face? That's the second hand—"

She slipped off her panties and tugged at my belt.

"C'mon Charlie. This watch has a real neat function on it. Better than scuba diving . . ."

I stepped out of my pants and took off my undershirt. She was grabbing at me. Tacky broad.

"Ow!"

"C'mon Charlie . . . get in."

"Hey, the ears wiggle too, with every tick . . . Hey!"

"Better than race-car driving too—"

I looked at the watch again before I climbed into the sack. The little guy on the face smiled back at me.

"Hiya Mickey," I said, "long time no see."

5

JOE CAME IN AND SAT DOWN ON THE FOOT OF OUR BED. HE was wearing nothing but his drawers.

"Good morning everybody," he said.

"Jeez, Joe, can't you get dressed before you come in here?"

"Why? It's only you and Sis. She's seen me like this a lot, right, Mare?"

She laughed a sleepy laugh. Sometimes, I thought, these Italians get too cozy for comfort. I got up and walked over to the bureau.

"Well look who's talking, for Chrissake! At least I've got pants on!" said Joe.

"It's different. I'm married to her," I said.

"Okay, you two. I think I've seen enough beef for this morning," said Mary wearily. "Especially considering it's not prime cut. Now I'm not going to get out of bed bare-assed in front of both of you, so get out."

"This any better, guy?" I held out my wrist to Joe and he laughed. I replaced the Mickey Mouse watch with the gold Omega, threw on my clothes, and went down to make coffee. Mary called after me from the bedroom. Were we going to church? No, Joe answered from the guest room, we had to go into Cambridge.

We had a quick breakfast of coffee and croissants, then

Joe and I left for the city in his car. Mary retired to her workshop. At a stoplight on Route 2 Joe didn't budge when the light turned green. Cars behind us honked.

"What's wrong?"

Joe looked as if he'd seen a ghost. He turned to me and said in a half-whisper: "His *pouch*."

"Whose pouch? Hey, move or pull over, guy, these polite Massachusetts drivers are getting impatient."

We moved ahead and Joe took the slow lane, staring ahead with his brows furrowed.

"Here we are with a dead courier, and the one thing we overlook is his carrying pouch. Hell, I never saw Johnny without it. It was an old newsboy's pouch. Gray canvas with a shoulder strap. It had the words *Lowell Sun* on it in dark-blue letters. Now he could have left it at his office. But as I remember, he usually took it home with him. Do you remember seeing it up in Lowell?"

"No. You know it wasn't there. I think the killers took it."

"Hmmm. That could be the motive. Gee, I remember Johnny telling me all about the pouch. Had it since he was a kid delivering papers up in Lowell. There weren't that many blacks in Lowell then. He'd have to go into white neighborhoods to make his route. He took a lot of abuse. As a result he learned to fight. But he told me it was the pouch that most often saved him. It was his badge of legitimacy, his reason for being in the strange neighborhood. It was his Saint Christopher's medal. I think that's why he kept it all these years."

He turned and looked at me as a car passed us at high speed.

"Wherever it is, we gotta find that pouch. Could be the key."

We took Memorial Drive to Mass. Ave., cut around the M.I.T. campus, and pulled up at a tiny cinder-block building, painted white, just off Kendall Square. It was surrounded by a high Cyclone fence. The windows were small and covered with grating.

Soon we heard a faint rumbling and popping sound growing louder and louder, a sound like a miniature artillery war advancing at great speed. An old red Honda motorcycle skirted the building and came to a stop in its own special parking space in a tiny niche in the Cyclone fence. It was a vintage bike, a 350 twin with loud pipes. As the driver revved the throttle prior to shutting it off, it growled and backfired.

The driver's passenger was a curiosity. It was a huge dog, wearing goggles, which sat on a specially made platform on the back of the double seat. The dog was big and blocky, and fawn-colored with brindle stripes on his big flanks. When the engine stopped he lowered his wide head and pawed at the goggles with the side of his front foot. The driver turned, pulled the goggles down so they dangled from around the animal's neck, pulled the bike up on its stand, and took off his helmet.

Sam Bowman, like his dead partner, was a black man. Also like the late John Robinson, he was a man who kept himself in shape. The man who snapped the heavy chain lead to the studded collar on the bull mastiff was whipcord lean and had wide shoulders. The shoulders sloped down like a barn's gambrel roof from a wide and sinewy neck. He walked toward us with vigor and purpose. The giant dog stayed right at his left leg. When he stopped to shake hands with us the dog sat down and looked blankly ahead. We all went to the front door, and Sam took a key chain from his pocket and unlocked three big deadbolts. Then he inserted a small key into a complex-looking box with a meter in it.

"Whole place is bugged," he said softly. "Anybody fool with this door, the *police* know about it. I just shut it off."

We walked inside. It was a single room with a sink and a coffee maker at one end, and an enclosed john. There were two desks. Sam sat down behind the bigger one, a hard rock-maple rolltop that had three large spindles on top which were stacked up with impaled receipts and slips. A big safe stood against the far wall. The floor was spotless linoleum, waxed. Sam unsnapped the heavy lead and the big dog ambled over to a raised platform covered with old carpet, where he sank to his belly and regarded us with a blank stare. He had a black muzzle, like all mastiffs, and a big steam-shovel mouth. His wide chest and heavy shoulders were bunched with wads of muscle, even in repose. Big blood vessels showed under the short, velvety coat. A whole lot of dog.

Sam nodded in the direction of the beast.

"That's Popeye. Nobody fool with Popeye. He all business."

"How you doing, Sam?" asked Joe.

"I been better. I been a whole lot better, Joe," he said.

"I know. We're real sorry. All of us are really sorry."

The man frowned and bunched his big shoulders.

"Somebody gonna pay," he said.

"Sam, as we told you over the phone, we'd like to look at Friday's log sheet to see exactly where Johnny went and when. Also, if we could find out what he was carrying . . . if it's known—"

Sam nodded and shuffled through a stack of papers on the big desk.

"Now the murder could be unconnected to any of this; it could be the result of something awhile back."

"I know. No way of tellin' is there? I think maybe it was something way back, Joe. Nothin' he did Friday was that important or valuable, except that fancy cup for the Harvard Museum, the Fogg."

"And the museum piece was valuable?" asked Joe.

"Oh yeah. About half a million bucks or somewheres. But it was delivered safe to the Fogg. I know because Johnny called me hisself after he delivered it. He called at—"

Bowman checked the log sheet.

"—lessee, ten twenty-seven. He just called to check in, see if there were any more jobs that come in over the phone, you know. There was nothing more, so that's the last I heard from Johnny. *Ever.*"

"Didn't you see him after the last job?"

"Naw. On Fridays we had a deal. If no more jobs came in over the wire after three, I split. Johnny would stop in after his last job with the log sheet . . . usually. That is, if the last job was pretty nearby. Otherwise he'd take the sheet home with him in the pouch and I wouldn't see him till Monday at seven-thirty. That's when we'd meet here every day, for coffee and to talk. About the only time we had to visit, except lunchtime, if he was nearby enough to stop in."

"Did he leave his pouch here, Sam?" asked Joe.

"No. He took the pouch home with him every night."

"Did he ever carry stuff home with him too?"

"Sometimes, if he couldn't make the connection. It was rare though. Generally, most of our business was right here in Boston and Cambridge. 'Course too, being black, we do some stuff for bidnesses in Roxbury and Dorchester. Fact, we do most everywhere around here but Charlestown and Southie."

This comment needed no elaboration to either of us; we knew what the racial climate was like in both of these Irish enclaves. In fact, it wasn't much better in the Italian neighborhoods of the North End and East Boston, either.

"I show you the log sheet he left here Friday after I was gone," said Bowman. He opened the notebook and Joe copied out the deliveries that had been entered:

8:30	Futurelife Laboratories—Cambridge	
9:23	Fogg Museum (Fabrianni)—Cambridge–Boston	
10:08	Harvard University Press—Cambridge	
11:00	Boston Public Library—Boston–North End*	
2:45	National Distilling—Cambridge	
3:41	Ramco Metal Fastener—Cambridge–Somerville	
4:10	Investment Alloy Labs—Cambridge–Concord*	

We studied this sheet awhile and asked Sam if he had any hunches regarding it.

"No. They're all routine things. Some of those companies, they want us to carry cash—not large amounts—to some of their truckers. Dunno. Maybe they not sposa be on the payroll. Hell, we don't ask questions, we just deliver. Don't truck for the Mob, though. We won't be bagmen. No sir-ree.''

"Sam, what do these asterisks mean?'' I asked.

"They mean the job wadn't completed. The pickup's been made but not the delivery. Hey wait a minute, Doc, this one here's *you*: Investment Alloy Labs. That's gold work, right?''

"Yes. And I was interested whether or not Johnny picked up the piece, and apparently he did. That means it was in his pouch when they got him, and lost.''

"You're not suggesting that as a motive are you?'' asked Joe.

"No. Certainly Dependable carried much more valuable stuff than that, like the museum piece.''

"I just thought you were thinking that because there are very few places where Johnny could have been nailed suc-cessfully. Here and his home are about the only places I can think of. Couldn't do it on the street without a lot of gunplay and noise. Since it happened at his home, and with a bomb that must have taken at least several hours to construct, I'm inclined to think it was strictly a revenge killing and had nothing to do with the stuff he was carrying.''

What Joe had said made a lot of sense.

"But then why'd they take the pouch?''

"Throw us off. Just like the missing fingers on the corpse in the chimney.''

"They must've wanted him dead awfully bad, Joe. Sam, if you think of anything that might point somewhere, I'm sure you'll let Joe know.''

Joe paced the small office nervously. Occasionally he glanced at the big green safe, five feet high, that stood against the wall so that it was visible through the front door and the windows. I saw two spotlights above it, angled so they would illuminate it fully at night. He dialed a number and talked to somebody at the lab at Ten-Ten Comm. Ave.

"Did you get any more latents? Well, there are some more

places we might want you to check out . . . Huh, for supper?
Gee Frank, that's nice of you. I don't know, uh, where I'm
eating tonight exactly . . ."

He glanced over at me, covered the receiver. Subtlety at
its best. I groaned inwardly and glared at him, saying nothing.

"Uh . . . wanta know where I'm eating tonight . . . uh
. . . what's Mary, uh . . . you know—"

"Marinated flank steak, sautéed mushroom caps, fresh
asparagus," I said with a weary sigh. An almost orgasmic
shudder passed through Joe's big frame and he snapped his
cop voice back into the phone.

"No Frank, I *won't* be able to. Something's come up out
in Concord."

We sat facing Sam, who had placed his big wide palms
down on his neat desk.

"I'm gonna be looking for whoever did this, Joe. And
when I find him I'm gonna kill him. Or them. Don't care
how many."

"Sam, I know how you feel. But it's unwise for you to—"

"—don't matter about wise. My partner's dead. My bid-
ness gonna shut down maybe. Got nothin' left now 'cept
Popeye."

At the mention of his name the big dog jerked his head
up.

"RRRRRRRRRRRRRRRR!" he said.

"Hush up, Popeye. Cool yourself," said Sam. He closed
the logbook, then stopped quickly, lowering his head and
squeezing the bridge of his nose.

"Gonna miss him, Joe . . ."

"Yeah. We all will. A better guy never lived. Listen: why
don't you put on some coffee?"

While Sam occupied his mind with the coffeepot, Joe
asked him over his shoulder, "What's this Futurelife Laboratories? Some kind of pharmaceutical company?"

"Naw. They a little far-out company. You know, one of

them places that takes little cells and bends 'em around, make a different kinda animal out of it—''

"Oh, you mean recombinant DNA? Gee, I didn't know you were involved with that stuff," I said.

"Yeah. They give us these steel buckets full of little-bitty growin' things, you know. Got big strong tops on 'em with bolts all around to hold it down tight, so nothin' leak out. Like a pressure cooker. All we do is tote 'em from one lab to another seven blocks away. Piece of cake."

"And you've had no trouble or anything with that account?" Joe asked. "Nothing strange lately?"

"Nope. Been four years now. No fracas."

"Okay. How about this Harvard University Press?"

"Man-u-script," intoned Sam. "We do a lot of manuscript deliveries for publishers 'cause they need 'em right away. Seems publishers always runnin' late. These books all the same; can't read 'em. Big thick suckers on stuff nobody ever heard of. Nothing unusual there either."

"All right. Now what's this pickup for the library?"

"Some guy in the North End, I think he was a lawyer, died a few months back and left his papers to the public library. It was just a bunch of papers. For some reason Johnny couldn't get ahold of whoever it was he was sposa give 'em to. So he still had 'em with him, just like your fancy gold dental work, Doc."

"And there was nothing of value there?"

"Naw, just papers."

"Okay," resumed Joe. "Moving right along, we come to the afternoon jobs. National Distilling and Ramco Metal I'm assuming are other routine deliveries like Futurelife?"

"Yep. Routine cash deliveries, same as every other Friday for the past four and a half years."

"How much did Johnny have with him?"

"Less than four grand. Here, I'll check."

Sam went over to the large green safe with the double doors and twirled the big black dial. In less than a minute he had the thick doors swung open and was reading off a lined sheet of notebook paper taped to the inside right door.

"Three thousand four hundred sixty dollars, even."

"And it was all delivered?" asked Joe.

Sam shrugged and stared into the safe.

"If it wadn't, we'd a heard I think." He continued to stare into the safe, which was divided into many small compartments and stuffed with papers. He began to rummage about in one of the upper compartments, reaching his arm deep inside.

"And when Johnny called you at ten twenty-seven—after he'd completed the first three jobs—he said everything was normal? Fine?"

"No," replied Sam, "but he didn't say nothin' to indicate it wadn't." He was feeling deep inside the safe, as if he were finding what he was looking for. It sure was a big safe.

"Then I think we can rule out anything out of the ordinary on the first three calls. And probably the last three in the afternoon, which includes your lab work, Doc. That leaves the errand for the library involving the lawyer's papers from the North End. What kind of papers were they, Sam?"

"Just some papers from a case a long, long way back. Forget it, Joe, it's old history. It was for the library, uh . . . *archives*. That's what they said: archives."

"Then I think we can rule it all out. It was a grudge hit, probably from the Mob. When we consider that it must've taken time to build the bomb and plan the thing, which happened like clockwork, then I think we can rule it all out."

"I think so too. But remember, Joe, I used to be a cop in this town. I still know cops all around here. And state guys, like you, and some of the Feds even. I got connections and contacts. I'm gonna keep an ear to the ground, hear? I'll keep pumpin' these dudes, hear? When I find out who it is I'm going huntin'."

We didn't say anything. Sam Bowman didn't seem to me to be a fellow to argue with. And if he had Popeye along, one would have to think not only twice, but a third time at least. Then I noticed that two of the lower cubbyholes in the safe were packed with stacks of what looked like bills. Legal tender. Coin of the realm.

"What's all that stuff that looks like money?" I asked.

"Money," said Sam. "That why it look like it."

"How much is there, Sam? Looks like a bundle," said Joe.

"Twenny thousand five hundred dollars. Small bills. It's our stash. Looks like it all mine now."

"Why don't you keep it in a bank?" asked Joe. "You'd get interest on it."

"Got plenty in the bank. Got about a quarter million bucks between us. This here's emergency cash money. Also, the bank blows up, we still got the loot here."

Sam was slowly drawing out his arm now. When his coffee-colored hand emerged from the cubbyhole it was holding a blue cardboard box. Heavy. I didn't have to be told what was in that famous blue box, even before I saw the S&W monogram on the lid. Sam placed the box down on the desk, took a long pull of coffee, and lifted the lid.

"Now what the hell are you going to do with that?" asked Joe. Sam was holding a giant revolver in his right hand. It was finished in bright nickel. Its bore was big enough to stick a palm tree in. Sam put the piece down quickly on the desk. The room seemed to shake a bit. He walked back over to the big safe.

"I told you, Joe. I'm goin' huntin'."

"No you're not." Joe stood up and started for the safe. In less than a second the big dog was in front of him in a crouch. The mouth was half-open, the front of the lips curled up in a combat snarl. A deep rumbling filled the room. Joe froze.

"*Be cool, Popeye!* Don't come no closer, Joe; he's trained to stay between you and the safe whenever it's open. Little trick I taught him."

Sam fished around further back in the cubbyholes and drew out another box, which he carried over to the desk. Joe squatted on his heels in front of the dog and held out his hand. The dog stared blankly at it.

"I'm good with dogs, Sam, right Doc? Watch. Here Popeye! Here boy! C'mon . . . caaaaaa-mon boy. Tchh! Tchhh! Caaa—"

"RRRRRRRRRRRRRRRR!"

Joe stood up, chagrined.

"Don't think you're having much luck," I said.

Sam looked up from the desk. He was loading the revolver with the cartridges he had just fetched. They were spilled out all over the maple desktop and looked as big as lipsticks. The ammo box said FIFTY CENTERFIRE PISTOL CARTRIDGES. 45-CALIBER LONG COLT. 185-GRAIN JACKETED HOLLOW POINT.

Big bullets that would go very slowly from the big handgun. I hefted one; it was heavier than a golf ball. And there was the gun itself. Perhaps the *Nimitz* could use it for a sea anchor.

"How much does Popeye weigh, Sam?"

" 'Bout a hundred thirty. Not too much fat on him."

There was a decisive *clack* as Sam slammed the loaded cylinder into the revolver's frame. He replaced the spare cartridges and put away both boxes. Joe stood up and came over to the desk. The dog likewise went back to his bed and sank to his belly on the old carpet. Sam opened a lower drawer in the desk and brought out an empty shoulder holster, which he ducked into, then replaced his light jacket. He slipped the big silver gun into its snug resting place underneath his left armpit.

"Johnny was the only one of us carried a piece. Now I'm carryin' this one every day."

He tapped the bulge under the jacket for emphasis.

"*Every day.*" He shut and locked the big safe.

Joe's sternness gave way to a helpless look.

"I assume you're licensed to carry, Sam. But be careful. How long since you've fired that howitzer?"

"Last month at the Deer Island range. It might surprise

you, Joe, but I pretty good with this ol' cannon. Here, you want this logbook anymore?''

We said no thanks, and told Sam how much we appreciated his coming to Dependable's office on a Sunday. He and Popeye led us out and then he turned and relocked the three big deadbolts and reset the electronic intrusion device. He faced us.

"I'm not kiddin'. I'm gonna have my ear to the wire. I hear who did that to Johnny—they're dead. I don't care if I go down with 'em. Got nobody waitin' for me . . . just like Johnny. Don't care if they take me with 'em. They're *dead*.''

"See you, Sam. Sorry about Johnny.''

"One more time,'' said Joe. He squatted down in front of Popeye. "Here boy. C'mon Popeye. Caaaaaa-mon!''

The dog seemed as interested in Joe as he would be in a snow shovel.

Sam fastened the lead and walked the blocky beast back to the motorcycle. As we drove off I heard the faint popping and rumbling of the old bike starting up. Joe said the lab at headquarters had some news.

"Two items. One: there was evidence on the corpse in the chimney that he was tortured. Cigarette burns on the sole of his right foot.''

"Oh Christ.''

"Yeah. Two: the emergency room of Union Hospital in Lynn treated—get this—an Italian fisherman for two amputated fingers late Friday night. The guy could barely speak English. Claimed he got his hand caught in a cable winch. Hah! You see how clever that was? Know how many illegal aliens there are in our fishing boats? Especially Portuguese down in New Bedford and Italians on the North Shore? Records show the guy paid cash, had no I.D. Don't you see how perfect it is?''

"Very clever. About as foolproof as the gas bomb. These guys are pros, or near it. I can just see that doctor who was on call in Lynn. He's sewing up the hand and thinking, this poor, poor fisherman. So far from home, working to support his starving family in Ragusa. And if word gets out, they'll deport him.''

"Shit. It's enough to make me wish Sam *does* catch up with them.''

"Think he will? And if he does, is he really going to try to kill them?''

"Oh yes indeed. Sam's no pussycat, in case you didn't notice. He was a paratrooper in World War Two and never got out of jump shape. He was a cop, like he said. I guess he's good with a sidearm. Sure hope he doesn't get himself killed. Whatever happens on this case, I'm keeping mum to Sam.''

We drove up Mass. Ave. through Central Square, which on a Sunday looked unrecognizably quiet and deserted.

"Where are we headed?''

"To the Fogg Museum,'' said Joe, driving through a thicket of Dunkin' Donuts wrappers that fluttered in our wake. "See if we can get any kind of line on that job Johnny did Friday morning. Then we'll go home, okay?''

"Fine. Except I think the Fogg's closed on Sundays, like everything else in this state is, except bars.''

"Except bars. Right. The Irish influence no doubt.''

The Fogg *was* closed. But Joe and I peered through the glass of the Federal-style front door and saw the display screens for the exhibit entitled "Renaissance Treasures of San Marino.'' On the screens were mural-sized photos of that tiny republic (reputedly the world's oldest as well as smallest) and its flag, showing the three stone castle towers on three summits that mark its crest. The museum was all dark inside though.

"Help you?'' said a voice. It belonged to a Harvard campus security guard, who wouldn't open the Fogg doors for us even when Joe flashed his badge. But he did give Joe the phone number of the right person to contact regarding Fogg exhibits and their sponsors. While Joe went off to make his phone calls, I went to the john in the lower level of a red-brick building that was pointed out to me by the guard. Standing in front of one of the urinals in the men's room, I was struck by the graffiti. Yes Virginia, there is graffiti on the walls of Harvard rest rooms. However, it was all neatly lettered and obviously not the product of average minds. For example, there was a running debate penned on the wall above me concerning the behavior of accelerated particles in cloud chambers at various temperatures. This was complete with lots of Greek letters and appropriate formulas. Underneath the arguments was the wry observation that perhaps the warring factions would do themselves and everyone else who used the facilities a favor by transferring to M.I.T. Then there was this:

CONSERVE GRAVITY; WEAR THICK-SOLED SHOES!

Followed by this, from the first book of *Gargantua and Pantagruel*:

> Come sit and cack
> With lusty back
> But leave no wrack
> Beside our closet.
> Void, spurt and pump
> Your turdous rump
> But leave no lump
> Here for deposit.
> He shall know shame
> Who misses aim,
> St. Anthony's flame
> Burn his scut sear,
> Who will not swab
> His thingumabob
> To the last blob
> Ere he leave here!
> —Rabelais

Well, I was impressed. I glanced around and saw the greatest names of science, literature, and philosophy well represented in the Crimson *maison de merde*. Perhaps fittingly, most of the quotes and diatribes concerned politics.

Finally, as I dried my hands and prepared to depart, I saw this terse warning:

> FOOL'S NAMES AND FOOL'S FACES
> OFT APPEAR IN PUBLIC PLACES
> —Shakespeare

Hell, I considered as I sprinted up the steps back out into Harvard Yard, I was wasting my money sending Jack and Tony to Bowdoin and Williams. I could save almost forty grand a year by making them hang around the Harvard johns.

Joe was still on the phone. I heard his cop voice haranguing some poor soul on the other end. He hung up and turned to me.

"Guess what? We're going to pay a brief visit—I promised her, and I promise you, it will be brief—to Lucia Fabrianni over at the Copley."

"You said we. Where do you get *we*?"

"Aw c'mon, Doc. It's only eleven-thirty. We'll only see her twenty minutes."

So we went to Copley Square, where the Fabrianni family was ensconced in Boston for the duration of their show. According to our information they owned the whole kit and kaboodle of the treasures from San Marino, and the senior Mr. Paolo Fabrianni was anxious to display the art treasures to increase tourism to his tiny country. But Joe told me during the ride over the Charles River to Boston that Lucia Fabrianni had sounded put out and wasn't at all eager for an interview with the police, especially on Sunday.

"Know what she said to me?" asked Joe as we strode into the ornate lobby of the Copley Plaza Hotel and punched the elevator button. "I spoke some Italian phrases to her, you know, to kinda break the ice a little. The extra effort, you know? What she says is, 'You're from the South, aren't you? I can tell you're from Naples.' Jeez!''

The elevator arrived, and we went up.

We sat in the small parlor room decorated with Louis Quinze furniture. Or was it Louis Seize? Well whatever, it was one of them. The furniture was white and gold with bent legs and claw feet. The chair backs and seats were overstuffed ellipses of velveteen. There was scrollwork and curlicues everywhere. Give me Shaker any day.

Lucia Fabrianni entered the room. She was everything we thought she'd be, and more. She was rich and beautiful. After a few minutes Joe suggested we get coffee. Lucia gladly accepted, and ten minutes later we were in the lobby sipping and munching. Lucia, educated in Switzerland, France, the States, and England, spoke perfect accent-free English. Boy, was she a looker too. Her dark-blonde hair was rather short and swept back soft and thick. I guessed her to be around twenty-five. Her face was finely chiseled and showed no sag or fat. Her mouth was almost too large and full. But not quite.

She puckered her lips over the steaming cup and sipped. A gold pin on her blouse glowed with bucks. Her nails were shiny beige. Bracelets twinkled. Four of them on her right arm, but thin, not overdone. Beautiful watch on her left wrist. I stared at it hard. Something wrong with the watch. Why did it make me uneasy?

"Well," she said, brushing crumbs off her hands. "it's Sunday, and like a good European I don't do business on Sundays, so what is it, please?''

Joe explained to her about the death of the messenger who had transported a piece for her exhibit. She was shocked and subdued at the news.

"Oh, I am truly sorry. The poor man. And he was so nice! He let me pet his big beautiful Alsatian dogs. I hope they are all right . . .''

"They were killed too, ma'am. It was a gas bomb. They were all killed instantly. Because of the nature of the killing we're investigating all possible motives. You say the cup is safe back in the museum?''

"Yes."

"And why was it taken out in the first place?"

"We took some pictures with it here in the hotel suite for a newspaper. The *World*, I think."

"The *Globe*?"

"Ah yes, the *Globe*. This man, he was a black man, sort of old with gold glasses, yes? Well, he brought the cup and then took it back. It is quite priceless. It was made by Baccio Bandinelli in Florence in fifteen thirty. But it is the legend surrounding Romeo's Chalice that makes it especially valuable, even though the legend is false. Supposedly it was the chalice used at the wedding mass by Romeo and Juliet. So it is still called that—Romeo's Chalice."

"And it is really pure gold?" asked Joe.

"Yes. Gold inlaid with silver and black onyx. It is a prize one might kill for, but as I told you the killing was quite unnecessary, since the cup was safely delivered by this man and his messenger service. Is this all now, please?"

"Uh, almost, Ms. Fabrianni. We just want to know if, when you met Mr. Robinson last Friday, anything seemed unusual. Did he seem nervous? Did he say anything unusual?"

"Well," she replied impatiently, "since I have no idea what his usual was, how could I tell if there was anything *un*usual, you see?"

"Yes, I understand. Well thank you, Ms. Fabrianni." He looked wearily at me. "That seems to clear this end up, eh Doc?"

I shrugged and nodded at the same time. Who knew?

Lucia rose from the table to say good-bye and return to her suite. Joe had his wallet out but she waved him off, saying she would have it put on her bill and charged as a business expense to her father's corporation. She said this as if she were used to doing it for many things.

"Uh, if anything further develops, we'll be in touch with you," said Joe.

"Oh. Why would there be any need for that?" she asked.

"Well I don't know. Just in case."

"Mr. Brindelli, I have been most cooperative, I think. Have I not?"

"Oh yes. We thank you."

"Well then, I see no reason to continue the matter any further, though I think it was unfortunate that the poor man was killed. Yes?"

She was lighting a Marlboro with a purple-and-gold lighter that had a tortoise-shell texture. It definitely wasn't a Bic. Probably cost a grand. Again I saw the watch on her elegant wrist and involuntarily shuddered.

As Joe stammered for an explanation we both saw the spoiled princess emerge from beneath the regal courtesy. Her irritation and impatience were less the product of a Latin temper or a nasty nature than the natural outgrowth of a centuries-old aristocratic view of life, in which the European wealthy were used to commanding obsequious armies of attendants, purveyors, merchants, chefs, valets, and chauffeurs at their beck and call. Sometimes America was a rude shock for them.

"I think his death had nothing to do with his errand for us," suggested Lucia.

"Plausible," said Joe, "except that Johnny wasn't the only one—"

"Uh, *Joe*," I said quickly, "let's talk briefly with Mr. Fabrianni before we go, okay? And also, Ms. Fabrianni, we really appreciate your help . . . I was just wondering if you could provide us with a quick rundown of the members of your party? Do you have any pictures we could look at?"

She balked a bit at this, but relented, and we returned to the Fabrianni suite where we met Paolo, infirm with old age and diabetes, and looked at many photographs in big albums. The watch Lucia Fabrianni was wearing had me on edge. Like the one on the wrist of the elegant young corpse in the old chimney, it was a Bulgari. We looked all through the photo albums, which were full of pictures of the art objects as well as the tour personnel. In none of the pictures could we spot a man who looked like the dead man. But Lucia explained that not all of the tour people were in the photographs; several of the younger assistants had not been around when the pictures were taken.

"Is everybody here now?" Joe asked Lucia.

"No. Several are away sightseeing this weekend. Two of them, I think Enzo and Michael, went down to New York on the airplane to see relatives—"

"They left Friday?"

"Yes. Friday afternoon," she answered after some thought.

Joe was leaning over toward her, his attention held totally by what she was saying. Why was he so engrossed? Then I realized he was staring down at the lighter. He was studying it as one might study a moon rock or the remains of a meteorite.

"And you have no pictures of either of them we could take a look at?" he finally asked her.

"No, I don't think so. Why? Are they accused of something?"

"No. Uh, would you call me, please, at this number if either one of them fails to turn up when you expect? Thanks."

We rose to go and she opened the side door, revealing another parlor and her aged father sitting in his wheelchair in front of a table with playing cards on it. Joe thanked her in Italian. She brightened up and answered him back.

"Mr. Brindelli, Dr. Adams, you must come for dinner soon. We will have a big banquet before we leave. Mr. Brindelli, you are the brother to Mrs. Adams?"

"Afraid so."

"Ah, and what village did you come from?"

"Oh, a little place south of Naples, like most of us who came to America."

"I see . . . interesting. And what is the name of the village?"

"San Mango d'Aquino, in Calabria."

"Oh yes," she said distantly, "I've heard of it, I think. It's very poor down there, isn't it?"

"Yes," said Joe.

We left the suite and walked down the hall toward the elevators.

"Notice the watch, Joe? Another Bulgari. Don't you think that's more than coincidental?"

"Yep," he said.

"What chance is there that the guy in the chimney was one of the Fabrianni party?"

"Some."

"And if he is, er, *was*, then what in God's name does it all mean?"

He shrugged his shoulders and kept walking. Joe wasn't saying much. But I knew what was bothering him.

Joe looked down at the patterned carpet as we walked. He didn't say anything. He scowled.

"That *norte* bitch," he said finally.

"Don't let it get to you," I said. "She doesn't know anything else. Like a lot of rich people she's both worldly and ignorant at the same time."

" '*It's very poor down there, isn't it?*' " said Joe, mocking her. "Well goddamn right it's poor down there; why the hell you think we all came over *here*?"

We got into the elevator and rode down alone. We didn't say anything. In the lobby we paused near the old gilded clock as if unsure of what to do next. Then we drifted along the corridor to the library bar. We sat in two leather chairs and gazed absently at the bookshelves and paintings. A waitress came by and we waved her off. I sighed and Joe rested his cheeks in his palms.

"Did you see that Orsini lighter?" he asked.

"Uh-huh."

"Jeez. Must've cost a mint. 'Course, she's probably got one of them for every day of the week and two for Sundays."

"Uh-huh."

Joe popped a Benson & Hedges into his mouth and lit it with a paper match. He dropped the matchbook on the table between us. On its cover it said in bold letters EARN BIG $$$$$$!

"I hate those *nortes*," he said. "They really think their shit doesn't stink."

"Uh-huh."

I waited patiently (I have the patience of a saint sometimes) while he moaned and pouted, then we went outside and crossed Copley Square to where Joe's cruiser was parked on Boylston Street.

"Want to walk down to the Boylston Street gym? Liatis Roantis is giving a savate demonstration today," I said. I thought it would take Joe's mind off Lucia Fabrianni, the stuck-up *norte*.

"What's savate?"

"French-Burmese foot-fighting. Roantis is really good at it."

"I bet he is. Why doesn't he cut the fancy bullshit and just use a machine gun?"

"I hear he's good with those too."

"I bet."

"Want to go over to the North End?"

"Nah."

"Want to go down to Dunfey's and get a couple of draft Harps?"

"Nah."

"Want to quit feeling sorry for yourself because your forefathers weren't from Florence?"

He shrugged and said yeah, okay. We swayed over to the storefront window of Ehrlich's tobacco shop. We stared at the pipes, pewter beer mugs, cigars, fancy ashtrays, and lighters in silence. Joe shifted his weight from foot to foot, his hands shoved down into his trenchcoat pockets. He moved his arms in and out, flapping the coat open and closed idly like a giant wading bird on its nest.

"Look at those lighters," he said.

"Uh-huh. What about Lucia's watch? Think it means anything?"

"Yep. It's a helluva coincidence if it doesn't. Remember I said the guy looked Italian. I'll make you a gent's wager that at least one of the Fabrianni staff turns up missing tomorrow. Hell, maybe we should get a post-mortem pix of the guy and check it out now. Question is, *why*? What's the connection between the dead guy in the chimney and the Fabriannis and their treasures? The cup was safely returned to the Fogg from the hotel, so Johnny didn't have it in his pouch."

"Okay, right. But maybe the thugs didn't know that. They're associated with the show and know the value of the piece. They set up the ambush—"

"You keep saying *they*—"

"*Two* gas masks, remember?"

"Right. *They*."

"They set it up, kill Johnny, and snag the pouch. But then they discover the cup isn't there—"

"Ah! Or maybe Johnny was carrying something else from the Fogg, something smaller that they could easily fence . . ."

Joe decided to have somebody from his office follow up with a post-mortem photograph to show to Lucia. Then he went back to staring at the window.

"Gee, I want to go in there and look at those fancy lighters, Doc. Too bad it's closed."

"There's a tobacconist's in the Copley Plaza that's open; we passed it on the way out."

That was all the invitation he needed. In three minutes we were back in the hotel, looking down through the glass of the counter display case, checking out the lighters. But the kind Joe was looking for wasn't there. He grew morose and impatient, asking the clerk if he carried Orsini lighters.

"We keep them in back, sir. They're not asked for that often. Excuse me a minute."

He returned shortly with two red leather cases which he unfolded on the glass counter. Set on the plush lining were about twenty lighters. They looked like the one Lucia had used. Joe was agitated. No, he was excited. He was all in a sweat to get one. Then he took a peek at one of the small tags underneath.

"Jeez! Six hundred twenty-five bucks! Uh . . . I don't know. Doc, whaddayuh think?"

"I think it's dumb. Get a Zippo for six bucks. You'll never lose a cheap lighter. Just like a cheap pen. But you get one of those, you'll lose it within a month."

But he couldn't take his eyes off the cases of fancy lighters. Some were blue and gold. Their labels said they were lapis lazuli and pure gold. Big deal. Others were platinum and onyx, tortoiseshell and gold, and so on. Joe was transfixed; he was going to be awhile.

"Yeah, yeah—how about this one? No, the blue," he said impatiently.

Now that I considered, I wished Ehrlich's was open; I needed tobacco. I bought a small tin and some Te Amo coronas. Joe looked at lighters. Finally he appeared at my side, ready to go. He hadn't bought anything. We left the shop and walked over to Joe's car. I put my bag of tobacco and cigars on the seat beside me. Joe eyed the bag enviously.

"How much did your watch cost?" he asked.

"You mean the black one? Why do you ask?"

"How much?"

"Uh, about four hundred bucks. Don't tell Mary."

"Hold on a sec."

He jumped out of the car and hoofed it back to the tobacconist's, reappearing shortly with a little paper bag in his hand. He got behind the wheel and opened it. He took out a small cardboard box, opened it, and held a jewelry case in his hand. On the blue case, in stylized lower-case letters in silver, was the word *orsini*. He handed it to me and I snapped it open. Inside was a blue-and-gold lighter.

"Very handsome," I said. "How much?"

"Three twenty-five. It was their second-cheapest one. But still nice. He just filled it for me."

"What does it run on, plutonium?"

"Butane. Nice, eh? See, the *nortes* aren't the only ones who can have these. I don't buy that much for myself, you know."

We headed home. For his dues Joe bought a sack of pears and some Brie in Fresh Pond, and we were home by four. But after the car rolled to a stop and I gathered our purchases to carry inside, I noticed Joe hadn't moved. He was still behind the wheel, regarding the lighter that he flipped around in his big hands. I thought he must really love it. Then he got out slowly, as if burdened by a great weight. He sighed as he walked up the flagstones, carrying the new lighter in front of him in both hands the way a priest carries the host.

"Dammit, Doc. Why the hell did I ever buy this thing?"

"Oh I don't know," mused Mary as she fingered the lighter. "It looks really nice, Joey. And don't worry so much what those *nortes* do or don't do. We all know they're not really Italians. They're Austrians in drag."

We had asked Mary to pass judgment on Joe's big purchase. We were sitting around the dinner table after a huge feast.

"The tortellini was a nice surprise," I said, placing my hand under the table and on her thigh, which I commenced to stroke.

"That's a ball, Charlie," she said with a sigh.

"Huh?"

"Low and outside," she said, patting my hand.

"That's tawdry, dear. Must you always be so tawdry?"

"Yep."

Joe took the lighter back. It had clearly become an object of guilt, an albatross around his neck. Poor guy. Mary had

the solution. She went upstairs and got my fancy black watch
and fastened it onto Joe's wrist. Then she took the lighter
from him and gave it to me. Pretend you've given each other
presents, she said.

"Great," said Joe, regarding the fancy timepiece. "Only
trouble is I don't need a watch."

"And I don't need a cigarette lighter."

"Well it's the thought that counts," said Mary. "Now
Charlie, make the cappucino."

After dessert we put on a Mahler symphony and sat in the
living room speculating on the Robinson/Fabrianni/dead-
guy-in-the-chimney connection. There still didn't appear to
be any, which made it all the more puzzling.

"Why are you guys so sure the poor man in the chimney
was working for the Fabriannis?" asked Mary, who was busy
flipping through a magazine.

"Well, the main thing is the fact that he looked Italian—
not Italian-American but real Italian, you know," said her
brother, scowling and fingering his new watch, which seemed
to confuse and disgust him. "And also the fact that Johnny
Robinson was carrying a gold cup for the Fabriannis earlier.
But mainly, he wore a watch just like the one Lucia Fabrianni
was wearing. It's called a Bulgari, and it's made in Italy."

"You guys are full of it," said Mary, looking at her nails.

"Now what makes you say that?" I asked.

"The man's watch. Two reasons. One: here's a Bulgari
watch right here."

She flipped the magazine around and showed us a full-
page color ad with the name boldly spelled out. I noticed it
was spelled with a Roman style *u* that was shaped like a *v*.
The magazine was her favorite: *Attenzione*, the magazine for
Italian-Americans, or anybody who likes anything Italian. I
liked the magazine a lot.

"Charlie and Joe, these Bulgari watches are the new thing.
No more Rolex or Patek Philippe. It's all Bulgari now; the
stores on Newbury Street are selling them like crazy. So
reason number one, again: everybody's getting Bulgari

watches now; the guy in the chimney could be an American.''

"No way," said her brother.

"Two: you're saying the guys killed Johnny to get the gold cup, or something else valuable? Then why didn't they take the watch? They could sell it easily for a couple hundred bucks. So one, two: you guys are full of it."

She returned to her magazine and her nails. We didn't exactly know what to say. Leave a woman to screw everything all up.

Just before Joe left to return to his Beacon Hill bachelor apartment he and I went over the whole thing again, just the two of us. We decided Johnny Robinson's death was a Mob revenge killing after all. So I said good-bye fully expecting to begin making a new bridge for Tom Costello's mouth the next afternoon . . . and not expecting to see Joe until next weekend.

But something unexpected changed all of that. It was a voice. A voice from beyond the grave.

Johnny Robinson's voice. Talking to me.

6

I REGARDED THE BLOODY OBJECT THAT RESTED ON THE STER-
ile paper. Clumps of clotted tissue clung to its lower extrem-
ities like limpets on a wave-washed rock. Although the patient
sitting in my chair would certainly enjoy newfound relief
now that the impacted third molar was removed from his
lower jaw, I could not help feeling a wee bit like Torquemada
every time I clamped my Hu-Friedy cowhorn forceps se-
curely around an offending tooth and began to rock it loose
from its socket. You do this after you partially lift the tooth
with a tool called an elevator; after the forceps are in place
you rock the tooth back and forth and then extract it. Sometimes there is a muted crunch of bone or crackle as a root
fractures under the strain. But always there is the sickening
wet sucking sound of the gum tissue, a sound like that produced when you sink up to your knee in a muddy bog and
then pull your leg out. To mute these noises I always have
my patient wear earphones playing classical music—on the
loud side. My current patient was listening to E. Power Biggs
playing Bach's Toccata in E minor. He felt nothing . . . yet.

The lower portion of Ronald Belknap's tooth was bent at
a thirty-degree angle. This dogleg had developed over the
years as the tooth tried to push its way up through the gum—
in the manner God and nature intended all good teeth to do—
and join its fellow teeth in the job of grinding up food. But

the tooth could not push its way to the surface because the jawbone was too small and there wasn't room. Our tiny mandible, like our appendix, is a curse of human evolution. So the tooth pushed against the twelve-year molar in front of it at an angle. And as it pushed against the molar, it began to bend. Finally all this pushing and bending leads to inflammation, pressure, and infection. Sometimes you need to section impacted teeth before you remove them, but in Belknap's case I didn't.

"Ohhhhh Jeeeez," he moaned, looking at the huge tooth that lay soaking the white paper with blood. "No wonder that sucker hurt!"

"Yes," I said, "and unfortunately, when the local wears off you're going to get some more pain. Notice, Ron, I'm not calling it *discomfort*, as so many of my colleagues do. I'm calling it pain because that's what it will be. Do you drink?"

"Sure."

So I gave him a blue card with instructions. For minors, or people who don't drink, I give a white card with a different set of instructions and a prescription for Tylox. But never do I mix instructions, or cards, because booze on top of a pain-killing drug can make some people drop where they stand after one snort. It's very dangerous.

"Hey Doc. This just says to go home and get bombed."

"Uh-huh. There's a good drink recipe on the back. Stay home tomorrow and watch the tube. You'll be in some pain for the next twenty hours because I had to remove a wee bit of infected jawbone. That's going to smart. Next day return to work and take aspirin. Keep the packing in your mouth until dinnertime and don't rinse. Good-bye."

"What about payment?"

"One pain at a time. Susan will bill you."

He regarded the devastatingly gorgeous Susan Petri, the one who could turn men into stone. Susan Petri should be a controlled substance. He addressed me *sotto voce*.

"Wow, Doc. If you'll pardon a personal observation,

you've got some really nice scenery around here. Must make coming to work uh, less of an ordeal.''

"If you're referring to Ms. Petri's physical attributes''— I sniffed—''then let me assure you they had next to nothing to do with my hiring her. And, speaking as one twentieth-century man to another, I regret your judging her solely on her physical appearance. It is sexist and archaic. Isn't she dynamite!''

"Yeah, I—*oooo*! I think I just got the first twinge!''

"You ain't felt nothin' yet, Ron. There's more where that came from. Go home and guzzle; I'll see you Friday.''

I saw him out the door just as the phone rang. It was Joe, returning my call to Ten-Ten Comm. Ave.

"Where the hell have you been? I called you before work.''

"Oh. You mean it was important?''

"Joe, listen: I've got a taped phone message from Johnny. he called me late Friday afternoon and left a message on my machine.''

"Well what's it say?''

"I'll play it over the phone. Hold on.''

I pressed the playback button on my phone answering machine and held the receiver right over the tiny speaker:

Hello, Doc? This is Johnny. Johnny Robinson, Dependable. Listen, I got your work from the dental lab but I'll be a little bit late with it. Can you hold on until just before suppertime? Sorry, but I'm totin' somethin' hot for my buddy Andy and I've got a—uh *[squeak, flap, squeak] complication*, dontcha know . . . *[bark, bark]*. Sorry for the delay . . . I'll stay in touch. *[bark, click]*

There was a pause on the other end after it was over. Then Joe asked me to play it again. I did. Then he asked me to play it a third time.

"Okay, I'll be out in an hour. I might bring O'Hearn with me. You hear that squeaking in the background? Phone-booth door . . . the old type. And the barking? Johnny's dogs. Somebody was tailing him.''

"Who's Andy?''

"That's what we're gonna find out. Stay put."

Joe and I listened to the tape three more times. We played the end of it over and over again to try and determine what the background noises meant. The problem was that the answering device was a crude recorder, and the speaker was a tiny arrangement barely an inch and a half across. Hardly concert-hall realism. Frustrated, Joe said he needed a big tape deck with three heads so he could make more copies. I had such a deck, but the one at the Concord police station was closer and Joe said he'd like Chief Brian Hannon's opinion of the message.

"You would? Really and truly?"

"Well why not?" asked Joe.

"Well why?"

We nestled ourselves in front of the police department's big Akai tape deck after we'd made four copies of the message, which ran 25.4 seconds, and listened again to the original tape. Brian Hannon sat between us, running his fat fingers through his thinning sand-colored hair as he cocked his ear at the voice. The details in the background were clearer with the better equipment. The squeak of a door hinge, the faint sounds of traffic and pedestrians . . . and a bell.

The three of us hunkered down there like sparrows on a wire, listening. I was at one end, a bit lean and graying at the temples. Brian, short, stocky, and almost bald, was in the middle. Bringing up the far side was good old Joe, with his paunch and his hound-dog eyes. Then I knew who it was we must've looked like: Larry, Curley, and Moe. The Three Stooges.

"Phone booth," growled Brian at the *squeak, flap, squeak*. "He's opening and closing the door of a phone booth, probably to get a good look at somebody who's tailing him."

"We agree," said Joe. "And the barking we're hearing is Tommy and Susie, who are on their leads right outside the booth. They usually didn't bark. It took a lot to make them squawk. All these things add up to the message: I'll be late, I got a *complication* . . . ''

"Uh-huh," I agreed. "Like somebody tailing me, trying to get what I'm carrying."

"What?" asked Brian.

"We're narrowing it down. But what about the chiming bells in the background? Which church is it?"

"Three bongs. Pretty deep bongs. Must be Park Street Church," mused Joe, "but somehow it doesn't sound like it. Three bongs means three o'clock. Let's consult Johnny's log and see where he was at three."

Joe flipped out his pocket notebook and checked the page that he'd copied the log information on. He ran his finger down the list.

"Let's see. At three in the afternoon Johnny was making a cash delivery to National Distilling in Cambridge. That's right over near the Museum of Science. Hell, there's no church there. None at all."

"It's gotta be Park Street Church," said Brian. "Do you know any other church that strikes the hours?"

Joe shook his head. "Doesn't sound like Park Street. The bongs aren't deep enough. God knows I hear that church often enough. They play a little song and then chime the hours. The bongs are slow and deep. These bongs are more like chimes; they're fast and higher pitched."

"Is it Trinity Church in Copley Square?" I asked. "I hear tons of people in the background—a lot of street traffic and pedestrians."

"I don't think Trinity strikes the hours," said Joe, rubbing his chin with his thumb. It made a raspy sound. He rewound the tape again, for the hundredth time. We were going to wear it out. There it was again: the barking, the squeak of the phone-booth door, and three bells, far off. Close by were lots of people walking and talking. Shouting and laughing.

"A mob scene," said Brian. "Sounds to me like lunch hour. Doesn't sound like three o'clock. Only on a weekend would it be so noisy at three. But it's gotta be either Park Street or Copley Square.''

"Wait a minute!'' said Joe. "I just heard the word *fiori*. That's Italian for flowers. Hell, Johnny's in the North End here. That must be Old North Church.''

We thought we'd solved the thing then. But several problems emerged. One was the fact that his log sheet showed him at the distillery at 2:45, over in Cambridge, not in the North End. Second, as Brian had observed, the mob scene outside the phone booth was too manic for three in the afternoon, even on a Friday. And finally, on Joe's suspicion that Old North Church did not chime, we called and had this confirmed. Old North was silent. Great for lanterns in the window, but not for chimes. We called Trinity. Also silent. That left us with Park Street, except the bells didn't remotely sound like those in the Park Street belfry. Then I solved it.

"Listen again,'' I said. "You'll hear that the bells aren't spaced evenly. It doesn't go *bong*, *bong*, *bong*. It goes *bong*, *bong* . . . *bong*. Two and then one. It's a ship's bell, don't you see? It's sounding three bells.''

"Three o'clock?''

"No. It would be, uh, five-thirty. Eight bells is four, then it starts all over again with a new bell for every half hour. Three bells is five-thirty in the evening. That would explain the heavy street traffic too.''

"I didn't realize the North End was so close to the harbor,'' said Brian.

"Right smack dab on it,'' said Joe, "except that it's mostly hidden by all the crowded buildings. But there's no indication in the log that Johnny went back there after his last job.''

"You remember two of the jobs had a star after them. That meant they weren't completed. One was for my dental work, which is why Johnny called me in the first place. The other unfinished business involved the public library and a party in the North End.''

"Uh-huh. And at the end of the day he went back to the North End to complete that errand, and he was carrying your lab work too. He called to say he'd be late, and right there on Hanover Street, or nearby, he realized he was being followed. And I bet the party in the North End is named Andy.''

Joe got on the phone and rasped out a series of commands to Ten-Ten Comm. Ave.:

1. He wanted the location of all phone booths in the North End near busy streets. Considering their rapid disappearance in favor of phone "enclaves," this wouldn't be difficult.
2. To check my theory, he requested information from Massport on any large vessels moored, anchored, or in transit near the North End on the day in question.
3. He called Sam Bowman at Dependable Messenger Service and requested further details on Johnny's errand to the library and the North End. Sam said he'd call back shortly with all the dope.

"Let's get coffee," said Brian, and while we sat in the police squad room and sipped, Joe's headquarters called back and gave us the location of four phone booths that would answer the set of variables he had described. They also said Massport had given them the names of three big ships in the vicinity of the North End of the previous Friday. One, a cargo container vessel named *Dunmore Hughes No. 8*, out of Bantry Bay in the Republic of Ireland, was making her way down the Mystic River channel from the Charlestown port terminal to Boston Harbor at exactly three bells.

Then Sam Bowman called back. We went back to Brian's office, where Joe took the call. His face clouded over. The big brown eyes took on a steely hard squint, and the mouth turned down at the corners. He was unhappy about something.

"Sam, say those two names again please, real slowly." He scowled. "Uh-huh. Yes, I know them. They're very familiar. I just wanted to make sure. It's just that when I hear those two names, Sam, I get a knot in my stomach and want to slug somebody. What? You don't understand? Well let's see now, what happens to you when I say Scottsboro Boys?"

Through the receiver end of the phone Brian and I could

hear faint yelling and cursing, even though the phone was pressed to Joe's ear.

"Well I thought so. So you see how it upsets me when I hear the names of Sacco and Vanzetti."

"*Sacco and Vanzetti?*" said Brian.

"Sacco and Vanzetti!" I said.

"Sacco and Vanzetti," reaffirmed Joe, who hung up and sat down wearily. He picked up his mug to take a sip; his hands were trembling. None of us said anything for a while. Then Joe spoke.

"Johnny's errand was to retrieve a portion of papers and effects willed to the Boston Public Library by the late Dominic Santuccio, a lawyer in the North End and a second-generation Italian-American. The papers and effects all concern the Sacco-Vanzetti case."

He stopped there and sipped again. His hands were still shaking. We nodded at his statement, as if listening to a university lecture. He continued.

"I met Dom a few times in connection with court cases and Italian-American functions and benefits. Nice guy, and rich. His obsession was collecting and verifying documents and evidence relative to the case. Like most of us he was certain the men were framed. He hoped to write a book proving their innocence and restoring their reputations. He was not popular with a lot of establishment people for wanting to do this. He died three months ago of cancer and never got the chance to do it."

"Yeah, I remember reading about him," said Brian. "What do you mean, *us*? You said that like most of *us* he was certain they were framed—"

"I mean us Italians, naturally. And also anyone who feels sympathy for the working-class immigrants in general. Sacco and Vanzetti committed no crime; they were radicals who questioned the system and fought for workers' rights, so the system big shots had them executed. So it's, ah, no surprise that I get a little upset when I even hear the case mentioned."

"I'm glad to hear you've got the case so goddamned buttoned up," said Brian, who was swiveling his chair around, back and forth, "because I've read about a lot of evidence that says they were *guilty*. Guilty as all hell of murder and armed robbery. The only reason, in fact, that a lot of idealists and artists *thought* they were railroaded is because of the propaganda stirred up for them by the Communists and Wobblies."

He leaned back and swiveled like a semaphore. If he was trying to get a rise out of Joe, then it worked.

"Oh yeah? Well what about that blackguard and murderer Michael Collins? Bloodthirsty pig—it's a good thing De Valera had him murdered, even though it was a double-cross. Of course, what would you expect from—"

"Don't you *ever* call Michael Collins a murderer," snapped Brian. "And don't ever accuse Eamon De Valera of killing him. Why I'd—"

"Now hold on a minute, you guys. Can't we just discuss—"

"Sacco and Vanzetti were doomed from the start. The mill owners and industrialists wanted them dead. Demanded their death. The trial was a mockery. Evidence was altered. Witnesses were led. A new trial would've—"

"Bullshit, Joe. You can't argue with a ballistics test. At least one fatal bullet was fired from Sacco's gun. Lots of reliable witnesses identified Vanzetti as one of the gunmen. When they were arrested, both men lied about what they had been doing. Both men were armed, too, with weapons like those used in the holdup."

Joe slammed his palms down on the table and jumped up, shaking his finger at Brian's face.

"Hannon, you don't deserve to be a police chief if you believe all that crap. There's a logical explanation for each of the things you mentioned, and the fact that they were even issues at the trial and turned against the men proves a conspiracy to obstruct justice. And as for that bullet, it's a direct misquoting of the witness summoned. A *lie*!"

"All I know is what I read, Joe."

"You don't know much. Those poor guys were tried and convicted not because of what they did, but because of what they were: working men, radicals, foreigners . . . Italians."

Then Brian really muddied the waters by remarking that maybe that wasn't so far off the mark, considering that Italians practically invented crime in America.

To which Joe replied—shouted back is better, actually—that ninety-eight percent of Italians were peaceable and law-abiding, and if Brian implied, directly or indirectly, that they were violent, he would personally take Brian's head off.

To which Brian replied—shouted back is better, actually—that the Irish never, as commonly supposed, looked for a fight, but if Joe wanted to start something with *him*, he personally knew of a place in Southie where seven or eight strapping young Sons of Erin would take delight in performing the Kilkenny two-step on Joe's face.

To which Joe replied—

But before he could reply the door to Brian's office burst open and two boys in blue, their batons drawn, jumped into the room.

"Everything all right, Chief?" asked the bigger one. "We heard shouting and—"

"It's okay, guys," I said calmly. 'It's just two officers of the law about to commit murder."

Brian dismissed them, and I got each combatant to his neutral corner. They glowered at each other over the table.

"I, uh, gather that the Sacco-Vanzetti case is fraught with externals. It's surrounded by issues of ethnicity and class. One might even say the judicial system was on trial as well as the defendants."

"Right, Doc. The trial did not prove they were guilty; it proved a man who didn't speak good English, didn't have a lot of money and prestige, and didn't agree a hundred percent with the exploitation of immigrants could not get a fair trial."

Brian started to say something, bit his lip a little, then said it anyway.

"But it's not by any means certain they were innocent," he said.

"Let's get back to Johnny Robinson," I suggested before Joe could reply. "Who's this Andy fellow he mentions?"

"Sam told me he's Andrea Santuccio, Dom's son. I've never met him. Johnny went to the Boston Public Library as planned at eleven on Friday and retrieved a certain parcel of letters and transcripts, given to the library by Andy after Dominic's death. Apparently this certain parcel was especially controversial . . . or *something*. Anyway, Andy later fought for a special injunction to get it back. I guess he wasn't aware of what the packet contained at first. When the court ruled that the Santuccio family was entitled to reclaim part of the papers, Andy immediately hired Johnny to pick them up and deliver them back to the Santuccio home in the North End. Clear so far?"

We nodded, and Joe continued.

"But when Johnny got to the Santuccio house apparently nobody was home. The mother died over ten years ago and Andy is the only surviving member of the family. He's also a bachelor, I guess. The fact that Andy wasn't there altered Johnny's plans. Andy was supposed to be waiting there but wasn't. So Johnny hiked over to Cambridge for the other errands, went to get your fancy dental work, Doc, and at the end of the day hoofed it back to the North End. Remember, all this time he's carrying the hot papers for Andy right in his pouch. We don't know, but we can assume that Johnny called you either right before or right after he went back to the Santuccio house for a second time."

"And delivered the papers?" asked Brian.

"No. And did *not* deliver the papers."

"How do you know, Joe?" I asked.

" 'Cause the asterisk was still there in the log, indicating a nondelivery. Sam said that before he called me back just now he called Andy's number. No answer. Now I'm going to try again."

And he did. Still no answer.

"Doc," he said wearily, "are you beginning to get the same queasy feeling I am?"

"Yep. I assume you're thinking that the guy in the chimney just might be—"

"Andrea Santuccio. The guy who was supposed to take possession of the papers but who wasn't there to get them."

"Where's that body now? In Boston?"

"It's en route from a Lowell funeral home to the Suffolk County morgue, where the autopsy will continue in greater detail. It may be there already. I'm going to make sure some locals from Hanover Street get a look at the corpse. Now."

So he got on the phone again to Ten-Ten Comm. Ave. to have some bluecoats from the North End take a peek at the grisly body we'd found in the chimney. But it wasn't necessary. As soon as the remains had come into the morgue it was identified. A subsequent check with dental records confirmed that the man was indeed Andrea Santuccio, son of the late and renowned Dominic.

"Well," sighed Joe as he twiddled a pencil between his big fingers, "at least we know why Johnny was killed, though it'll be small comfort to Sam."

"And a lot of us policemen," said Brian. "Can you work up some sort of scenario on this thing?"

Joe rubbed his stubble and thought for a minute. His face darkened.

"Old Dom Santuccio had those papers for years. He always claimed he'd uncover some kind of evidence that would clear Sacco and Vanzetti. But he obviously never did or he'd have been pounding on the governor's door night and day, shouting and screaming. Old Dom was quite a character—a fire-eater. Finally, about a year before he died—he had the cancer already and was on all kinds of drugs—he said he'd have a great announcement to make. One that would shake the world. Trouble is, nobody would believe him. Including me. He was batty by then from the pain and the drugs. Then he had a stroke and lost his speech and most of his memory. Andy had to hospitalize him because he got so violent. Now

I say this, and I don't like to, being Italian: if there's anything hot in that pack of papers, I'm afraid it's something that drives the last nail in the coffin of Sacco and Vanzetti. If not, then why didn't he let it out?"

"Why did he will the papers to the library then?"

"He didn't. After he died, his son, Andy, donated them."

"Now wait," said Brian. "Is there anyone who'd go haywire if they knew the stuff had gone into the public domain? If so, they'd be mighty annoyed at Andy. Mad enough to kill him."

We all considered in silence for a minute. Then Joe cleared his throat and raised his big bloodhound eyes up at us.

"Okay. Assuming the evidence is damning—and I can reach no other conclusion—then there's only one logical candidate for a group who'd get totally unglued at the mere thought of its revelation."

"Who?" asked Brian.

"Ever hear of the Sons of Italy?"

"Oh no. No way," I said.

"That's what I hope too. After all, I'm a lifetime member."

"Say it ain't so, Joe," I said.

"I hope—I hope to God it ain't so, Doc."

There was more silence. Then Brian spoke.

"Wait a minute, Joe. Wasn't Andy in Sons of Italy?"

"Sure. One of the real leaders, and so—oh shit. I see what you mean. They certainly wouldn't harm him. In fact, the Sons wouldn't hurt anybody . . . I don't think."

"Here's what happened," I said. "After old Dom's death Andy, being a good citizen and interested in the case and his father's lifelong passion, donates the papers. Fine. Then sometime later, and we'll probably never know how, he discovers that there's something hot in the papers: a potential bombshell. He has to get the papers back to save the last vestiges of Sacco and Vanzetti's tarnished reputation. Because if scholars dig out the facts and publish them, every American, and especially every Italian-American, will have to face the truth—that Sacco and Vanzetti were indeed rob- bers and killers. Right?''

''That's it. So far so good . . . *But*, he also knows that somebody else wants the papers. Or else why hire Johnny Robinson?''

''Yeah, but who wants them?''

''I don't know,'' said Joe. ''But I've seen the archives room at the Boston Public and it's a virtual vault. The people who wanted the papers would have to take them from Andy after he got them back, or else during the delivery itself.''

''It would seem to me that taking them from Andy would be easier and safer,'' I said.

''Yeah, but you don't know the North End like I do. It's the tightest of all the Boston neighborhoods. Maybe they thought pulling something against Santuccio on his home turf would be very risky, so they took or lured young Andy away from the meeting with Johnny. Maybe they thought he al- ready had the packet. Under interrogation he tells them it's on its way via courier, but one glance at Johnny and the dogs and the thugs know it's no-can-do. So they know if Johnny can't make contact he'll either leave the packet at Dependable's office or take it home, where they set up the ambush—''

''Doesn't sound right,'' I said. ''Let's suppose that by eleven in the morning the bad guys already have custody of Andy away from his house. He tells them the drop is being made right then, and they're too late to connect. He describes Johnny to them—maybe they're already familiar with how formidable he is—and they set the ambush with the bomb by early afternoon. One or two guys are in Robinson's place waiting. Another guy stations himself at the Santuccio house to see if Johnny comes back, which he does at around five. Still no Andy, so he leaves and starts home. He stops to call my office, knowing I'm waiting for the bridge. At that time he discovers he's being shadowed.''

''Right!''

''Okay. So he's struck out twice with an important meet- ing with Andy and thinks he's being tailed. 'A complication, dontcha know,' he says. He's put two and two together and it spells trouble. But he's cool; he's been through worse. He does stop at Dependable to drop off the log sheet and get into his Cutlass to head for home. He takes his pouch with him because he wants to touch base with Andy, and me, over the weekend. Probably the lookout notices this, and calls ahead to some guy waiting near a pay phone in Lowell. Johnny's coming home with his pouch: get ready.''

"Yeah. So the hit goes pretty much the way we figured it. As soon as he's dead they take Johnny's pouch and skip. They kill the Santuccio boy so he won't talk, and as an afterthought remove two of his digits.''

"Would you guys tell me what's happening?" asked Brian. So we did. And he thought about it.

"But you said the boy was tortured too. That's terrible. It also has to be explained. Why torture the kid? Who would want to do that?''

"Hatred,'' said Joe.

"Maybe. But that's only one of the three reasons for torture,'' said Brian. "The other two are information, and the verification of information.''

"Ah yes. Well then, they tortured him in order to find out about Johnny and how to get their hands on the packet,'' I said.

"Maybe,'' he said, "or maybe it happened afterward . . . Maybe they tortured and killed him as a last resort because they didn't get what they wanted.''

"They got it,'' said Joe. "We know they got the pouch; we can't find it anywhere. Neither can Sam.''

Brian Hannon set fire to a Lucky, inhaled deeply, and let the smoke stream out his nostrils like a dragon.

"Mmmmm. You can't find it. But that doesn't mean for sure that the bad guys have it. Yet. Johnny was no dumbbell. He was cool and sharp. Maybe he stashed the pouch at the last second. Who knows? All I say is, I say the torture thing is not only ugly, it's mysterious. It needs explaining. If I were you, Joe, I'd hang in there like a sash weight. Go at it tooth and nail; I'll help any way I can.''

We got up and left the chief's office. But Joe ducked back in to thank Brian, which I thought was nice. Then he said: ''About that ballistics test performed at the Dedham trial. I just want you to know a few things about it, Brian, because like any cop I'm aware of how decisive they are nowadays. This was the first ballistics test and comparative analysis of fired bullets ever performed. The guy who did the test was a Massachusetts state cop, like me. His name was Captain William Proctor. My boss remembers him. Anyway, the results proved that one of the fatal bullets could have been fired from the pistol Sacco was carrying at the time of his arrest. *Could have.* What they didn't give Proctor a chance to say was that it could have been fired from *any* thirty-two-caliber automatic. Later investigations by the defense showed that the spent cases had a peculiar mark on them made by an ejector claw common only to foreign-made automatics. Sacco carried a Colt. The defense later showed that the pistol that fired the bullet probably belonged to Antonio Mancini, a professional killer and member of the Morelli gang of Providence.''

Brian stared dumbstruck during this discourse. Then Joe and I headed for Old Stone Mill Road. I had a question that was gnawing at me.

''Joe, if the defense proved that the bullet was probably fired by this other guy, then why didn't they let Sacco and Vanzetti off?''

''Because they had already been electrocuted. Read the books on the case, Doc. It's not very pretty. The whole thing makes the Commonwealth look like a ninety-pound pile of dog doo.''

Mary was out shopping. I made a big sandwich for my brother-in-law, and while he ate lunch I drank two mugs of coffee and ate half a banana and some yogurt. While we ate I asked him lots of questions about the Sacco–Vanzetti case. Then he left for Ten-Ten Comm. Ave., taking the tapes with him. I returned to my office to look at X rays and do preliminary work on a mandible resection that I was to perform the following week. After all my appointments I stopped at the library before going home and emerged with seven books, all about Sacco and Vanzetti.

Quite a case.

7

Tom Costello was miserable, and irritable.

"But the insurance will cover everything, Tom. Every buck."

"Great! But what about *me*? Know how thilly I thound over the phone?"

"I've still got the casts; it won't take as long as the first time."

We made the necessary appointments for the rebuilding of the anterior bridge. It would take a lot of extra time and neither of us was happy about it. I would not bill him for the extra hours it would cost me, of course. As he was leaving I asked him what he knew about Sacco and Vanzetti. He harangued me for twenty minutes about what a raw deal they'd gotten, mostly because they were Italians. Considering his name was Costello, it figured. But then I bumped into Jim DeGroot at the liquor store. I asked him and he shrugged his shoulders, saying that if a Massachusetts court found them guilty and all the appeals and motions of delay and new trials didn't work, then they probably were guilty.

"But what's the sense in talking about it now? They're dead anyway, right?"

Figured.

Then I asked Moe Abramson, and he said that he pitied not only the two innocent men who were sent to their deaths but the whole sick and bigoted Yankee–WASP establishment plutocracy that set them up. Then he went into a discourse on punishment and guilt, and quoted by memory whole passages from Dostoevski, Freud, Malraux, and others.

Figured.

"You know who I think really convicted them, even more than that bastard Judge Thayer? It was the jury foreman, Ripley. He hated Italians. He was a cop who wanted more than anything to 'get the dagos.' Can you imagine allowing ga jury like that? They should've had some Jews on that jury. It never would have happened."

"Why?"

"Simple. Of all the people who have suffered from prejudice and persecution, we've suffered the most. But we're not like the other groups, who then can't wait to dish out hatred to the next bunch of unfortunates. The Jews don't do that. We've never done that and never will; we stay with the underdog. Listen Doc, more than anyone else it was two Jewish men who tried to get Sacco and Vanzetti off the hook: Felix Frankfurter and Herbert Ehrmann. Wanta see my new tank?"

"No."

"Get in here this instant." He held his office door open and I followed reluctantly. I stayed two feet behind him and got ready to shield my eyes. The new tank was high and narrow and filled with bright coral fans. Several brilliantly colored fish wafted about. Surprise, surprise; Moe's taste was improving.

"Salt water," he said. "Those are tangs. Nice, eh?"

"Great. I'm surprised that you—"

But I stopped short, speechless with revulsion at what I saw at the bottom of the tank. The sand there came alive in a flapping, rolling, undulating mass of writhing flesh.

"Good God!" I groaned.

"What? The skate? He belongs there, Doc. Part of the scheme of things."

The horrid bulbous eyes darted about as if on stalks. Four

vents behind each eye opened and shut rhythmically. The scaly tail twitched. I spun about-face and departed.

" 'Bye, Moe. We'll resume our chess game when you get rid of the tank."

"Remember, Doc," he yelled after me, leaning out of his doorway, "every creature deserves a home, even ugly ones."

"Don't be a sap," I said.

I went home at five-thirty, went for a run, took a sauna and shower, sat with a cold mug on the porch, and started to read the first book about Sacco and Vanzetti. After twenty pages I was disturbed. After eighty I was distraught. Surely this was some kind of joke. Certainly the author did not know what he was saying . . . So I put it down and tried another. Worse. Okay, I told myself, the third time's the charm. So I picked up tome number three. Disastrous. I put the books down and gave the far wall a thousand-yard stare. I felt bludgeoned. If it weren't so sad it would be almost humorous. The proceedings of the case, and the various assumptions, allegations, denials, and refusals, had all the earmarks of a vaudeville skit.

Mary came home. I heard her high heels clicking and snapping around the kitchen linoleum. I heard a shopping bag rustle, the refrigerator door open and shut.

"Charlie?"

"Mmmmph."

"What are you doing home? What's the matter?"

I explained the reading material. She replied that of *course* they were innocent men. Of *course* they'd been railroaded to the chair. Where had *I* been?

"Our folks talked about that case all the time when we were kids in Schenectady. Didn't Joe tell you?"

"Joe just left here. He ate the biggest submarine sandwich ever constructed. He just ate a Trident-class sub. He's taking us to dinner tonight at Joe Tecce's. Now let me be; I want to reread key parts of these books again to make sure there's no mistake."

I did. Then I read them again. Mary came in and said it

was time to get ready. She asked me why I was reading and rereading the books.

"Because I'm hoping that I've overlooked something; that something will change if I keep reading it over."

But it didn't. It was with a weary heart that I donned the fancy duds. Even the sight of Mary prancing around in her undies didn't cheer me up, and she looks nice in 'em. We got in the Audi and got on to Route 2 for Boston. I had a tape of Mozart's Concerto No. 2 for Horn playing, and it helped a bit, but not much. By mistake Mary first popped in the cassette of Jeannie Redpath singing Scottish ballads. That can have you bawling in five minutes even if you're in a good mood. We drove along and I puffed on my pipe in silence. Mary turned off the tape.

"Okay, Charlie. Tell me about it. What's gotten you so depressed? We've got the time now. Spill."

"Everything I read about Sacco and Vanzetti points not only to a trial that was unfair but to an inexorable machine of destruction pointed straight at them."

"So what's new about that?"

"I've got to read the stuff more carefully, but getting into it fast, I saw the sweep and size of the monster. Most people have now acknowledged the unfair-trial part. After all, Sacco and Vanzetti, while never even accused of any crime whatsoever prior to their arrest, *were* radical anarchists. Anarchists killed President McKinley in 1901, and started the First World War by killing Archduke Ferdinand in 1914. So they were unpopular. This is old. What's new to me is the sense of *orchestration* behind the events of the trial and subsequent appeals. I keep seeing in my mind's eye a smoke-filled room somewhere with a small group of very rich and well-dressed men puffing on cigars, planning the whole thing. And this cabal could set the machinery in motion, Mary. Ah, yes . . . just as easy as throwing a switch in one of the textile mills, setting all those flywheels spinning, those loom arms thumping, those bobbins twirling . . ."

"Well hasn't that been said before?"

"Kind of. It was alleged vaguely. It surfaced during the seven years of the trial and appeals—"

"*Seven years!*"

"Oh yeah. During the ordeal some of the undercurrents were visible. But when you look through seven books all at once you see the entire thing, as if from a space satellite. I can't help seeing a great mechanized thing, fueled by power and wealth, running down those two steerage-class trouble-makers without even missing a beat."

"You sound like Jack London."

"Don't mean to. And, of course, they could have even been guilty. But guilty or not, they had that machine set after them like the Hound of Hell. As sure as we're sitting in this car."

"What happened? The crime, I mean."

"On April fifteenth, nineteen twenty, there was an armed robbery of a shoe factory in South Braintree. It was the Slater and Morrill factory on Pearl Street. The spot is probably less than a mile from where the South Shore mall is now. In the robbery the two payroll guards were shot dead. They didn't try to go for their guns or anything; they were just shot down in cold blood. Murdered. About fifteen grand was taken by five holdup men, who escaped in a large touring car."

"They stole money, not shoes?"

"They robbed the payroll. It was payday. In those days workers weren't paid by check; they got cash in pay envelopes which were toted around in strongboxes and armored cars like Brinks trucks. It was like the old Westerns, in which gold was carried on trains and stagecoaches. But your point about stealing shoes is interesting, because only people with a great familiarity with the factory and its procedures could have pulled off the heist, which went like clockwork. They even dribbled out a stream of tacks behind the car so pursuing vehicles would rupture their tires. They got clean away."

Mary sat in silence for a second before asking the obvious

sequitur: "If they got clean away, then when were Sacco and Vanzetti arrested?"

"Twenty days later, on a streetcar in Brockton. It was about ten at night. Both men were armed with handguns. They had spare ammunition too. When asked about their business that night, and where they were on the day of the robbery, they lied."

"*Huh?* I never heard it that way."

"Probably not. Not in an Italian-American family you wouldn't. But it's true. So you see they weren't off to a good start. Add these circumstances to the fact that they had both gone to Mexico as draft dodgers during the Great War, and the fact that Sacco was not at work on April fifteenth—he missed that day and only that day—and the fact that Vanzetti, a fish peddler, had no regular job or employer who could vouch for him, and you can see how their troubles multiplied pretty quickly."

"Jeeez, Charlie. Maybe they *were* guilty!"

"May be."

We drove on past the Fresh Pond Bowladrome and fruit stand. I could feel Mary glaring at me.

"Don't play games, dammit! You've got me hanging now. Did they or didn't they?"

"Did they what?"

She punched me in the arm. It hurt. She'd make a good featherweight, I thought, and I told her so. She hit me again.

"Okay, okay," I said. "An interesting thing was this: right after the South Braintree robbery the police in New Bedford were closing in on a known gang of robbers they were watching because of a suspicious license plate and a stolen car that might have been used as the escape vehicle. This gang, called the Morelli gang, was based in New York and Providence. One of the Morelli brothers lived in New Bedford. But the New Bedford cops cut short their investigation."

"Why?"

"Because in early May they heard that the criminals had

been arrested: Sacco and Vanzetti. So they dropped it. It's a shame they did, too, because the Morelli gang had a history of robbing factory freight cars, especially those of Slater and Morrill. In fact, some of its members had cased the Slater and Morrill plant more than once . . .''

"And how did they know that the cops in Brockton had the right guys?''

" 'Cause the cops in Brockton *said so*. Chief Michael Stewart of Bridgewater was obsessed with the idea that a band of anarchist robbers was living in the South Shore area, and that they kept their getaway car in a shed. Finding such a shed and having been told that the car usually kept there wasn't running well and was being repaired, Stewart ordered a stakeout on the local garage that was fixing the car. It was an Overland, a now-defunct make of auto. Four men came to the garage to claim the car. Told it wasn't ready, they departed. Two left riding a motorcycle. Two left on foot and boarded a streetcar: Sacco and Vanzetti.''

"And what were they doing at night getting a car and carrying guns? Huh?''

"They wanted to use the car to collect some radical literature they'd recently distributed. An associate of theirs, a guy named Salsedo—Andrea Salsedo—was held illegally and interrogated by the FBI in New York. He was also detained for eight weeks in a fourteenth-story room of a building there. All this was done without formal criminal charge, you understand, in violation of his fundamental rights. On May third his crushed body was found on the pavement below. The Feds said that he must have leaped to his death. Suicide, or so they said. Sacco, Vanzetti, and the rest of the anarchists were scared stiff. They feared the same fate. That's why they were armed; that's why they were out trying to get the car rolling so they could make the rounds and get rid of the incriminating literature.''

"And why weren't the two other guys accused of the crime too?''

"They were. One had an alibi through his employment

and the other was very short—so short all of the witnesses agreed he couldn't have taken part. So the police got Sacco and Vanzetti by process of elimination. Even then, their fingerprints did not match any found on the getaway car when it was discovered abandoned. The prosecution later dropped the whole question of prints.''

"Charlie: *were they guilty*?''

"From what I've read, I'd say no. Armed robbery was against their characters as revealed by their lives. They simply weren't violent men or criminals. Protestors, yes. Angry men who disagreed with the status quo, yes. But killers and robbers, no. And the prosecution's claim that they pulled the job leaves too many ends dangling, too many details unexplained and floating in a vacuum. Where were the guys who helped them? Not only did the defendants not tell, but there was nothing about their past histories or personal associations that connected to the robbery. The fifteen grand that was taken—where was it? The defendants didn't have it. Moreover, there was not a trace of it anywhere around the two men. Certainly the sick old car they came to collect wasn't the one used in the lightning-quick robbery. No sane person would use it in *any* robbery. The guns they were carrying seemed to be the most damning and inexplicable pieces of evidence. Yet the ballistics tests performed by the prosecution were misinterpreted and used to mislead the jury. Finally, both men did have alibis.''

"Well if they had alibis what was the problem?''

"The alibis, on both counts, had serious flaws: they depended on the testimony of fellow Italians.''

Mary snapped her head around and let out a few choice exclamations. I blush even now to think of them.

"Uh-huh. That's how a lot of your countrymen feel about it. Now as a comparison, when the case against the Morelli gang is considered, all—not some, but *all*—the loose ends are gathered up neatly and tied into a bow: the gang's need for money to pay for upcoming defense lawyer's fees and bail; the money itself, which appeared at the right time and in the right amount; the getaway car, which as I mentioned earlier first tipped off the New Bedford cops; the getaway route, which was accurately described by the guy who should've been the defense's star witness in a new trial; and finally . . . three big things.''

"What were the three big things?''

"One: the fact that the Morelli-gang hypothesis explains each and every participant in the crime, down to the last detail as described by the witnesses. Two: the Morelli gang was composed of robbers and killers; the past of each gang member ties him with robbery and crime as a way of life. And three—are you ready? Remember I said there should have been a star witness? He was a guy in jail with Sacco and Vanzetti at Dedham. He was the guy who sparked the investigation of the Morelli bunch in the first place. Know why? Because in nineteen twenty-six, six years after the holdup and a year before Sacco and Vanzetti were put to death, *he confessed to taking part in the robbery* and described it in every detail. Know what else? He wrote out a sworn statement that *Sacco and Vanzetti weren't there*!''

Mary squirmed in her seat and drew her breath in sharply, her eyes bugged out in her anger.

"You're shitting me!''

"Nope.''

"And those bastards executed them anyway?''

"Yep.''

"Charlie, you're shitting me!''

"Cross my heart . . . ''

"Bastards!'' she shouted, smacking the dashboard with her fists. She does this on big slabs of clay to get the air bubbles out before firing. The clay could take it; the Audi, despite its engineering, probably couldn't.

"Easy, kid. The guy's name was Celestino Madeiros, a Portuguese boy who was already indicted for murder in another holdup. He was executed the same night as Sacco and Vanzetti. He had nothing to gain by the confession. He said he felt sorry for the two guys held wrongly. He felt especially sorry for Sacco's wife, Rosina, and their son, Dante.''

We were now passing Mass. General Hospital, and swept around it and over to Causeway Street. Then a right turn onto Washington and we were there. The whole time Mary sat silently, glowering through the windshield. We met Joe in the open-air patio court for a drink. I ordered a dry Tanqueray martini and got it wet, which invariably happens in any Italian restaurant, and we waited for our table. Mary sipped on a Campari, having forsworn peppermint schnapps forever.

"What's the matter, Sis?" asked Joe, who couldn't help noticing her subdued state. She told him, and we launched into the case again.

"I agree with you, Doc. There was an invisible hand behind it all, pulling the strings and pushing the buttons. The worst thing though was the prosecution's constant claim that this and that evidence showed that the defendants *could* have committed the crime. Their alibi witnesses *could* be lying to protect their friends; therefore they *were* lying. The men *could* have been in South Braintree, so therefore they *were* there, and therefore they *did* commit the robbery. Bullshit! American law says the prosecution must prove guilt. It does not say the defense must prove innocence. They were marked men.''

He rapped the table twice as he said the words again. *"Marked men."*

We went in and ordered dinner. I had the house specialty, which is steak à la Mafia. It was great. We all shared the antipasti and pasta, and a liter of good house red. Three couples came in, obviously young studs and foxy mammas from the North End. They wore the local outfit. The women, who were gorgeous, had on tight blouses, choker necklaces, and pants that were sprayed on. This ensemble was set off by four-inch stiletto heels. Their hair was swept back, short, thick, black, and slightly wet. Their faces were heavily made up and their cheeks bloodred. Their lips were purple and wet and slick as the underside of a lily pad. Mary said that she didn't care if the punk look was the rage, they looked like cheap whores. No doubt about it, they looked a bit tawdry. They looked wanton. They looked wicked and nasty. They looked terrific.

The guys, among the three of them, were wearing more gold than Fort Knox. Necklaces, crucifixes, St. Chris medals, St. Francis medals, St. Jude, St. Anthony, St. Peter, and so on. Rings, I.D. bracelets, watches, buckles. If they tried to board a plane at Logan Airport the metal detector would get a hernia. They wore continental-cut jackets with a little sheen to them, black calfskin boots with heels—they needed the heels to be taller than their dates—and pants that were skintight at the crotch to show the world that they were hung like seed bulls. Their hair looked a lot like their dates' hair. All of them had mustaches; one also wore a beard. Their white silk shirts had big collars and were open to the navel, this to reveal both the array of chains and charms and medals and the chest rugs. Each guy's bosom looked like a coconut-fiber doormat. I've heard it rumored that Caesare's Men's Boutique sells not only hairpieces but chest rugs too, for those who aren't naturally endowed. I could use one. Another item that purports to move well at Caesare's is a padded-cup jock for guys who want to look hung like a seed bull but aren't. I could use one . . .

"Well at least you can tell the boys from the girls here," I said. "That's refreshing anyway." Never had I seen such blatant sexuality; never was human sexual dimorphism more exaggerated. "And don't bother staring at their pants, Mary; they're just wearing those padded jocks."

"If I have another glass of wine I think I'll go check," she said. "By the way, I notice you haven't taken your eyes off that tall girl's ass since she walked in."

"Huh?"

"Don't 'huh' me, buster. How would you like me to dress like that?"

"I'd love it."

"Hey Joe! Joey!" A fat man with an enormous mustache was working his way over to our table. Joe jumped up and pumped his hand. Then his arm slowed down. He was looking at the man's face. He had obviously been crying.

"Joey—" the man said quickly, and he leaned over and whispered in Joe's ear.

"I know."

"Oh, sorry," the man said, turning to us, "didn't mean to do that. Something sad just happened. Sorry."

Then he turned back to Joe again and leaned over him. "Can you come for a few minutes anyhow?"

"Yes," answered Joe. "We'll be right over when we finish."

The fat man left, his eyes glancing to and fro as if looking for others to accost. We dove into our ice cream, and Joe explained that they had Andy Santuccio laid out at Langone's funeral parlor a couple of blocks away and that he was going to stop by and pay his respects. We said we'd come along.

The place was crowded. People of all shapes and ages milled about, talking in low tones. They kissed each other, embraced, sobbed quietly, and said the rosary. About half spoke English, half Italian. There was a lot of black, especially worn by the older woman. Men wore dark hats. It almost resembled a congregation of Orthodox Jews on the Lower East Side. The parlor room which held the remains was packed with flowers. Two old aunts stood at the casket, shaking hands with mourners and wiping their eyes. Many people came and went from the chapel room. The only things missing were the street procession and the men with the trumpets following behind, playing the dirge. Otherwise it very closely resembled the Sicilian funeral scene in *The Godfather*. I made this observation to Joe, who suddenly realized something.

"Follow me," he said, leading us back past the offices to a small room crammed with mementos and pictures on all the walls. Joe looked through several volumes of photographs and newspaper clippings before showing me a picture of Hanover Street crowded to overflowing with spectators as a pair of hearses inched down the street. All the men wore hats: skimmers, fedoras, bowlers, even top hats. The women wore wide hats with flowers on top and big, full-skirted dresses. The hearses looked about 1920s vintage.

"What's this?" I asked him.

"The funeral procession of Sacco and Vanzetti. Look. See the armbands worn by all the mourners? Look, here's another one."

He turned the page and I saw a grisly photo of two dead men on slabs. They were partially draped, but their upper torsos and heads were visible. Their faces had the vacant, collapsed look of death. Then Joe turned another page and we saw the two men formally laid out in suits, placed in caskets with the lids propped open, and covered with flowers, much as poor young Andy was next door. But a crowd was tightly pressed around the corpses. The people in the crowd were holding up a huge banner, which read: DID YOU SEE WHAT I DID TO THOSE ANARCHIST BASTARDS THE OTHER DAY?

"Do you know about that quote, Doc?"

"Yeah. It was supposedly said by the judge at the trial, Webster Thayer, when he was playing golf with friends in Worcester. It showed he was just a wee bit biased. It doesn't say very much for American jurisprudence, does it?"

"Nah. It sure doesn't."

The fat man with the watery eyes and walrus mustache came into the room and looked at the pictures with us for a few minutes. He kept apologizing for interrupting us and Joe kept telling him he wasn't. His name was Gus Giordano, and I liked him immediately and intensely. Like Moe Abramson, he seemed to be a giving person.

"So sad," he said, looking down at the photographs of the funeral procession. "So very sad."

Big drops were falling on the pictures. Giordano was crying. He wiped his eyes and looked at Mary. He managed a weak smile and she hugged him.

"But you should see the real thing. The films of it. Joey, you know Frank Bertoni?"

"Never heard of him."

"He lives just up the street. He's a film nut, you know? Collects all kinds of old movies. He's put together a film based on old newsreels of the trial. Took him years to get all the footage. We've shown it at Sons of Italy and sometimes—"

"Wait a minute," said Joe, looking up quickly. "Hey, I think I've seen that film. It's like old-time movies? Like Chaplin?"

"That's it," said Giordano. "Well, if you've seen it already . . ."

"But we haven't," said Mary. "Do you think it's possible for us to—"

"For you, the world," said Giordano, and went to a phone.

He returned in less than five minutes and handed Joe a slip of paper with a name and address on it.

"He's a great guy and he loves to show the film; it's his pride and joy. I'd go too but I really should stay awhile. *Arrivederla.*"

After Joe spent another ten minutes pumping hands and giving hugs, we left Langone's and walked four blocks to the apartment building of Frank Bertoni, who let us in at the front door and walked us up two floors. He was young and blondish and wore wire-rimmed granny glasses. His apartment was small but neat, the walls covered with old movie posters. There was a photo of Charlie Chaplin in a repairman's suit, wielding a huge wrench to giant machinery. There were posters featuring Gable and Lombard, Tracy and Hepburn, Jane Russell, and lots more.

Frank had prepared for our arrival; armchairs were set up in the living room in a row facing a screen. Behind the seats sat a projector on a table. He switched the projector on, the house lights off. The whirring of the projector was the only noise in the room. The movie was silent, the seconds ticked off by a line like a radar blip that moved counterclockwise in a circle: 5 . . . 4 . . . 3 . . . 2 . . . 1 . . . and then we saw the title in black and white:

THE NEVER-ENDING WRONG
a film by
Francis J. Bertoni

The window was open, and the street noises of babbling pedestrians and car traffic that filtered up through the window were a natural accompaniment to the crowd scenes and protests we saw on film. The film was, of course, a spliced collection of the original film footage. The moving images on the screen bore all the earmarks of age, with ropelike streaks that moved back and forth across the pictures, making them look like it was raining, and great white blobs and flashes that exploded continually all over the screen. Most striking, though, was the high-speed, Chaplinesque puppet dance of the people, which failed to lend the necessary comic relief to the grim scenes that paraded before us.

The first thing we saw was a huge crowd of protesters carrying signs and banners in the rain. I was puzzled to see a gigantic pillar in the center of the picture. A shot from farther back revealed it to be the base of Nelson's Column in Trafalgar Square. Tall-helmeted bobbies milled around the fringes of the mob. Flash to Paris, where a similar throng stood and pranced around the Arc de Triomphe, the primitive camera making the solemn marchers look like square dancers as they jumped and turned and sashayed arm in arm. On to Moscow, where, as one would suspect, they were going bananas. Whole trainloads of protesters, probably encouraged by the state, filed off railroad cars and drummed through the wide streets as they met farmers driving troikas and ox-carts. Around St. Basil's the multitudes in tall hats and billowing skirts shouted and raised their hands together, sang, and hopped about like bunny rabbits. In Rome the crowds were tumultuous, as might be expected in the home country of the accused. Though lightly clad in comparison to their northern cousins, the crowds in St. Peter's Square engaged in the same tragicomic square dance.

Shot of a building. Bertoni announced that it was the Dedham courthouse, scene of the trial. Pan down the street toward another biggish building, which we cannot see. Then another shot. It is a prison, complete with high brick wall and coil of barbed wire, barely visible, creeping over the edge. Two watchtowers, and the big cell-block building itself, with barred windows. The Dedham jail looks the way we think a jail should look—perfect for a movie set. A crowd coming toward the camera, with all the people doing that old-time-movie polka dance that's usually funny but now is not. Close-up of four men. I see instantly that the two in the middle are Sacco and Vanzetti. They look young . . . and hopeful. Sacco even manages a weak and fleeting smile. Vanzetti looks stern. He is talking. He is holding hands with his fellow prisoner, a nice gesture. No, wait. They're handcuffed together. Their outer arms are also handcuffed, to the marshals beside them. Vanzetti is trying to say something, but he wants to use his hands and he cannot. He finally manages to bow his head and remove his worker's snap-brim hat, which he holds, and speaks to the camera. Shot of Sacco, saying nothing. Vanzetti is tall and handsome; his giant drooping mustache gives him the air of an orator. Sacco is short, stocky, and trim in his dark suit and bowler hat. Very close shot of Sacco's face. Typically Italian. Dark, with rather prominent nose and cheekbones. Intense and handsome. The face aroused much controversy because witnesses swore that it was Nick Sacco they saw at the scene of the robbery and murder. Nobody claimed to have seen Vanzetti. And yet Herbert Ehrmann, the young, bright assistant defense counsel, showed the striking resemblance between Sacco's typical Italian face and that of Joe Morelli, leader of the holdup gang in Providence. A resemblance that was not twinlike but clonelike. The prosecution and the state refused to consider the evidence.

Back to Vanzetti, who finishes his speech and replaces his

cap. The crowd moves on, jump-stepping fast down the street. Policemen in double-breasted coats with brass buttons bring up the rear, carrying shotguns. Switch to big car pulling up in front of courthouse. Car is fancy, probably a Stutz or Packard or Cadillac. Out pops a man in tails and top hat. Close-up as he tips his hat and smiles. Judge Webster Thayer. His hair and mustache are trim and white. He looks prosperous, and is. Switch to beefy, truculent man charging down the sidewalk. Military carriage, firm bouncy step, skimmer straw hat. Fred Katzmann, the district attorney and chief prosecutor. He looks competent, trained, thorough, and absolutely merciless. He proves himself to be all of these, especially during the cross-examination of Sacco, in which his questions are directed toward Sacco's political beliefs, his American patriotism, his home and family life, and a dozen other subjects not related to the South Braintree crime but designed to inflame and prejudice the jury. Katzmann gives a false smile and quicksteps on. Crowd going up courthouse steps. They jump and swing their way up in double time. One can almost hear the dance caller and fiddle. As each person appears Bertoni identifies him for us. Then we are surprised to see the interior of the courtroom, and Bertoni explains that this was before the Lindbergh kidnapping trial, at which cameras of any type were banned from courtrooms.

"It keeps getting darker and lighter," said Mary, breaking our silence. "Why's that?"

"It was before high-intensity lamps," explained Frank. "They're lighting magnesium flares, one after the other."

The courtroom is packed. Shot of curious-looking wire cage in back of courtroom. Sacco and Vanzetti are sitting in it. Cage is solid except for space to peek out in front. Close-up of Judge Thayer. Shot of someone testifying. Slow pan of pistols and bullets and cartridge cases on table. Shot of defense table, with attorneys Thompson and Ehrmann nodding and talking to each other. Shot of Katzmann again. Scary. Evil. But then the film was designed to convey that . . .

Final close-up of Sacco and Vanzetti. Then the strange,

snakelike scratches in the film, the dark vertical lines that weave about on the screen, seem to converge on the two men in the dock. They snake forward and back, growing thicker, almost blotting out the two faces. Close-up of Vanzetti, whose face has lost all of its former defiance and sternness. One now sees doubt in the handsome, youthful face. Doubt, and the beginnings of fear. The lines grow thick again. Big white blotches explode around the face.

Cut to Boston Statehouse. Big crowd on Beacon Street and up the steps. Cops with brass buttons and billy clubs holding the crowd back. Huge car pulls up. Much bigger than Judge Thayer's. A real limo. Out pops a man in a sporty three-piecer, with skimmer. He jumps up the statehouse steps, removes the skimmer, and waves it to the crowd. Governor Alvan Fuller. He looks rich, and is. He owns the Packard dealership in Boston. He wants to be President. Close-up of Fuller speaking. Then a shot of three middle-aged men. Very distinguished trio. Bertoni tells us they are the special commission chosen by Fuller to review the case. They look as alike as Winkin, Blinkin, and Nod. All have white hair and trim mustaches like Judge Thayer. All have well-cut suits with tails, and top hats. They look as if they're going to a ball. The credentials of the commission were flawless: Robert Grant was a former judge, Samuel Stratton was president of M.I.T., and A. Lawrence Lowell was president of Harvard. In fact, the towns of Lawrence and Lowell were named after members of his family, who put up the money to build the factories and dams and canals to make even more money. But they meant well, those three top-hatted gentlemen. I guess.

Cut to crowds of protesters on Beacon Street again. Cut to Trafalgar Square, Paris, Moscow, and Rome again. Cut to a grim crowd of silent people standing around a big prison. Now, even the old-time movie camera cannot make them jump or dance. They are frozen. Waiting.

"This is Charlestown Prison, the afternoon of the execution," said Frank.

The camera pans the faces of the crowd. All is still. Then the shot we aren't ready for: a small crowd of prison officials opening the gates, and behind them people carrying out the two black coffins.

The film hissed and crackled. The wavy black lines snaked along over the picture. The white splotches exploded on the screen.

Cut to Langone's funeral parlor, the place we had just been to see Andy Santuccio. Then a shot of the inside, where the open caskets are resting on sawhorses, the big banner with Judge Thayer's quote up behind them. It looks just like the photographs we'd seen earlier. Then the final scene, a slow procession of the two hearses down Hanover Street, decked in flowers. Cut to a quote:

> None of my enemies will be mourned as I am.
> —Bartolomeo Vanzetti, 1927

The film crackled loudly, snapped through the gears of the machine, and flipped round and round until Frank Bertoni switched it off. We sat, stunned. Mary's mouth was halfway open. She didn't twitch a muscle. Finally Joe broke the silence by thanking Frank.

"Was it really that big, Frank?" asked Mary. "People protesting all over the world?"

"Oh yeah. In fact a lot of people, in retrospect, think that the protesters did as much as anything else to send them to the chair. It got too big. Too threatening. The big shots in the system felt that half the world was against them and willing to help 'the reds.' It scared hell out of 'em, and they convinced themselves they *had* to snuff out this radical menace before it got out of hand and overpowered them. It became a battle of ideology and class, not a criminal trial."

We had some of Frank's Amaretto and departed. We stopped to buy coffee beans and spinach pasta, then went to the car. Joe asked us over to his place on Pinckney Street, so we went. After all, he treated us to dinner, and I think he wanted a chance to pay us back for the weekends in Concord. But my heart wasn't in the visit. The film had done me in. Mary too. We sat and listened to records and shared a bottle of bubbly. Joe sensed our depression.

"Movie got to you eh? Yeah. Thinking back now to when I first saw it, I remember feeling pretty depressed too. Well as I said before, the case makes the Commonwealth of Massachusetts look like a ninety-pound pile of dog doo."

"Any luck on finding Johnny Robinson's courier pouch?" I asked, changing the subject.

"Naw. It'll never turn up. They destroyed it I'm sure."

"You say he wore it every day?"

"Yep. Wore it to bed practically."

"Did he wash it often?"

"Huh? How the hell do I know? What kind of question is—"

"Nothing. I was just wondering. Well Mary, let's get moving."

So we went and got home forty minutes later. It was close to midnight. I sat on the couch reading a book about French vineyards.

"Wait here, sport," said Mary, disappearing upstairs.

Ten minutes later I heard labored footsteps on the carpet, and felt a tap on my shoulder. I looked up and couldn't believe my eyes.

Mary was standing there in skin-tight pants and a pink sweater that would've been too tight on a Barbie doll. She had half her makeup cabinet on her face, her hair down, and was scarcely able to retain her balance on five-inch spiked heels.

"Where the hell did you get *that* getup?"

"Been savin' it for the right guy . . ."

"How can you walk in those? Or stand?"

She shrugged and sneered.

"Don't plan on stayin' upright that long."

"Those pants are even tighter than the ones in the North End."

"They're dance tights. You like?"

She turned her back and wiggled, then sat down on my lap and kept moving.

"Seriously, Charlie"—she kissed me—"do you like it?"

"Be still my heart."

8

I TOOK MY COFFEE INTO MARY'S ATELIER AND WATCHED HER throwing big slabs of clay around. Fifty pounds apiece. Wham! Splat! She hefted them up and slammed them down on her sturdy bench to force the air bubbles out. If the bubbles remain inside the clay, the air explodes in the heat of the kiln during firing and your pot blows up—shatters all over the place. She bounced the big wads of clay around as if they were little hunks of cookie dough. That can make you strong; no wonder she was so good at arm wrestling. I pinched her on the butt.

"Thanks for the cheap thrills last night," I said.

"Aw don't mention it; the others never do."

"Want to go on an adventure today?"

She eyed me warily, then grabbed my wrist. She was relieved to see that I was still wearing the respectable, if boring, Omega dress watch.

"Can't be too dangerous, you're not wearing that black watch Joe finally returned when you gave him his wop lighter back. What's the adventure?"

"I've got an idea of how to try to find Johnny Robinson's courier pouch."

She eyed me again, even more warily. Yours Truly is not famous for good ideas regarding adventures, as was borne out when I nearly got my brains splattered all over the place in the old Plymouth Cordage warehouse and factory. Mary reminded me of this past misadventure and it gave me pause. I shuddered.

"And I was reading your Sacco–Vanzetti books this morning early when you went running. Did you know that Vanzetti lived in Plymouth and worked in that cordage factory? He even led a strike there."

"Yeah I know. I try to forget about that place."

She attacked the clay hunks with a new ferocity now, and threw them around like Liatis Roantis throws people around in karate class. She sank her fist into the clay, leaving a deep mark.

"Bastards! God, I hate that Thayer. Even if I were a WASP I'd hate him!"

"After you put those in the bags, follow me," I said. She did, still dressed in her white bib overalls and striped jersey. I carried a walking stick and a flashlight. We got into the Scout, bound for Cambridge.

"Have you told Joe about this? And how smart is this idea?" she asked.

"No, and not very," I said.

We rang the bell at Dependable Messenger Service but nobody answered. I knew Sam Bowman was expecting us because I had called him earlier and set this adventure up. He had agreed eagerly.

We rang twice more and finally heard loud cussing from behind the thick door. Along with the cussing was a deep growl.

"I told ya I don't want none! Now *git*! I set the dog on ya!"

"It's us, Sam. Mary and Doc."

He let us in, apologizing. He said that two of the pushiest salesmen he'd ever seen had just come by and wouldn't leave.

"They tryna sell me some roofing compound. It's silver-colored and dries up like metal, you know? I say I don't need no roofing compound, but they say we can take a look. Won't cost me nothin'. So I let 'em. Had their own ladder on top of the van.''

''Ah! And—surprise, surprise—they then informed you that yes indeed, you *do* need roofing compound.''

''Zactly. And then they came inside to write out a estimate, even though I said I didn't want it. Who knows . . . might be closin' the place. *Watch it!* Watch it, Miss, he'll *bite*—''

But it was too late; Mary was already close to the huge dog and bending down over him. Popeye went wild. He flattened his stubby black ears, squinted his eyes, and lunged at her.

He licked her all over, then flopped over on his broad back and piddled up in the air. Embarrassed, he jumped back up again and tried to sit so she could pat him. But he couldn't sit because he was wagging his stumpy tail too hard. In fact, he was wagging his entire big butt. He sniffed and snorfed, whined and yelped softly as she patted his wide, flat head. He squatted and leaked again briefly in ecstasy, then turned, wagging and whining, in a tight circle.

''Silly boy . . . silly old boy,'' cooed Mary.

''Now would you look at *dat!*'' said Sam in amazement. ''Popeye my man, whatsa matter wit*chu*?''

I was looking at the interesting objects on Sam's rolltop desk. He didn't see me looking at them.

Popeye pawed at Mary's leg and whined until she patted him again. Then she walked around the tiny office and the dog followed her. She went to the safe, which was open, and the dog didn't do squat.

''What happened to your guard dog, Sam?'' I asked.

''Damn! Don't know, Doc. Strangest thing I ever—''

He stopped in mid-sentence because he saw me looking down at his desk top, where the jeweler's saw and the big fat cartridges lay strewn over the blotter. I picked one of the forty-five-caliber rounds up—still as big as a lipstick—and examined the tip of the bullet. Sam had used the fine metal saw to delicately score the metal casing that reached halfway up around the lead core. He'd made two cuts across the top, perpendicular to each other, in a cross, then two again in between the first two cuts, resulting in a delicate eight-pointed star in the front of each load. A finely wrought flower of death.

"You do nice work," I said.

He swept the rounds up in his big coffee-colored mitt and put the saw in a drawer.

"That's no dumdum, Doc. I was just teasin' the noses a bit. Just *teasin'* 'em—"

"Shall we go? You ready? Can you call off your big vicious attack dog?"

"Gut-*damn!* Never seen ol' Popeye like this. C'mon, dumbhead."

He shut the big safe with a heavy clunk and spun the dial. Then we got into the Scout, with Popeye and Mary in back. But before Sam joined me in front he called out to a man who was walking toward the office. The man wore a blue guard uniform and carried a small satchel. He was about fifty years old, with a paunch and a Rudolph-the-Reindeer nose. Sam spoke to him briefly, reopened the office, and soon reappeared with a small bundle which he inserted in the man's satchel before sending him on his way again.

"Don't know how long he'll last," growled Sam as we pulled away from the curb and headed north. "I went through two guys already. All of 'em too old and sometimes too drunk. Damn! Looks like we closin' down. All I get is old broken-down cops."

I thought of those big pistol cartridges with the fancy tips, trying to imagine what kind of horrendous wound channel a doctored slug like that would leave in its victim. Not that the plain old undoctored ones wouldn't do plenty. What Sam had done was illegal, but I wasn't going to mention it. I let it drop from my mind. Then I thought of those pushy salesmen who had bothered him before we arrived. I asked him how long they'd hung around. When he answered that it was quite a while, it set me to thinking.

As soon as we got into Lowell we headed straight for Johnny's apartment in the gray house. It was locked and sealed, and even Sam did not have the key, but all we wanted to do was lead the dog up and down the outside stairs a few times to fix the scent firmly in his mind. As soon as Popeye was led into the stairwell he began to whine and carry on. He bounded up the stairs, almost pulling Sam off his feet, and whined and scratched to get in. It was sad to see—rather like the movie of Lassie who travels all across the Highlands to sleep finally on her master's grave. We hung around the stairway for another fifteen minutes so the big pug-ugly pooch would know what we were looking for. Then we got back in the car and went over to the old blown-out factory where we'd found Andy's body in the rubble of the chimney. All the way there Popeye was fawning over Mary; couldn't get enough of her. Sam told me he was worried the dog had lost his mind.

We climbed up the rubble mound in the chimney with the big dog on a lead. He sniffed around but showed no further interest. We assumed then that neither Johnny nor his pouch had been near there. We walked into the big building itself and cruised the first floor, which was empty. The dog showed no interest and didn't even pause, except to lift his leg and leave an odoriferous sign that said in dog talk: Hey, all you cute bitches, I am a swell stud and will make you thrilled and happy. Follow this smell and you can't go wrong. P.S. You other guys beat it or I'll rearrange your face and body.

He spent a lot of time doing this routine, and growling when he sniffed a smell he didn't like. Nix on floor one.

On to floor two. We climbed the musty stairway at the end of the building. It stank of stale urine, dust, and mildew. Faint shafts of sunlight came in through ancient grimy windows. There was no old machinery on this floor, but it was strewn with discarded furniture: ancient desks and chairs, timekeepers' booths, homemade footstools and cabinets. The rancid odors seemed to delight the dog, which didn't surprise me. Our doggies love dirty socks and underwear. Still, Popeye showed no recognition sign. On to the third floor, which contained some old carding machinery and canvas bins with dolly wheels on them for moving the wool. None of the items had seen service in a long, long time. From the far dark corners of the gloomy place came the flutter of wings hitting glass and wood, the dry skitter of rodent feet, and faint twitterings. We saw a group of old stinky mattresses that smelled of vomit. Wino haven in the abandoned factory—a place of refuge from street toughs and cops. We cruised the place and struck out.

"Don't look like pay dirt, Doc," said Sam.

I looked out of one of the windows. We were high up. I admitted to Sam and Mary it was a long shot. I knew the Lowell and state cops had given the building a going-over too. Just before we started back down I noticed two more buildings that seemed deserted. They were big as well. Not as big as the mill we stood in, but big. I peeked lower and saw a wire fence separating us from them. I dismissed the whole thing from my mind. But then I saw a break in the fence that led to a bridge which was almost hidden by locust and sumac trees. The yards connected. And those other buildings were sixty yards farther away from any street. It made me think.

With a huff the giant dog was beside me looking out, his paws on the rotten sill. He huffed and puffed with heat, his tongue lolling out the side of his wide black mouth. It looked like a two-pound slab of used bubble gum.

"We goin' now?"

"Yeah, c'mon, Charlie. It's a bust. Sam, I'll buy you a beer at Johnny's old bar."

So we left the big mill and walked out onto the cracked and buckled asphalt. Mary took the lead from Sam and walked the dog. I had them follow me to the fence, then to the opening and the bridge beyond. They protested, but I convinced them to try once more. The bridge spanned a stagnant canal once used to provide water power and barge transport. Now the water was dead quiet and thick with duckweed and scum. We walked over the small bridge in dark shade, then over gravel that crackled beneath our feet. I still carried the blackthorn walking stick, which I thumped along the ground. When we got to the door of the first building Mary announced she'd had enough of traipsing through depressing old buildings. She sat down on a concrete pier to wait. We went inside.

This building was full of machinery. Rows and rows of it, all covered with the grease-soaked lint. All of it old and fuzzy-wuzzy. It looked as if the people just stopped work one afternoon and never came back. Nobody had cleaned up. Cotton and wool waste still littered the floor, black with dirt and age. Some bobbins and spindles were still in place. Old time cards with inky fingerprints were scattered all over. We walked through the rows of frozen metal, looking at scores, hundreds of things meant and made to move: worm and drive gears, wheels, cranks, ratchets, rollers, belts, levers, swing arms, hinges, drive shafts . . . all still and grease-clogged. We saw the embossed names of manufacturers on the knitting and spinning machinery: E. HASTINGS & SONS, MILLENOCKET, MAINE. D.R. WHITNEY, WORCESTER, MASS. KOEBLENTZ BROTHERS, TORRINGTON, CONNECTICUT. All still and silent.

This was it, then: the underside. Or what was left of it. This was the New England not presented in the college catalogues and travel brochures. The one hidden in towns like Lowell, Lawrence, Manchester, and Fall River. Places where there weren't colleges, lawns, and quaint inns, but factories. And in England too, in many cities with identical names that were described by George Orwell and Jack London. And places worked in by people like Nicola Sacco and Bartolomeo Vanzetti, a shoe trimmer and rope spinner who worked in factories just like these in the towns of Stoughton and Plymouth.

"Kinda spooky, eh Doc? Can't wait to get out of here and dive into a beer. How 'bout you?"

"Let's cruise the next two floors and beat it. I'm getting the creeps in here."

It was on the second floor, almost dead in the center of all the rows of machinery, that we first heard it.

The dog reacted first, freezing and half-lifting his right front foot. His nose was lifted, and a low growl rose in his throat, the back of his neck turning dark with raised fur. We all stood still and listened. It was a distant pounding. It sounded deep and heavy, not the sound of a light hammer driving a nail. Popeye backed up two steps and raised his big head still more. The blank stare was fixed on the ceiling twenty feet ahead of us. Sam whispered to the dog and we crept forward until we were directly beneath the sound. It was muted clanging that came at regular, slow intervals. After each clang came a softer sound, like heavy raindrops on a shingle roof.

Sam whispered: "Somebody up there breakin' through the wall. Hammer and cold chisel, then plaster and masonry fallin' on the floor."

"Yep. Let's sneak up there."

"Let's not."

"C'mon, fraidy-cat," I said, and holding the cane up, I began a slow, tiptoeing, silent, George M. Cohan stage shuffle down the grimy factory aisle. All I needed was a hat. *I'm a Yankee Doodle daaaaaaan-deeee* . . .

Sam looked at me as if I were crazy.

I'm a Yankee Doodle boyyyyy . . . The song was playing slowly in my head as I crept along the floor as quiet as a cat. Right above me came a big thump. Dropped the hammer. Why? Then footsteps, slow and steady, walking toward the outside of the building. Toward the windows . . .

I quickstepped it to the windows and looked out. Down below, Mary was still sitting on the concrete pier, bored. She had one leg cocked up and her hands clasped around her knee, like Marlene Dietrich in *The Blue Angel*. She turned and waved, but something made me uneasy. I realized she wasn't looking at me; she was looking ten feet above me.

She waved again, smiling. There was no sound from above. I tilted open the big metal frame of the pivot window and waved down at her. She saw me and frowned. I held my forefinger to my mouth, but it was too late.

"*Charlie?* Then who's *that?*" she yelled, pointing over my head. I repeated the *shhhhh* sign and motioned for her to move away, to get lost. She jumped up off the concrete and began a brisk walk through the yard. More footsteps from above, quicker this time, then back again to the windows. Mary was now out of sight. More steps and clanking of metal. Clanking, not pounding. Putting the tools in a bag? *What?* Sam and I walked toward the stairwell door. Popeye needed no urging to climb. He strained ahead on the leash, the fur on the back of his neck still raised. I walked right beside Sam, holding the knobby-headed cane by the bottom end. Sam slid his jacket zipper down halfway.

We reached the top of the stairs and stood on the landing. I looked through the door and saw a wall with another door. The old wooden door was almost shut; we couldn't see what was beyond it. This floor had been divided up into smaller rooms, either for offices or for small work areas. We walked slowly into the first room and listened. I thought for a second I did hear footsteps, but then it did not matter because the dog blew it. He barked and snarled and dove right at the door, slamming it shut. Fast running steps now, going away from us. Sam's hand made a quick motion on his chest and the zipper was down all the way. That big hunk of bright nickel winked at me. He held the dog tight but it took effort. He opened the door. I could see the man just disappearing toward the far end of a narrow hallway, scarred with ruined plaster and lath, that ran down the center of the building, with small doorways opening off of it. He wore a tan trenchcoat and a brown hat. He never turned around, just whisked around the corner outside the far door and was gone. The big dog leaped ahead, pulling Sam off his feet. I heard the distant pounding on the stairs. I jumped through the door and after the man. When I was halfway down the narrow hall

I seemed to hear footsteps below me, running back in the direction I'd come from. I turned and shouted to Sam, who was being dragged along the old plank floor like a dogsled, that he was doubling back on the second floor. As I made the top of the stairwell I saw Sam back on his feet trying to go down the other end. But Popeye didn't see it that way and in the heat of the chase was hard to convince. I reached the second floor in time to see the stranger begin a leaping descent down the stairs. Sam, being pulled by the dog, followed an instant later. When I began down I heard distant running, a shout or two, and an explosion. A big hollow boom. Sam's revolver. I thought he'd lost his head until I heard another explosion from farther away. So the stranger in the tan coat who liked to chop at walls also carried a piece. I was beginning to think that this excursion was indeed a dumb idea as I shot out the building. As I cleared the doorway an arm snaked out and grabbed me by the collar, jerking me back hard against the brick wall. I found myself standing next to Sam, who'd released the dog to grab me. He held the big revolver near his chest, with the barrel pointed up. A slug thumped into a wall somewhere and a big noise with it. I didn't know where the dog was. We hugged the wall.

And then I heard a long scream.

It was Mary.

We both left the wall on the run to the gate and the old bridge. I heard the dog snarl beyond the sumac. We were running hard on the gravel and I think I was crying. We didn't hear any more screams. Then we saw why. Mary was lying on the old rickety footbridge, just above the still brown water.

She didn't move, even when I knelt down and shook her.

9

THEN SAM WAS NEXT TO ME AND I WAS MURMURING A prayer between clenched teeth and everything was blurry but clear when I blinked. The bridge seemed to rock like a roller coaster. I lifted my eyes up and saw the big fawn-colored dog wandering over the yard far, far away. It was a dream. A very bad dream.

"It's okay . . . goin' to be okay, Doc," I heard Sam say softly.

Then Mary opened her eyes and stared at me. She didn't say anything, just stared. Then she looked confused. She frowned, and tried to sit up. We held her back. I heard Popeye barking far away.

"Charlie?"

"What?"

"He hit me."

"I know."

"He hit me with his coat I think."

"You're not shot anywhere? I can't see any blood."

"No. I was standing here on the bridge when he ran past. He held out the side of his coat at me—"

"Probably had a sap in his coat pocket," said Sam. "You'll be all right in a minute. Just don't move fast."

Sam should've been a doctor, I thought. Then I saw that her face was all wet. Wet with tears. Mine. I wiped it dry and she got up. When I saw that she was really honest-to-God okay, I dropped her arm and went over to the railing of the bridge and puked.

I'm as tough as they come. You bet.

I led her to the car and was about to slide behind the wheel when I looked back. I saw Sam walking up behind the dog with his gun in his hand. The dog was going through the blown-out doorway of the big mill building in the front yard. Popeye was walking slowly, stiff-jointed, in a stoop-shouldered stalk. Sam was looking up at the rows of dusky windows where a bad guy could lean out and loose off a couple of rounds. They needed help.

"Can you drive? Good. Get out of here and find a pay phone at least five blocks away. Call the local fuzz and have them send a bunch of cruisers here. Then hang up and dial Joe in Boston. Don't come back here no matter what. I'll meet you at a pub called the Dubliner on Market Street."

"But I don't know where Mar—"

"Just ask; they'll tell you."

"I'm not going unless you come too! You can't—"

"Get out of here or I'll knock your block off!" I said, gripping her upper arm until she winced. I watched her speed off. Marital discussion is nice and everything, but when a couple of bad-asses are walking around the place with heaters drawn, discussion has no part in the program. Discussion is *closed*.

I dogtrotted back through the gate and into the yard, headed toward the old wrecked chimney and the big building next to it where the man and dog stood frozen, straining forward yet still, like hunters in a field of quail. I trotted along a zigzag path, deliberately making myself bounce. I wanted to keep moving. I caught up to them. We all scanned the dark windows above.

"He in there, Doc. That sucker in there. He tried to split the scene but ol' Popeye head him off."

Still looking up, the gun muzzle raised to guard himself, Sam ran his sinewy arm down the leather lead and unsnapped it from Popeye's collar. The collar was big enough for a Clydesdale. He pointed at the near door and said *stay*. The dog placed himself in front of it in a half-crouch, mouth open, panting. Then the heavy flews drew back, revealing a mean grin. Popeye growled.

"Ain't nobody goin' through that door," said Sam as he led me around the other way. We stood on each side of the old wooden door for several seconds, listening. Then we went in.

The first floor was deserted. There was nothing in it but dirt anyway. We went to the far end where the dog was, then walked softly back to our side of the building, leaving the dog to guard the other, and went up. This was the floor with the old mattresses and office furniture piled high and strewn about. Dark and dirty, with a thousand places to hide and ambush.

"Now I wish we had the dog," whispered Sam. "You stay behind me now; don't get off to the side, you'll get shot."

He didn't have to tell me. I was beginning to feel like Huck Finn on the old steamboat wreck: I was sorry I'd come. Halfway through the building and nothing. Then Sam stopped and held a finger to his lips. We waited motionless in the gloom. Then I heard it, a faint sound at regular intervals. Breathing. Somebody was in the building not far from us, breathing. Almost panting. I held the cane four inches above the ferrule, ready to wing it at the first thing that moved. Its knobby end was heavy, but it was a pathetic weapon against a handgun.

Sam led me to a spot behind a plaster-covered column and an old tipped-over desk. He held his motorcycle keys up and began to jingle them softly. Then louder.

"C'mon, Popeye," he said in a coarse whisper. *"C'mon!"*

Instantly there was a rustling and scrabbling in the far darkness. Sam drew back the hammer of his piece with a loud clack. "Stay down," he said. I saw the dim figure of the man jump up from behind old boxes and furniture. He wasn't where we'd thought. A brightness and a big explosion, and at the same second Sam returned fire from our refuge behind the column.

If you ever have the chance to be in an enclosed place with somebody letting off a large-bore pistol, don't take it. My ears hurt, and there was a silent ringing in them as I crouched deeper in the junk furniture. I finally raised my head when I again heard the scrabbling sound of someone moving fast in a crouch. The place was brighter now, owing to the fact that one of Sam's big slugs had torn away part of a metal window frame and let more sunshine in. Nothing like a little cheer . . .

"Stay put," whispered Sam, inching ahead. The man had not left the building. Apparently he now knew that the dog wasn't really with us. Since I was not armed—and totally unprepared mentally for using a firearm against a human—Sam thought it best that I remain safely tucked behind the pillar. And I agreed.

Sam catwalked to the next column. The rustling sound was moving to our right. I could see nothing there. The bright shaft of sunlight was a hindrance because it made the darkness beyond even blacker. All I could see was the explosion-bright dustswirl in the sunlight. I heard the clack of the hammer as Sam cocked the revolver. He shouldn't have done that, because less than a second later a big clunk of the column blew away inches from his head. Sam fired twice at where he'd seen the muzzle flash, but after all the roaring and ringing died away I could again hear that scrabbling and rustling sound that told me our quarry was still moving around. He was a cool one, too. Chances are he'd been in scrapes before. Hunkering down in the dust and dirt, I remembered my previous adventure in another old factory, where I'd almost lost my life because of people shooting each other. The morning had indeed taken a nasty turn. I couldn't help wishing I were someplace else. Like Bhutan, for instance.

I crept forward and to my right. I didn't want to pull any

fancy stuff; if Sam mistook me for the other guy I'd have *nowhere* to hide.

More scraping and rustling. Then I heard breathing pretty close by. Or was it farther away and I was just nervous? I *was* nervous, no doubt about that. More creeping forward. Two quickish jumps to my left. Sam. I *thought* . . .

Next there was a long period of quiet. Which I did not care for at all. I'd rather have them shooting now and then just so I could keep my bearings. Then I heard the breathing coming closer, but before I had a chance to creep forward with my cane, Sam fired again. The shot was dead on, or almost, because I heard a distinct running and shortly afterward saw the upright rectangle of light which meant the far door had been flung open. Sam fired again as it swung shut. We charged the door and I saw the baseball-sized hole in it where the doctored bullet had spread out on impact like a pancake. Running footsteps on the stairs. Another door. Where was the dog? We followed down, around, down, and out into bright daylight.

There sat Popeye, who hadn't moved a muscle. He seemed glad to see us; obviously our stranger-marksman hadn't come out this way. Then the dog was off, sprinting around the corner of the big mill. Sam reloaded, and we followed in time to see our trenchcoat-clad friend making a beeline for one of the smaller buildings. When we got around the side enough to follow the action, we saw him rush in and slam the door behind him. The dog never broke stride, and must have been doing at least thirty when he hit the door. Popeye left the ground fourteen feet in front of the door. For an instant he seemed to sail through the air like one of those gazelles in a slow-motion nature film. His black muzzle was down, and he hit the door just like the Billy Goats Gruff. It exploded, and he sailed right on in.

"Gutdamn!" said Sam as we closed the distance. We backed up tight against the doorway, then Sam peeked around. We went in. The dog was standing in front of yet another door at the opposite end of the building. He was so far away, and the interior so dark, we could scarcely see him. We trotted toward him, flinging glances over our shoulders, and opened that door, and the dog went out trailing, nose to the ground, in the direction of the fence.

"He's not inside anymore?" I asked.

"Naw. Popeye would smell him. He gone now. And *look*."

He pointed at a dark spot on the buckled asphalt.

"Winged him too. Just a sliver, no more. But I winged him."

We stared at the fence. Sam called the dog back. Popeye wasn't moving so fast. His eyes had lost their brightness. I realized how the beast had gotten his name. The eyes protruded from the flat, mashed face. Now they looked tired. I felt tired. Sam looked tired. Our weary trio went slowly, half stumbling, back to the main gate. The dog sat, then sank to his belly. Popeye was working on a monstrous concussion.

Two cruisers pulled up, sirens blaring, lights snapping, and we all got in.

10

THE CRUISERS OF THE LOWELL PD SNAKED AROUND THE OLD textile compound looking for the man we described. No luck. He was a slippery one, was the guy in the trenchcoat. More cars were dispatched to continue the search while we were dropped off at the Dubliner. The Market Street section is the New Lowell, the phoenix arising from the ashes of the abandoned mills. Across the street were new condos made from converted mill buildings. The Dubliner was an attractive pub that bordered an area increasingly filled with fine shops and busy offices. We found Mary pacing out front. Our greeting wasn't peaceful, but I realized through it all that her anger was the result of worry. We sat in a booth with one of the officers and I bought beers. The officer had coffee. We told him what had happened. Not only was he not impressed, but he informed us we had trespassed. Fortunately for us, Joe arrived shortly thereafter and smoothed things over. The squad car left for the factory, and we had lunch. The others dug into their bacon-cheeseburgers on bulkies, and I had a small Greek salad. Unless you're a lumberjack you've either got to skip lunch or go light. If you don't, before long you'll look like Santa Claus. We had more beer and then coffee. The strings were beginning to loosen, the tension of the O.K. Corral incident receding.

The manager, who had refused to let Popeye into the establishment, stopped by our booth in a distressed state. The bull mastiff had sprawled in front of the Dubliner's door for a little post-adventure snooze. Patrons and potentials, seeing the beast in their path, were afraid to enter or leave. I looked out the window and saw pedestrians glance down, shift into high gear, and move right on. They were avoiding the place like a herpes hooker. So we brought the big lug in and he went up to Mary and started wagging his tail and big fat butt around and whining and piddling. The manager looked on and shook his head slowly. Joe tried again to pat Popeye, who growled at him. Then Joe reached over and gave Sam a quick pat near his upper arm. Joe winced.

"Use it?"

"Uh-huh."

"Score?"

"Uh-huh. Indirectly; clipped him with a splinter I think."

Joe groaned softly and pinched the bridge of his nose, his eyes shut.

"You guys give me a pain in the ass," he said. He reached over and tapped me under the arm. "You packing iron too?"

"Of course not, dummy. I don't even own a shoulder holster."

"Well I just never know with you, Doc. You're a strange one, with your fancy watches and—"

"Pooooor baaaaaaby!" cooed Mary as she patted the dog's head. "Baaaaaby got a headache, hmmmmm?" She wrenched open his mouth and popped in three Excedrin, closed his mouth, held it shut, and massaged his throat until his big pink tongue popped out, which meant the pills had been swallowed. Sam watched, amazed.

"Let's split," said Joe, getting up. "The state lab team will meet us at the factory. They're probably already there."

The manager was glad to see us go. On the way I stopped at a hardware store and bought a small crowbar, a pony sledgehammer, and a broad mason's chisel. I knew there were tools left at the scene, but in all likelihood the lab boys would want them.

Within thirty minutes eight of us wound our way up the dismal stairs and onto the landing where we'd first spotted our man. The room was halfway down the hall on the right. Right in the center of the big building. We went in. There was a very faint aroma in there I didn't like. A burnt smell. Popeye went over to the wall on the left and jumped up, sniffing. He whined and wagged his tail, then dropped to all fours and turned in a tight circle. Whined louder. Cried. Wailed. To the dog's left, near the door we had entered, the wall was torn. The plaster and lath had been hacked away from the studding and lay on the floor in a heap. This had been the falling noise, the patter of debris like heavy rain, we'd heard from the floor below before our mysterious friend had knocked off work and fled, shooting at us.

"He picked the wrong place to look," I said. "That's why he didn't find it."

"Find what?" asked Joe.

"Johnny's pouch. It's in there. In the wall. Didn't you notice the dog's reaction? That's why we brought him in the first place. He just also happens to be good at bulldozing old doors. I'm going into that wall to get the pouch because I bet my anterior bridge is inside. Now you see why our errand doesn't look so dumb?"

"I just wish you'd told me is all," he said. "And you're not doing any banging and digging until the lab boys case this place."

And they did. While we watched from the doorway, they took photographs of everything, and one guy made a sketch showing measurements, the window and door, and the location of the old desk that was in there. The team dusted the place for prints, collected fibers and dust from the floor, placed some cigarette butts in vials, and carefully collected the tools (a hammer and cold chisel) left by our mysterious friend. Then they left. Joe, Mary, Sam, and I stared at the wall. Then Joe examined the floor closely and drew our attention to large scrape marks on the floor. They led to the heavy old desk. His eyes went back to the wall, which was ruined along its upper edge where it joined the ceiling. There was about a two-foot line along the top where the plaster and lath had been removed from the timbers a long time ago, perhaps in the expectation of installing plumbing pipes or heating ducts. But it had never happened. That meant there were deep troughs between the studs that ran all the way down the wall toward the floor. The big gash in the wall was as high up as a basketball net.

"What they did was," said Joe, "they dragged that desk from the middle of the room over to the wall here, then dragged it back. Yeah, they dropped something down behind the facing all right."

I watched the dog jump up again, forelegs on the wall, nose pointed straight up, whining. I took hammer and chisel and poked through the wall just above the floor, right below him. Nothing but space. I tried farther up and ran into horizontal cross bracing between studs. So I tried right above the bracing, and before half a minute was up I was seeing glimpses, through the plaster dust and crumpled, splintered lathboard, of gray canvas. When the hole was big enough I pulled at the cloth and then was holding the pouch in my hand. On it, in dark-blue letters, were the words LOWELL SUN.

"Well, gutdamn!" said Sam.

The dog took it in his steam-shovel mouth and sank to his belly, holding it between his paws with his chin resting on it. He whined and thumped his tail on the old dirty floor. Popeye seemed to know Johnny wouldn't be back.

I returned to the hole and kept pecking away, hacking and tearing off slabs of plaster the way a pileated woodpecker works on an old dead tree. My mouthpiece was in there. I just knew it. And I'd save Tom and me a week's work if I could get it out. In fact, I was in such a sweat to retrieve my dental work that I didn't notice Joe. I heard him mumbling something but I couldn't—

"Why?" he shouted. I turned to face him. Joe had Sam get the paperboy's pouch for him, since he didn't want to lose an arm. He turned it inside out. Examined the seams, the carrying strap.

"Why?" he repeated. "They got the pouch, took the packet inside, then ditched the pouch behind the wall just the way they ditched the gas masks . . . and for the same reason. But what happens? They come *back* for it. Why?"

"Because they failed to get what they were after," I said. "They got the packet of documents from the public library all right."

"What makes you so sure?" said Mary.

"Because here's the envelope," I answered, gingerly pulling out a crumpled manila bundle that was slightly torn. Clearly visible on it was not only the Santuccios' address but the receiving stamp of the Boston Public Library.

"Well done, Doc. *Well done*. You shoulda been a cop."

I continued to punch, pry, smash, and chip at the wall. My reasons, and reasoning, were simple: there were two things in Johnny's pouch when he was murdered, the Sacco–Vanzetti documents in the packet and my anterior bridge in a small cardboard box. One they wanted, one they didn't. They'd taken the pouch to this location to examine it. Therefore, they'd disposed of the dental work the same way they'd hidden the pouch. In the old wall.

Only it wasn't working out that way. When I'd demolished the rest of the wall, with Joe's help and encouragement, it yielded nothing except what we'd already found. I'd helped Joe a bit but struck out on my personal quest. I led them back down and outside, trudging across the old buckled asphalt and cinder. The tools clanked and clinked under my arm. I was down. Joe was up; his star would rise at headquarters. I would have to spend a lot of time and trouble redoing the piece. Damn it all.

We asked Sam to dinner. He thanked us but declined, saying he had a lot of extra work to do at home. As we dropped him off I got out and walked with him over to the door, where he switched off the electronic alarm.

"I want to thank you, Sam, for all you've done."

"Hmmmph! Should be me who's thankin' you, Doc. We almost got that guy today. Next time, I promise you: I won't miss."

"Call it a hunch, Sam, but if I were you I'd take that cash out of your safe for a week or so."

"Huh? Why?"

I shrugged my shoulders and repeated that it was just a hunch. Sam went in and reappeared with a shopping bag full of bills. He asked us to drive him to Somerville. We did. Following his directions, we soon found ourselves winding our way through tiny labyrinthine alleyways that were lined with small businesses dealing with the automotive aftermarket. Muffler shops, radiator repair, engine rebuilding, front ends, rear ends, bumpers, windshields, tires, shocks—the Cambridge–Somerville line was to cars what Boston's South End was to leather and shoes. We passed a radiator joint and I smelled noxious fumes of zinc galvanizing and acid baths. We stopped at Nissenbaum's Auto Parts on Columbia, right down the street from the Nike running-shoe factory. I went inside with Sam; Maurice Nissenbaum put the cash in his big safe, gave Sam a signed slip, and we returned to Dependable where we finally parted. Sam left on that rumbly, popping old Honda with Popeye, goggles and all, right behind him. It seemed as if we could hear him three blocks out of sight.

At home I poured large dollops of Laphroaig into brandy snifters and added some room-temperature soda water. We sat outside on the flagged terrace and looked at the two pink dogwood trees that were in full bloom. Joe and I stuck our noses down into the bowl-like glasses and inhaled the warm malty smell of the whisky. Mary sipped on Amaretto liqueur.

My lawn was bright green and wide. In one cozy corner of it was a cluster of paper-birch trees, and in the midst of this copse was a rough wooden table with benches. Moe and I like to sit there and play chess on a crisp fall day. Moe brings his old samovar and we make Russian caravan tea and play and push our little chess clocks down and he beats me. And we pretend we're Tolstoi and Chekhov. We wear warm sweaters in the afternoon and play balalaika music on a tiny cassette player. The birches are gold and white, and it's very Russian.

Mary has part of the side yard bounded by a walk-through arbor. The side of the house there is set with some Florentine tiles and a bronze wall fountain. There are Lombardy poplars around the other two sides, and two gas lamps. It's a romantic Latin courtyard, and only about twenty feet square. My favorite spot is still under construction, and borders on the small garage-sized guest cabin far back on the lawn. It is enclosed by birches and wild evergreens and wide bamboo stakes. Inside this tiny court are boulders, a pond, a curved concrete footbridge, a small torii, and two dozen dwarf bonsai in old pots or pots made by Mary, or set into rock crevices, or lining the miniature waterfall. Then in the middle, surrounded by all this miniaturized countryside, is a tiny teak teahouse with ungawa and rice screens. By the time I'm a hundred I may finish it. It's only forty feet square, but inside it one has the feeling of great space, privacy, and timelessness. Not a lot of talking in there. No laughing or loud noise. Cats but not dogs. You go there alone, or with someone you really care about, and sit quietly. Little bronze temple bells chime in the wind, and the squat bronze lantern by the miniature lake glows, and you can sometimes see the dull golden flash of the bug-eyed goldfish who live in the lake. I wanted to be there right now. I wanted to be drinking hot Keemun, not Scotch, and meditate on the past few days. I wanted the dust and events to settle, find their place, and begin to make sense.

"Charlie! *Charlie!* My God, how many times do we have to *ask* you?"

"Hmmm?"

"What's it going to be tonight, rack of lamb or bouilla-baisse?"

"Oh, whatever." I got up and paced the flagstones. I looked up at our house. It looked big. I felt insulated and spoiled. Then I thought of what I'd read about Sacco and Vanzetti. Sacco and his family lived in a tiny cottage in Stoughton. He worked eighty-hour weeks and kept a big garden. He gave his spare vegetables to the "needy" families in the area. Vanzetti was a boarder in North Plymouth who, if the testimony of his neighbors in that town could be believed, made pennies at a time, yet gave the kids in the neighborhood dimes. Not only was there testimony as to his good character and generosity not believed by the jury (because the neighbors, too, were Italians and therefore in league with him), but his giving away of dimes was taken as evidence that he had stolen fifteen grand from the Slater and Morrill shoe company in South Braintree. Of course this line of thinking failed to explain why both Sacco and Vanzetti had none of this fortune in their hands, and why they then perversely chose to continue to live in tiny workingmen's dwellings and to work eighty-hour weeks.

Looking up at our red-brick house on Old Stone Mill Road, which looked very big and splendorous, I thought of Sacco and Vanzetti and all the old ladies on the oil-soaked floors who were deaf from the looms, and felt guilty.

"I think we should sell this place, Mary," I announced, "and get something a bit smaller. What do you think?"

"What?"

"Well, don't you think it's a bit big for us? Jack and Tony are off at school now, and I just thought—"

"You're losing your mind, Charlie. Okay, sit out here and moon and pout all you want. We're *not* selling this house; we've got way too much at stake here. And a large part of it's mine, kiddo. You forgot that? See you later; Joe and I are going in to make bouillabaisse. And if you're not a good boy you won't get any."

But I couldn't have cared less. Oh, they tried to distract

me, all right. A few times I almost weakened. First the aroma of the olive oil with onions, shallots, and leeks sautéing in it. I didn't even flinch. Then Joe brought out a glass of cold Soave, and shortly afterward I heard the strains of Mozart's Clarinet Concerto in A major. I sipped and listened and sniffed, but not a quiver. I just kept thinking of the pouch, the *empty* pouch . . . the anterior bridge, and those two working-class Italians strapped into the electric chair at Charlestown Prison and coming out in those black boxes.

I heard the hum of the microwave. Mary was defrosting frozen fillets of striped bass and containers filled with little-neck clams and mussels, shrimp, lobster claws, and maybe even some king-crab legs . . . big, thick, spiky golden sticks full of white meat . . .

I squirmed a bit and stared out over the wide lawn.

The pouch was empty. Why had they come back for it? Maybe it was somebody else who'd come back. Some other party entirely. That would explain why the guy we'd gotten the drop on had been digging in the wrong section of the old wall. He hadn't been there when the pouch was dropped down into the—

"How you doing?" asked Joe, who had sneaked up on me. "Mary just added the *fumet*. Smell it?"

"Yeah. Hey, Joe, how did your old man get to be president of his company, anyway? That's pretty good for an Italian peasant who landed broke at Ellis Island. I know the broad details. But you know Mary doesn't talk about it that much. I know he started out as a carpenter, right? But how'd he—"

"Pop made it on hard work and luck. And common sense. He was no genius, but he wasn't dumb, and he listened to the right people. I tell ya, Doc, next to common sense, genius isn't worth shit."

"I agree."

"Well, Pop went from New York up to Schenectady, where he had some relatives. He learned to be a plasterer, and he earned good money, which he saved. He got married and Mom worked too, as a pastry cook. They saved and saved. Just before World War Two, rock lath came in. Most people dismissed it as a fad, but Pop saw the writing on the wall— no pun intended. He knew rock lath was here to stay, and that it would put him out of business. I don't know if you know this, but it took a week to put up a real plaster wall. The wooden lath, sometimes wire lath, then the rough coat. Day or so later the brown or scratch coat. Finally the finish coat. A great wall, but a lot of time and dough. So Pop, using his common sense and some of the saved money, got some young greaseballs off the anchovy boats and trained them to put up rock lath. That was the start of his contracting business.''

''Ah *soooo*.''

''It was small at first, and Pop worked with them, doing the fancy cornice work and stuff. Before long he hired more greaseballs to work as carpenters, putting up studding and door frames. About that time Pop ran into a young Polack named Ray Woznicki, who was a plumber. Well, both guys were looking for a shop and some rolling stock, and they thought if they could go together on the capital equipment both would benefit. Ray wasn't Italian, but he was Catholic, which was almost as good. They were in the same parish. So they went in as partners, and each guy moved out of his garage and into their new rented building in the center of town. Result? Central Construction Company. Hah! Original, huh?''

''And so it just grew and grew.''

''And so it just grew and grew. Right. Pop went overseas in the war and fought at Anzio and all up through his old country, then came home. Ray didn't come home; he got shot to pieces on Iwo. Broke Pop's heart. Old Mrs. Woznicki, Ray's widow, she still owns a lot of the company. Anyway, Central Construction grew like Topsy in the postwar boom, and they went into retail . . . started a lumberyard and supply house along with the contracting company. Now Pop was hiring greaseball *architects*, for Chrissake.''

"Amazing!"

"No, not amazing. You're forgetting it all happened real gradually, Doc, over years and years. And sometimes, growing up, I remember some pretty lean years. But it kept growing mostly, and Pop paid off his notes, and then he did the smartest thing of all.''

"What?"

"He got out. As Kenny Rogers says in the song, he knew when to fold 'em. Around nineteen sixty Pop saw the dramatic rise in union scale. The greaseballs were now making more than he was. No good. It was the rock-lath story all over again to Pop. You couldn't pay a guy nine bucks an hour to slam nails. Again, common sense. Forget the financial rags and the guys with MBAs . . . good old common sense, eh?''

"Right."

"So in sixty-one Pop sold the contracting business for a bundle, and put the money into three big retail stores specializing in what Pop saw would be the new thing: do-it-yourself home improvement. So there you are.''

We sat in silence for a minute.

"America is a great country," I said.

"It sure as hell is. Got some warts, but we're the best around. You bet! So come on in now and have some bouillabaisse.''

When the fish stew was ready Mary served it in big crocks she had made. Each one held over a quart of bouillabaisse, which we ate with huge wooden spoons. There was a long baguette of French garlic bread, and more cold Soave. Okay, they'd done it to me.

"Well I wish you luck on this bad business, Joe," I said, refilling my glass. "I really hope you catch the guys who did Johnny in. And I hope Sam doesn't get hurt, either. But one thing's for sure: I'm *out of it*. My mouthpiece is nowhere to

be found. So they chucked it into some old trash can somewhere and it's gone for keeps. So that lets me out. Exit Doc.''

''About time,'' growled Mary, who was cracking a lobster
claw in her teeth. ''No more screwing around in old factories
and getting shot at.''

But she was wrong, and so was I. Because my mouthpiece
was about to surface in a most surprising manner. And like
so many things that come back at you—like the late John
Robinson's voice—it came with strings attached.

11

LIFE'S BIGGEST PROBLEM IS THAT IT'S BORING. AT LEAST IT'S boring most of the time. When it's not boring it's terrifying. But when the panic subsides the needle does *not* settle back to mid-range, which consists of stimulating, interesting, exciting. No. Instead it drops right back into boring. There's no middle ground in life, or precious little of it.

So, in accordance with this zero-to-red line-to-zero pattern of life's tachometer, I was bored and depressed following work the next afternoon. My day's labors had consisted of removing impacted third molars. It's a painful but necessary procedure. It's how I make the bulk of my living. I hate it. None of my patients had been happy to greet me. Afterward, though glad the operation was over, they departed sullenly, with swollen jowls, in anticipation of the pain to come when the local wore off. *Bad.*

I went for a slow run out along the Old Road to Nine-Acre Corners, then back around to Old Stone Mill Road where we live. I took a sauna, assembled and fiddled with my new compound archery bow, and took the mail into the study to go through it. I listened to Wagner. It was the funeral march from *Seigfried.* Very stirring. Heroic. When the Chicago Symphony plays Wagner, with that great brass section, you can hear the alpenhorns echoing off the purplish far walls of the Jungfrau . . . The only trouble with Wagner is that if you listen to too much of him, you get to actually *believe* it. And then it's not too difficult to imagine yourself walking out to the nearest aerodrome, climbing into your Stuka, and roaring off into the wild blue to strafe civilians.

Got to watch it with old Richard Wagner.

Halfway through the mail call I came across a government form bearing a U.S. Postal Service inscription. It was from the post office in Lowell, informing me that "an item of personal property" had been found in one of their postal facilities, and that I could claim said item by appearing there in person, bearing the proper identification, within thirty days.

An item of personal property . . . found in a postal facility . . .

It couldn't be. It was too good to be true. To hell with thirty days; I hightailed it to the phone and dialed the Lowell P.O. It was after four; I had forty minutes to get there before they closed. After much runaround and holding, I finally got to the young lady who was familiar with the item.

"Well, we were wondering when you'd call back, Doctor Adams. You see, you gotta have the slip in your hand, as well as the I.D. It's just the rules."

"I understand. Well, I'll be right up, so stay put. You want me to describe it?"

"No, not again. I'll be here. 'Bye."

On the drive up I couldn't help thinking that part of her phone conversation had sounded funny. Did she have the correct item? Was she confusing me with someone else? It wouldn't seem likely in a town the size of Lowell.

I arrived just before closing, and soon was facing the young woman across the counter. I showed her the proper identification.

"Should I describe the package?"

She gave a little giggle, as if I were obviously kidding, then gave me a questioning sidelong glance with furrowed brow.

"Your voice change?"

"Hmm?"

"Your voice. It sounds different. Gotta cold, mistah?"

I stared around the building. I was beginning to think I was in a Franz Kafka novel. A fat man appeared next to the young lady and glared at me over his droopy glasses. He looked at me, looked at the slip, looked at me, looked at the slip, looked at me. Later on in the year he was going to try something really challenging, like toilet training.

"Whatsa big idea?" he asked me.

"What big idea? I'm here to claim my personal item. I have furnished the required identification and am prepared to describe the item. It's a small package from Investment Alloy Laboratories in Cambridge, which is a dental lab. And the piece is valuable to me."

"Must be, the way you been buggin' us about it," he said.

Back into the Kafka novel again.

"Excuse me. I only called once."

"Frank, he don't sound like the other guy," said the girl. "I asked him if his voice changed."

"What other guy?" I asked.

"A guy named Charles Adams has been callin' us continual for the past two days, did we fina box, you know? But we ain't found no box, till yesterday. Then we send the note out, right?"

"Did he call you today?" I asked.

"Uh-huh. About forty minutes ago."

"No dear, that was *me*."

She giggled again. Frank looked at me, looked at the slip, looked at me, looked at the slip . . .

"That's just what he said each time: *it's me*." She laughed.

"But I described the package."

"Yeah," said Frank, *"four times."*

I sighed, and swept my eyes around the place. Somebody else wanted the package. Somebody who knew what it looked like. And also somebody who knew the post office would have it. Who was it? Not the guy chipping at the factory wall, because he thought the package was still in there. Or maybe he was after the newsboy's pouch . . . the empty pouch . . .

They finally let me have the package because they knew I wasn't leaving without it, and it was closing time. The best way to win an argument with a government employee is to do it just before quitting time. I filled out another special form and departed with the box, which was only as big as a pack of cigarettes. It had been opened, and the post-office people had not opened it. The letter carrier had found it, as is, in a letter box near the old factory. It could have been there all weekend. The mouthpiece was there, in perfect condition. They had never seen the other caller at the post office, nor had he left any phone number or address. One thing for sure: he knew where to find me.

But he didn't even wait until I got home. At the third light I knew the dark-blue Olds behind me wasn't there by coincidence. I did a double cloverleaf on and off of 495 and he was still on my tail. He was following me, as Brian Hannon might say, like stink on a skunk.

South on Route 3 he sped up, swerved to the left-hand passing lane, and tried to come alongside. But I swerved left too and blocked him. He tried to pass on the right and I blocked him again. Then I pulled out the light switch while I tromped on the gas pedal. He braked hard when he saw the rear lights flash on, and I had the edge for a few seconds, but it didn't work and I wasn't surprised. An International Scout is no match for an Olds sedan on the highway. He tried the passing routine again and this time I let him. But as he passed me he tried to run me off onto the shoulder. And we weren't alone on the road, either. My mystery friend wanted that cardboard box pretty badly. When he tried to head me off I got a little belligerent and swerved right into him. *Kawhunk!* Our fenders banged and shrieked, and I even saw sparks. A Scout may not be fast, but it's heavy-duty and good on the body punches . . . just like Dempsey. I had bloodied Blue Olds's nose a bit and he backed off.

I couldn't see the driver clearly at all. He had no front plate, either. I guess I was a little heated up by this time and didn't care what happened to the Scout's body. I wanted to put Mystery Man into the opposing lane, right smack into a Peterbilt or a Mack. But I think he sensed this, and stayed back. He got no closer than a hundred feet but stayed with me like an echo. We crossed the Bedford line, then on into Concord. I went along to the town and hit Walden Road. Half a mile along it I swerved into a parking lot and Mystery Man followed me in. But he did a three-sixty right away and barreled out of there on two wheels. And as it was, it was lucky for him he wasn't tagged right then and there. I went inside and told the desk sergeant to follow that car. Then I went upstairs to Brian Hannon's office.

"Smart thing, coming to the police station," he said as he ignited a Lucky and waved out the match. "Usually crooks feel unsafe around them."

"Except for this one."

"Your comedy is not appreciated, Doctor Adams. I'll have you know that the people of Concord, and of the Commonwealth, depend on me and my staff to—"

"Listen to this. I want to tell you what's been happening lately. Maybe you can help me figure it out."

"Maybe I can, maybe not. I'm very busy right now."

"So I see," I said, pointing at the unfinished crossword puzzle on his desk.

He frowned and squinted at me and leaned back in his chair, blowing smoke rings. When I finished he scratched the side of his balding head. Then he spoke.

"What happened was, they went through the pouch in the room at the factory, okay? They not only opened it there; they went through the contents. The empty envelope from the Boston library proves this. They sorted through the papers and discarded the envelope. They opened your box from the lab and decided they didn't need it. So on their way home one of them, who decided to do his good turn for the day—"

"God bless him—he saved me weeks of work."

"Uh-huh. He drops your box into the nearest mailbox so you'll get it back. So then afterwards, when they've gone through the Sacco and Vanzetti stuff real carefully, they realize something's missing. So they think, where could this thing be? They knew Robinson had it on his person. It turned up missing from the bundle, so the first place they look is back in the pouch."

"But they never got to the pouch . . . or the envelope. I think they thought Johnny hid the thing in my box to throw people off if by chance they snagged the pouch. Right?"

"Yeah. That's it. But you say somebody was looking for the pouch too—tearing up that old wall. I think that either there are two rival groups after this thing, or else the original outfit is searching everywhere they can, covering all the bases."

"Whatever it is, Brian, it's small."

"Yep. Sounds like negatives to me. Either microfilm, microfiche, or plain old thirty-five mil. negs. They're all small and potent."

We ambled over to the tiny lab and I produced the cardboard box and the piece for them to examine. We watched them work on it for half an hour, slicing away at it with scalpels, shining bright lights through the cardboard, dipping shreds of the cardboard in solutions and dyes. Nix. Plain cardboard box. *Containerus ordinarius.*

We went back to Brian's office where I called the Boss. She told me Joe was looking for me. I called him at his office and found him in. He was glad to hear about my find in Lowell.

"Got some interesting stuff from the lab. One: the cigarette butts' snubbed ends contain residues of human flesh, burnt blood, epidermal tissue, and fat."

"They did it up there. They tortured Andy up in that room where nobody could hear him scream. The bastards."

"Right. And what they did was, they tied him to that big old desk. Remember the scrape marks? They dragged the desk over to the wall so they could stand on it to reach the gash in the wall. They went up there tippy-toe and dropped the pouch and the envelope inside. Then they dragged it back and tied Andy to it. Get this: fibers from the suit coat he was wearing were found on the floor. Likewise, the old oil and dirt on the floor match the smudges on his coat. No doubt about it then.''

"Anything on the pouch or envelope?''

"Nothing. Pure blank.''

"Then they'll keep looking.''

"Think so?''

"Know so. Whatever the hell it is, they want it bad.''

"You're right. Don't you see too how the evidence proves that the pouch and the packet didn't yield what they wanted? Because, see, if they moved the desk back from the wall to torture Andy, it was done *after* they discarded the pouch.''

"Yeah . . . they tortured him hoping he could tell them where the thing was when it wasn't where it was supposed to be. After all, it was impossible to ask Johnny; he was dead.''

"I told you so . . . I told you so,'' sang Brian as he swiveled in his chair, exhaling smoke. "Torture is performed for three reasons: revenge, information, or verification. They wanted information from Andy and the poor guy didn't have it.''

"Who's that?'' asked Joe.

"Brian, in the background.''

"Put him on a sec.''

After they talked Brian and I chatted a little. I was hoping he'd get a call from a cruiser saying they'd snagged the blue Olds, but none came in. This bunch was tough and slippery. I didn't like it. I asked Brian how the bad guys didn't know that the object wasn't in the hands of the police; now that we'd recovered the pouch.

"They don't. They only know that Robinson had the item when he left the library, and that sometime between then and when he arrived home to meet his death it disappeared. Andy must have told them that before he died. Therefore they're desperately concentrating their efforts to uncover every possibility within that time gap. And one of the leading figures in that gap, Doc is *you*."

"So this poor slob who casually chucked my little packet into the mailbox later regretted it."

"Yeah, I'd say. He's probably got his boss all over him like a fire blanket. Steer clear, Doc. Use your mental faculties, limited though they might be."

I thanked him for the compliment and left. I went home and told Mary about the auto chase. Needless to say she was not pleased. She called me a meathead and a jerk. I was beginning to feel just like my old self again.

Tom Costello sputtered and lisped with ecstasy over the phone when I told him that his mouthpiece was ready for installation.

"Jeeth! It'th about time. Now I can get thtarted thelling again. Tomorrow?"

"Seven-thirty sharp."

I glanced at a brochure Mary had left on my study desk explaining a new high-efficiency boiler and blower for our furnace which was guaranteed to cut our heating bill by thirty percent. If true, considering New England's climate and fuel prices, that meant we could make an extra trip to Europe each year. I studied the pamphlet carefully and called Mary in.

"Didn't Patriot Oil install something like this two years ago?"

"Uh-huh. But this guy said improvements had been made since then. He said his company would reimburse us for our present unit, so the net cost would be only nine hundred for the whole thing."

"Oh bullshit," I said, and tossed the packet into the circular file. "If it's not this, it's driveway coatings or roof sealant. Then there are the lawn doctors, tuck pointers, gutter rats, and chimney sweeps. Honey, if you listened to all of 'em we'd be broke in a year."

"Then just forget it; he said call him only if we're interested. Janice called and asked us over for supper at seven."

"During the week? Ha! A meal at DeGroot's calls for a two-day recovery."

"No. They want to see us before they fly to the coast. Janice said it would be a pretty dry evening."

"I'll bet. The last time we went we should've worn Aqua-lungs."

But true to their word, the night held only moderate supping and sipping, and pleasant cards and conversation afterward. It was fun. Janice had on a pair of tight tennis shorts too. Her ass is, like Fujiyama, the Bay of Naples, and Grant's gazelle, *Sequoia sempervirens*, a sable antelope, or other wonders of nature, awesome to behold. I could watch it for hours. On a scale of one to ten it rates a fourteen. Easy.

When I was dummy (my natural state, claims Mary) I followed Janice into the kitchen to help make more coffee. She was walking right in front of me.

"Janice, you have the nicest—"

"Ohhhh *you!*" she cooed, throwing a little more twitch into it. "You and your thing about my butt. Hmmph! Fat old thing; I just can't understand you, Doc. Here you're married to the most gorgeous piece on earth and . . . well—"

"I know she is. But it's funny, you know, sometimes you're attracted to somebody else just because they're somebody *else*. Know what I mean?"

"Yeah, I—now where *is* that thing?" she said to herself, bending over to get in the cabinet. She was leaning right in front of me, so I could see the outline of her panties underneath the shorts. Planned. She filled the decanter and poured the water into the machine.

"I do know what you mean, Doc," she said, brushing my hair aside. "Gee I think you're just gorgeous—"

"Oh of course."

"No, I really do, and you know it. You know what's going to happen someday don't you? We're going to find ourselves alone somewhere . . . sometime. Maybe after a party where we've had a few drinks and our guards will be down . . . and we'll hop into the sack.''

"Oh no we won't.''

"Yes we will.''

"Oh no we won't.''

I hoped we would.

"Listen, I think the best thing to do about this thing you have for . . . for my ass, is to get it out of your system a little.''

"Janice, that's the dumbest—''

"I think if I give you a nice big feel, you'll feel better.''

"I might feel better but I don't think it's going to—''

"Here,'' she said, taking my wrists in her hands. She pulled them behind her until our tummies were touching. Then she moved our hands around in back of her, fast, and wrapped my hands around so they cupped her lovely, meaty hams. I had two handfuls of luscious bun. It was a flagrant case of a 112-pound woman sexually abusing a 174-pound man. Despicable.

"How's that, Doc?'' she purred.

"Great,'' I said. I could not tell a lie.

"Are you getting it out of your system a little?'' she whispered.

"I'm getting it, but not out of my system.''

"Then I think we'll have to—*whoopsie!*''

She disengaged, spun a pirouette like a dancer, took two fast steps sideways, and was demurely fiddling with the coffee machine as Jim strode through the doorway.

"What's goin' on? Where's that coffee? Oh, there. Well come on then.'' He was gone faster than he arrived.

A deep smear of crimson had invaded Janice's neck and cheek. She grinned at me and giggled.

"Whew!'' she whispered, then frowned. "Sorry, Doc.''

"Let's get out of here,'' I said, taking the tray of cups, cream, and sugar. "And we should never do that again.''

"It's going to happen at the lake I bet,'' she whispered as she walked steadily beside me, holding the tray of coffee and spoons. "Up at the lake. We'll be having a party at the dock, and the others will leave for Wolfsboro to buy food and booze and there'll just be us on the dock . . . in only our bathing suits . . ."

"Nope. Never happen."

She half-closed her eyes and grinned.

"Oh I can just see it. We'll be rubbing oil on each other, then go into the boathouse and—"

"Never happen."

"Gonna happen, Doc. Gonna *haaaaaaa*pen . . ."

"No. No. A thousand times no," I said, trying to convince myself. Trying not to imagine her skinning out of her wet tank suit in the shadows of the boathouse.

"Well it's a pleasant fantasy anyway. Now here we are; stop smiling."

I put the tray down and poured coffee for everyone. Mary was frowning at the cards on the table. She sipped coffee and looked up.

"You're still dummy, Charlie," she said.

"You're not kidding," I said.

I felt the eyes on me. The dreaded *mal'occhio*—the Evil Eye—of southern Italy.

"Why are you staring?" I asked.

"I think you know."

Ha. A bluff. How could she knew what I knew? I gripped the wheel a bit tighter and swung around the curve back to Old Stone Mill Road.

"Whatever do you mean?"

"Don't kid around. You grabbed Janice's ass in the kitchen, didn't you? I can tell because you've been smiling. You don't know you're smiling, but you are. It's the smile of Charles Adams the ass grabber. Not Doctor C. Adams after he's performed a beautiful operation, but Charles Adams the *lech*. And you're going to get it, buddy. Just you wait."

I didn't say anything.

"Oh I'll give you some credit; I bet it wasn't your idea.

She probably set you up for it. I sort of like Janice, but she's going to have to be taught a lesson."

"What's going to happen to her?"

"I'm going to hit her on that behind of hers, so the punishment will fit the crime. I'll use an implement."

"Belt? Paddle?"

"No. Chain saw. A Homelite will also render her anatomy less attractive to you. Thus I'll kill two birds with one stone. And as for you—"

"Hmm?" I gulped, feeling a damp flush on my brow.

"I haven't decided. But it will be *exquisite*. I promise you."

I didn't like the cold smile she was wearing. In the dim light her swarthy features and high cheekbones gave her the appearance of an Indian squaw. I remembered that the Indians, when they captured the lone white man after a battle, handed the poor guy over to their women. Of course he would beg to be killed, but they'd refuse and tie him to an old wagon wheel and invite the squaws out. Then he'd sit there, tied to the wheel, while the womenfolk assembled a gruesome array of equipment: rawhide thongs soaking in water, glowing brands, sharp flint shards, smoked hornets' nests . . . and so on. I'm sure the poor guy didn't know exactly what was on the agenda, but he would have a vague hunch that it wasn't Dinner at the Ritz.

At home we exited from the car and walked up the flagstone steps. I put my arm around her shoulder.

"Nothing bad happened," I said. "And Janice is okay."

"Sometimes I just get mad—"

But she didn't finish her sentence, because I had opened the front door and we were staring inside at our living room. Chairs were overturned. The sofa was shredded and hanging open like a disemboweled cow. Pictures were off the wall. Mary's desk was apart and all its contents spread over the room.

"Charlie!"

I walked through the dining room. Compared to the living

room it was almost untouched. They had broken no china, yet all the pieces had been shifted in the cabinets. The silver, worth perhaps thousands of dollars, had been extracted and tossed in a heap. But none of it appeared to be missing. Same story in the kitchen. My study was a wreck, with its desk in the same condition as Mary's. They'd hit every room, and obviously spent time and effort in each in direct proportion to the room's capacity for concealment. I was boiling mad, but inwardly relieved that nothing had been taken.

I was still thinking this when I entered the darkroom; then my heart sank. It wasn't a total wreck; it was just gone. The enlargers were still there. But the cameras were gone. All gone. The two multidrawered Shaw–Walker metal cabinets were *gone*. Twenty years' worth of negatives, our life on film, *gone*. Mary found me leaning against the bench. She told me later I looked like I was ready to sink right through the floor.

"Good Christ," I groaned, "I wish they'd taken anything but that. The paintings, rugs, stereo stuff, jewelry . . . even the cameras can be replaced. But not those negatives."

"That cardboard box, Charlie. That little box with Tom's front teeth inside. That's what they were after."

"And dammit, if I'd left it on my study desk where they would have found it right away, they wouldn't have done all this."

"Where did you leave it?"

"In Brian's office, for safekeeping. Safekeeping! And look!"

Mary crinkled up her face a bit and her eyes got shiny. The corners of her mouth turned down.

"Oh no," I said. "This is something to get upset about, but not to cry over. You don't cry over property; you cry over people. You cry over Roy Abernathy, not stuff like this."

Roy Abernathy was a thirty-three-year-old father of four who, a year and a half ago, had noticed pain in his right testis. In the space of fourteen months he had been transformed from a strong carpenter into a moaning, panting, babbling, ninety-four-pound, shriveled sack of agony. As a registered nurse, Mary had performed the post mortem care on what was left of him while Moe Abramson had done his best to arrest the avalanche of despair and depression in his now institutionalized wife. The children were fast changing from floating, speechless zombies of shock into truants and thieves.

So much for the Abernathy family. It's just one of those minor incidents that makes it a wee bit tougher to put on the spruce duds of a Sunday morning.

Mary let out a low moan and came apart at the seams. Now why did I have to mention Roy Abernathy? But perhaps it was best to have her cry. I walked her downstairs and we sat on the ruined couch together. I wondered. If there was a plan to the Great Going On, was what had just happened to us retribution for my clutching those luscious globes of flesh? And then a little self-hatred and guilt went into the stew pot along with the disaster and the horrendous, pyrotechnic trauma and injustice delivered to the Abernathys.

And I realized life had outdone itself. The needle had now fallen below boring. It was all the way down into the Dead Zone.

12

"Everybody should believe in somethin'," mused a dejected Sam Bowman as he hefted the jug of Cutty Sark and poured himself a magnum load. "I believe I'll have me another drink."

It was two in the afternoon the following day. We were having a powwow in the Adams kitchen. If you could call it a powwow. I couldn't. It looked more like a wake. I opened a bottle of Bass ale while Joe set the Krups machine to growling and produced cappucinos for Mary and himself. Kevin O'Hearn took the whisky jug from Sam when he was finished and gave himself a double-barreled slug, then returned to fiddling with the little Sony television, tuning in a soap. Brian Hannon was smoking one of my Montecruz coronas and sipping a Sprite. O'Hearn eyed the soft drink with disdain.

"Don't you want some Cutty, Brian?"

"Yes I do, Kevin. But if I had some, then I'd have more and more and more. Then things would go blank and I'd disappear and you wouldn't see me for months, and I'd wake up in an ash can in Panama City. So I'm having a Sprite."

"Oh. Had it bad eh?"

Brian's big balding head swiveled like a gun turret and two streams of pungent smoke cascaded out of his nostrils.

"How many people have you known who've had alcoholism *good*? Hmmm?"

O'Hearn returned to his soap, and Brian to his Sprite and stolen cigar. Brian's story, replete with fled wife and kids, wasn't a happy one. This somewhat accounted for his rather acerbic wit and sarcastic humor. But a nicer guy never lived. Except Moe.

"Okay Doc, we hand it to you. That makes two in a row. You're batting a thousand. So spill. How'd you know they'd burn Sam's safe?" Brian interrogated me.

"Didn't. Like I told Sam, just a hunch."

"Good hunch," returned Brian. "You got any more hunches?"

"Yeah, like on the Sox game Sunday?" asked O'Hearn.

"They just about done it to me," said Sam, tossing off the last of the amber fluid. "They just about broke me down now. Kill my partner, break open my place. S'all ruint now."

He shook his handsome head slowly. He was dressed in a cream-yellow Windbreaker. His hands and forearms were veiny, his chin clean and taut. Tiny little white pinpricks of whisker showed on his nut-brown jowls where he hadn't shaved—the reverse image of my Calabrian brother-in-law, who patted him softly on the back.

"C'mon, guy," said Joe. "Remember, the damage done to the office and safe is all covered. Covered well. You'll lose a coupla hundred, max. Thanks to Doc here you took the cash out and stashed it at Nissenbaum's. Good thing too. You had no proof of it at all. It was just a giant-sized hunk of petty cash, right? You wouldn't have gotten a dime on it, I'll bet. But it's safe, so don't worry."

"What I gonna do for a partner?"

We all stared at the table and sighed. There was a lull in the talk, which added further to the gloom. Mary asked Joe about Johnny Robinson's car.

"They towed it four blocks away in the dead of night to a deserted garage, which is where the Lowell police found it. The rocker panels had been ripped off, seat upholstery torn open—"

"And they also, what did they do, burned up Sam's safe? What do you mean, burned?" asked Mary.

"They broke into Dependable's office—came in through the roof—and burned the safe, honey. *Burned* it," I said, lighting a pipe.

"See, Mare," said her brother, "there are several basic ways to open a safe without the combination. The famous one is by cracking it, or moving the lock dial delicately back and forth until the tumbler pins fall into place. Then the safe can be opened. This is a great method, but it takes infinite skill and hours of time. Most crooks nowadays have neither. Also, the old pin-tumbler safe locks have been replaced by disc locks and other sophisticated stuff. It's almost impossible to crack a safe anymore. Now Sam's safe is—was—an old pin-tumbler Mosler. It could be cracked, but it would take a long time and it's in an exposed position. That leaves the other methods: peeling, blowing, punching, and burning."

Brian erupted in a choking fit; he had tried to inhale my stogie.

"That's a no-no, fella; you'll kill yourself," I warned.

"Peeling a safe is strictly for amateurs," continued Joe. "When you peel a safe you don't have the knowledge, skill, or tools needed to do a professional job. What you're doing is, you're attacking the steel casing of the safe rather than the door. You're going after the body, and you start at an edge of the casing and peel away the layers of steel with cold chisels and sledges, wedges, pickaxes . . . anything. It takes about eight hours of sweaty work to peel even a small safe, and it's noisy as hell. You can only peel a safe that's isolated in some old warehouse where nobody will hear the noise."

"Right," said Brian, whose eyes still watered. "Had a junkie tried to peel the safe in the lumberyard last year. Could hear him a mile away. Caught him before he'd even made a dent in it. Poor slob. But punching's different. Now that takes a little skill, and it's much quicker. Problem is, it's also noisy."

"Yeah, noisy, but it is quick," said Joe. "Usually the guy who punches a safe will plan to skedaddle before the heat arrives. What you do is, you drill into the safe door with a low-speed, high-torque drill with a good Swedish bit. You put the hole just to the side of the dial in the door, angled in toward the center. Then you stick a heavy metal punch into that hole and whang it with a baby sledge. *Ping!* The back of the lock is knocked right off, and in you go. Noisy but quick."

"But you gotta have a good drill, and it takes an hour, and several bits, to get that hole," said Brian.

"I wanna tell about *blowing* a safe," said Kevin, who'd spun around in his chair to face us. Cops. They'll talk your ear off. "Everybody's seen the movies about this, where the guy packs in the vials of nitro, called soup, and then hides behind the mattresses while the building blows up. Well, it ain't like that. Now they don't use nitro, which is dangerous as hell. They use *plastique*. Black-market *plastique*, and they place it just right. Then they tamp it with a hemp-and-cable mat and detonate it electrically. *Boom!* Off comes your door and you're in."

"Yeah," said Brian, "but not as easy as that. One: how and where do you get the funny putty? Not so easy, and a federal offense if you're even caught with the stuff. Two: you still gotta drill the holes and know how to place the charge. You gotta study the box beforehand. Blowing a box is like cleaving a diamond: you get one shot . . . and you can wreck the box and everything that's inside. Also of course, you can kill yourself."

"True, true," said O'Hearn philosophically. He returned to "The Young and the Restless."

"Still," mused Brian, "blowing a box remains the quickest way in. If speed is all that counts, and you don't worry about the noise—"

"—or the danger—"

"—or the danger, then you can't beat it. But burning's the most popular method now."

"Oh for sure," said Joe, lighting a Benson & Hedges with his Orsini lighter.

"Where'd you get that fruity lighter, Joe?" asked Brian.

Joe cuddled the instrument in his big hairy paw and glared back. "This is a class lighter, Hannon. Cost three hundred bucks. Made in Italy. In Florence. Only reason you think it's strange is because it's class."

"I just said it looks a little fruity is all. I guess a lot of stuff made in Italy is fruity, like those chacha boots."

"*Izat so?* How fruity is a nine-millimeter Beretta? I guess the Israeli army doesn't think it's so fruity. How about a Lamborghini, or a Ferrari? I notice there are no high-performance racing cars named O'Grady. Eh?"

Brian squinted at him, like a leopard on a limb.

"About the only thing they make in Ireland is Guinness . . . as if the Irish need any more of *that*—"

Brian slammed his palms down on the table and rose to his feet. O'Hearn slammed down his shot glass and rose to his feet.

"Shut up, Joe, or I'll paste you one," said Mary.

"Everybody keep quiet, or I'll paste everybody," I said.

"But you're just a doctor," said O'Hearn.

"Kevin, you obviously haven't seen Doc Adams in the gym or on the pistol range," said Joe. Gee, he made me feel like Captain Marvel. I liked hearing that. Any guy who's almost fifty likes to hear that.

"I want to hear about burning safes," I said.

"Aren't they steel? Then how can you burn them?" asked Mary, getting another cappucino.

"You use an oxyacetylene torch, Mary," said Brian. "It'll cut through anything. Burning is pretty slow, but it's dead quiet and safe. In the old days the only problem was lugging those big gas tanks to the box. How can you hike those big cylinders up to a roof and through a skylight? Can't. But recently they've come out with these little bottles, tanks you strap on your back just like scuba tanks. With hoses and gauges. Only instead of a mask on your face you're carrying the torch. You climb into the joint and walk up to the box and start burning it. Right around the lock face. She falls away when you cut through the facing. It's kind of like punching, only slower . . . but dead quiet.''

Sam Bowman spoke up. We'd almost forgotten him, he'd been so polite and quiet.

''Doc. What tipped you off was those guys come to look at my roof.''

''Yep. Seemed to me they came and inspected your place at a pretty convenient time. So I warned you. But it was only a really vague hunch. I wish I'd have caught on to *this*.''

I glared down at the crumpled brochure describing the high-efficiency oil burner, which I was holding in my hand.

''Mary says she let the guy into the basement for a quick look at our furnace. She stayed upstairs. He was down there for maybe ten minutes.''

''Enough time. Plenty,'' said Joe. ''He was a real pro. He cut through your alarm wires in two lower windows, and so skillfully you can't detect the cuts on casual inspection. He slipped the snib on one. He left the bogus literature and split, knowing he could come back at his convenience and get in. Which he did.''

''Only question now,'' said O'Hearn, ''is how many of them are there? Twenty? Keee-*riste*, seems like there's an army of 'em.''

''Don't like it,'' said Brian. ''But as far as Doc and Mary are concerned—as far as the town of Concord is concerned— I think the worst has passed. Don't think I can say the same for you, Sam.''

''The worst ain't passed for *them*, I tell you that,'' Sam said.

The phone rang. It was for Joe. While he nodded and grunted into the instrument, Mary began making a pizza. She had delegated tasks to everyone: Sam sliced the pepperoni, Kevin opened the anchovies, Brian sliced mushrooms and green peppers, and I grated mozzarella. Joe grunted and nodded. Then we all froze in our tracks.

''DeLucca!''

Stunned silence on the part of all the cops. Mary and I stared at each other dumfounded, as if someone had just told a joke and we didn't get the punch line.

"*DeLucca!*" echoed O'Hearn.

"DeLucca shmalooka," said Brian contemptuously. "Carmen DeLucca is dead."

Joe held the phone, frozen. He was wearing the Thousand-Yard Stare, like a G.I. who's been in combat for two days, or a football coach who's just lost the title game in the last thirty seconds because of an interception runback. He replaced the phone without saying good-bye, returning it to its cradle carefully, as if it were filled with "soup." I didn't like the look on his face.

"Lab finally did a make—a twelve-point positive make—on the dog-biscuit fingers we found at Johnny's," he said.

"Not DeLucca's," said Kevin.

"DeLucca's. Positively DeLucca's. Carmen Salvatore DeLucca, the East Coast buttonman and Wise Guy."

"They found Carmen DeLucca in a lime pit," said Brian. "They found what was left of him in Elizabeth, New Jersey, in a quarry lime pit. Don't tell me different."

"I tell you different. Fingers in the doggie's mouth belong to Carmen DeLucca. *Twelve-point positive make*. The bag of smelly jelly they dragged out of that lime pit was some other poor bastard."

"You mind?" said his sister, who was rolling out dough for the crust.

O'Hearn glared at the other two cops.

"Bull-fucking-shit, Joe," he yelled. "I say bull-fucking-shi—" He stopped, ashamed, as he realized Mary was there. She hadn't even turned her head.

"Uh—sorry, Mrs. Adams, I didn't, uh—"

" 'S okay, pal. I'll survive," she said, never taking her eyes off the rolling pin. "I've heard worse."

"Worse? You've heard *worse*? Jee-sus Keee-*riste*!"

"Lemme get that name," said Sam between clenched

teeth. "DeLucca killed Johnny. This guy Carmen DeLucca killed my partner."

While all this was going on, Joe's expression had not changed. Still the zombie look, the Thousand-Yard Stare. He announced he was going outside for a little walk. We watched him go, staring after him as the door shut. Joe does not take walks. Joe does not like the New England countryside; he likes crowded bars and sports events. Something was wrong.

We finished our tasks as Mary trimmed the dough on the big pan and spread her homemade tomato sauce on it. We slid it into the hot oven, heaped with all the cheese and goodies, then looked out the kitchen windows at Joe, who was pacing back and forth through the grape arbor. His head was down and he was smoking furiously, lighting one cigarette off another. Kevin, who worked with him almost daily, was especially concerned. He told us he hadn't seen Joe so worked up since the Blue Hill Butcher case.

"If it is DeLucca, then that means several things," he explained. "First, it's a giant-sized headache in general for all of us, since he's as brutal and bloodthirsty as they come. It's like Dracula coming out of his coffin. Second, as regards this case, it means it's big. It involves the Mob, the Wise Guys . . . and that alone makes it big."

"But Kevin, it was the Outfit that wanted DeLucca dead in the first place. Two of their henchmen swore to this. They talked, then walked," said Brian.

"Yeah I know. And that's another thing too: it doesn't figure. But even if he's not working for the Wise Guys, then he's gotta be working against them, or something like that. Any way you lay it out, Brian, the Mob's got to be *involved*. Jeez, DeLucca was into the Outfit like Folger's into coffee. But to even show his face around . . . I just don't get it—"

"You mean either he's off their shit list or else he's risking his neck," said Brian.

"Exactly. And there appears to be quite a number of guys

involved in this. How many to kill Johnny? The way we've got it figured, at least three: one to tag Johnny in town, the other two at Robinson's with the bomb. How many to pull these B and E's? At least two at Sam's for a burn job like that, plus the hole in the roof, right? Add to that one, maybe two guys here. Then there's Johnny's towed car. I figure two more. There are probably half-a-dozen men working the street side of this caper, which means two or three times that many upstairs. Now you see why he's upset.''

"Could be more than that. Don't forget the guy in the mill and our hot-rod friend on Route Three.''

Mary slid the hot pizza out and onto a rack. It smelled great. "It's more than that," she said. "I know Joey better than all of you put together. It's something else he's not telling us.''

She watched her brother pacing and smoking outside, then went out to call him in. We saw him turn and shake his head.

"Not hungry?" said Kevin as he leaned on the countertop and stared out the window. "Joe Brindelli *not hungry*?''

They came in and Joe sat and smoked in the corner while we ate. He had a Laphroaig on the rocks with a splash and fiddled with the television. He said nothing, and we left him alone. When we all finished he rose first and went to the door. He turned and faced all of us.

"The way I figure it," he said, "this thing has taken an unexpected turn. All I've got to say is—and Kev, I'm not trying to speak for you, so disagree if you want—all I'm saying is that it now appears to be a Mob action. Therefore I'm turning any business I may have had with this thing, or any I might have in the future, over to the O.C. unit. As far as I'm concerned, it's a local killing—as much as I loved Johnny, Sam, and I mean that. I'm out of it and the state is out. Let O.C. handle it if they want. Good-bye.''

He turned and left and got into his cruiser. We all stared after him.

"What the hell was *that* all about?" asked Brian.

"I have no idea," said Kevin, "except I don't believe it.''

We walked the rest of them out to their cars. Kevin got in the shotgun seat next to Joe. Mary stuck her head in and kissed her brother; her long black hair hung down and cascaded all over the door. Most women over forty say they can't wear their hair long. But Mary can. She looks under thirty. She leaned back and brushed her hair aside and Joe motioned me over with his finger.

"Doc, stay away from this business. *Stay away from it!*"

He and the others drove off, and Mary and I went back into the house. She sat down and put her chin on her fists.

"What's the O.C.?"

"Organized-crime unit. But I can't understand the sudden turnaround. Nobody liked Johnny better than Joe. And he was keen on this case too, especially since it involved us. Can't understand it."

"I can."

"What?"

She narrowed her eyes and glared at me. *"Not telling!"*

"Why not?"

"You know why. Remember, I said I'd get even with you. Well here's round one: Joe told me why he's dropping the whole thing, and why he's upset. But I'm not telling you and neither will he. Then maybe next time you and Janice—"

"How'd you know that—uh—what makes you think I—"

She waved her hand through the air impatiently.

"I just know, Charlie. And the next time you get even a pinky finger near her it's going to be *all she wrote!*"

She jumped up and stomped out, leaving me to clean up the luncheon mess. I opened another Bass and regarded the task before me, contemplating recent vicissitudes.

The needle wasn't moving up out of the Dead Zone. Sumbitch appeared to be *stuck*.

13

I FINISHED CLEANING UP, RELIGHTED MY PIPE, AND WENT
to find Mary. It was time for a Long Talk, in which I would
tell her that I really hadn't meant to grab Janice like that. I
would explain that it was all her fault, not mine. That's all.

Swell, Adams.

To hell with it, I decided as I passed the door of her workroom. Besides, Long Talks are like summit meetings; when
they're over things are more screwed up than they were before. I went for a medium-long run, did a hundred sit-ups on
the inclined board, and took a sauna. I dressed and left the
house as the first of the insurance claim officers arrived, and
I left a warm note for Mary which explained that I would be
at the residence of Morris Abramson, M.D. I thought it best
to communicate by diplomatic note until the crisis *à la frot-
tage au derrière* blew over.

There was a darkening cloud cover, with a chilly blowing
drizzle, as I turned into Walden Breezes trailer park. It's right
across from Walden Pond, where Thoreau wrote the famous
tract. But old Henry David would get the fantods if he
glimpsed the horrendous assemblage of mobile homes per-
manently parked across Route 126 from the pond. Most are
vintage fifties and sixties, with a few more recent additions.
Moe's dwelling was at the end of the circle, right by the deep
pine woods. This was a good thing because he keeps two

Nubian goats in a miniature corral and they can be noisy. I got out of the car and felt better immediately. Although I have no firsthand knowledge of how good a therapist he is, I can say that being with him is good therapy for me. After being in his company even briefly, you begin to sort out what's important and what isn't. And it's amazing how many things in twentieth-century middle-class American life aren't at all. I sauntered down the tiny gravel path lined with myrtle and climbed the two narrow wooden steps to the side door of the old Airstream trailer.

One could say that Moe is antimaterialist. He claims that cluttering your life with too many possessions fetters your mind and soul. Aside from the old Airstream and the battered Dodge sedan (1963, white over blue), he has nothing.

I rang the little cowbell and waited. Above the door, painted in Gothic letters, was the vehicle's name: "Der Schleppenwagen."

Moe says that there are three basic ways to measure a person: by what he *is*, by what he *does*, and by what he *has*. The first is the most important, the second slightly less so, and the third almost meaningless. America's primary fault, he says, is that it foolishly persists in paying attention solely to the third item. Remembering this made me feel guilty again that I had so much, and I thought of Bartolomeo Vanzetti in his little rented room in Plymouth, giving the kids dimes. Moe was like him. Moe was like Thoreau too, with a modern-day, riveted-aluminum version of Henry David's hut.

A gravelly, irritable voice answered my yank on the cowbell.

"Who's dat?"

"Electrolux!" I chirped.

"Oh yeah? Well make like a vacuum and suck. I'm busy."

"It's me."

The curved slab of aluminum opened and Moe's angular, bearded face peered out. He was dressed in a soaked running suit.

"Oh hiya, Doc. What brings you here? Some masochistic desire for humiliation at the chessboard?"

I entered the tiny residence, which was akin to boarding a miniature, stationary airplane. I stood next to him but detected no locker-room stink from the sweat-soaked garments which hadn't been washed in weeks. Moe runs over fifty miles a week and his sweat has about as much poison in it as distilled water. He rattled a metal Band-Aid box at me. It had a coin slot gashed in the lid and was wrapped with tape. It was his charity-of-the-month box. I heard the rattle of the coin of the realm inside. I pointed at the battered tin box.

"What this time?"

"Saint Bonaventure's Home for Runaways."

"Since when are you giving to Catholic charities? You're not Catholic."

"So? A runaway is a runaway. Let's have it." He rapped my trouser pants with his knuckles. No coins. He glared at me.

"It'll take folding green, Adams. Gimme a bill. One wit' double digits."

He took my ten-spot and folded it quicker than a beer vendor at Fenway, stuffing it into the slot. We were standing in the tiny galley kitchen of the trailer, whose cracked and crumbly linoleum counters were littered with banana peels, orange rinds, yogurt cartons, sprouts, granola, chocolate bars, and thick dark breads. All around us hung bags and baskets of dried fruit. On the tiny icebox was a photo of Albert Einstein. Underneath was a clipped headline message that said SMARTY PANTS. I grabbed a handful of dried apricots and followed Moe through a bead curtain, past the minuscule bathroom, and through his bedroom.

"Is someone in there?"

"Uh-huh. My friend is taking ga shower in there. Come on out back."

Whoever his friend was, he was a shrimp; the tiny shoes Moe kicked aside showed that. We went through a rear door of the Airstream, which connected it to the addition Moe had built to double the size of his dwelling, leaving it tiny rather than microscopic. The addition was a single room, twenty feet square. Three of its walls were bookshelves, broken only by windows, paintings, and stereo equipment. The fourth was glass and screens that slid open. The view was of the woods and goat corral. A wood stove provided heat; its big black box crinkled and tinked, and the air above it danced. The tiny color television was on; Moe was listening to Dr. Mortimer Adler discussing ethics.

Another of Moe's aphorisms is that the amount of contentment and happiness you get out of life is directly and inversely proportional to the amount of time you spend worrying about yourself or trying to make yourself happy. Seek happiness, he says, and you'll never find it. Seek the welfare and happiness of others and you'll have more happiness than you'll know what to do with.

He is probably right about this. I say he's probably right because I have never known him to be wrong about anything. I suppose the idea is rather akin to that of Zen. Happiness, says Zen, is not seeking or expecting it. So these Zen Buddhist monks sit around in orange robes and shaved heads, keeping terrible hours and a starvation diet, whopping each other with bamboo stakes. Hey, c'mon and get happy . . .

"Wanna play?" Moe growled, hauling out the chessboard from beneath a photograph. The photograph was taken in 1967 and shows Moe with his then wife, standing in front of their big house in Lexington. A Mercedes and a Jag are visible in the picture off to one side. Moe is clean-shaven, suited, and trying his best to hide his strained smile. This is Moe Abramson in his former life—Moe the Big-shot Psychiatrist. The material success was supposed to make him happy but it didn't. Underneath this portrait was another clipped-out headline: WHY IS THIS MAN SMILING?

Moe and his wife split and he underwent a startling metamorphosis, a reincarnation of the personalities in part of Jesus, Buddha, Gandhi, Thoreau, St. Francis, and Florence Nightingale. The only trouble with Moe is that he's the world's biggest soft touch. Moe's such a sap he'd buy tickets to the Arsonist's Ball, bless his heart.

As he set up the wooden pieces I heard a soft patter of feet behind me and turned to see Moe's friend. Her long hair flowed over her shoulders and almost covered her breasts. But not quite. As for her bottom half, it remained in full view as she swung into the room, making no attempt to cover herself.

"Doc, this is Loretta Popp. Lolly, this is my friend Doc. Lolly honey, I think you better put something on, okay?"

She stopped, dumbfounded, as if the thought hadn't occurred and there was no need for it.

"Oh yeah . . . sorry, Moe, it's just that I'm used to . . . you know . . ."

"I understand. You go put something on now."

She turned and sashayed out of the room, swinging a luscious tail section and gorgeous legs. My knees quivered and I had the cold sweats. Soon the fantods would set in.

"What was that?"

"Mmmm. One of my charity cases. Lolly's been hooking these past two years. Started when she was sixteen, can you imagine?"

"Lolly Popp? *Lolly Popp*, for Chrissake?"

"Loretta. Then they nicknamed her Lolly. It was her, uh, *nom de guerre*. It seems to have stuck."

"Well she certainly is tasty-looking. She part black?"

"Half-Jamaican, which explains the tawny skin and aqua eyes. She looks great now—a beautiful girl. But seven months ago she was a sick kid: hepatitis and V.D. Got her all squared away now. She's en route to a foster home."

"But I'm not going," said the lovely creature as she glided back into the room. She curled up on the sofa next to Moe and ran her fingers through his thinning hair. Then she pouted and let her head fall against his. She was wearing a big floppy Celtics sweat shirt. It became her. But then, an ox yoke would become her. She could glorify a slag pit. Moe rubbed her back. Then I saw his hand fall down behind her. Almost instantly he withdrew it, clucking his tongue like a scolding mother hen.

"Loretta. Loretta dear, I said *get dressed*."

She rose, still pouting, and began to return to the old trailer portion of Moe's dwelling. As she walked past, the sweat shirt rode up a bit and I saw the cause of Moe's rebuke. It seemed that lovely Loretta had neglected to put on pants. She turned and paused, a faint smile of apology played about her full lips.

"Sorry, Moe. I'm just used to . . . you know . . ."

"Of course," said Moe, watching her disappear.

"Killjoy," I said.

"So what's wit' you? You've just moved your bishop like a knight."

Lolly came back in a flash. In the truest sense, since she was still bottomless. But old Lolly Popp had a sense of humor all right. I have to hand it to her. She scowled at Moe, one hand on hip, and held a pair of black underpants up, as if for inspection, in her other hand. That is, I think they were black. So much light was coming through them it was hard to tell. I wouldn't exactly call them flimsy, but if she held them at shoulder height and dropped them, they'd take five minutes to reach the floor.

"An extremely gratifying choice of undergarments, Lolly," I said. "Bravo."

She smiled at me—my God, she was gorgeous!—and dutifully held the panties out in a little rectangle and stepped into them, pulling them up. Then I discovered that a girl looks just as sexy squiggling into a pair of slinky panties as she does wriggling out of them. Why is that? And also, though you'd eventually tire of viewing the Taj Mahal by moonlight, or the sunset over Morro Bay, a beautiful woman slipping in or out of her drawers is a sight that never ceases to enthrall. Why is that?

Lolly Popp smiled at me and then gave an exaggerated blush, realizing that I was watching her pivot back and forth as she drew up the lacy pants. Gee, they were snug. She grinned, turning around.

"Here's the good part," said Moe intensely.

"You're not kidding," I answered as I stared at the sumptuous globes of tan flesh that jounced and jiggled as they fought their way into the slinky nylon casing. Lolly made a final adjustment, then smoothed out the fabric—if one could call it that—with her hands. The pants were nearly transparent except for a tiny pie-shaped wedge of darker material at the crotch. Perhaps this was for reinforcement, but I know better. Like the seams in nylons, it was designed by some kinky frog in Paris at the turn of the century to make the wearer yet more seductive. Bless him (or her), whoever he was. He should be canonized.

"Ah, this is *terrific*!" said Moe. Then I realized that he wasn't referring to his friend; he was engrossed in Dr. Mortimer Adler. He leaned over and turned up the volume. The good doctor said: ". . . and so by the term *goodness*, we could be referring to the classic Judeo-Christian concept of purity . . . or perhaps in a more modern sense the Sartrian view, so well expressed by Gabriel Marcel, of goodness as a *behavior* template—an active as opposed to passive concept, if you will—which leads to the individual's own responsibility to immerse himself in the upward march of humanity . . ."

Lolly stared at the tube and sighed. She turned to me.

"Moe's so smart, isn't he? Isn't he terrific?"

"Yes he is."

She sank silently onto the couch between us. Our sides were touching. Above the dark wedge of material on the front of her pants the top of her bush peeked through the thin material. It looked cute. They tend to.

"Pay attention, Doc; here's the essence of life," said Moe, leaning forward. "The real *essence*."

"I know," I said, staring at Lolly's sport section. My head refused to budge. Hydraulic levers couldn't move it. I heard Mortimer Adler continue: "And so we ask—literally for goodness' sake—what we each can do, every day, to contribute to the general welfare. Now this daily game plan, mundane as it may seem—a sort of Boy Scout ethos, if you will—remains a salutary mode of living. It is reflected in the New Testament . . .''

Lolly sighed again and shifted her bottom. She leaned over, and in a cloud of delicious scent whispered to me.

"I'm finally able to show Moe how grateful I am. Do you know he's paying for my junior college?"

"A wonderful guy . . ."

"I don't have any home now but this; I hope he'll let me stay."

I was about to offer her alternative residence, but some vague voice in the old gray matter told me it was unwise.

"Loretta, dear, those pants are inappropriate. Why don't you put your gym shorts on over them, okay?"

She stalked off toward the bedroom, giving me a last fleeting glimpse. I could've killed Moe.

"What kind of cockamamy chess game *is* dis?" He scowled. "Your king gand queen are switched and you just moved your pawn like a rook!"

I set the chessboard aside. "I can't play chess with her around, Moe."

"Why not?"

The cowbell rang. We heard Lolly answer it. A second later she hobbled around the corner, yanking on a pair of faded cotton shorts. They became her. But then—oh, skip it.

"Doctor Adams?" she inquired, but the visitor had come on in anyway and now stood behind her, gaping. It was Joe.
"There's a john here to see you—oops! I mean, a man . . . "

"Thanks, Lolly. Hiya, Joe."

"Doc. I gotta see you."

"Sure. You remember Moe. Moe, Joe. Joe, Moe."

"What is dis, the *mojo* song?" said Moe irritably as he put away the chessboard and pieces. "Joe, want some food? Dried pears? Tofu? Celery? Wheat-germ muffins? Bean sprou—"

"No thanks," said Joe, his mouth curled in revulsion, "that stuff will kill you. Doc, I have to talk with you privately a minute. Got to. Sorry, Moe."

I rose to go and looked at Lolly, who winked at me. It was not a teasy wink; it was a good-luck wink. She looked terrific in the shorts. The more clothes she put on, the better she looked, because I knew what she had on underneath the shorts. But I couldn't see those slinky panties. And I knew what was underneath those, but I couldn't see. That would be the ultimate striptease, I thought as I drew on my jacket, to have a girl come on the stage naked and get dressed, piece by piece.

"Nice meeting you, Lolly," I said as we left through the airplane-style doorway. "You've made my day."

"You're in enough trouble at home," Joe reminded me, pausing on the doorstep. He was looking at two old photographs that hung side by side on the kitchen wall above the tiny sink. "Who the hell are those guys?"

"Two of the greatest chess masters who ever lived," said Moe, who was showing us out. "Great but tragic. On the left is the American Paul Morphy, the first true chess genius. On the right is Akiba Rubinstein, a rabbinical student from Lodz. Both of these men had their careers terminated by mental illness. Specifically, it was schizophrenia. Both died in asylums."

"I might as well get to the point, since you're leading up to it so brilliantly," I said, reaching for a taped oatmeal carton with a slot on top. It was heavy in my hand as I held it out to my brother-in-law. I rattled it under his nose.

"Give to mental-health research, Joe," I said. When he dropped two quarters in I asked for more. He claimed he had no more change.

"It'll take folding green, Brindelli. Give!" I said.

"All I got's tens. I can't give a ten."

"Ten bucks for leaving," Moe announced, blocking the door.

We skinned Joe for a tenner and then he and I left. Joe

paused outside the old trailer, still in shock. Through the thin walls of the domicile we could hear Lolly cooing at Moe.

"Not now dear. Not *now*; I just have to see this second tape."

And then came the voice of Mortimer Adler: "—and so to leave Reinhold Niebuhr for the moment and explore the existence of a Supreme Being as expressed by the systems philosopher Alfred North Whitehead—"

"C'mon, Moe," cooed a sultry voice, husky with desire.

"Not now, Lolly; I've got to hear the rest of this lecture."

"—in relation to what he calls *absolute entities*, which become the building blocks, the molecular and atomic structure, if you will, of his system . . ."

"Moo-*ooe* . . ."

"Now as you'll recall, Russell and Moore attacked the dilemma differently . . . and posing the dilemma, merely asking the question, you see, flips ordinary language analysis and logical positivism into the proverbial cocked hat—"

"Stop it, Lolly, or I'll send you to your room."

Joe shook his head sadly.

"Can you believe it, Doc? Can you believe that dirty old man in there with that young piece?"

"You are in error. Moe is many things, some of them a little strange. But one thing he is *not* is dirty. Not in thought, word, deed, or body. And not in soul. Nobody is cleaner than Morris Abramson."

"Yeah, but that girl, Doc. You should've seen what I saw as I walked in!"

"That and more. Hey Joe. Cut that out. We're in public view."

"What? I jus—oh. Sorry," he said, withdrawing his hands from his pockets. He got in his cruiser and followed me home. As I drove through the drizzle I reflected on luscious Lolly and couldn't help but think that Moe's philosophy worked.

* * *

Forty minutes later Mary slid back the rice-paper screen of the tiny teahouse, kicked off her slippers, and placed a rough clay pot on the low lacquered table near where Joe and I sat with robes of white raw silk wrapped around us and tied with big sashes. We didn't feel the cold damp. Silk is warmer than wool and as strong as steel, though most people cannot believe this. The pot was filled with boiling hot water which surrounded a bottle of saki. Mary sat down between us.

"Tell him, Joey."

Joe poured a tiny cup of the hot wine and sipped it, staring out through the open wall at the gray-brown water of the pond, which rippled infinitely in the light rain.

"I've been thinking of what the killers have been searching for all along," he said in a tired voice. It was weary—husky with emotional fatigue. "From the start it interested me, of course. Mary can tell you how we were weaned on the Sacco–Vanzetti case. It's funny, but the event seemed to spark the Italian-American community instead of depress it. It was the thing that galvanized and united it. It made us sad, but it made us proud and defiant. So you can see how disastrous it would be if . . ."

He paused to let out a slow sigh.

". . . if it were proved that they were guilty."

Joe let the hot wine roll around on his tongue, swallowed it, then let out another deep breath as he shook his head slowly.

"I've already talked to Gus Giordano about it. That's where I went right after I left your place earlier. Hotfooted it right down to the North End to talk to Gus. Now what we think is . . . what we *think*, is that the thing the hoods are after, whatever it might be, is some kind of proof. Probably a document or photo—*something*. And what we're really afraid of more than anything is that old Dominic Santuccio had something in his files that he didn't tell Andy about before he died. And that something is pure dynamite. Probably Andy found out about it last week and so asked for the bundle back. I checked with the library; they hadn't opened it yet, just sent it back to Andy via Johnny Robinson. Maybe Andy was ordered to get the envelope back. Who knows?''

"Ordered? Who would order him to do that?''

"You know who.''

"The Mob? Oh, and that's why DeLucca's name upset you. You knew it was the Mob. Why would they be interested in evidence from the case? And how do we know the thing doesn't *clear* Sacco and Vanzetti?''

"Those two questions exactly were what was bothering me earlier when I was pacing around in your yard, while the rest of you ate lunch. They bothered me a lot. Okay. Either the Wise Guys want the damning evidence to blackmail the Italian-American community—to threaten to make it public if they're not paid off—or else they simply want to destroy it. I kind of suspect the latter possibility. Much as I hate the Mob, I admire the way they usually look out for the rest of us, especially us Calabrians and Sicilians. But you never know. For the past twenty years the Wise Guys have had everybody believing they don't traffic in hard drugs. Everybody thought it was the blacks and Hispanics. Not so. The Mob is heavy into horse. Why? Because it pays. Pays like there ain't no tomorrow. Now, if they knew the evidence or whatever in Andy's envelope could pay, they might steal it and hold it for ransom.''

"And if it got out? The effect on the North End?''

"Disaster. My talk with Gus confirmed that. It'd be a major blow to the community's morale. The thing would travel across America like a shock wave. And Italians wouldn't be the only ones hurt by it. The labor movement, the entire liberal left—hell. The neofascist bunch they've got in the White House now would get that much more ammunition to go after every splinter group, every bunch who's not lily white and WASP. I could see a major backlash.''

"I couldn't. And frankly, I don't see how anything carried in that envelope could be hot enough to kill over.''

"Yeah, but it *was*. Why don't you go say that to Sam?''

"Joe? What if whatever it is proves they were innocent?" asked Mary.

"I just can't see it, Mare," he said, shaking his head, "and Gus can't either. That's why he's even more upset than I am. He's not telling a soul about this and neither of you better either. Mary, how can you sell good news? You can't. And there's no reason to hide it. There's no money or leverage in good news. The only reason people are going after that packet is because there's something Andy didn't want to get out. There's just no other explanation."

I was afraid Joe was right. But I didn't say anything.

"Charlie, you said there was no way they could've been guilty."

"Yeah I know. And I still say it. But then, just as guilt was never really proven and there was no confession, innocence has never been proven either. I feel the weight of evidence remains overwhelmingly in their favor. But it was never a hundred percent."

"*Sacco's alibi*. That's it. That's what Gus thinks," said Joe.

"What about that other guy's confession?" asked Mary.

"Madeiros? He was doomed anyway. Again, you can take it strongly either way, just like the rest of the case. Pro: Celestino Madeiros knew he was going to the chair and didn't have anything to gain by clearing Sacco and Vanzetti; he did it out of the last twinge of conscience he had left because he didn't want to see two innocent guys get fried. Con: just as he didn't have anything to gain, he also had nothing to lose. Why not make a last-ditch effort to save a few partners in crime?"

"Unbelievable. Hollywood couldn't have written a better script," said Joe.

"It's like one of those optical tricks, Mary. Is the picture with the curved lines an outline of a vase or two faces staring at one another? Is that stairway the top of the basement stairs, looking down, or the bottom of the attic stairs, looking up?"

"Sacco's alibi," repeated Joe. "Both men had lots of witnesses swearing they were with them during the holdup. Sacco claimed he was in Boston that day, right in the North End, getting his passport ready so he could visit his relatives in Italy. He said he went to a local restaurant, a coffeehouse, and met a lot of people as he strolled around during the afternoon. But the jury found that suspicious. Why had this guy missed work—not shown up at his factory in Stoughton—on the very day of the holdup, when he never missed work? Ha! they said, very convenient.''

"And Vanzetti?" asked Mary, drawing her silk robe tight around her against the chill.

"Vanzetti's alibi depended on neighborhood friends, who were mostly Italian too. But one legit Anglo-Saxon vouched for him: Melvin Corl, who was mending nets on the beach in North Plymouth. Also, Vanzetti was not absent from his place of business as was Sacco. Reason? He *had* no place of business; he came and went as he pleased.''

"The whole thing is screwy," Mary said.

"Yeah," I said. "But Joe's right. The jury tended to believe Vanzetti a bit more than Sacco. It's the old double reverse again, don't you see? Sacco's alibi was doubted because it was so good, so coincidentally foolproof. Why would a man decide to go into Boston and be absent from his work on the very day the robbery was committed? To the jury it meant only one thing: a false and carefully prearranged alibi. Add to this Sacco's twinlike resemblance to Mike Morelli . . . and there you have it.''

We struggled to our feet and stood over the lacquered tea table. I felt as if a great weight had descended upon me. I knew what they were thinking, and felt sad. Everybody knew—had known since the arrest and trial—that there was always a chance that it would be shown that the shoe trimmer and the fish peddler had really pulled the job. That they were both guilty of armed robbery and murder and deserved to die.

We trudged back to the house. Joe was silent. He finally announced that he might resign from the force. Mary told him to cut the bullshit and help plan dinner. This helped some, but I was quick to notice that he did not pitch into the kitchen activities with his usual gusto. Instead he trudged around like a robot, slicing and peeling here, tasting there, trimming here, all with a look of black depression on his big dark face.

I called Tom Costello to confirm our appointment for early the next morning, since the original appointment had been scrubbed because of our wrecked house. During the course of our conversation I happened to mention Joe, and Tom replied that he'd like to see Joe again soon. I remembered then that the two men liked each other. I told Tom in all frankness that he'd be pretty sore tomorrow after my work on him, and suggested that perhaps a little jaunt with us would take his mind off the discomfort. He agreed, and it was set up.

"I told ya, Doc, I don't want to go," Joe said a few minutes later. "I'm dropping this thing and so are you. Frankly, I hope the whole thing blows over. All I want to do is to get Carmen DeLucca. Dead or alive. Preferably dead."

We sat on the high stools near the butcher block and talked and smelled the onion soup and halibut cooking. Joe got a wee bit brighter over the deep sadness. He still said he wasn't going.

"After today I don't wanna hear about those two grease-balls anymore. Not now. Not *ever*."

"We're going down to Braintree tomorrow at ten. Be at my office, Joe. Be there."

"Not on your life."

He was.

14

I HAD TOM IN THE CHAIR, TILTED FAR BACK, FOR AN HOUR and a half. He was getting purple in the face. If it had been a set of lowers I was putting in, he would have remained sitting upright, but the uppers require the patient to be almost horizontal so I can look right into the upper gums and sockets from the tooth's point of view. The saliva ejector squeaked and hissed and kept his mouth dry.

I had prepped Tom's eyeteeth, or canines, by grinding them into pegs over which the ends of the six-unit bridge would fit. I spent the better part of an hour checking and rechecking the fit, using De Mark and articulating paper to locate humps and high spots I wanted to remove. I checked his bite and removed the interferences with a greenstone and the polishing wheel. When the occlusion, or bite, was perfect, I was ready for Susan to mix the cement. Susan mixed it perfectly in one minute. It was a brand-new wonder cement that creates a chemical as well as physical bond between the bridge and the teeth. Called glass ionomer, the cement contains ions of fluoride which slow-release into the teeth constantly and prevent decay. Great stuff!

I applied the cement, inserted the bridge firmly and finally, and it was done. The entire upper permanent bridge fit in flawlessly—better than any glove. There would be no wiggle or waggle. No fuss, no muss. Tom could eat anything and

175

his permanent front dentures would not come out or slip. He would not have to put them to sleep in a glass every night. He would not have to buy Polygrip, Dentu-Creme, or any of that elderly stuff.

I liked doing this kind of work because it demanded a lot of skill and patience. And when I was finished my patients were always very happy with the result.

"You do good work, Doc," said Tom, admiring himself in the mirror. "And I can talk now too. You can't imagine how sick I was of sounding like a dress designer. The only thing is, my mouth feels all tingly and fuzzy."

"Well enjoy it while you can, old sport," I said as I cleaned up and hung up the white smock. "Because when the local wears off there'll be some discomfort for a while. Now here's Joe in the parking lot. Let's go."

Out on 128 Joe told Tom about recent developments in the case, including a brief and bloody bio of one Carmen De-Lucca. Tom said he was sick of hearing about the Mob the way the Germans must be sick of hearing about Hitler. But like me, he couldn't believe for a second that Sacco and Vanzetti were guilty. However, the more we explained to him, the more silent he became.

At the South Shore Plaza shopping mall we got coffee and studied a map of Braintree. Pearl Street, where the old Slater and Morrill factory stood, was about a mile away. We drove over there, and found nothing.

Joe drove while Tom and I consulted the street map and one of my library books which had a detailed map of the robbery scene. As we passed up and down the section of Pearl Street indicated, we saw not even the slightest indication that it was anything special. No historical marker, no privately erected sign, not even a memorial water bubbler for the two watchmen killed. Nothing.

"I'll be damned," mused Joe as he nursed the cruiser along in a crawl. The guy behind us leaned on his horn and finally passed us right in the middle of an intersection. As he flew past he glared at Joe and shouted, then roared on and ran the next red light.

"Where the hell are the cops when you need 'em?" said Joe, staring out of his unmarked car.

"Pull over here," said Tom, pointing. "This is right smack dab where it happened."

We got out and walked around. Nothing was left of the Slater and Morrill factory. In its place was a rubble-strewn field of weeds. About a hundred yards down the road and pretty far back I saw the remains of the Rice and Hutchins factory: a rickety red-brick smokestack just like the one Andy Santuccio had been found in. I pointed it out to Joe.

"Surely that's more than coincidence, Joe."

"Don't be too sure. There are lots of old smokestacks left behind when they pull down factories. It's because they're too tall to wreck; they can't get the wrecking ball up high enough, even on the biggest derricks. The only really safe way to take them down is to build a scaffolding around them and do it piece by piece, which is too expensive. Only way to do it cheap is to dynamite 'em, which they should do, because they're a hazard. They fall over and it's like a bomb."

We strolled along the fields, using my books as a reference to key spots. The railroad track was right where it had been in the 1920s, minus the depot shack where the money was delivered in the morning. On the day of the robbery, the payroll had been kept there until mid-afternoon, when the two guards, Parmenter and Berardelli, came and took it away in two locked boxes. But they never made it to the factory. We walked through the scene, trying to reconstruct it, and half-closing my eyes, I could almost take myself back to April 15, 1920.

The men in the depot shack received the money as scheduled when the train pulled through that morning. They paid little attention to the men lounging nearby, watching the train. Later, on the witness stand, they recalled that these early-morning visitors were obviously casing the job, making sure

the money had indeed arrived. Things were quiet until just
before three o'clock . . .

I squint my eyes and look across the road to the rubble field, but
now it's a red-brick factory with a belching smokestack and people
in skimmer hats in the yard. Some of the workingmen wear cloth
caps. Two men emerge from the building and walk purposefully
along the road, which is Pearl Street, then across it toward the
shack. They go in. A few minutes later they come back out, each
carrying a metal bank box. They are armed but guns aren't drawn.
They usually make the transfer by car or wagon, with a shotgun
guard, but today for some strange reason they walk.

Back across the street, then up along the road past Rice and
Hutchins, they approach the grounds of Slater and Morrill. As they
near the big red-brick factory, two men who have been leaning idly
against the wall step out and walk toward the street, intercepting
the two guards with the metal boxes. As they get within a few feet
of the guards, guns appear in their hands. There are a few shouted
orders. Quickly and without warning one of the bandits shoots, and
the chief guard, Frederick Parmenter, falls mortally wounded,
clutching at his middle. Alessandro Berardelli, his assistant, panics.
He drops his box and begins to run back across Pearl Street, where
he is cut down by pistol fire. Then one of the gunmen raises up his
pistol and fires a lone shot into the air.

This appears to be a signal, because an instant later a large touring car, a big Buick, roars down the street and stops. The bandits
begin to jump in, but one of them hesitates and walks back to Berardelli, lying in the street. He takes deliberate aim and shoots the
fallen man point-blank, killing him, then returns to the car and gets
in. The car, a dirty greenish-brown in color (or was it dark-blue?
The witnesses later argue), speeds off down the road, a wicked-
looking shotgun protruding from the rear window.

At the railroad crossing gate the big car stops and the bandits
order the gatekeepers to raise the drop gate immediately or they will
be shot. They do this, but not before one of them gets a good look
at one of the killer bandits and hears his voice. The car roars off,
turning left at the intersection and speeding away, the occupants
flinging special round-headed tacks (which always land point upward) behind them.

Ingeniously, the driver of the big car reverses direction in a two-
wheeled hairpin turn half a mile down the road and heads back
toward the scene of the crime on a parallel road. This incongruous
reverse has its intended effect; the pursuing police are totally confused and allow the big Buick to proceed unchallenged out of town.

The robbery, planned carefully and executed like clockwork, is successful. But two men have been gunned down in cold blood. Neither guard had a chance to draw his sidearm; they were shot down without reason. Parmenter didn't die right away, however; he lived just long enough to describe to the police the man who shot him. Other witnesses, leaning out of factory windows when they heard the noise or watching the car speed by, saw him too. And these, along with the gatekeeper, described a man who looked exactly like Nicola Sacco . . .

"What did you say, Doc?" asked Tom, who was staring at me. I came to and realized I had been standing dead still and staring at the rubble field and smokestack. And worse, I had been muttering to myself too.

"I said that of all the days to pick to miss work and go off on an all-day errand, Nick Sacco had to pick April fifteenth. And at the same time here's a guy standing right about where you are now who looks just like him, pumping shots into those guards . . ."

Tom scraped gravel back and forth with his toe, like a batter at the plate, and shook his head slowly. His hands were deep in his coat pockets and he was hunched over. Joe was behind him, standing near the road in silence.

"Oh I don't know, Doc. Jeeez. I mean, maybe he did do it. Sure looks like it anyway. I was so sure he didn't because all my life I was told he didn't. Like all good Italian boys I was taught the basics, you know: don't eat meat on Friday, go to confession, FDR is the greatest president who ever lived, Joe DiMaggio is the world's greatest ballplayer . . . and Sacco and Vanzetti were innocent."

"Sounds pretty good to me," I said. "So what's changed?"

"Lots. For instance, we eat meat on Fridays now, right? We don't go to confession much anymore, right? And it looks like Roosevelt made some mistakes."

"What about Joe DiMaggio?"

"You kiddin'? He's *still* the greatest. That's not changed. Except there might be one just as good since—"

"Who might that be?"

"Rico Petrocelli. Who else?"

"Let's get out of here. I'm getting depressed. *Hey Joe!*"

We got in the car and rolled away. Joe didn't say much either. We stopped at the McDonald's across the street and bought coffee. I asked the girl at the register if she knew the significance of Pearl Street. She didn't. And she'd never heard of Sacco and Vanzetti either. She couldn't have cared less.

"Sounds like a kinda spaghetti, dudn't it? Like Ronzoni?"

In a few minutes we were purring along on 128 again, heading back north. Neither Joe nor Tom wanted to make the second stop at Dedham after what we'd encountered at Braintree, but I insisted. The old film clips had entranced me and I wanted to see the courthouse and the jail where the two defendants had spent seven years while the whole world watched and waited.

The courthouse had not changed a bit; it was still the gray, quasi-Greek classical building with a high dome and an American flag on top. When we reached the second floor, which was the entrance to the courtroom and judges' chambers, a security officer approached us quickly and asked if he could help us. In a case like this everybody knows that "Can I help you?" really means "Get the hell out of here." But Joe flashed his badge and we went inside. The courtroom had not changed at all except for one detail: they had removed the medieval prisoner's cage at the far end. Otherwise I could almost see Katzmann and Thayer, Thompson and Ehrmann, the jury and its foreman, Harry Ripley (who was a former police chief and who hated "dagos"), and the two defendants locked in their cage.

We cased the whole place, looking for photographs on the walls, plaques or markers, perhaps a framed statement or scroll. There was nothing. I asked the rather plump, pale woman in the county clerk's office about the case. As soon as she heard the names she brought her index finger up to her pursed mouth.

"*Shhhhh!*" She giggled. "We don't talk about *that*!"

We left and walked around the courthouse. Twice. Aside from a historical plaque set in a boulder telling about some early schoolhouse, there was nothing. Not any kind of plaque or marker—even one hostile to the defendants. There was nothing. And that seemed strange, considering the fuss New Englanders make over history. They're forever holding parades for people who've been dead a hundred years. But here, where the world's attention had been riveted during the summer of 1927, there was not a thing to mark the occasion or any mention made of it.

We went on to the jail. Things had not changed much there either. Again Joe flashed the badge and we went through the lobby and into the cell blocks. We were shown the cells that Sacco and Vanzetti occupied during their long incarceration. We saw the courtyard where they exercised. It was in this very courtyard that Celestino Madeiros caught Sacco's attention one day. He whispered:

"Nick! I know who pulled the South Braintree job!"

Sacco ignored him and returned to his cell. Why? Ehrmann said it was because he feared that Madeiros was a plant, a spy put there by the government to get a confession out of him. They had tried that the year before. But there could be another reason Sacco had ignored him: because he, Sacco, had pulled the job.

The courtyard was ringed with barbed wire and a new, shiny type of concertina wire that was drawn from a flat strip of metal with prongs extruded from its edges. It looked like old ripped-apart tin cans. It looked about as attractive as a swarm of maggots. Then I recalled two things from the reading I'd done. One was the reminiscence of a guard who one day overheard Sacco and Vanzetti arguing about who had the best singing voice. To resolve the dispute, each convict sang to the other. The song they sang was "Let Me Call You Sweetheart." The other thing wasn't so cute; it was the recurring periods when one or both of the prisoners had to be taken to Bridgewater State Mental Hospital for treatment and observation. It seemed that the length of the confinement, and the men's inability to accept or believe what was happening to them, drove them crazy now and then. It was supposedly especially hard on Sacco, who missed his wife, son, and infant daughter dreadfully. Of course, the other side of the coin was the argument that the men were faking to buy time and public sympathy.

Is it a vase, or is it two faces? Is it the top of the basement stairs or the bottom of the attic stairs?

"Let's get the hell out of here," said Joe with a groan. "I've had enough for one day."

We walked back inside and down the corridor and overheard one of the guards yelling at an inmate.

"I am held here wrongly, mon," said a deep booming voice. "I am held on suspicion, nothing more. And because I came here in a leaky-sponge boat, does that take away all my rights? You hear me talkin', mon?"

The guard slammed the door with a clang and passed us in the hall. "Fuckin jig," he muttered under his breath so we could all hear, especially the man behind bars. He was huge and rich chocolate-brown, with green eyes. He gripped the bars, and the big muscles of his jaws bunched and leapt at the sides of his face. He rocked sideways, back and forth, back and forth, as he gripped the steel in front of him. He swayed to and fro on his feet, like an elephant eating hay.

"What's the huge black guy in for?" Joe asked the superintendent.

"Vagrancy and resisting arrest. Don't think it'll stick though. He'll probably walk in a week. Why, you want him?"

"Naw. Just curious. He one of the Caribbean boat people?"

"Uh-huh. Jamaican. Nothing but trouble, the whole bunch of 'em, and they're coming farther north every day now. Oughta kick 'em right back out. Oh, but he'll walk; you wait and see."

On the way out of the cell block something—I'm not sure

what it was—made me retrace my steps to the cell that held the giant Jamaican. He looked at me.

"What did you do that they put you in here?" I asked.

"Nothing. They call it vagrancy. I am an illegal alien. I was arrested loitering at a bus station. Are you a policeman?"

"No. A doctor. What is your name?"

"Amos Railford. Fisherman and carpenter. You will help me? I cannot pay now, but later—"

"Amos Railford, are you innocent of any crime except being here? You've heard of a polygraph, or lie detector? Would you take a polygraph test?"

"Hmmmmph!" He snorted, and jerked at the bars two inches in front of his face. His forearms bulged like Popeye the Sailor's. His chest was a bronzed, chiseled slab of muscle two feet wide. I was a little thankful for the bars.

"Will you take it?"

"Yes, mon."

"And what is your bail set at?"

"Bail? I don't know."

"Thank you Amos. Good luck."

I walked back down the corridor, smelling that peculiar and depressing jail smell so well described by Raymond Chandler. On the way out I could not help thinking that nothing much had changed since 1927, except perhaps the appearance of those on the lowest rung.

We walked back to the courthouse building. It was just a couple of blocks. Sacco and Vanzetti made the trip there and back every day during the weeks of the trial, surrounded by armed guards. I stood facing the courthouse steps and recalled the film. Turning toward the jail, I took myself back in time. The small, squared-off Datsuns and Vegas became rounded Packards and Overlands. The people wore wool and cotton instead of polyester. The women had on wide hats with flowers on top; the men wore top hats, boaters, snapbrims, and bowlers. A crowd came dance-stepping around the corner, heading my way. Throngs of onlookers pressed close. Kids shouted and ran around the edges of the crowd. A big square of blue-coated policemen formed the nucleus of the mob, each one toting a Winchester pump scatter-gun. Here they came bouncing fast up the street. They were jump-roping without rope. The cars zigged and zagged. People waved their arms and hopped around. Where was Harold Lloyd? Buster Keaton? The mob was close now, approaching the courthouse steps. I could see the two defendants: Vanzetti with his proud carriage, tipping his snap-brim hat, gesticulating to the crowd with raised fist. *Injustice!* he is crying, and for him it certainly is. Almost everyone agreed that Bartolomeo Vanzetti was innocent. The other man, though—what's going through *his* mind? Sacco walks on silently, having to pause when his companion does because they are chained together. But he says nothing, looking straight ahead, noncommittal. Is he scared? Seething with outrage? Bored? Or is he lying? Is he merely disgusted with himself at having been caught?

A car horn jerked me out of my reverie, and I moved off the street. The driver rolled down his window and grinned.

"Don't tell me. Don't tell me—I know what ya wuz lookin' at. Yuz lookin' at the jail and then the court building. Well, I tell ya, mistah . . . they wuz *guilty*!"

He drove on, and we got back into Joe's cruiser and went back home.

After dropping off Tom, Joe and I went back to the house. Joe's mood was still dark. He paced the living-room carpet, drink in one hand, cigarette in the other, muttering to himself. The only words I caught were "can't believe it . . . just can't believe it," over and over again.

"Can't believe what?" I finally asked. "That they were probably guilty?"

"Not that so much. I'm thinking of Andy. I can't believe the community would turn against him. You know the Sons of—oh hell, skip it."

He returned to pacing and muttering until the phone rang.

Mary answered it in the kitchen and called Joe. "Joey, you know anything about Christopher Columbus?"

"Sure. He discovered America in—*what*? What the hell are you asking me a stupid-ass question like that for?"

"No, dummy. There's a guy calling you from the Christopher Columbus. What's that?"

Joe rushed toward the kitchen like a fifty-yard man out of the blocks. "Gimme that," he said, panting.

There was a short, intense conversation in the kitchen, with hoarse whispers and oaths. Comments like "you're goddamn right that's what I thought. What would *you* think, for Chrissake?" and "I didn't mean you, Mike. I was thinking of the young guys—"

Mary and I waited in the living room until he was finished, which wasn't long. He came stomping through the room and hooked his finger at me. I followed him out the door as Mary sank dejectedly onto the couch and stared at the wall.

"Don't worry, Mare. This is just a short visit in the North End. Be back in two hours. Promise!"

"I'm coming too then."

"Can't. The Christopher Columbus is a men's club. See you."

The neighborhood social club was on Fleet Street between two others. The North End is famous for these men's clubs. On any weekend in nice weather the front doors are generally open and you can hear the television blaring out the progress of the Patriots or Red Sox games and, further in the background, an aria.

The weather was slightly chilly and the door, with no markings or signs on it whatsoever, was closed. Joe opened it and walked in. The men inside stared at us. Then I realized they were staring at me. I was a stranger. My presence in this private drinking and social club was tolerated only because I was with Joe, who was an ex-officio member.

We walked through the front room, which contained the TV, bar, and pool tables, and into the back one, which had a carpeted floor, a smaller bar, a stereo from which a rich baritone crooned, and a big green felt card table. As we entered, all seven men at the table rose at once. Three of them, younger men, left as if on prearranged signal and went back to the front room. The cards had been turned face down, the play having stopped in the middle of a hand.

Of the four men who approached us smiling, I recognized Gus Giordano immediately. He came up and hugged me first, which set the mood of acceptance right away. The men beckoned us to sit down in the leather chairs, which looked as if they were purchased secondhand from a bar that went bust. They drew theirs up around us, facing us like a panel. Or perhaps a tribunal? The leader, a man named Mike, spoke first. He was at least seventy, razor-thin with a veiny forehead, pale skin, white hair, and a thin beaky nose. He had piercing black eyes and wore a big old-fashioned hearing aid. He chain-smoked as he drank coffee.

"Joey, that big Irish guy you hang around with, Heeney?"

"O'Hearn. Kevin O'Hearn. My partner."

"Yeah, him. Well, he told Angie Catardi, who walks the beat here, that you thought we were behind the Santuccio murder. Joseph, shame on you."

"I didn't say you were. It crossed my mind is all. And I didn't mean you guys. I was thinking of the young hotheads. You know. They'd do anything to save the community morale. Maybe get carried away."

Mike pulled a piece of newspaper out of his trouser pocket and handed it to Joe.

"Take a look at that. It appeared in today's *Globe* and will appear for another two weeks. The Sons of Italy and the North End Improvement Association, which you will recall Andy was president of, are putting up a ten-thousand-dollar reward for information leading to the arrest and conviction of his killers. Now c'mon, pal—don't say those things about your friends, huh?"

Gus leaned over and put his hand on Joe's shoulder. I thought my brother-in-law was going to cry.

"I guess I never really believed it. But who else, *who else* would give a shit about those papers enough to do that? Tell me, *who*?''

I swept my eyes around the circle of four faces, three of them with big mustaches. All were solemn and silent. I saw them shake their heads back and forth slightly, slowly, in bewildered sadness and resignation.

''All I know is Carmen DeLucca—may he drown in his mother's blood—works for the families. An enforcer. Scum. We would never do such a thing and never truck with his kind of filth. Shame on you, Joseph—a member of the Sons yourself. Shame on you and may God and the saints forgive you for thinking it,'' intoned Mike. He did not look angry. He was profoundly hurt. His eyes were glistening.

The message delivered, we had coffee and beer and talked for fifteen minutes to leave the meeting on an upbeat note.

''Will you keep in touch, Mike? The rest of you?'' asked Joe as we left the back room. ''Tell me anything you hear, okay? And listen: you guys know Paul Tescione well. No no—forget that crap. I know you know him. I've met him briefly once. I know he does some good around here. Stay on the wire with him, huh? Let me know if DeLucca's back with the Outfit, okay? I gotta know.''

''Thanks for coming, Joe. Doctor Adams, nice to see you.''

''Hey. Thanks for asking us,'' said Joe.

We left, and heard the young men called back to the game.

''Okay,'' said Mike as we left. ''Seven-card stud and Gus is showing a possible straight!''

Things settled down a bit afterward. Life's petty pace ground forward, trying to churn out the yardage. The needle moved up out of the Dead Zone and into Boring, its natural home. The days rolled by, tasting like wet cardboard. A few incidents of note occurred, but they served only to punctuate the tedium. To underscore it.

One: Sam Bowman got a new secondhand safe and retrieved his loot from Nissenbaum's. He still lacked a partner however, and the future of Dependable Messenger Service was none too rosy.

Two: Moe Abramson was finding another foster home for the luscious morsel Loretta Popp, better known as Lolly. He had told her it was only a matter of days before she would start packing. She raised a fuss, but it was no use. She proposed marriage, but he wouldn't listen. She proposed to continue living in sin with him, but he turned a deaf ear. And that figured. Moe's not only a sap, he's the world's biggest puritan too. As soon as he finds anything the least bit pleasurable, he drops it like a red rivet. Old John Winthrop had nothing on him.

Three: Joe told us the Boston Public Library reported vandalism in the archives. This, and the fact that somebody broke into my office and rifled my files, told us all that the Wise Guys were still hunting for the hot item. But Joe figured they'd never get it now. He also figured they'd leave me alone, finally. He said his activities had now turned to focus on the apprehension of Carmen DeLucca.

Four: Mary and Janice went to play tennis out at the country club. A minor point dispute then erupted into a full gale, force eight. Mary told me afterward that she'd ''had words'' with Janice. Considering what her version of ''words'' meant, Janice was lucky to be alive. Worse yet, Janice called me the next morning at work; I wasn't sure whether Susan Petri was listening in on the line or not. I hoped not, because the gist of the brief conversation was that Janice was going to give me no more quick feels if I was going to kiss and tell.

''Blabbermouth!'' she said, sniffing.

I went on to explain to her that I hadn't said a thing. Mary knew. She would always know.

''And that's why there's no future in it, Janice, don't you see? There are certain immutable laws. Two and two is four; the sun rises in the east; and Mary will always find out.''

''But what about in the boathouse? When all the others

leave to go into Wolfsboro, and there'll just be the two of us in our bathing suits, and—''

''Won't work. There'll be a crack of lightning and a pillar of smoke . . . and Mary.''

Janice said that it was still her favorite fantasy, and that I was in that fantasy and there wasn't anything I could do about it. She hung up.

To top it off, Susan and I had two fraidy-cats in a row in the chair. Now I'll be the first to admit that visiting the tooth-puller isn't everyone's favorite pastime. In fact, a lot of the time my job makes me feel somewhat like Bela Lugosi and gets me down. But life is life, and involves some risk and pain, and it should be borne with as stiff an upper lip as one can muster. We had to face two twenty-five-year-old cry-babies back to back. They fought the needle; they were afraid of nerve damage; they broke into tears when I described what was going to happen. Now I've tried it the other way: *not* telling them what will happen. That's when pandemonium really reigns. We've had shouting matches, tantrums, threats, the works. As the second fraidy-cat filed out whimpering, I collapsed behind my desk and switched on WBUR. They were playing a nice piece by Luigi Boccherini, the Baroque cellist and composer. I like the cello anyway, and the music was particularly soothing.

''Why didn't you just put her out?'' asked Susan as she cleaned up.

''I really don't like to do that. Too many things can happen when they're out. Besides, in a fearful patient the effects of sodium pentothal are uncertain; sometimes it makes things a lot worse afterwards.''

''Well, thank God that's all for today. Did I tell you Mrs. Reubens canceled?''

I brightened. ''No, you didn't.'' I looked at my watch. It showed three-twelve. I could go home. Or I could go some-where else. Somewhere that had been on my mind a great deal lately and wouldn't let me alone. I called Susan over to my desk.

"Listen carefully," I said. "I've got some business to attend to up in Lowell. I'm going up there alone for a few hours and I'm not telling anyone. I'm only telling you in case of an emergency here or in case I don't come back."

She stiffened; her eyes widened.

"Don't do that; it's not really that daring. But I'm afraid I'm going to break the law a little teeny bit. That's one of the reasons I don't want a lot of people to know about it."

"Not even Mary?"

"Most especially not Mary."

"Oh . . ." There was a hint of accusation in her voice. "Who are you uh, going to break the law with?"

"*What*? With nobody else. This is a solo operation, Susan; I'm going alone."

"Oh, I just thought . . . you know. There was that woman on the phone and—"

"Well, you thought wrong. Now I should be back here, or home, by between six and seven. Don't tell anybody where I'm going, but if something big comes up, give them this number—it's a bar—and tell them to tell the folks there to come find me around the corner."

"Okay, Doctor Adams. I'm sorry I thought—"

"Forget it. It's just that certain people, no matter how sincere their intentions and how noble their character, can't stay out of trouble. My life is living proof of that. Good-bye; be sure to lock up when you leave."

I went out into the lot, climbed into the Scout, and headed north to Lowell. I'd left Susan the number at the Lucky Seven, and right underneath it the address of Johnny Robinson's apartment. Joe said the place was closed and sealed by the fuzz.

But I had to get in there; that's where the hot item was.

15

I PARKED THE CAR A BLOCK AWAY FROM THE LITTLE GRAY house and walked up to it from the front. The day was warm and mostly sunny; the birds were singing. A gray squirrel sat on a low limb with a nut in his mouth and scolded me. He flipped his tail and cluck-clucked. Then he cried *chaaaaww, chaaaawwwww*! and went back to clucking again. I strode up the walk purposefully, opened the side door, and went briskly up the stairs. At the top Johnny's door was locked solid and had a Middlesex County Sheriff's Department seal on it. I walked quickly back down and out to the car where I put on an old Levi's jacket and a long-billed fisherman's cap that I always keep in back. I was wearing khaki-type slacks which weren't as good as jeans but would have to do. I grabbed a roll of friction tape and an oversized screwdriver from the glove box and returned to the house. But instead of going in the front, I walked around to the back. The ladder in the garage made it easier to mount the small shed roof. But had it not been there I was prepared to climb up. With the ladder in place I stepped back and gazed at the scene. The back of the small house was invisible from the neighbors'. I returned to the front porch and stood at the downstairs door and rang the front bell twice, stomping around impatiently like a repairman. No answer. Still vacant.

I was up on that little roof in two winks. In another two I

had crisscrossed the windowpane with tape. I took a final look around, and holding a thick rag up between the windowpane and my arm, I swung at it with the screwdriver handle. The window broke with a low, grinding crackle. It sounded exactly like pond ice breaking underfoot. With the wind in the trees and the bird-song outside, it was scarcely audible. I poked the remaining glass away, and it fell inside in a jagged stringy mess of tape and shards. The tape had prevented the explosive tinkling sound of glass and had kept the mess together too. Old Joe had taught me a lot.

I stuck my head in and hollered hello three times, waiting awhile between each call. I climbed inside. Nobody home. Except me.

First I made a quick and silent survey of the apartment. It appeared fine—just as we'd left it almost two weeks previously. Next I unfastened the front-door lock and opened the door, thus breaking the seal. I was in triple Dutch if caught, but I wanted a quick way out. I left the latch on, though, just to buy myself some time if anyone tried to come in that way. I returned to the bedroom, went back out onto the low roof, and tipped the ladder over. It fell back onto the grass, which was tall enough to hide it from casual view. Nothing looks more suspicious than a ladder beneath an open window. To hide the broken pane I raised the window, then lowered the top sash into the bottom position. With the shade halfway down, a passerby would have to look carefully up at the top pane to see that it was missing. I figured I was safe for the time being. I had maybe an hour to find what everyone was looking for. Whatever *that* was.

I began my search by closing the hall door and peering out through the peephole that the killers had constructed in it. I assumed the lighting would have been about the same the day that Johnny and the dogs bought it. Through the peephole I could clearly see the hallway and the front door. I could also see into the living room, and a large portion of it. None of the lights was on, and they wouldn't have been that day either. But the light was more than adequate. I studied the killer's view for several minutes because it told me something. It told me that Johnny had been in plain view from the time he entered his apartment. And he had not gone into the john, or his bedroom, or around the corner of the living room. Because if he had, then those rooms would've been turned inside out by the killers in their efforts to find the hot item. The rooms would have all been ransacked like my house and Sam's office. After torturing Andy and murdering him, the killers had certainly returned here, but they had left the apartment alone. Ergo, Johnny was never out of their sight from the time he entered until he drew his last breath. Perhaps a total of thirty seconds—probably no more. Then maybe this errand had been a mistake.

I sagged down in the shoulders and sighed wearily. I ambled down the semidark hallway and into the living room, where I sat on the couch. Way to go Adams. You pull a B and E to discover that he couldn't have hidden the whatever-it-is in his own house. And sitting there, I was struck by the possible consequences of what I had done. Breaking and entering. What did it carry? Five years in the slammer? If I was caught, would the fact that I was a physician and respectable citizen with a clean record help me? Maybe not. Would the fact that I had enough money to get the best defense and grease a few palms help me?

Immeasurably, without a doubt.

And again with my thoughts got on that trolley track which clickety-clacked back to the fish peddler and the shoe trimmer. They certainly hadn't had much money. In fact, one of the first items of business in the Italian community after the arrest was the establishment of the Sacco–Vanzetti Defense Committee, headed by a man named Aldino Felicani, to raise funds for the trial. The trolley track kept clicking away . . . I had been over this same path many, many times in the past two weeks: then why . . . *why* was the defense committee even necessary, if indeed the two men had knocked over a shoe factory three weeks previous for fifteen grand?

And then my thinking went back to the biggest question in

my mind, which revolved around the characters and personalities of the defendants. Why and how would two working stiffs
like Nick Sacco and Bart Vanzetti—anarchists and idealists,
yes, but guys who had earned their meager livings for over a
decade without any brush with the law—get involved with four
or five other guys, two big cars, armed robbery and murder,
and then . . . and then *go back* into their drab working-class
life, with no car, no big house, no bankroll . . .

No. It didn't fit. Unless they had drunk some magic Jekyll-
and-Hyde tonic the evening of April 14, pulled the job the
next afternoon, then returned to normal, it didn't fit.

And that was the reason I had entered illegally. Since it
now seemed certain that at least one of them—Sacco—was
guilty, I had to find out what horrendous aberration in the
human personality had occurred to make it so. And I wanted
to see the implication, the proof, in black and white.

A bluejay cawed outside. Through the front windows I
could see the elms and maples flopping and swopping around
in the late spring breeze. A robin sang. I got up and walked
over to one of Johnny's fight posters. I was staring at it when
I heard a car whisper by on the street, and I jumped a bit. I
looked down to see a tan sedan turning toward town. I walked
through the rooms once more, hoping to get a spark, a faint
beam of light . . .

In the bathroom, looking at myself in the mirror, I thought
of it. The thugs had searched the office and Johnny's car and
his person. It was not in the pouch. Therefore he'd ditched it
between the car and the hallway. I went to the door and opened
it cautiously. I crept down the stairs, then stared out the tiny
curtained window at the bottom which looked out to the street.

As I watched, a black-and-white police cruiser oozed by
in a crawl. I nearly fainted.

But they didn't stop, just drifted by ghostlike and went off
down the street. Thank God for the white lace curtains. They
acted like a one-way mirror and I wasn't seen. When I was sure
they were far away I went out and looked at the door. My eyes
followed every shingle, every inch of door-frame molding. I

looked up. I reached up as far as I could and ran my hand along the joints and crevices. Johnny was shorter than I, so I knew by stretching up I was overlooking no place he could reach.

The door revealed nothing, so I walked toward the street and stood on the sidewalk. I walked slowly to the doorway. Now what if Johnny had a warning, a premonition something wasn't right? Perhaps a flutter of motion in an upstairs window? Maybe the dogs began their low growling as they came up the walk? I went over and looked down at the porch steps and floor. There was no hiding place I could see or feel. There was not even a crack in the boards through which a photo negative could be dropped or slipped.

Returning to the enclosed side stairway, I opened the bottom door and went back inside. Behind me the street was empty and the birds chirped; the leaves hissed and whispered in the breeze. The sun came out. I closed the door softly and stared up the dark stairway.

I crept up, step by step, searching the walls and wood every inch of the way. I took out my penlight and swept it everywhere. I grabbed the stair tread boards by their lips and tried to raise them. I kicked at the risers to see if they were loose. No dice. The stairwell walls were painted a flat yellow. No cracks. Light-switch plate was firm, ceiling fixture too high to reach. Up at the top I examined the outside door frame with eyes, light, and fingers. Nothing there. The door was left ajar; I pushed it open and re-entered, standing near the living-room door. I examined the walls, the chair rails, the small table under which the lethal bomb had been placed, the rug runner, everything. No dice.

I reached my hand up and swept it all around the walls. Same result.

"Johnny, damn you," I whispered aloud in exasperation, *"what the hell did you do with it?"*

I trudged back to the living room and stared out the windows. The faint happy noises of springtime wafted through to me. I was a fool to suppose that I could uncover the object if the determined efforts of the professionals, whose handiwork I had seen firsthand in my own house, had not. I decided I had overstayed my luck; it was time to depart. But first I went into the john a final time to take a leak. Had he flushed it down the toilet? I asked myself. No; the thugs had him in their sight the entire time. I decided to ask Joe to let me look at Johnny's clothes. Though they had been gone over by the killers and the cops with a fine-tooth comb, they seemed the one possibility remaining out of reach of the competition.

I washed my hands. The water seemed to be making a rather strange noise: a faint thumping and grating. I thought the pipes needed fixing; they had water hammer. Put dead-end air-capped pipe on the feeder line to soak up that water shock and—

I looked at myself in the mirror. I didn't like the look on the face that stared back; it was afraid. I turned the water off. The grating and thumping were still there. They were coming from beneath me. When I got out to the hall I was sure what the noise was.

Somebody was coming up the stairs.

Cops or crooks—either way, Adams was cooked. Luckily, like any decent burglar, I had an alternate exit route chosen. I was going to leave via the back window. And quickly.

But it was no go; when I got there and reached down to pull up the intact pane I saw a rough-looking character standing in the small back yard. He wasn't looking up at me; he was glancing sideways, back and forth. He had seen the fallen ladder too. He was no cop. I went back into the hallway; I heard the double scrape of feet—faint yet clear, which told me the stairs had been climbed. My visitor had reached the top landing.

As I ducked into the john again I looked back. The door was open a crack; a gloved hand crept around it and pushed. The door swung open.

16

THE FOOTSTEPS STOPPED IN THE HALL, ALTHOUGH FOR A second I could not tell them from the beating of my heart. They paused there. No doubt the intruder was on the same errand I was. He was studying the hall and the small table. Then they commenced again, going away into the living room. Again silence. I crept from behind the door into the tiny shower stall, letting the curtain fall behind me. If I squatted over the drain and tilted my head down I could see about four feet out below the edge of the curtain. What did I have to defend myself with? Not a damn thing. I took out my briar pipe and my Zippo lighter, the only objects of hardness and substance I had on me. Pretty poor equipment against a hoodlum. I held the lighter in my left fist; I grasped the pipe by the bowl so that the stem stuck out straight ahead, like a pistol barrel. It was the best I could do.

The footfalls came again, louder now, and stopped right outside the bathroom door. I heard the door creak a bit, then stop. The footsteps continued down the hall to the kitchen, then over to the bedroom. Was the guy going to search there? If so, he'd find the broken windowpane and the big screwdriver I'd been stupid enough to leave there. And he'd know, as if the open front door hadn't already told him. Real smart, Adams. I knew there was more than a good chance that I could be killed in a few minutes. I tried to make myself accept this by arguing that anyone so stupid deserved to die, as part of the Divine Plan, in much the same way that those who are stupid enough to explore underwater caves deserve to drown.

This was supposed to make me feel better, but it wasn't working.

Faint voices came to me in the shower stall. It was probably the two men talking. From everything I had heard, it seemed that they did not suspect I was in the apartment now; they probably had surmised that the entry had been made earlier. If I could only get *out* . . .

I pushed the curtain aside and slipped out of the stall, heading for the door. I had the door partly opened when I heard the footsteps returning. I jumped back into the stall and noticed that the curtain now was not back straight. There was an inch-wide gap along one side, through which I could peer. The footsteps passed back down the hall and stopped near the front door again. I was beginning to know this little apartment like the back of my hand. The intruder was again studying the hall. No doubt now about what he was after. I began to breathe easier; it was pretty clear he was on his way out. They had not seen my car, and both would depart soon, leaving me to creep down the stairs again and *leave*.

I heard the footsteps again, finally. But they were getting louder; he was coming back.

I saw the same glove slide around in the side of the door like a moray eel slithering out of its lair, and swing it open. The quick glance I got through the tiny slit was enough to see the trenchcoat, the hat, and the glasses of our old friend the wall-smasher from the mill building scarcely a mile distant. And almost instantly a change came over me; all the fear turned to anger. I remembered Mary unconscious in the mill yard. I remembered the way he'd shot at us. I didn't like the skulker in the raincoat, hat, and glasses. I didn't like him at all.

As the gloved hand appeared at the curtain's top I drew back my left foot as far as possible and steadied myself by pushing my hands (both of which held objects) lightly against the metal sides of the narrow stall.

The curtain was drawn back. A face stared at me from two feet away. I realized just before I began my kick that the man wore very thick glasses.

My foot shot upward toward his groin as fast and hard as I could make it travel. I connected, and saw his mouth widen. He had begun to scream from fright when he saw me, but it turned to agony half a second later. I thrust my right arm forward in a short, snappy punch. I was aiming for anywhere on his face, but as it happened I drove the pipestem smack into his open mouth and halfway down his throat. Before he could recover from this unpleasant duo, I stepped out of the stall and swung my left hand around in a hook to the side of his head. The rectangular steel lighter helped give the punch more authority, and I had enough adrenalin going to give it some oomph, but I don't think I hurt him much. I just can't throw a punch worth a damn.

He bent over double, shuffling backward in very short dance steps, and let out a gurgling bellow that was half the dry heaves. Old Four-Eyes wasn't having much fun, and I was glad. I cocked my right forearm tight and came down with the point of my elbow on the nape of his neck, and that finished him.

But just as I was feeling proud of myself, I heard a loud rushing and stomping on the stairway, which would be the watchman out back coming to help. Then the man on the floor, who I thought was holding his crotch, had produced a pistol from underneath the big coat. I dove for it and wrestled it free, and suddenly was more scared than I'd been in a long time. I was now holding a loaded firearm in a situation where I might have to use it on a human being.

Kneeling, I closed the bathroom door all but a crack and pointed the revolver barrel through it. A dark shape came around the corner from the hallway, crouched low and moving fast. I could have fired. Perhaps I should have. But I didn't. I think I yelled something. The man hit the door with his shoulder, like a lineman, and slammed it into me. The thick edge of the door hit my forehead full force, and I felt also a sharp pain as the wedge-shaped metal latch piece bored right into the front of my skull. I fell back on the bathroom floor, then spun to my feet. The man in the trenchcoat was just getting up too, and before I could raise the gun he did a strange thing.

He grabbed his coat flaps and held them out wide. He looked like Count Dracula. He seemed to hover over me for an instant like a giant bird of prey.

And a bird of prey he was, too. Yes indeed, because he brought those big wings down around the sides of my already hurt head and I felt a monstrous, heavy thump on each side of it, like two wrecking balls swung from either side.

And then everything went away and it got dark.

17

BLOOD!

I was floating in a sticky sea of drying blood. My own. It had a faint metallic smell, which was underlaid by the salty aroma of lymph and pus, as when you change a dirty gauze bandage. I smelled a lot of blood every day. But I didn't like smelling a lot of my own on a tile floor. And I didn't like the dark rivulets and puddles that spread out on the tile a few inches from my face, either. I had opened and closed my eyes quite a few times, I thought. I had awakened and gone to sleep four or five times. When I was finally able to move, I drew my hand up to my throat to feel the deep fissure where it had been slit.

For I was a hog on a slaughterhouse floor.

But try as I might, I could find no evidence of the slit throat. And I was glad. The cause of all the bloodletting, I finally remembered, was the gash on my forehead. What reminded me of this was the throbbing in that location. My hand felt a puffy swelling and a huge sticky crust forming on it. Head cuts bleed like Niagara Falls anyway because the human head is laced with blood vessels. When you're pumped up, as in a football game, a boxing match, or a less orthodox fight, your blood pressure soars and makes even a scratch on the head bleed like there's no tomorrow. I had a deep gash up above my eye—perhaps even a skull fracture too, and I had indeed bled like a stuck pig. I sat up on the tile floor. I felt cold beneath me. I was cold. I was freezing. The place was dark now. I saw the dark, chocolate-colored stains everywhere, especially on my clothes.

I staggered to my feet and turned on the light. I looked at myself and wished I hadn't. I washed the dried blood from my face and neck but left the wound to clot over. All the time I stood at the sink my stomach churned and my knees trembled. Then I felt sick and scared. I was scared at what had happened—at how close I had come to dying. I was afraid the police would find me in the house and throw me in the slammer. I tried to check my watch but it wasn't there. They had taken it, perhaps to make the thing look like robbery. Then I realized that my belt buckle was unfastened and my fly was unzipped. Why? Had they molested me? Were these guys fags as well as crooks? But then I noticed my shoes and socks were off and my pockets turned inside out. No. They had searched me, and thoroughly too, to see if I had recovered the item.

I crept dizzily along the hallway, leaning on the wall and breathing hard as I went. The couch seemed a mile away. I sat down on it and almost threw up.

I'm as hard as nails, I am.

I sat there for some time, moving my head back and forth, up and down, and rubbing the back of my neck. I patted my feet against the floor to stop the pins and needles. Then I staggered back to the john and took three long drinks of cold water. It almost made up for the blood I'd lost. They had taken not only my watch but my car keys and wallet. The phone in the apartment had been disconnected. The only way out was to trek over to the Lucky Seven and call Mary.

But before I could get started I heard steps on the porch below.

Adams, this just isn't your day.

I heard the door at the foot of the stairs open. Then once again came the scraping tread on the stairway. We just had this tape, I told myself. Why are we playing it *again*? Well,

I could barely stand; I was certainly in no condition to fight. As the steps grew louder I panicked. How did I know it wasn't the two men returning to finish me off? Perhaps their boss had told them to go back and do the job right . . .

I searched around the dim living room with my eyes; my body was too slow and sore. I unplugged a lamp with a turned wooden base, unwrapped the cord around it, removed the shade, and held it like a billy club. With this I snuggled against the wall near the door so I'd be out of sight when it opened. It did, and in the near-darkness I saw a stocky, menacing profile stalk into the hall. His deep, noisy breathing was almost a growl and made him more ominous. He was wearing a narrow-brim tweed hat and a droopy coat. Lord only knew what was in that coat—maybe an antiaircraft gun. I was taking no more chances; I had gotten the drop on this hood and he was going to pay. After dimming his lights I was going to get his gun and go outside, putting a hole into anybody who blocked my way.

The shadow half-turned and came right into range, and I swung the club down on the hat . . . hard. The man fell without a sound. It was only after he rolled over and his hat slid off that I had the sickening feeling I knew him. Getting to my knees and peering down into the face confirmed it.

"Oh sweet Jesus," I moaned. "I'm awful sorry, Brian."

I had our chief of police propped up on a low pillow with his feet raised. Suspecting at the last instant that I might be doing a damn fool thing—which I do often enough to realize I'm prone to it—I had eased off on the blow in the last millisecond before its delivery. Also, the thick tweed hat helped cushion the blow a little. Still, knowing Brian Hannon well, I predicted he would not regain consciousness in a very sociable mood.

It so happened that this was the one thing I was right about that afternoon. When he finally managed to open his eyes, stare at me, and speak, his words were not encouraging.

"*Listen*, butt-wipe," he growled, "do you have any idea of the kind of trouble you're in?"

"Don't worry; I can explain everything," I replied, placing a soaking cold towel on his head. He ripped it off and threw it at my face. Brian was going to be okay. He struggled to a sitting position and sat against the wall, glaring at me. Then he called me more bad names. I finally helped him to his feet, and he seemed to see my injury for the first time.

"You look like shit warmed over, Doc. Know that?"

"Yes I know that. And I obviously didn't mean to clip you; I thought you were the bad guys come back to finish me."

"I'm not the bad guys, Doc. Know who I am? *I am the law.* You have assaulted a law officer. You're going—"

"All right, Brian, all right. Pipe down. You've been watching those Broderick Crawford reruns again. Let's get out of here."

He took a pair of handcuffs from his hip pocket and told me to put them on; I told him to shove it and walked him down the stairs. He grumbled and cussed all the way down, and together we limped over to his cruiser. I said I'd drive, and put him in the front seat beside me.

"Know how I happened to come up here?"

"No."

"Mary called me. Didn't know where you were. Know how much trouble you're in with her?"

"I can guess."

"Well, we got your assistant to spill the beans on where you'd gone. You're just lucky I'm not going to fill out a report."

"You're not?"

"No. Not my jurisdiction here, dummy. Although as an off-duty policeman I'd be well within line if I did."

"It surprises me that you're not."

"Yeah, well I figure that after Mary gets through with you, you'll wish you were in Walpole instead."

I thought of what awaited me back home. It made my forehead ache, so I must have been wincing to myself.

"Can I spend the night in the Concord jail?"

"No. You may not."

We drove on into Concord, and I noticed that Brian seemed to doze off and on. I didn't like this, or his slurred speech. I pulled into the emergency parking lot at Emerson Hospital, where we dragged ourselves out of the car, across the lot, and into the waiting room. We were a couple of tough guys, all right. We were right out of a Charles Bronson or Clint Eastwood flick.

"You poor, poor old men," purred the young nurse who examined us.

"We're not old," snarled Brian.

"*Aaaannn*ything you say, sweetie," she said, patting him on his stubbly cheek. Then she went to get us booked for the CAT scan. The very fact that they thought we should have the scans disturbed me. When the attending physician said he thought everything appeared normal I felt better, but Brian was diagnosed as having a mid-sized concussion. Needless to say, I didn't feel good about this, and neither did he. They laid him down in a bed with his head between sandbags, and he was to remain *in situ* for at least twenty-four hours.

"I'm going to get you for this, Doc. Count on it. Sooner or later you're gonna pay. And I'm in this case now too. I've got my damaged skull invested in it. I'm going to be hanging around like a wind chime."

A dark hand shot in front of me and swept gently over Brian's forehead. He smiled at its owner.

"Hi Mary. See what your husband did?"

She bent down and kissed him and murmured kind words. He reached up and squeezed her arm. It was a touching scene.

"That's nice of you, honey," I said. "I'm sure that—"

"You be quiet!" she snapped without turning around. "The car's outside waiting. We're going home and you're going to stay there. You're *grounded*."

"You can't do that to me."

"Hell I can't." She turned around and looked at me for the first time. "So you'd better get—Charlie! Your head!"

She stared at me for a few seconds and then started crying and swearing at me. I was glad she was letting off the steam, anyway. But closer examination of my head convinced her that I needed stitches. It was good to be with her; it almost made me forget the pain.

They had to drain the swelling first, since enough time had elapsed for the lump to grow and spread the cut wide apart. They were able to use butterfly bandages instead of sutures. Scarring would then be absent or minimal, and my forehead would not look like something Dr. Frankenstein put together. After it was over they had me wait in the recovery room. It was a sit-up recovery room and had a TV. After all I'd been through I sat rather mesmerized, watching a special report on the upcoming gubernatorial race. Apparently the reporters expected a close race, with Joseph Critchfield III having announced his candidacy a week before.

Mary sat with me, her gaze leaving the television now and then to glare in my direction. At quarter to ten we were finally ready to leave. We went in and said goodnight to Brian. He was not in a particularly good mood. Neither was Mary, considering other minor matters like my stolen wallet and car keys. I sat in front on the way home in Mary's Audi. We got settled on the couch and she wanted to hear all about what happened in the little gray house up in Lowell, and I told her. She listened intently, and I felt confident she'd approve of the way I attacked old Four-Eyes, since he had whopped her with his loaded coat as well. But she just sat there holding the bridge of her nose and squinting. She was repeating a word over and over, mumbling it. I listened close and heard it: "dumb . . . dumb . . . dumb."

But little by little she began to calm as we sat and visited. Some music, some beer (I was still terribly thirsty), and some rock lobster tails and we were as good as new. Except that during dinner I realized that my left rib cage had been aching. I pulled up my shirt to reveal a mass of dark bruises there. The sumbitches had kicked me when I was down. I swore inwardly to get even with them. But I didn't tell Mary. We had hot raspberry tarts and vanilla ice cream for dessert, and Irish coffee. I had talked myself into believing I really wasn't beat up and weak. But halfway through the laced coffee I felt the room shift a bit, as though we were dining in a stateroom on the Cunard Line. I began to nod, and Mary helped me into the bedroom and into the sack.

When I woke up I realized how seriously I'd been hurt. My left side had stiffened up badly, and I had a permanent headache from the blow to the head and a forehead that itched and stung from the dressing. I sat up in bed and drained the ice water waiting for me on the bed table. Under the big frosty tumbler was a note:

> Dear Charlie:
> I meant what I said: you're grounded. I will be out till four. I had Susan cancel all your appointments. Stay in bed. If you get up, don't leave the house. Joe's coming for dinner.
>
> M.

Well of all the nerve, I thought as I drew on my clothes. I'd show her who ran things; I was going to hop in the car and go in to Louis's and buy a sport coat, then go over to the Rod and Gun Club for some silhouette shooting. Grounded my ass. But as I was eating breakfast it occurred to me that I had no car; it was sitting up in Lowell on a side street. I had no car keys, and Mary had taken the other car. I looked at the key rack and noticed she had also taken my motorcycle keys. That made me angry.

But I had a spare set hidden away in the garage. I put on my jacket, grabbed my helmet and the extra keys, straddled the big BMW, and started it. Those big transverse cylinders thumped and purred with about as much fuss as a Singer. I would show her who was grounded. Then I tried to put on my helmet and almost fell off the bike from the pain. There was no way that that snug Simpson full-face brain bucket was going to fit around my swollen and bandaged head. And also, I considered as I hefted the big machine back onto its stand, riding a bike when you're not 100 percent is just dumb. I switched it off, dismounted, and went back inside.

Well, she was right. Two hours were spent calling emergency credit-card numbers to report my lost cards. I wanted to run but knew it was unwise. So I took my ten-speed out and rode over to the hospital to see Brian, who was due to be released that evening. His mood had not improved, and in fact he had reported the incident to Joe, who was none too pleased either. As I left the hospital I was considering joining the Foreign Legion, except I doubted they'd take me.

It was only half a block to the Concord Professional Building, so I went to the office and did some paperwork and went over some castings. A gaunt, shaggy head poked in through the doorway.

"Well well well, if it isn't da cat burglar," said Moe. "I saw Mary earlier when she was chewing out Susan for letting you sneak off like dat. Wow! Some clout, eh? Did they knock any sense into your thick skull?"

"No. I'm still the same."

"Pity."

"Where's Lolly? I need to be cheered up; the sight of her prancing around bare-assed does me a world of good."

He frowned and *tsk-tsk*ed at me.

"Loretta is a problem. She's too old for a foster home and I can't have her staying wid me. It's just . . . well, it's not right. So she's both too old and too young. I'm putting her up for now in a rental room with an older couple; it seems to be working."

"She happy?"

"Uhh. No. But there's nothing gI can do right now."

"Listen: if you want to help somebody, call the Dedham jail and help spring a guy named Amos Railford who's being held there on the most tenuous grounds." I told him the story of the big Jamaican, which I knew would touch his soft heart.

"It's the least we can do in memory of Nick and Bart, Moe." He agreed.

I pedaled back home and saw a New England Telephone van parked in the driveway. I eyed it warily, considering the untoward events of late. But it appeared to be a genuine phone company truck. As I passed it I heard a loud *psssssst!*

A large and heavy-set lineman sat smoking a cigarette and listening on a phone in the van's driver's seat. He was sitting sideways on the seat with the door open and had his hard hat on, which was a white helmet with a blue telephone-company symbol in front. He annoyed me, sitting casually and uninvited in my drive. I heard a thumping sound and the van rocked slightly. The smoker had friends in the back. I liked the whole scene less and less, but considering the shape I was in, I sure didn't feel like getting tough. The man nodded, said good-bye, and put the phone back. He looked up at me.

"Hiya Doc," said Joe. "Where's Mare?"

I approached him and saw Kevin O'Hearn, also dressed as a lineman, peer around the corner.

"Hi Doc," he said. "Hey kid, you're in trouble."

"Oh really, what else is new?" I said, leaning the bicycle on its kickstand and moving over to the door. "What's all this for anyway?"

"We're going to go and get Carmen DeLucca in about half an hour, that's what," said O'Hearn.

"We know he's holed up in Lynn, right above a sub shop," said Joe. "Been watching the place two days. Way he's moving lately, we figure it's time to make the tag. I'm just waiting here to get the word to start up there. Don't want too many of us converging on the place at once. But Kev's right, you know. You are in trouble. You wanna take a fall for B and E?"

"Of course not."

"Then stay out of it, Doc. Really. You're either going to get yourself killed or get me canned."

"Can't I just go up to Lynn and watch you nail DeLucca?"

"Naw," said O'Hearn. "It might get rough. DeLucca's no pussycat."

"What you could do, though" said Joe, "is to drive up to Lynn so I can get a ride back here for supper."

"I don't have a car. I'm grounded."

"Oh. Well look, I'll do you a favor. If you promise to stay out of this thing, I'll write a little note to Sis saying you're riding up with us. You can watch all the preparations too. But when the hammer's about to fall I want you safe in the back of this vehicle, on the floor. Deal?"

"Deal."

"Okay with you, Kev? After all, we're only the communications team. The SWAT boys will pull the dirty stuff. Remember, Doc: mum's the word."

So I parked my bike and climbed in. The inside of the van was crowded but comfortable. A phone-company van was perfect cover; it allowed the fuzz to plant stakeouts just about anywhere and stay as long as they liked without attracting attention. Most important, the cops wore headsets or talked into phones as they waited around the van or up on poles. Thus they could stay in close touch without attracting the least suspicion—and they could tap into common phone lines to do it, which meant their messages weren't subject to radio surveillance.

I sat amidst a sea of props, most of them functional. There were orange traffic cones, *Men Working* signs, yellow blinkers . . . The van was equipped for protracted engagements too. There was a chemical toilet and a tiny gas cylinder stove for making coffee. The cops had added all these touches after they purchased the vehicle from Ma Bell.

We bounced and swerved along Route 2, then around the rotary at Fresh Pond and on to 16, which is called Alewife Brook Parkway there and soon becomes Revere Beach Parkway. I sat hunched on a carton right behind the two men in front. Before long the view opened up a bit, revealing distant smokestacks and fuel storage tanks, factories and warehouses.

"Where's my wop lighter?" asked Joe, frisking himself. He found it and lit a Benson & Hedges and Kevin's Kent. The smoke in the tiny van was awful, and I scooted back to open the plastic rooftop vent with a steel crank. It worked; the smoke got sucked out the tiny hole faster than the two smokers could put it in. I liked the cozy van, which reminded me slightly of the cabin in our little cat-sloop, the *Ella Hatton.*

"You really love that lighter don't you?" said Kevin.

"Yeah, and I know you do too. Listen, Doc, we got the lead on this place from a snitch in the sub shop. But anyway, it was the hospital where DeLucca got sewed up that helped us focus in on the North Shore. Then up comes this little snitch, see, who's a two-time loser under suspicion for a string of robberies which he knows—he knows, see—we're gonna pin on him. So what does he do but comes forward last Thursday with a nice leak for us if he can work out some kind of deal when we go to sock the rap to him."

"And it sounded too good to be true, so at first we doubted it," said Kevin.

"I still do a little; I'm not convinced it's him. But if it is . . . we'll get him sucked in and sealed up so goddamn tight a mosquito can't get out."

Joe gripped the wheel so hard his knuckles were white. Kevin glanced at him out of the corner of his eye with a worried look. It was not like Joe to be so worked up. We were passing through Everett now, toward Revere. There was the Teddy peanut-butter factory on our left, with its steamy stack and a smell like a candy bar, and a small GE plant. As we passed into Revere the scenery got positively bleak, and I knew it would get worse. Shallow pools of standing water lay on both sides of the roadway in places, and tired gulls circled overhead. Smoke and smells drifted across the sky. We went through Revere, and I could see the big red-and-white-checked watertank that marks the Veteran's Hospital in Chelsea. Strobe lights winked from tall stacks that spewed white steam clouds. All around was that grayish, dusky coloration of industrialization. We turned onto highway 1A and headed north toward Lynn.

Lynn is filled with nice working people, but it is not a pretty city. In Lynn, even the dogs are ugly. They have mangy coats, bloated bellies, and spindly legs. They have a black spot around one eye and bobbed tails that wag too fast.

We swung along 1A, which was now called the Lynnway and which took a straight shot over bleak marshy meadow after crossing the Saugus River and headed back toward factories, railway yards, and oil tanks. Joe was chain-smoking; Kevin drummed his fingers fast on the dash. I stretched my legs out hard one at a time to relieve the cramping. To our left loomed the General Electric River Works plant, the largest factory in New England. It was here that America's first jet engine was built during the Second World War. Just opposite Lynn Gas and Electric on the harbor, we eased left off the Lynnway, went three and a half blocks, and came to a stop along a low and dirty curb. Joe turned to me.

"Put on a helmet, Doc, and one of those jumpsuits."

"I can't; it hurts my head too much."

But we could find no alternative, and so I slipped on the biggest hard hat there was in the van. After a few seconds I forgot the ache. With my lineman's jumpsuit and dark glasses I was one of the crew. We opened the rear doors of the van and Joe set out a few orange traffic cones and blinker lights. Hell, it even fooled me.

In accordance with state law, a cop was present at the site to help direct traffic. Our cop was really a detective in a local Lynn uniform. He ambled up and chattered with us and filled Joe in on the other teams. There were three of them: another phone van up the street and around the corner, an unmarked car a block up on our street, and a milk truck in the alleyway opposite the unmarked car.

"Don't turn around fast," said Joe to me, "but when you get a chance, look at that sub shop down the street, just opposite the unmarked car. DeLucca's been holing up right over it in rented rooms. The snitch is working in the shop;

in a few minutes we're going to go see him. Give me those cables, Kev; here comes Powers.''

O'Hearn uncoiled some wire in the back of the van and fed it out to us. A lineman was walking up the street toward us smoking a cigarette with a big coil over his left shoulder. It could have fooled me. Frank Powers nodded hello to us and spoke under his breath as he puffed on his smoke.

''We expect him just after four. It's the time he's been showing up. I doubt if he's got a steady gig going, but Rizzo says he's been showing up every day almost like clockwork. Joe, can you call the rig? I'm about ready. Excuse me.''

He stepped forward and hooked the big cable over his shoulder to the ones Kev had snaked out of the little van. Almost as soon as he was finished a big phone truck with a cherry-picker hoist slid around the corner. Powers got into the crow's-nest and soon was up above us all, hooking the big cable to the pole. In the van Joe and Kevin put on earphones and I listened in on a phone extension fastened with clip wires. Pretty soon both phone trucks could communicate clearly and talk to the men in the unmarked car as well, since they had a remote device. Powers swung down from the treetops and said good-bye, adding that he'd station the hoist truck two blocks away and keep the platform up so he could keep an eye on everything and advise all parties what was happening from his vantage point.

''That guy seems like a real pro,'' I told Joe as Powers jumped into the truck.

''He is. He's a real phone person we borrow when the need arises. And that big cherry-picker rig is a real phone truck too. Now come on. I hope you're hungry because we're going to go and buy a sub from Johnny Rizzo, the snitch who's responsible for this whole setup, bless his heart.''

We left Kevin at the van, diligently twiddling with wires and cable and looking very professional, while we ambled up the street to the sub shop.

''This snitch—this Rizzo guy—he's in a bind, isn't he?''

''Oh yeah, it's death if DeLucca ever finds out. But what

choice does the poor stupid bastard have. He's got those robberies hanging over him that are worth the rest of his life in the joint. We dropped in on him three weeks ago and he knows we're on to him. The fact that he subsequently came forward with this tip all but proves he's in on the robberies. Now if we get DeLucca, Rizzo can cop a plea and get off light. It's not a perfect system, Doc. In fact, sometimes it downright stinks, but it's all we've got that's workable right now. Most of the busts we make are crooks ratting on other crooks.''

"Hmmm. And Kev once told me you've got to screw up several times before they even hand you a jail term. It's pathetic. It's as if these clowns can't stay out of the slammer.''

"You're right. They can't stay out. And know what? A lot of them don't want to. They like it inside.''

"That I don't believe. I've been with you on enough visits to Concord, Walpole, and Deer Island to know that isn't true. Nobody could like it in there.''

"They do. They get used to it and they get to like it. Know why? Because basically they're too screwed up to make it outside. And that's the truth. Come on.''

As we passed the beat-up car on the opposite side of the street facing us, the driver gave Joe a quick nod. Both men in the car were dressed shabbily in old, greasy work clothes. They looked like two factory workers getting off work. The car was no treat either. It was an ancient Plymouth, dented and scarred, with a cracked side window. It was a dull, dirty brown color with patches of gray primer paint. All in all, I thought it fitted into Lynn quite well.

"Are you sure those guys are cops?''

"Look at the tires,'' he said. I did, and was surprised. The tires looked new, and wide.

"Those are racing slicks. Last week that car was used in Fall River in a high-speed chase. We caught a drug dealer. On the interstate that crate hit a hundred forty. That's Keller at the wheel. Underneath those grimy clothes he's wearing a

Kevlar vest. So's his partner. And they've got a couple of pump guns on the floor. Here we are.''

We went in. The skinny, pockmarked man behind the counter was dressed in old khakis and a clean undershirt with a white apron around his waist. He was quick and nervous, like a ferret. His hair was thin and greasy, his skin pale and shiny. He looked indeed like a jailhouse punk. Joe glided over to the counter and laid his big palms on it. He spoke softly, even though there was nobody else in the shop.

''Hiya Johnny. How things?''

The man's eyes didn't meet ours. He looked nervously down at the counter and wiped it back and forth, back and forth, with a damp rag.

''Who's he?'' Johnny finally asked, not looking up at me.

''A friend. Don't sweat it. Now look, when he gets here and goes up the stairs, we just want you to come outside and. fool with the awning crank, okay? Just give it a couple of spins, then back inside to get the two-wheeler.''

He nodded and began kneading the rag on the countertop as if it were a hunk of pizza dough.

''If he finds out, I'm cooked. I think he knows, Joe.''

''Nah. No way. And in an hour we'll have him put away. Just put those empty bottles on the two-wheeler and march them outside and around the side of the building. Stack 'em up like you always do there, then just keep walking around the building and down the alley. Simple.''

''He knows. I know he knows,'' said Rizzo in a thin, reedy voice. He looked like a cornered animal. He smelled of fear. I saw the look of death about his eyes. He gave me the creeps.

''You got no idea what'll happen to me if you don't get him. You got no idea—''

''Shut up, Johnny. Be cool. I gotta *good* idea of what's gonna happen to you when we put the wrap on this string of armed robberies.''

''Look, I got nothin'—''

"Yeah sure, Johnny, you got nothing to do with 'em. You're just being a good citizen."

"I don't care no more. I'll go back to the joint. I don't give a shit."

"That's your problem, Rizzo. It's your problem and all those punks like you. You just don't give a shit. Wash your hands and get us two large Italians. And two coffee regulars."

Johnny made the sandwiches with the same quick and jumpy movements, and kept twitching his shiny pale head around to look out the front window to the street. The old battered car with the racing slicks was still there. Joe asked Johnny what he was going to do when DeLucca showed. He wanted to be sure Johnny had it right. Rizzo repeated the plan and shoved our sandwiches at us. I took the coffee and sipped but let the sandwich stay on the paper plate. Johnny looked up past us and his eyes widened.

"Jesus Christ! It was *him*," he wailed.

"Who?" said Joe, turning around with one elbow resting on the counter.

"DeLucca. I swear to Christ it's him in that cab." Rizzo was past trembling now, and there was a line of dampness on his brow and above his lip. I smelled again the sweet, sickly odor of fear and decay about him. I wasn't going to touch my sub; I was sure of it. Joe looked at the departing cab as it vanished up the street, and turned languidly back to his meal. He shook his big head slowly.

"For Chrissake, Johnny, you're scared shitless. Willya calm down, eh? You got any booze back there? Take a shot and have a smoke. Settle down; it'll be over before you know it."

Joe had finished his sandwich. He can demolish a sub faster than anyone I know. He drained his coffee and winked at me under his New England Telephone hard hat.

"Let's go, Doc."

On our way out a girl came into the shop and called for a pizza. Johnny skittered back round the corner and we saw him pull open the big Blodgett oven and take out the pizza and pan with a flat wooden paddle. Engaged in serving the customer, he seemed a bit more relaxed. But as he was making change he glanced quickly up at us again, and he seemed to come apart.

"Don't leave. Don't leave me, please."

"Take it easy. Remember what I said and take it easy."

We got out of there, followed by the girl. Joe looked at his watch, swore, and kicked little stones as we walked down the street. We weren't heading to our van, but in the other direction.

"Stupid little shit; he'll blow the whole thing."

"Where are we going?"

"Just to check the other teams. I guess I better warn everyone that Rizzo's clutched. Look over there; there's Powers up in his crow's-nest."

I was sure he saw us. From up alongside the high pole he could see everything. But he never seemed to take his eyes from the box on the pole that he was fiddling with. Around the corner was another van just like ours. We stopped by and hefted cables for a minute, talking to the men all the time and warning them about the snitch's mental state. It was twenty past three, and Joe and I ambled back toward our van, taking an alley route.

"There's the milk truck," said Joe. It was backed up to a convenience store. The driver, dressed in a blue cotton uniform, lounged on the loading dock with a cup of coffee. We walked over near him. He spoke to us softly, scarcely moving his mouth.

"Anything?" he said.

"Nah. About forty minutes more. How are the little toddlers? They behaving themselves?" Joe walked closer to the milk truck and glanced in the partially opened rear door. I was right behind him and looked over his shoulder. Inside, sitting on two benches reading skin magazines, were four of the meanest-looking dudes I'd ever seen. The SWAT team. They were wearing flak vests, funny-looking headgear, and blackface. Neatly laid out on the floor of the truck were shot-guns, tommy guns, and sniper rifles. They didn't even look up at us.

"Just be ready when we holler," said Joe, and we walked on.

"Hope we don't have to use the goon squad," he added as we drew within sight of our van. "It'd mess up this nice neighborhood."

We found Kevin fiddling with some bogus Ma Bell equipment and talking softly into his headset, looking very professional. We told him he should get coffee now because there wouldn't be time later.

"Mainly I want you to let Rizzo know we're still here, Kev. Calm him down a little. If he sees me again he's going to come all unglued."

So Kevin went and returned shortly with a steaming cup of java, shaking his head sadly.

"Says DeLucca's gonna hit him, Joe. Says DeLucca ain't coming at four. Says he was riding in a cab and saw you two in the shop with him. He wants to go back to Deer Island where it's safe. What about this guy inna cab, anyway?"

"Aw, bullshit. He's just spooked. I just hope he doesn't screw up the drill and get some bystander killed. Now Doc, listen: we want you to get in the back there. If I yell, you're to fall flat on your face. Nothing should happen—our van is really just a lookout. But we've got to be ready to pull out and block the street if he's got friends with a car. If that happens, Mary would never forgive me for bringing you along. But I really expect it'll go smoothly. And if, God forbid, any rough stuff starts, we've got the gorillas in the milk truck."

I was not in a jolly mood. While I dearly hoped Carmen DeLucca the mad-dog killer would be snagged, I had seen a lot in the past hour that had me down. The town depressed me, with its grimy, crowded streets, dilapidated buildings, and ragged, worn-out people. Of course they were the victims, not the culprits, but it was depressing nonetheless. The goon squad in the milk wagon depressed me. Most of all, Johnny Rizzo the jailhouse punk depressed me. He was a sad case, and frankly I didn't see much future for him no matter what happened.

Kevin sat at the wheel. Joe sat in back just behind me, with his legs stretched out on the floor and his headset on. Now and then I listened to my phone receiver and heard the conversations. There was none of the static crackle and buzz of the radio. Code words like *over* weren't needed either. It was a conference call of four parties, clear, subdued, conversational. And unlike talk on the police radio, it was private.

At four DeLucca still hadn't shown. At four-thirty I was surprised to see Rizzo leave the shop, fiddle with the awning crank, and disappear. I heard Powers alert all of us from his lookout. Right according to plan, Rizzo reappeared a second later, pushing the two-wheeled cart loaded with empties.

"Did you see him?" Joe asked Powers via his headset. "He must've come in the back way. Bill, get your guys ready. Keller, you guys see anything inside from where you're sitting?"

The answer was no. We waited, and pretty soon Bill said that the milk truck had seen no sign of Johnny, who was supposed to saunter down the alley in their direction after he stacked the bottles. Then a disgusted voice from van number two told us the answer.

"Hey Joe, your prize snitch is *here*. The little asshole is pounding on our van. You believe it?"

I hadn't seen Joe so mad in a long time. We unhitched the line cables, started up, and tore up the block and around the corner in less than half a minute. There he was, complete in undershirt and white apron, whining and dancing around the telephone crew of van number two and yelling that he wanted to go back to the Big House. Talk about blowing the stakeout. I thought Joe was going to kill him. The other guys thought so too, because they kept between the two men. Finally we had a plainclothesman march Rizzo back to the shop and we went back to our stations. But it wasn't any good; we all knew it wouldn't work after that.

We waited till five-thirty, then decided that it really looked fake to see all these workmen putting in overtime doing nothing. To continue the stakeout now would only wreck our cover for any future ones. Joe arranged to have a heavy surveillance of the place and neighborhood for the next twenty-four hours and we all went home. Kevin was to drive the van back to headquarters at Ten-Ten Comm. Ave., where he and Joe would pick up their cars.

Joe and Kevin were irritable and glum. Joe's mood was so dark it was dangerous. I went and bought them a pint of Johnny Walker, some soda and ice, and some plastic glasses. I said I'd drive the van for them, which I did. They sat stretched out in back and grumbled, swore, and drank. I heard Joe say more than once that he hoped DeLucca *did* catch up with Johnny Rizzo. We stopped on the way for Joe to make a call to Mary, and then I got on the line too. She was mad all right, but it could have been worse. Joe promised to buy a big leg of lamb in the North End before we started home.

"No, Joey. That means we won't eat until midnight. Get loin chops. And hurry up, it's past six!"

We promised to be home by eight, and continued on our way. At headquarters Joe didn't even go into his office; we got into his car and headed over to Storrow Drive. In fifteen minutes we were in the North End and, miraculously, parked right off Salem Street. We walked two blocks and then turned onto a little side street. I mentioned that this wasn't the way to Toscana's, and Joe nodded. He had a desperate look on his face. He said he had a little errand before we bought the meat.

"But it's important, Doc. That's why I thought of telling Mary we were going to Toscana's; there's something I just have to do here. It won't take long."

18

JOE WENT INTO A CANDY STORE AND PUMPED COINS INTO A pay phone, speaking into it softly and hunching into the alcove. I was standing next to him and couldn't hear what he said. Then he held the phone and waited. Finally I heard him say, "I'm right beneath you, in the store." Then he hung up and motioned me to follow him. We went out into the street again, through a small door, and up a flight of stairs to the office of a little realty company. The office was closed, since it was almost seven. But we waited in the hallway, looking in at the dark office through the glass door. I was beginning to think Joe had lost his mind, that the strain of the past week had been too much for him. But soon a young man appeared in the dark office, turned on the lights, and unlocked the door for us.

"Come this way, Mr. Brindelli," He said, leading us through the thickly carpeted office to a solid oak door in the back. This door was thick-paneled white oak mounted on heavy brass hinges. It looked bullet-proof. I found out later it was. The attendant heaved it open and it hissed against the hydraulic closer.

We found ourselves in a large, dimly lighted club room that was plush indeed. Burgundy pile carpeting. Walnut bookcases. Brass and pewter sconce lights. Leather club chairs. Ten-man walnut conference table with club chairs neatly arranged. Illuminated globe. It could have been the Harvard Club, except it was newer.

"Gee Joe, this is really tweedy. Veddy British."

"Yeah. Too bad it's High Sicilian. Listen, you're to be my man in this little visit. My witness. My second. Capish? Keep your eyes and ears open, and your mouth shut afterwards. Capish?"

We sat down in two of the leather club chairs. The guy who showed us in, the Sorcerer's Apprentice, asked us if we cared for anything to drink. I asked him if he could fix me a dry Beefeater on the rocks. He said no problem, took Joe's order, and oiled off.

"He's not even Italian, Joe; he looks like a Swede or something."

"Oh yeah. The big guys always hire WASPy help. That peon's probably a Yaley."

"Uh, Joe? Would you mind explaining—"

"Not now. It'll be quick, I promise. Just keep your eyes and ears open, mouth shut."

I sipped my drink. A polished rosewood door swung open and a tall, distinguished-looking man oozed forward on the thick carpet.

"Mr. Brindelli?" he said in a silken voice. "And Mr. Adams?"

We stood and shook hands with the man.

"I am Bernard Aldorfer, Mr. Tescione's personal assistant. We are honored by your visit, gentlemen. Mr. Tescione is in a brief meeting and will be with you shortly."

I had heard the name Tescione mentioned more than once by Joe. I had also heard it on television, read it in the papers.

"Ehhh . . . Mr. Tescione wishes me to ascertain the precise nature of your enquiry, Mr. Brindelli, so that, ehhh . . . he may be of more service to you in the short time he has at his disposal."

Joe leaned forward and looked into Aldorfer's eyes.

"Tell him it has to do with Carmen DeLucca," he said quietly.

Mr. Aldorfer's eyebrows went up; he slid the soles of his wing-tip brogues nervously on the burgundy pile carpeting.

"I, ehhh . . . see. Well, I shall go and inform Mr. Tescione then. We won't keep you waiting much longer."

"You both are very kind," said Joe. I could see he meant it sincerely. I leaned over and whispered to him. We were alone in the big club room except for the flunky with the J.D. from Yale, who was keeping an eye on us from the entrance hall. But I thought the place might be bugged, so I whispered.

"But I thought you hated Tescione and all he stands for. You keep saying he's a disgrace to Italian-Americans. That he—"

"Yeah yeah, I know. But right now I need him; I need to muddy my feet a little. Just keep—"

"I know: eyes and ears open, mouth shut."

He nodded in silence and the rosewood door swung open again. Mr. Aldorfer came forward, making as much noise as a cat, and requested that we accompany him. I set down the half-finished drink (the way they poured them, it had to remain half-finished if I wanted to walk) and followed Joe's wide form through the rosewood door.

We entered a dark and narrow hall. Stairs rose at the end of it. As we began to climb a faint beeper went off. Mr. Aldorfer apologized and requested that we accompany him back into the club room, which we did.

"I'm terribly sorry, gentlemen, but one of you—perhaps you, Mr. Brindelli—seems to be in possession of, ehhh . . . some sort of firearm. Correct?"

"Oh, I forgot," said Joe, drawing back his coat and producing his nine-millimeter Beretta. "Was on a stakeout; I don't usually carry a gun. Here." He removed the magazine and snapped back the slide, flinging out the chambered round, and then handed the empty gun to Aldorfer, who carried it over to a cabinet with a look of fear and distaste, as if it were a black mamba.

"Don't be fooled by that," whispered Joe. "He's probably trained to pump the whole clip into a twelve-inch circle at sixty feet.''

We tried the stairway again and this time reached the top. In the upstairs hall a man sat in a big leather chair. There was none of the Ivy League about this fellow. He sat in a big chair because he needed it. And he wasn't a WASP either. He looked like Primo Carnera. He glanced up at us as we walked by. His expression was totally blank. Aldorfer knocked at the third and final door, and opened it. We went in.

It was dark inside. The only illumination came from a desk lamp that threw a small circle of yellow light down on the desk top, and from the skyline of Boston and the harbor that was visible as a panorama through the wide plate-glass windows that swept around two sides of the spacious office. I was told later that the glass was bullet-proof. The tall man sat silhouetted against the city lights. The setting seemed appropriate, I thought, for a man of great power and perhaps, metaphorically speaking, a man of darkness.

He rose and shook hands with us. His grip was firm; the hand was wide, strong, and dry. I was looking dead level into the face of Paul Tescione, fourteenth most powerful underworld figure in America and the world. He was very handsome. If an Italian man can keep his hair and stay thin, he is usually good-looking. Tescione was as thin as Jacques Cousteau, with strong, sharp features, dark skin, and snow-white hair. His suit was cut perfectly in the European style, but not flashy. He looked like an ad out of *GQ*.

We sat down, Joe and Paul facing each other across the wide desk, with me on Joe's right and Aldorfer on Tescione's right. It was like a chess game. Joe and Paul would be the *caporegimes*, the warlords, and Aldorfer and I were the *consiglieri*, or counselors who were to sit in on any important meeting for protection and to listen carefully so that afterward, in discussions and decision making, we could clarify points, remember details. It was very Old World. It seemed to me like a pretty good system.

Tescione broke into a wide grin that revealed perfect teeth and a touch of gold work on his upper bicuspid. He slapped his palms gently but decisively down on the desk.

"So! Carmen DeLucca. Tell us about Carmen DeLucca, Mr Brindelli."

"He's alive. You knew that didn't you?" said Joe.

"I have heard that. Very, very recently I have heard that."

"Okay," said Joe softly. "Well it's true. He didn't die down in Jersey. He's alive and he's been up here. Now I came here tonight to ask you something and to tell you something, okay?"

"Okay," said Tescione, his eyes never leaving Joe. I don't think he had blinked in two minutes.

"Friday before last, Andy Santuccio was murdered up in Lowell."

Tescione's eyes blinked and fluttered down briefly to gaze at the desk top before returning to Joe.

"I know. I was at his funeral; God rest his soul."

"The same people who killed him killed another friend of mine, and a friend of the doctor's here too. The man who killed Andy is Carmen DeLucca."

Tescione's eyes widened slightly. He put his palms back down on the desk top and leaned over close to Joe, still looking him square in the eye.

"We know he killed him," Joe continued. "We have laboratory proof. Now what I wish to ask you is, do you know who had DeLucca kill Andy?"

"No. But I do know one thing."

"What's that?"

"That if he were in this room now I would kill him. And if you tried to stop me I would kill you first, then him."

"Do you know what Andy Santuccio had in the Boston Public Library that people would kill for?"

"I know his father had important papers from the Sacco and Vanzetti trial. That is, if you could call such an outrage a trial."

"Yes. I know that too. But do you, or anyone you know,

have any idea exactly what part of the papers could have caused his death?''

''No,'' said Tescione, who sank slowly back into his chair and propped his chin on his knuckles. ''Until a week ago I thought DeLucca was dead. I don't know why anyone would have Andy killed. He was a friend of mine and a good man in the community. Did you know that at the time of his death he was working on a housing project for the elderly?''

Tescione opened a silver case at his elbow and drew out a black-and-gold cigarette. He stuck it in his mouth and patted his pockets. Joe put his Orsini lighter on the desk top and slid it over to Tescione. Having lighted the cigarette, Tescione began to slide the lighter back, but Joe pushed it away.

''Keep it,'' he said.

Tescione held the lighter up and examined it.

''But this is a very expensive lighter, Mr. Brindelli. I can't—''

''No, please. Keep it. I got plenty.''

Tescione pocketed Joe's lighter as a man brought a carafe of coffee and four cups. He detained the man by his sleeve, got up and walked with him a few steps, and whispered some instructions. Then he returned to the desk and poured coffee for all of us. I wanted a cigarette. I haven't had one for twelve years and it takes a helluva situation to make me think about them. But now I wanted one. A Camel. Joe sighed.

''Then,'' he pursued, ''who had DeLucca kill Andy, and why?''

''I don't know,'' replied Tescione, setting down his coffee cup and dragging on the Du Maurier cigarette. ''And also I don't think I know anyone who knows.''

Joe looked blankly, and bleakly, ahead with his Thousand-Yard Stare. ''I guess I have no alternative but to believe that.''

For a second a look of annoyance crossed Tescione's aquiline face, then it was replaced by a smile. I could see how people could be afraid of him.

''Then believe it. Because it is true,'' the man said, thumping his palms down on the table. ''Now. You have asked me. You said also you were going to tell me something.''

Joe hesitated for a moment, then crooked his finger at Tescione as a signal for him to lean over the desk, which he did. Joe leaned over too until they were cheek to cheek, as if embracing. I heard him whispering right into Tescione's ear. The whispering stopped; the two men began to part, then Joe grabbed Tescione by the shoulder and drew them close again. The whispering continued. Then the men sat back and Tescione nodded slowly at Joe.

"Very well," he said. "Then it appears, Mr. Brindelli, Mr. Adams, that our business is concluded. Thank you very much for the visit. And thank you for the fine lighter too.''

"Don't mention it. Enjoy it.''

We shook hands. The attendant returned to take the coffee tray and leaned over and whispered quickly to Tescione, who nodded and smiled at him. Then he left, and we followed. Mr. Aldorfer led us back downstairs and said good-bye. The Yaley lackey appeared with a paper sack for Joe. It contained his pistol. We were once again walked back through the dark and deserted realty office, let out through the front glass door, walked down the stairs, and soon found ourselves on the street near the candy store where Joe had made the phone call. It was as if the whole thing hadn't really happened.

"I had no idea that the notorious Paul Tescione was so approachable," I said as we walked back to Salem Street and headed for the car.

"He usually isn't. I don't think we'd have gotten in if I weren't Italian. He knows of me; we've got some mutual friends, like Giordano. Ha! Meeting him like that, you'd never know how he makes his money would you?''

We walked on in silence. I didn't mention the lighter; I knew it would be unwise. Joe had loved that lighter and had given it up as a sign of fealty to a man he hated, but needed. I wondered too what he had told Tescione. I had an idea.

"Why the hell did they give me back my gun in this damn

sack? Wait a sec; I'll slip into the car and lock it up under
the seat.''

I waited outside while Joe locked his Beretta in the special
strongbox bolted to the frame of his sedan under the driver's
seat. He hated to carry guns. He emerged, shut the door and
locked it, and came to my side chuckling. He held in his big
hand a blue cardboard box.

"Look what I found in that paper sack along with my
gun.''

I took the box and opened it. It was a lighter. A Cartier,
dark blue and gold. The gold seemed to be real.

"Shit. I'm moving from a wop lighter up to a frog lighter.
I'm moving up in the world. Do you believe how fast he did
that?''

We both laughed, and went into Toscana's and bought six
extra-thick loin lamb chops. Up the street at Beninati's we
bought some fresh bread sticks, the white nougat candies
with the bright wrappers that Mary loves, some fresh bread,
espresso beans, and six cans of flat anchovy fillets. It's practically impossible to go into these little North End stores and
buy one thing. Back on Storrow Drive, then home by eight-
forty. Not too bad, considering all we'd done.

Joe and Mary talked in the living room while I sliced
tomatoes in the kitchen. I alternated slices of tomato, cucum-
ber, and onion around the outsides of three large plates, putting a bed of romaine lettuce in the center. On this I placed
a big chunk of white tuna, a handful of Tuscan peppers and
semihot banana peppers, pimentos and black olives, Greek
olives, provelone and feta cheese, Genoa salami, and pro-
sciutto, and I topped it with anchovies. Off to one side of
this was a big scoop of marinated eggplant chunks and arti-
choke hearts. Then I crushed fresh basil over the tomatoes,
added salt, coarse black pepper, olive oil, vinegar, and a
little lemon juice. The lamb chops had been basted with
garlic butter and were almost done. With the meat we would
have bread and white beans with lamb drippings.

We started with the antipasto, and when we were almost

through it Joe showed Mary the lighter and told her about
our visit with Paul Tescione. She sat at the table wide-eyed
and silent, her eyes never leaving her brother. She fed herself
by touch. I brought in the meat and the rest of the meal and
squirted a few drops of fresh lemon juice over each buttery
chop. Joe had demolished his first chop and almost the second one when the phone rang and Mary went into the kitchen
to answer it. She came back with a message for Joe.

"It was your office at Ten-Ten Comm. Ave. A man called
the office there asking for you, saying it was pretty important. A Mr. Aldorfer?"

He was in the kitchen quite a while. His chop got cold.
He came back, sat down, stared at his plate a minute, and
then excused himself, saying he'd be in my study.

Mary asked me who Mr. Aldorfer was and I let on I didn't
know. Just a little white lie to keep her from getting worked
up. I finished Joe's chop for him and told Mary I'd see him
alone in the study for a few minutes.

I found him in there playing with the dogs. He was patting
them and talking to them, and smoking.

"What's up?" I asked.

"What's up? *I'm* up. I'm up shit's creek without a paddle
is what. Aldorfer just told me that some of his acquaintances
up in Lynn stumbled across a corpse up there."

"Then they got DeLucca?"

He exhaled smoke through his nostrils like a dragon and
shook his head.

"No. The body they found was the late Johnny Rizzo, tied
to a chair in his rooming house. He'd been gagged. Then
somebody—gee, I wonder who—broke both his legs with a
billy club and went to work on him with a knife. Poor bastard. And it's my fault."

"Where were the cops?"

"They were still watching the sub shop, not Rizzo's place.
None of us took Johnny's fear seriously. He was such a
chicken-shit all the time. But he was right; DeLucca did

know he was being set up. Maybe that *was* him in the cab. Jeeee-sus Keeeee-*riste*.''

''Now I know what you whispered to Tescione.''

''No you don't. You can guess, but you'll never know. We made sure of that. Listen, Doc: the stakeout was blown and I didn't think we'd snag him. And if we did, chances are he'd walk, or get life. And Ill tell you one thing: I want Carmen DeLucca dead. On a slab. He's a goddamn animal.''

Joe stalked out of the study and through the hall to the little phone booth underneath the stairway. Before he could close the door after him I held it.

''Joe. What would happen if O'Hearn and the others at Ten-Ten Comm. Ave. got wind you'd met with Paul Tescione in his office?''

He stood there glaring at me with the phone cradled in his big hairy paw and a new cigarette dangling from the corner of his mouth, trailing smoke. He needed a shave. Joe always needs a shave. He smelled of stale sweat and old smoke and food and booze. I saw a corner of his shoulder holster peeping through his coat. He was straight out of a Cagney flick. He was scary.

''Seewwww *what*!'' He snarled. ''They wouldn't particularly give a shit. But anyway, they'll never find out. Know why?''

''Why?''

''Because you don't want to take a fall for a B and E, remember?''

He slammed the door after him and pushed buttons while I went back into the study. They say when you fight an enemy long enough you begin to take on his characteristics. Maybe they're right; all Joe needed was a big white fedora. He marched from the booth.

''Where are you going?'' Mary asked him as he went to the door. He kissed her on the cheek, thanked both of us, and said he'd just alerted his own people to check on Rizzo. Knowing what they'd find, he thought it best to be on hand.

''At least the Mob wasn't in on the Robinson-Santuccio

hit,'' he said as he paused at the open door. "I mean, I think he's leveling with us."

"I do too. I don't think it was the Mob."

"And if the hot item never surfaces, then so much the better. All I want now is DeLucca on a slab and I'm happy."

He left. Mary and I went into the kitchen and started up the coffee machine. She sat at the kitchen table and rubbed her fingers nervously over her eyes and forehead. Then she played with her hair, kneading and pulling at it like a grumpy child. She gazed down at the table, ignoring her coffee. Mary had had it. She was wrung out and exhausted. I patted her back.

"I can't wait for the trip," she said, resting her head down on her forearms. "When do we leave? The third?"

"Yep. Day before the Fourth of July. The flight to Milan is out of New York, and I've heard the Tall Ships will be in the harbor . . ."

"Good. Jeeez, I can't wait to get out of here for a while."

I opened the swing-out, lead-pane windows and let the spring breeze in. Mary sighed.

"At least it's just about over . . . this thing."

"Yep," I said, and went to get a magazine. On the hall table I spotted a manila envelope with no writing on it. I opened it. Inside were some police circulars on Carmen DeLucca and some glossy photos of him. He had black eyes like a Gila monster. He did not look like a nice guy. Joe had left the envelope with us, probably by mistake. I pulled one of the big glossy prints out of the envelope and took it in to Mary. It would be interesting to see if she could recognize a mad-dog killer just by his face and eyes.

She was slumped against the table, playing idly with her earring. She looked tired. I slid the photo in front of her. She glanced at it and looked up.

"Where'd you get that?"

"Joe left it here. What do you think of it?"

"It's a good photo. It's him all right. Joe works pretty fast."

"What are you talking about? What do you mean, it's him?"

"The guy who came to fix our furnace. I remember he had a bandaged hand, too."

"Oh," I said, putting the photo away. Danny, our yellow Lab, raced into the room, his toenails clicking on the linoleum, and jumped up to the window, paws on the sill. He sniffed and began a low growl, the fur on his back rising in a dark patch.

19

I NEVER LEFT THE HOUSE THE NEXT MORNING. HE CAME IN through the front door wearing a green jumpsuit. Mary thought he was the UPS man.

"Charlie . . . ?" I heard her call to me in a high, thin voice that wavered. I came around the hallway to see her standing straight up, as if stretching back, with a green arm around her neck and a small black gun pointing at the side of her head. But I wasn't looking at the gun; I was staring at the four-inch blade that extended down from the right fist of the green sleeve. The tip of the blade was pressed into the material of Mary's nightgown right over her left breast. The fist twitched. The knifepoint dipped into the soft fabric.

Mary gave a yelp and a high, whining shudder.

My knees began to shake and my mouth and throat felt numb and full of electric currents. My hair was moving.

And from around in back of Mary's head of long black hair crept a face.

I was expecting the black Gila-monster eyes, the black hair and wide face. But the face that glared at me with animal hate was not that one. And I was still rational enough to realize why: Mary would have recognized it. A blondish baby's face sat round and pink under the driver's cap.

"Listen real good," it said quietly. "We see three dogs out back. Two big ones and a little one. Any more in here?"

"No."

We. He'd said *we* . . .

"Now: anybody else in the house? Any kids, old folks? Anybody?"

"No. We're alone."

"Now you don't wanta lie."

"We're alone I said."

"Okay. Now where's the switch for those lights at the front door? Walk over to it but don't touch it."

I did, and he walked Mary along until he was directly opposite me. She was looking at me and at the ceiling. Her eyes weren't focused, and her breath was coming in little whiny pants, like a dog crying.

"Charlie? *Ohhh* . . ."

He silenced her by a short, hard rap on the head with the barrel of the pistol. It must have hurt terribly. She clenched her teeth and squeezed her eyes shut. Tears rolled down her face. I wanted to kill the man. But I knew better than to move a muscle.

"Now you flip it on while I count three, then you turn it off, hear?"

I nodded, and flashed the light on for three seconds. Almost immediately afterward I heard a distant car door slam. Then footsteps on the gravel walk, and two men dressed in street clothes came in. The door had been left open, and they were inside in a hurry, shutting the door behind them.

"Good morning everyone!" said the man with the wide hat.

His right hand held an automatic. I couldn't see his face. Then his left hand went up and grabbed the hat brim. The hand was bandaged. The hat came off and we could all see him now.

It was Carmen DeLucca. He stared at me, smiling. Then suddenly the smile dropped. The lizard eyes bored into mine.

"Hear you been looking for me, Doctor Adams. Well, I saved you the trouble. You both do exactly as we tell you or you'll die."

He walked farther into the hall, and motioned the third man to bring the large carton that had been the ruse for Mary to unfasten the chain bolt. He turned and looked at both of us again.

"Matter of fact, you might just die anyway."

20

IT WAS NOW ALMOST NINE; AN HOUR AND A HALF HAD PASSED since the three hoods had forced their way into the house. It felt like a century and a half. Mary had become hysterical and Babyface had led her into the downstairs john, seated her on the toilet, and handcuffed her left wrist to the radiator pipe in there. The door was left open a few inches so we could all hear her. They had me in the living room, my right wrist handcuffed to the arm of a heavy desk chair.

In the hour and a half I had phoned Susan Petri and announced that I was not coming in to the office. There was a two-second hesitation on the other end of the line—a pause that I'm sure was noticed by DeLucca, who listened in on the kitchen extension. But finally she had said fine and the conversation closed. Had she guessed something was amiss? I did not think so. Damn.

Through it all I sleepwalked as if in a dream, the trembling and electric buzzing clouding my senses and thinking. What was happening was happening to someone else, not Charles and Mary Adams.

The men had helped themselves to coffee and eggs. They rifled through the place—for a second time—and took clothes that fit them. Babyface slid outside fast to make sure our dogs were locked in their runs. The men put their tan Chevy in my garage and locked the doors, but only after they backed out our cars and switched their plates. The plates they took out of the big carton that Babyface had carried with him up to our door an hour and a half earlier. They took out the handcuffs first, then the license plates. They were New Jersey issue, and I knew they were what hoodlums call cold plates. Joe had told me cold plates were stolen but not used for several months so that their descriptions would not appear on police hot sheets.

They were going to take our cars someplace. They were on the run.

What about us? If pursuit was immediate, they would take us as hostages. If not, they would leave us tied up in our house and take off, buying themselves probably ten or twelve hours' time. Enough time to get to another big city and take a plane far, far away. Or they could decide not to leave us tied up.

They could instead decide to kill us.

And knowing Carmen DeLucca, who had killed so often he had nothing to lose, I knew this last possibility was real. And I didn't like it. Mary, seated in the semidark john and looking up through the red-print curtains, knew it too, and did not like it either. That's why she was crying and hysterical.

It was not knowing what course they would take, and the complete powerlessness over it, that was so frightening. It was not only scary, it was exhausting. I was scared to death and weak and tired, all at once.

And then DeLucca came into the room where I was handcuffed and asked me what I had done with the strip of photo negatives.

At quarter to ten I came to and looked down at the wires taped to my left forearm. DeLucca was good with wires and juice; he could set off gas bombs with them and make people unconscious from pain. I smelled singed hair and skin. Mine. And all because I couldn't answer his question.

Then DeLucca and his gang said they were going to work

on Mary until they got an answer. I could hear her saying "Don't—please don't," over and over again. I knew if I ever got a chance to kill any one of the three I would do it. They came back and sat down and told me Mary was not injured.

"Marty just got a little fresh with her, didn't you?"

Babyface leered at me. I tried to lunge at him but was now tied into the chair with a strap. I felt like a marionette. I swore at him until he cracked me across the mouth with the back of his fist. I didn't mind the pain; it seemed to wake me up.

"Okay," said DeLucca. "So you don't have it and don't know where it is. I didn't think you did, but I hadda make sure."

Then he sat on the sofa, hunched over, and clapped his hands slowly together, thinking. He turned to his confederates.

"We got nowhere to go now, except away. We can't go back to Lynn now. We can't go to Andover. The Doc ain't got it; we can't get it. The whole Mob's after us. We can only get lost."

The third man, a tall, thin, and morose lout with pale skin and bad teeth, stood up and paced.

"Don't forget the money, Carmen," he said. "We got the cars; now we need the loot."

Carmen DeLucca looked at me and said they needed five thousand bucks in cash, and it gave me a little hope. Because I knew that as long as I was in the process of getting him the money, Mary and I were safe.

"I can get that for you, but it won't be before this afternoon, even if I started now. We've got very little money in savings and checking accounts; it's mostly tied up in investments and term accounts that take some time to free."

"How soon?"

I shrugged. As used to big money as a guy like DeLucca was, he probably had no experience with or knowledge of the ways in which straight people keep money. A thug gets a bankroll and spends big bills until the roll is gone, then works at getting another.

"There are a lot of papers to sign. I'd have to see two bankers and my tax lawyer to free most of it. About eighteen hundred you can have in twenty minutes."

"Not enough," said DeLucca. He did not bridle at the fictitious red tape I spewed about bankers and lawyers. There would be penalties for tapping the term accounts, but no red tape. I told him I could furnish the deposit contracts and explain them to show I was telling the truth, but he shook his head. He believed me. He knew only street money and bad checks; anything else was beyond him.

Then the tall one called Carmen out of the room for a talk, and I didn't like that at all. They could just decide to put both of us on ice now and get moving. I heard arguing in low voices, both urgent. The men were cornered and scared, and very mean to begin with. That spelled danger. But by the time they came back I had a better idea.

"I know where you can get twenty thousand in small bills. In a sack, ready to go, unmarked. Twenty thou. and I can have it delivered."

It was some time before DeLucca answered. He sensed a trick.

"How soon? And how many people you gotta visit?"

"One phone call and it's on its way. I don't have to see anybody, DeLucca, so you don't have to worry about me blowing it. But the deal is, you get the cash and we go free."

"The deal is like it was planned: we get the dough and Marty and Vince and your wife hole up in a motel room we've rented near here. You and me, we take the red car and drive away. Someplace deserted I let you out of the car and keep going . . . and you remember that your lovely wife is still in that motel room. They are not to touch her unless I say otherwise or unless the law comes in. Then she dies. But *if* I get where I'm going safe, and I figure you haven't called any law, and *if* when I call this motel room everything is cool there, *then*, but *only* then, they tie your wife inna chair and wrap a hanky around her mouth and turn the TV up loud and leave. Got it?''

I nodded. So this was not a last-minute effort on their part. They had planned it pretty carefully, perhaps arriving in town the night before and staying in the rented motel room, wherever it was. After I was released it would be perhaps an hour before I could reach a phone. Even then I would know that Mary wouldn't be left alone in the room until DeLucca gave the word to his confederates over the phone from God knows where. And he might not call them until late. In a way the plan made me breathe a little easier; it indicated that they did not want violence, only escape. For this they needed another car and cash—and they knew that I had both.

''Now where's this twenty grand? What bank?''

''No bank. It's at Dependable Messenger Service in Cambridge, in the safe.''

''No it ain't. I *know* it ain't.''

''Oh yes it is. When you burned that safe the money was out, sitting inside another strongbox. I had a hunch that place was going to get hit. But there's a new safe there now, and the money's back.''

''Let's get to a phone,'' said Vince, ''and see.''

Before I went I demanded to see Mary, who looked fine, considering. I didn't know what Marty had done to her and for the time being didn't want to—I was afraid I would lose control and lunge at him and both Mary and I would get shot. They gave me definite instructions for the phone conversation, which I followed to the letter. It was rather brief. I told Sam I had a private problem. *Private.* He was to tell nobody about it, or else the problem would get a lot bigger immediately.

''You've got to believe me, Sam.''

''I believe, Doc—I believe. Come by and get it. I'll have it ready and nobody'll know.''

''No. Can you bring it to the Minute Man Park off Route 2A? Bring it—alone—to the park at eleven-fifteen. Walk in the park, which should be empty, until you see my red-and-white International Scout. It looks like a Jeep. Nobody will be inside but the door will be unlocked. Put the sack inside on the back seat, close the front driver's door so it locks, then go back to the office. Okay?''

"I got it."

"Sam? Don't call anybody after we hang up. It'll go bad for us if you do."

"I won't. I'll do just like you say."

"How much is in the sack?" said DeLucca, who was listening in on the extension.

There was a slight pause, and Sam asked me if he should speak to the strange voice. I told him yes.

"Just about eighteen thousand seven hundred dollars in bills. Nothing larger than fifties."

"It all better be there. And remember what the man said: don't mention this to anyone. Go right back to your office and be cool until the doctor calls you. Got it?"

"I'm hip. Well, I'm startin' now."

In five minutes we were ready too. Vince was to stay behind with Mary while I drove DeLucca in the Audi, and Marty the baby-faced psycho was to drive the Scout. Apparently even DeLucca was anxious about leaving the punk alone with Mary. I don't think she even knew when we left. We went out to the cars. Something was wrong with Marty. I could tell by the way he walked.

We were waiting at Minute Man National Park at eleven. I was sitting at the wheel of the Audi, my left hand cuffed to the rim of the steering wheel, while DeLucca sat in the front passenger seat watching me and the Scout, which was parked way over on the other side of the big lot. There weren't many visitors at the park this early in the year. There were only two other cars and a couple riding ten-speed bikes, who'd stopped to look around and drink from their plastic water bottles. Marty, who'd driven the Scout, was leaning into a public phone alcove up near the park building. From this vantage point he could see everything. DeLucca had instructed him to phone Vince at the first sign of trouble so he could put a bullet in Mary.

My palms were sweaty and my heart was going like a jackhammer.

"Stay cool," purred DeLucca, drawing on a cigarette, "and nobody gets hurt. Keep telling yourself that all we want is the car, the cash, and a head start. You get us those and you're all set."

He grinned at me as his mouth dribbled smoke. On the seat, cradled in his right hand, was his little pocket auto pistol. The grin was wide but the eyes black and cold. I did not trust him even a little. And like an ice-cold serpent crawling up my spine, a thought that entered my mind dropped the bottom out of any slight hope and optimism I'd allowed myself to have.

The thought was simple, and devastatingly logical. DeLucca and his two sleazy sidekicks had absolutely nothing to lose at this point. With the police of the entire Eastern seaboard, the Mob, and practically everybody else after them for murder and betrayal, they faced certain capture and death if they remained in the area now that word of their presence in Boston was out. As DeLucca had said, they needed a head start. And the longer that head start was, the better their chances. With Mary and me alive there was a ceiling on that lead; with us dead there wasn't.

They might kill us in the house, hide our corpses in the attic or basement, and leave. They might kill us in the motel room, but that seemed unlikely. Today was Friday. If friends saw nobody home and the cars missing, they would assume we'd gone down to the cottage on the Cape for the weekend. Our two sons weren't due back from school for another three days.

They would have plenty of lead time that way. Plenty. Enough to drive the stolen cars with the cold plates clear across the country.

Maybe they wouldn't kill us right away. Perhaps they would begin the plan as DeLucca had outlined it to me. When he and I were far away in the Audi, he would have me pull off the road near the woods or scrub, do me in, and dump me in a green tangle. Then they'd kill Mary and leave her in the motel bed, naked and violated. When the local authorities found her, Brian would proceed with caution, sensing a possible scandal. Or would he? Would he—

"Hey! Snap out of it!" snarled DeLucca. I turned my attention back to the red-and-white vehicle sitting all alone at the far end of the huge lot. Was Sam going to show? Or was he bringing in help to get us off the hook? An hour ago I would have hoped more than anything he would do what they wanted. But not now. As soon as I realized how much more getaway time they'd have with us on ice, I was sure we were done for. I looked back at DeLucca. The lizard eyes glowed and darted in the wide, dark face.

"Look," he said, and pointed past me with his cigarette, which he held in his bandaged hand.

A red Buick Regal had pulled into the lot and stopped next to the Scout. A man in a gray jumpsuit was getting out. He carried a dark-green canvas bag. It was Sam. He approached the Scout without ever looking up or looking around. He opened the front door, leaned in, flipped the bag into the back seat, stood up, pushed down the door-lock plunger, closed the door, tested it to make sure it was locked, and got back into his car. I could see no sign of the big dog. My heart sank. He was following the instructions to the letter. I couldn't understand the jumpsuit, except that if he felt he was being watched, the jumpsuit would signify his occupation as a messenger. The Regal backed up, swept around, and was gone.

As per the plan we all waited for ten minutes without moving a muscle. Nothing happened. No battle weapons filled with fuzz roared into the lot. No choppers descended. It was quiet; the plan was working.

DeLucca had me start the car while Marty sauntered down to the Scout. He unlocked the door and got in. We saw him reach back for the moneybag, and seconds later the headlights flashed once. That meant that there was really money in the bag, not paper. We cruised out of the lot with the Scout right behind us. DeLucca had me go along at a pretty good clip, then turn off 2A onto a small dirt side road for about thirty yards and stop. He took the keys and left me cuffed to the wheel while he went back to see Marty. The kid's face looked funny.

They opened the bag and set it on the hood of the Scout. DeLucca examined the loot while he kept looking over his shoulder toward the highway. He pawed through the satchel, flipping through wads and stacks of bills. He seemed more than satisfied with the haul. If he were an ordinary guy, without a string of grisly murders and betrayals to account for, I might have reason to expect that this fortune I got for them would make him spare us. But more and more I realized he would not. He couldn't. He now had his hands on enough money to live for months without risking his neck or even showing himself. So the lead time for his escape had become that much more important.

They crept down to the highway and watched it for a while to see if there was a tail. There wasn't. DeLucca got back in, handed me the keys, and told me to drive home. As I swung the car around I was hoping we wouldn't get there. Instead of getting the gang off our back, the sack of money was rushing the final act. I should never have called Sam, but now it was too late.

We pulled up the drive and into the turnaround in back. Vince came out the door and met us on the flagstone terrace. He was scared. He pointed down the slope at the orchard and woods beyond the low stone wall.

"There was shooting there ten minutes ago," he said to DeLucca. "I heard a gun, firing fast."

"Well?" DeLucca asked me. I shrugged.

"A lot of kids hunt rabbits down there with four-tens," I said. "It's illegal, but they do it."

"I don't hear nothing," DeLucca said. "Let's get inside."

Vince followed us, but not before glancing back at the woods and the apple trees.

I heard Mary crying as soon as we entered the back door. They unlocked the cuff that held her to the radiator and she clung to me. The episode in the Lowell mill yard flashed back into my mind for an instant, and I couldn't believe that what was happening to us was related to that incident, with the stranger picking away at the old factory wall. I gripped her tightly and spoke to her. I told her we only had to wait it out and it would be over and everything would be back to normal. I was lying. I don't think she knew it. They cuffed us together and had us sit on the couch while Vince got one of Mary's raincoats and some casual shoes. He found a scarf too, and a pair of dark glasses for her to wear. They got a medium-weight jacket for me, saying I'd have a long walk later that night.

Maybe they weren't going to kill us after all, I thought. But I didn't really believe it.

They counted out the money on the coffee table. DeLucca moved fast, looking at his watch. He had trouble with some of the bills owing to his bandaged hand, so he let Vince do it. Marty, the kid, was hopping up and down on the seat, grinning from ear to ear.

"Stop it," said DeLucca.

But the kid kept it up. His eyes were shiny, and I noticed a string of saliva snake down out of his mouth.

"I said stop it."

Marty stopped, and tried to wipe his mouth with the back of his hand, which didn't seem to be working right. He quieted, then rocked to and fro on the couch making sucking sounds. DeLucca and Vince looked at each other. Vince scowled, looking at the kid.

"When it rains it pours, eh? Why now?"

"It won't work," said DeLucca softly. The kid didn't hear him.

The money was divided into two equal piles. DeLucca and Vince each took one.

"Where's my-un?" said the kid, who was bouncing again. His teeth were clicking. He took out the four-inch sheath knife and tapped the blade into the table. His tongue was hanging out. He looked at Mary and managed a laugh. Then he looked sideways at the other two men and tried not to. He stood up and wobbled, then hummed. "Where's mine?"

"Vince's got it, Marty. He'll give it to you when you get to the room. Now come on, Mrs. Adams, time to get your coat on."

They unfastened her cuff, leaving it dangling from my left wrist. Mary put on her coat, shoes, scarf, and dark glasses. They had me put on the jacket and we started toward the back door. Then Marty started to bleat like a sheep. He took out the knife again and Vince grabbed it. DeLucca walked up to him and slapped him across the face. That seemed to straighten him up.

"I promise I won—" he began. "I promise . . . I *prom-ise*."

DeLucca hit him again. The kid bounced back against the kitchen wall. He was gurgling, and his face was slack. DeLucca looked at his watch. Vince had the door open. I heard the dogs barking outside. DeLucca told him to shut it and led the two of us back to the hallway, where he passed the chain from my handcuff through the banister railing and fastened Mary to the other end. I would have tried to whang him with one end of the handcuffs if Mary hadn't been there. As it was, Vince stayed three feet away with his pistol pointed right at me.

"Get him down the basement," DeLucca said softly to Vince.

Vince went over to the kid, who was leaning in the corner, and put his long arm over his shoulder, comforting him. He patted him on the back hard, just like old buddies. He led him over to DeLucca, who put his arm around him too. They helped him along. I heard the kid crying. We could just peek around the hall corner and see the three of them standing at the head of the basement stairs. Then Marty realized what was happening. He stared into that black hole and bawled, grabbing the edge of the door frame with hands that didn't work.

"Come on, Marty. Be good. I just want you to sit down on the floor," said DeLucca softly, as one rebukes a child.

They hauled at him but he wouldn't budge. He still had enough strength and control left to hang on and keep from going down that dark stairway.

"We just want you to sit down on the floor and rest," DeLucca repeated softly, tugging at the kid's waist.

"Puuuu-*leeeeze*!" wailed Marty, his feet pointed out and his knees bowed like a toddler's. His lower half was shaking violently now.

"Mister Deeee-loooo . . . Deeeee—"

Vince took his pistol and struck Marty's hands, which slid away from the door frame. The two men helped the kid down the stairs. We heard him blubbering and wailing. Then a door slammed shut and everything was quiet. I looked at Mary. Her teeth were clenched tight on her lip. There was a little blood. I kicked at the railings with my feet and knees with all I had, and finally managed to break two of the oak uprights, which weren't very thick. I yanked them out of their sockets, leaving a wide hole under the banister.

"Hurry, Charlie. *Hurry*!"

I pulled Mary underneath the banister. We were still fastened together. I ran down to the front door and yanked. No go. I flipped the bolt; it still wouldn't open. It had been deadbolted.

As we went back down the hall and into the kitchen we heard a sound beneath us. A muffled explosion. Then fast feet on the stairway, coming up.

I had the back door open now and we went through it. Out of the corner of my eye I saw Vince in the kitchen raising his arm. His hand held a pistol.

We were running across the terrace when I saw a piece of the brick wall fly away. I jumped over the wall and yanked Mary after me. She was making little high sounds. Vince was raising the pistol again when I pulled Mary off to the right and began to circle the house. I knew we'd never make it across the open meadow to the woods.

But around the first corner we stopped dead, looking right down the muzzle of DeLucca's automatic. His meaty chest and shoulders were heaving as he panted. He'd gone around the other way and cut us off. We heard Vince coming up behind us. I grabbed Mary tight and shut my eyes, waiting.

I felt a rap on the head and opened my eyes. I was half-stunned. I looked up and saw Vince grab the chain that held us together. DeLucca, panting loudly, was behind us, pushing the gun muzzle into our backs.

"You blew it, shithead," he growled. "Now you're gonna have to go down the cellar."

Again I felt tingling around my head and mouth. The ground shook under my feet. I was afraid to look at Mary.

"Let her go. Have Vince take her to the motel."

"Too late," he said, smacking the back of my head with the barrel. I felt a warm trickle down the left side of my neck from the previous blow. We were back around to the terrace again. The kitchen doorway was only twenty feet away. Once they had us through that door we'd never get out again. I decided to shout for help at the top of my lungs before all hope was gone, and had just taken the biggest lungful of air I could manage when I heard a gigantic roar. Instantaneously I felt a stinging on my right cheek, and the arm tugging the handcuffs went slack.

Next to us, Vince was falling. His head had come apart into a big red wet cloud. And part of that cloud was stuck all over my face, stinging it.

DeLucca had his pistol up. He was pointing it at a huge dark shape that was flying at his head. The thing hit him with a deep rumbling snarl and threw him to the ground. Popeye had him by the upper arm, right near the shoulder. He had his big steam-shovel mouth wrapped around DeLucca's upper torso and was shaking it, tearing it. DeLucca couldn't

hold the gun; nobody could have. Then the dog was off him
and waiting by in a crouch.

DeLucca sat up for a second, then lunged for the pistol
and brought it up. But before he could fire the roar came
again and he was flung backward, spinning around like a
top. He lay on his stomach and didn't move. There was motion in the yew trees, and Sam Bowman came walking toward
us, the big silver revolver held up in his hand. He came up
and looked down at Carmen DeLucca, who was now moaning and flipping his left arm on the grass like a seal pup. The
big soft-nosed slug had left his back just below the left shoulder blade. A lot of his back was gone. I peered down at him
and could see a shiny pink balloon sliding around in the gore
beneath his splintered ribs. It was his lung.

Sam shoved his big piece back into its shoulder holster
and zipped up his Windbreaker. He was no longer wearing
the jumpsuit. He reached down and laid his large coffee-
colored hand on Mary's cheek.

"How ya doin'?" he asked, and she began to bawl.

I was certain DeLucca was dying. I thought he knew it
too. Sam went through the pockets of the former Vince and
retrieved the keys to the cuffs; he had us free in a wink. I
crawled over to DeLucca and looked at his face. The lizard
eyes fluttered, then opened. Carmen DeLucca stared at the
blades of grass inches from his eyes and the terrace wall
behind them. The big wound in his back began to bubble
and sputter.

"Carmen. It's Doc Adams. Remember?"

A nod.

"You don't have very long. Tell me what the negatives
showed. Hear me, Carmen? What did the pictures show?"

A faint shake of the head.

"You don't know?"

Headshake.

"Who hired you to get them? It wasn't Paul Tescione, was
it?"

Headshake.

''Then who was it, Carmen? Who?''

I heard a thin rasp of expelled air. I bent over and put my ear close to his mouth. He said a name in a barely audible voice. Then there was a long sigh. When I next looked at the cruel black eyes they were open and staring. I watched them and the face for a minute. There was no motion, no change, nothing. Carmen DeLucca was dead. But not before he had told me who it was who'd hired him to snatch the Sacco–Vanzetti papers. I looked up from the corpses and turned my head around. Mary and Sam were sitting quietly on the terrace chairs while Popeye sat looking up at Mary and whining. I had been alone with DeLucca when death overtook him. Nobody had overheard him tell me the name. That was awkward.

It was especially awkward because it was no ordinary name. I knew if I mentioned that name nobody, not even Mary, would ever believe me. Ever.

21

WITH THE TENSION AND THE ADRENALIN RUSH WORN OFF, Mary and I collapsed in fatigue. After I took her to the hospital to be treated for several small gashes on her breasts—the sad result of Marty's warped idea of "getting fresh" with a woman—I took her home in time to meet Joe out in back. He stared and stared at DeLucca's body. He thanked Sam over and over again. He was one glad cop.

"Except I'm kicking myself in the ass for leaving so suddenly last night. I should've thought of the possibility he'd sneak out here. Anybody with the balls and cunning to slip back into Lynn and grease Johnny Rizzo would try anything. But it seems to us that it was that psycho kid who did all the wet work. He sure loved to hurt people."

"Well I'm not going to miss him one bit. He may have been ill, but I don't feel sorry for what happened to him. I'd hate to think what he would have done to Mary if he'd had the chance. As it happens, she's probably not even going to have any marks when she heals up. Jeez, I bet Moe has a field day when I describe Marty to him."

Joe's men had found Marty wedged up behind my workbench with a hole behind his ear. Then they carted the three of them off in a meat wagon. Good riddance. Joe said he guessed the whole thing was as good as wrapped up.

"Not quite," I said, leading him into the study and closing

the door behind us. I sat him down and told him the name
of the person who had hired Carmen DeLucca.

"*What?* Where did you get that load of shit?"

"From DeLucca himself. His dying words. You're the only
one I've told. I didn't think you'd believe me."

Joe walked over to the window and looked at the dogwood
petals that littered the lawn. He had his hands thrust deep
into his pants pockets, and he rocked back and forth on his
heels.

"That's a big name, Doc. Not as big as the Kennedys or
Saltonstalls, but big. The only thing I can't figure out, assuming he was even involved, is why *he'd* want the papers."

"Could you question him?"

He spun around. "Are you kidding? Based on something
you overheard? No way."

"Isn't there a rule about deathbed confessions?"

"Yes. A dying declaration is admissible evidence since it
is assumed to be, as the deceased's last words, the truth. But
dying declarations almost always concern something the dying man himself did or didn't do, or else the identity of the
man's assailant."

"So it means nothing?"

"Oh no. It means a lot. A hell of a lot. I just don't know
what yet."

The door burst open and Brian Hannon entered, shaking
his right fist like a crapshooter. The fist emitted a metallic
rattle.

"Thanks for knocking, Brian," said Joe.

"You're entirely welcome . . . *lieutenant.*"

He held his fist up under our noses and opened it. Resting
on his wide palm were four ammo rounds as big as lipsticks.
They were Sam's forty-five-caliber long-Colt cartridges.

"Seen these?" asked Brian. Joe picked one of them up
and looked at the nose. He saw the snowflake cuts hacked
across the lead.

"Well hush my mouth," said Joe.

"Great, Brindelli. Just great. Know what it looks like to

have dumdums used in my jurisdiction? You just wait: the city council's gonna be on my case like cheddar on Ritz.''

"You gotta admit they do a job," said Joe.

"Don't you be a wise-ass. You been hanging around *him* too long," said Brian, jerking his thumb at me. He bent over and pointed to the top of his head, which had been shaved and bandaged. "See this? Seven stitches on account of your friend the doctor. Now what do I do about Sam?''

"Nothing. It it weren't for him my brother-in-law and sister would be dead.''

"That's what I mean. Take 'em. Lose 'em someplace. Though God knows the medical examiner's going to ask a lot of questions. Jeez, you see those slobs? Look like they were hit by mortars.''

Joe slipped the rounds into his coat pocket and turned to me.

"How'd he do it, Doc? How'd Sam get back here for the ambush?''

"After he took the call and got the money from the safe, he took a couple of minutes to study a road map. Seeing that the drop was on 2A, he thought there was a chance something was happening here. It was a lucky guess. He knew he couldn't tail us without being noticed. He got a friend of his to drive the Regal to the Mobil station near 128 and Route 2. He followed with the dog and the cycle. They met at the gas station, where Sam took the Regal to make the drop. He wore a hat and a jumpsuit so he could change his appearance fast. He went up 128 to 2A, which is less than a mile, and into the lot. After the drop he hustled back to the station, doffed the clothes, and sped along Route 2 into Concord and over here by the back way. With the bike he could cut right across the orchard, which he did. That's what Vince heard. It wasn't shooting, it was Sam's old Honda backfiring. Hell, he and the dog were staked out in position behind the far wall even before we got back.''

Brian looked at me. "I think you owe him dinner," he said. "And Joe, don't forget to ditch those rounds.''

* * *

Next day, as I fitted the shiny prongs of my Hu-Friedy forceps over the crown and shank of a deeply impacted third molar, the idea came to me. I was struck by how the metal of the instrument obscured the tooth completely. The metal surrounded the object . . . *hiding it* . . .

"Eureka!" I whispered.

"What?" asked Susan Petri, who stood, white-smocked and plastic-aproned, to my immediate right. "Did you ask for a beaker?"

"No. I said *Eureka*. That means 'I found it.' "

"I know. Found what?"

"The place where the negatives are hidden. I think I've found it."

She stared at me. I couldn't see her lower face since it was hidden by her surgical mask. The eyebrows went up; the forehead wrinkled in a frown. "Swell, Doctor Adams."

She dipped her siphon tube into the patient's open mouth to draw off the blood that was fast collecting there. Fortunately the patient was asleep, having been given a shot of sodium pentothal. Mrs. Habersham couldn't hear us. I withdrew the bent and buried tooth, which I had twisted up with the cowhorn forceps. There was a deep, sucking, squishing noise as the molar came out, then we sutured and packed the wound, injected Mrs. Habersham with a hefty slug of penicillin, and watched her carefully while she came to. You must be really careful with a general anesthetic so that your patient doesn't choke or drown. This is especially true if you've worked in the mouth. She woke up without a hitch and we sent her on her way. On foot.

At the earliest opportunity I returned home to the darkroom (which I was painstakingly rebuilding) and got an eight-inch strip of 35mm film. I headed out to the Concord Rod and Gun Club and the outdoor range. I heard those big Magnums blasting off long before I reached it. Then another sound: the thump of iron silhouettes being hit by slugs and slamming against the ground. Silhouette shooting, imported from Europe in the sixties, is all the rage now at gun clubs. It consists of shooting at thick metal plates cut out in the shape of animal profiles, at long range, using big-bore Magnum handguns. No rifles. It's a silly sport, I guess. But then so is chasing a little white ball around on grass and whacking at it until it falls into a cup.

I was out at the silhouette range because I needed a big-bore revolver to experiment with. I found Chuck Norgaard at one of the stations, poised at the line with a revolver held out in front of him with both hands. There was a blast I felt in my chest, and the gun and his arms went up. He stepped back and flipped out the cylinder, pushed the ejection rod, and dumped out the spent shells.

"Hiya Doc. What brings you here?"

"I want to borrow that thing when you're finished."

He nodded, and I saw him drop six more silver rockets into the cylinder. I was sick of looking at big handguns.

"Got any idea what those things do when they hit people instead of steel plate?" I asked.

"I can imagine."

"No you can't," I said, and waited for him over at the bench. I should have brought earmuffs.

Half an hour later I left the club, went home, and got hold of Joe.

"What do you mean, not there?"

"All Johnny Robinson's personal effects went to Sam, except for the stuff his sister took. It's all at Dependable, or Sam's apartment."

"Okay; I'll get in touch with Sam. Meet me at Brian's office at six tonight. I think I know where the hot item is."

"Okay, sport, strut your stuff," said Brian Hannon, leaning back in his armchair. He glanced over at Joe, who was lighting a Benson & Hedges 100 with the new gold-and-blue lighter. A look of confusion crossed Brian's face.

"Hey, that lighter looks different, Joe. Not as fruity. What happened?"

"This is a new one. Classier."

"Where'd you get it?"

"I got it, if you must know, from a Mafia chieftain."

"No, really."

"Let's talk about something else. C'mon, Doc, I'm getting starved. Sam's late, but tell us anyway. Where the hell's this filmstrip?"

I laid Inspector James Bell's Smith & Wesson on the desk, and next to it a new, unsharpened pencil. I explained that I'd gotten the idea while fitting the barrel of my tooth extractor around an old lady's molar. They weren't impressed. I handed Brian the revolver and asked him to check it out. This he did in standard fashion by swinging out the cylinder, which was empty, and looking down the chambers as he spun it on its crane arm. Then, the cylinder still out, he looked down the muzzle of the barrel and handed it to Joe, who repeated the procedure, then stuck his thumbnail under the barrel throat so the light would reflect off it up through the tube.

"Empty," he said, handing it back. "I don't have a screwdriver to take off the grips or sideplate. I assume that's what you're going to do."

"No," I said, taking the pencil and inserting it into the barrel. I pushed it down carefully. The coiled celluloid sprang out of the barrel throat like a jack-in-the-box, and there was the filmstrip on the desk.

"Sure looked clean to me," said Joe.

"That's because the film was rolled emulsion side out, leaving the inside of the roll shiny-slick. When you roll up the film this way and stick it in the muzzle end, which is nearest the viewer's eye, he's got to be looking very closely to see it. In regular room light, like this, it's just about invisible."

"Hmmm. And Johnny put Santuccio's film there? You sure?"

"Just about positive. He was carrying it the day he was killed. From his phone message to me it's clear he knew he was being tailed . . . and he knew why, too. He didn't leave it at the office, or in his car. Those places were searched thoroughly by DeLucca and you guys. It wasn't in his apartment. Not only was the place searched several times, but the killers nailed him as soon as he walked in. I thought for a while it was tucked away somewhere on his apartment's porch, or in the stairway hall going up to his place. But I was wrong. All I got out of that expedition was two broken heads: mine and Brian's.''

"Tell me about it," the chief growled. "Although I admit this is kinda clever, Doc. Now it'll be even better if you're *right*."

"Where else can it be? He didn't put it in his shoe. Joe, your men checked his clothes. He didn't mail it to himself; we've watched his mail. He wanted it ready to deliver. But I'll tell you something else: this is my second experimental filmstrip. The first one disintegrated. When you put a roll of film inside the business end of a thirty-eight, there's nothing left of it after you touch the gun off. It shreds and burns into vapor.''

"When we found Johnny's body up in Lowell, Mary noticed that the carrying strap of his sidearm was unfastened.''

"Uh-huh. Which meant that if indeed the film was in there, Johnny knew he could both conceal the evidence and destroy it immediately if he had to.''

"Sounds too good to be true," said Brian as he swiveled in his chair and watched a red Buick Regal swerve into the CPD lot beneath his window.

Well, it was. Too good to be true, that is. As for the film negatives which should have been tucked neatly, invisibly, into the barrel of Johnny Robinson's S&W model ten, they *weren't*. They weren't hidden in his little leg pistol either. They also weren't in any of the clothes and shoes that were in the cardboard carton that Sam hauled into the office with him.

"Well close, but no cigar," said Brian, drumming his fingers on the desk. "Sorry to have brought you all the way out here, Sam.''

I cussed. Sam folded up his dead partner's clothes and placed all the belongings neatly back into the carton.

"My guess is Johnny ditched the stuff somewhere on his way home, at some drop, intending to return to the drop later Friday night or Saturday morning when the heat was off and retrieve it. Of course he never got the chance."

Following this bit of deduction, which seemed plausible, we called the Lucky Seven tavern again, just to make sure nobody there had seen Johnny that day, or whether indeed a letter, package, or message had arrived there with his name on it. The answer was no.

"I'm back to first base," I said.

"Wrong, Doc. You're back in the dugout," said Joe. "Now Brian and I have some paperwork to do for the De-Lucca thing. It's just routine and will take about an hour. Let's meet afterwards in case there are some last-minute questions."

"Yeah," said Brian, "minor things like dumdum bullets and breaking and entering."

"Mary and I are going to buy Sam a big dinner at Yangtze River. Brian, seeing's how I accidentally banged up your head, I think I owe you one too. Why don't the three of us wait for you two at our place?"

They said it was the first good news they'd had all day. So Sam and I left. At home Mary set a blood-rare round steak down in front of Sam's big pooch. Turns out he is not a fussy eater.

"It's the least we could do for him, Sam," she said. "And now Charlie, you want to show Sam his present from us, since we're still alive?"

It was sitting behind the little tool shed with a canvas cover over it. A new Honda CX-500, with full fairing and a special platform for Popeye covered with thick acrylic carpeting in silver-gray, which matched the bike. Sam rubbed his hands over the satin finish of the tank, the brightwork of the cylinder casings, the flat black of the cockpit instrument panel. He was speechless. The big dog at his side sniffed the machine and waggled his fat butt.

"She's quiet as a graveyard, Sam; I took her for a little spin yesterday. With this you won't give away your position to the enemy."

He and the dog walked in silence around the bike. Something looked different about the dog. I couldn't figure out what it was. We had drinks on the terrace. Sam couldn't seem to take his eyes off the bike. We let our doggies out of their runs and watched tensely as they approached the big bull mastiff, who was reclining sedately on the flagstones, digesting twenty ounces of steak. Danny, the yellow Lab, approached growling with a lot of braggadocio. Popeye looked at him through slit eyes over a wide mouth, bored. What was different about Popeye?

After fifteen minutes of bluffing and retreating, charging and dodging, the four dogs reached a truce and began to play.

"I know what's different about our friend," I said at last. "He's got a new harness on."

"Oh yeah," said Sam, taking the set of keys Mary handed him. "He got that last week; I threw the old one out. Doc, I've had a drink, but you think it's all right if I take it down the end of the drive and back?"

"Sure. But watch it—you've got about twice the power of your old bike, and a shaft drive too. It'll feel different."

Sam started the bike, eased it off its stand, and purred down the gravel drive slowly. He scarcely made a sound. He came back grinning from ear to ear.

"Doc, Mary," he said, "I just don't feel right abut taking it without paying you. It's so nice and I just feel—"

"Cut it, Sam," snapped Mary. "It's really quite simple: if you hadn't been here, risking your own life, we'd be in the ground now. So let's not hear any more about it." She went inside to freshen up our drinks and I patted the huge dog and scratched his ears. Popeye was used to all of us by now. The new harness he wore was about the scale of those used on Budweiser draft horses.

"This doesn't look new," I said. "It looks bigger and better than his old collar, but it's not new."

"Naw. It was Tommy's. It's heavy-duty and cost Johnny a bundle to have it made, as I remember. So instead of throwing it out like I did Susie's, I kep' it. Makes him easier to control; he's got plenty of power."

"And Johnny had it custom-made?"

"Um-hmmmm. Can't buy those."

"Take it off a minute. I may want to get some made for our dogs."

Mary brought the drinks and said she wondered what was taking Joe and Brian so long. She and Sam sipped and talked and played with the dogs. I turned the big harness over and over in my hands. The strap that held the lead ring was three inches wide and very heavy, with a lot of coarse stitching done in heavy welting twine. Strong enough even for a dog who could smash through doors.

A car door slammed out front and we heard low chuckles and guffaws coming to us on the cool evening air.

"Out here you guys!" yelled Mary, and the footsteps approached. I was fiddling with a rivet snap on the underside of the big leather strap. The men came around the corner, smoking. They oooh'd and ah'd the new Honda, and ordered drinks. Mary went, and came back with a mineral water for Brian and a Campari for Joe. We all toasted Sam. Then Popeye. We settled back in the redwood lawn furniture.

"Well," groaned Brian tiredly, "so what else is new?"

"This," I said, leaning forward with the leather harness in my hands. I had unsnapped the rivet fastener, which held the folded-back leather upper in place on the underside of the wide top strap. Unfolding this flap revealed another one, done in thin, fine leather, underneath. Snaking my index finger down inside, I realized it concealed a slip wider than a matchbook that ran the length of the big strap. It was like a money-belt slip, only bigger. I felt something in there. I pulled at it, and it slid. Soon we were all staring at the yellowish glow of manila paper. A thin envelope, whose flap I peeled back. Another envelope inside. Glassine. The old heart was thumping away now like a pile driver. I could feel my pulse in my neck. I slid out the gray glassine envelope and looked in. Inside was the slick, smoky-gray sheen of photo film.

"It appears we've just found the hot item," I said.

"Hut damn!" said Sam.

Carefully, I pulled out the filmstrip. Four frames. One of them was a picture photo. The other three appeared to be documents of some kind. I slid the strip back into its casing and stood up.

"I could perhaps make a silly joke and suggest that this could wait till after dinner, but I know where that would get me. Besides, two good men were killed because of this little strip of celluloid. *Shall we?*" I walked toward the kitchen door, and the little ragtag procession followed close at my heels.

22

THE DARKROOM HADN'T BEEN TOTALLY RESTORED SINCE THE
burglary, but it was certainly operational enough to run some
big prints from the negatives. It was obvious to me immediately that the film was not old. If the shots were of old
things, then they were copies, and probably made within the
past five or ten years. After running a test strip I made a big
print of each negative on sixteen-by-twenty-inch Brovira paper. I put the prints into fresh developer, then stop-bath, and
then fixed them. We tried to decipher them in the dim illumination of the safelight but couldn't. Then I took them from
the fixer and put them in the wash tray. I had to stack them
to fit, so we could only see one print at a time. I lit up the
room. The five of us crowded around the wash tank when I
was finished. We looked down at the first of the four big
sheets that lay stacked underwater when I turned on the light.

Well, it was hot all right. It was so hot I'm surprised the
wash water didn't start to simmer. Here's what we saw:

The first print was a photograph of an old letter, written
in longhand and without letterhead, to Frederick Katzmann,
the prosecuting attorney. It was from John Vahey, the attorney for the defense who was later replaced by Fred Moore
and finally by William Thompson. It was Vahey who told
Bartolomeo Vanzetti *not* to take the witness stand in his own
defense for the first crime he was tried for: the attempted

holdup of the White Shoe factory in December 1919. Vahey told Vanzetti, an accomplished orator, that to speak in his own defense would only prejudice the judge and jury against him. Wishing to cooperate, Vanzetti finally agreed. His failure to speak on his own behalf was later mentioned—twice—by Governor Fuller as the single most incriminating piece of evidence in the entire trial. Apparently his special commission agreed with him, and as a result they supported the earlier convictions of the Dedham courtroom. The letter proved beyond any reasonable doubt

- that Vahey, the defense lawyer, and Katzmann, the prosecuting attorney, were in cahoots. No surprise then that they later became law partners.
- that the trial was rigged from the start, with the prosecution and defense planning and executing an entire scenario that would railroad Sacco and Vanzetti straight to the electric chair. This, then, was the origin of the orchestration, the smoke-filled room and the mysterious "third hand" that I had sensed from the moment I began to read the histories of the case.
- that Judge Webster Thayer knew of this cabal and perhaps even had a hand in its formation. The letter was not clear specifically as to the second point, but left no doubt as to the first one.
- finally, that Katzmann and Vahey owed much of their plan's inspiration and execution to a brilliant and energetic young industrialist-lawyer: Joseph Carlton Critchfield.

We read and reread the letter, which was copied in typescript underneath the original photographed copy of the handwritten note. Brian broke the silence with a low whistle.

"Unbelievable! Dynamite, eh? The whole damn thing was rigged. Except I can't believe that stuff about Critchfield. That's hooey. Pure bull."

Joe looked at me quickly. We didn't say anything. We read the next letter. This was typed, and bore the letterhead of Whitney & Steele, a textile firm in Fitchburg, now defunct. The letter was written to a Mr. Lloyd Prill, Katzmann's assistant, and was dated January 23, 1927. It explained that the greatest obstacle to the final conviction of Sacco and Vanzetti, which, as the assistant prosecutor knew, was vital to the interests of American democracy and industry, lay in the broad sympathy the pair of renegades had managed to stir up in the working class. This must be undermined, the author of the letter said, and at the same time the alibis of both men must be discredited. He then proceeded to outline two alternative plans to accomplish these goals. The letter mentioned several other actors in the drama of Dedham by name, among them Brockton Police Chief Stewart; Harry Ripley, the jury foreman who hated Italians; Judge Thayer, who apparently was a close family friend of the letter writer; and others. It was signed by the house counsel for Whitney & Steele: Joseph Carlton Critchfield.

Underneath, instead of a typed copy of the letter, which was unnecessary, were three affidavits from handwriting-analysis institutes in Albany, Paris, and Toronto, stating to Mr. Dominic Santuccio that the signature affixed to the letter matched other specimens known to be those of Mr. Critchfield and that it was genuine. Below these were two notarized statements, one from a museum and one from a laboratory, attesting to the authenticity and age of the letterhead, paper, and typeface.

We stood in silence reading and rereading this second tidbit.

"I still don't buy it," said Brian. "The Critchfield family . . . it's as big as the Adamses, the Lowells, the Peabodys. His grandson's going to be *governor*. Hell, the old man wouldn't be involved in this."

"There's a good reason for you to start buying it, Brian," said Joe. "Just before he died from Sam's bullet, Carmen DeLucca whispered the name of the man who paid him to put the hit on Johnny Robinson and Andy Santuccio. Tell him what Carmen said, Doc."

"He said three words to me: *Old Joe Critchfield*. Then he died. Where does Critchfield live, anyway?"

"I think he's got a big estate up in Danvers or Andover," said Mary. "Someplace like that."

"It's Andover. When they had you locked in the john, DeLucca mentioned that they had nowhere to go, not even Andover. Well Brian?"

Our police chief paced back and forth as if doing a slow waltz step, looking at the floor.

"Hmmmph! I'll be damned. Well, assuming that only part of it's true, it's no wonder old Critchfield wanted the film. I wonder how he knew it even existed, unless Santuccio himself told him. But I wonder why Santuccio didn't make it public."

"We'll never, ever know those answers," said Joe. "In fact, we still don't know the answer to the most important question of all: were Sacco and Vanzetti guilty? We know now that their trial was rigged, their lawyer was crooked, and so on. But we've always suspected that. But were they *guilty*?"

Then we examined the last two prints. One was a typed page. It was not a letter; it was a typed explanation of the photograph, which was the fourth and final frame in the negative strip. And that was the heartbreaker.

The photograph was an old one. It was a street scene in Boston. We could tell it was taken a long time ago by the old landmarks, now gone, and the absence of present-day buildings. Also, of course, we could tell by the clothes the people in the photograph were wearing. It didn't take us long to fix the location: Boston's North End, right along Atlantic Avenue at the Commercial Street intersection, looking northeast across the harbor to East Boston. The warehouses of Battery Wharf were unmistakable. The picture was filled with pedestrians, some faintly blurred because of their walking. A lot of the harbor was visible, including many boats and ships that spouted great black plumes of coal smoke as they headed out to sea or up toward the Mystic and Chelsea river channels. In fact, we soon decided the picture was of the harbor, not the street. Two old tin lizzies were parked along the Atlantic Avenue curb. In the foreground was a group of three men who stood chatting, oblivious of the camera. They were standing quite still, because there was no blur about them. They stood out clear and crisp.

"That's him," said Mary, "on the far right. See? He's holding his derby hat in his right hand."

She was right. There stood Nick Sacco, bare-headed and instantly recognizable, talking with two friends. In his left hand the one nearest the camera, he held a piece of paper that was not newsprint. It appeared to be a picture. If it was, then I knew the tremendous significance of the old photograph, for Sacco's errand to the North End on April 15, 1920, had been to take a family photograph to the Italian consulate as the first step toward applying for passports to Italy. As it turned out, the photo he took to the consulate office was too big. He was turned down, and consequently had no written proof of his visit that day. I explained this to Joe and Brian. Both were slightly skeptical.

"Too pat," said Joe. "That picture was taken from about twenty feet away. Why would anybody do that? And it just so happens that you've got Sacco in the picture, posing, with his passport photo very conveniently displayed. Nah. Sacco was a typical southern Italian type. Somebody got a ringer for him and posed that shot."

"I agree," said Brian. "I'd like to think it was genuine, but I guess I want to know how come a passerby just happened along at just the right time and decided to snap that shot."

"But wait," said Mary. "the shot isn't of the men: they just happened to be in the foreground. The picture is of the harbor. It's a good view too."

We all stared at the scene in silence. Sam's finger went to the very center of the picture and rapped on it.

"What's this?" he asked in a low voice. "What's goin' on here?"

He pointed to a steamboat, bow toward the camera, that was heading for a pier abutting Atlantic Avenue. Directly in the path of the steamer, and broadside to it, was a smaller steam launch. Upon looking more closely, we finally saw what it was that had drawn Sam's sharp eyes. The launch was canted over unnaturally. It was then clear to us that the bigger vessel was in fact colliding with the smaller one, about two hundred yards out in the harbor. And the collision scene, though by no means major, had been sufficient to draw the attention of a sightseer with a camera at hand, for the picture was framed around the two boats. They were the object of the picture, though casual inspection wouldn't reveal it.

"That's one of the old penny ferries," said Joe. "I've seen a lot of pictures of them. They operated between Eastern Avenue in the North End and Lewis Street in East Boston. Fare was only a penny for foot passengers. It was before the Callahan Tunnel was built."

"I *remember* the penny ferries," said Sam. "They were for the working people, the people who worked in the factories . . . it was the only way they could get to their jobs, so they kept the fare low."

"Listen to this," I said, laying out the dripping print of explanatory text on the worktable. I then read aloud to them the following explanation:

This photo was taken on the afternoon of April 15, 1920, by Mr. Louis Perez of Pawtucket, Rhode Island, during a visit to Boston. Mr. Perez's widow claims he was walking down Commercial Street when he came within view of the harbor. Having his camera ready for a panoramic picture, he planned to walk to the water's edge. However, at the intersection of Commercial and Atlantic, just opposite the old ferry landing, he saw that a collision between the ferryboat *Ashburnam*, inward bound from East Boston, and the cargo launch *Grenadier* appeared to be imminent. He took the picture, unaware that Nicola Sacco was standing on a nearby corner talking to his friends Dentamore and Guadagni, who promptly left the scene for a coffeehouse. Unfortunately, they were also unaware of the photographer.

Damage to the vessel *Grenadier* was minor, and the incident, in spite of delaying the *Ashburnam*'s four-minute channel run by eight minutes, was soon forgotten by both crews. However, the Coast Guard, which dispatched the rescue vessel *Felicia* to stand by, recorded the collision as having occurred at approximately 3:26 P.M., April 15, 1920.

I replaced the print into the washing tray with the others. Nobody said anything. Sam went to the tray and picked up the wet print again. He held it up, and I looked over his shoulder at the face of the little dark man holding the picture. He was smiling. He was smiling because he was going on vacation to Italy to see members of his family whom he hadn't seen in years. But at the very instant the shutter was released, Alex Berardelli and Fred Parmenter lay dying on the roadside twelve miles away in South Braintree while the Morelli gang piled into the big touring car and sped away with the loot. And probably at the same instant Bart Vanzetti was sitting on an overturned dory on the beach at North Plymouth, thirty-five miles southeast, talking with Melvin Corl, the Yankee fisherman. They were probably talking politics, workers' rights, socialism, and all the other things that got Bart into trouble. And the events in Braintree would sweep along and engulf these two men who scarcely knew one another, would sweep them along as if they were in a riptide, so that within a month they would find themselves taken off a Brockton trolley car and arrested. And from the police station in Brockton they would follow an inexorable course that ended in the low, rambling, dusky hills of Charlestown, in the prison death house. Ironically, Sacco's ultimate destination lay just outside the photo, to the left.

And it broke my heart.

23

"THING IS," SAID JOE AS HE LUNGED SO HARD INTO AN EGG roll that the cooking oil ran down his big chin, "thing is, we gotta make the thing *stick*." He commenced chewing, and his big soft eyes glazed over in ecstasy.

We sat around a big table in the Yangtze River Restaurant in Lexington. I had just inhaled a tureen of hot-sour soup, an egg roll, won-ton shrimp, and four pork dumplings with hot sesame oil. I had warned my mouth, esophagus, and all parts below that they were in for trouble, then thrown caution to the winds. Nothing beats a good thing like too much of it.

"How?" asked Mary, whose mouth was swollen with Szechuan spicy beef and fried rice.

Joe shook his head like a big bass fighting a hook. The headshake meant that he didn't know, couldn't talk, or both. We were thinking of an airtight way to nail Joseph Carlton Critchfield to the wall, even though he was ninety-two years old.

"His grandson's the active one now," said Brian. "Maybe he's the one we're really after. One thing: we're not going to get anything firm on him because of that letter. It's damning; it'll wreck his rep . . . but it won't put him away."

"We got to get him for killin' Johnny," said Sam.

"I've got a nasty hunch," said Brian, "based on a lot of

experience, that if we don't make it tight on the first pass, he'll slip through the net. He's got too many connections."

"You're dead right," Joe said, rolling up a pancake filled with mu shu pork: He fed the tube into his mouth; it disappeared like a branch into a tree shredder. "I suggest entrapment."

"Isn't that illegal?" I said.

"Yep. I suggest it anyway. Just for openers. All Critchfield now knows are two things. One: nobody's found the incriminating photographs. He therefore has good reason to suspect they'll never be found . . . at least in his lifetime. Two: the thugs—all three of them—who could testify against him are dead, and nobody's come knocking on his door. He thinks he's in the clear. He's finally breathing easy. He's *ready*."

"Count me in, Joe."

"Forget it, Sam. We count you *out*. You're up to your ass in alligators already. You've done your part and we all thank you, but now you've got to be cool. Nope, there's only one logical person to spring the trap."

"Who?" asked Mary.

Joe pivoted around in his chair and leveled a big fat finger at my chest.

"You."

"Oh no."

"Oh yes. You're the only one, Doc."

"Now wait a minute, Joey," said Mary. "Wait just a goddamn min—"

"I know, I know. But listen, the thugs are dead and the evidence is missing. But there's one guy around that if DeLucca did report in to old Critchfield—and we have every reason to think he did—could be a possible threat. And we all know who it is."

Everybody stared at me. I felt like Caesar crossing the forum on the Ides of March.

"But I . . . but I . . ." I protested.

"Not to worry, Doc. Take it easy, Mare," Joe continued,

scooping a pint of sweet-sour pork over a heap of steaming rice. "There's nothing to worry about."

He commenced shoveling in the food, and I felt a little better. I guess. But I had my doubts. After all, the last person he said that to was the late Johnny Rizzo. I felt the first of the gas pains shoot up my rib cage like a napalm rocket, and winced. Mary saw my expression and rubbed my shoulder. She attempted a weak smile.

"Nothing to worry about, Charlie," she said. I stared glumly at the table and asked for the garlic shrimp and snow peas.

"Here you go, pal," said Brian as he handed me the platter. "You're gonna need it."

I peered down at the L-shaped brick-and-stone mansion at the foot of the hill. There was an iron fence all around it, and the tall, ornate gates were closed. In back of the house, enclosed by the L, was a pool, and off to one side a formal French garden. The roof was slate, and heavily gabled. It sure looked like a big house for one old man. But then he wasn't alone; he had his staff too.

A portly black man in a dark uniform came out the back door and walked along a curved gravel path to the garage. He had white hair and carried a leather case. He disappeared into the garage, which was a four-car structure with a sizable apartment over it. It matched the house. Seconds later one of the doors glided up and a Fleetwood brougham limo the size of a boxcar rolled silently out, swung around the house, and eased to a stop in front of the terrace steps. It was the same one I'd seen earlier, at the younger Critchfield's fundraiser on Beacon Hill. The man got out of the car, putting on his cap, then opened the rear door and stood at attention with his white-gloved hand on the door handle. He could have been hewn from stone. It was right out of a movie.

I felt a jabbing at my shoulder and handed the binoculars to my companion, who was also sprawled prone on the granite ledge above the estate on the outskirts of Andover. On the northern horizon we could see the forest of giant smoke-stacks in the city of Lawrence. They were still nowadays; not great white and black plumes of steam rose from them. They were like a forest of dead trees.

"Here comes somebody," said Liatis Roantis, adjusting the focus of the marine glasses. "Looks like the big shot himself."

Without the glasses the two figures descending the front steps of the mansion looked very small, but there was something familiar about the man who accompanied the old man into the limo. Was it his walk, his appearance? What? Before I had a chance to get a look through the glasses, the two men had entered the car and settled themselves in its vast interior. The black chauffeur shut the door and got back behind the wheel. The big car glided around the drive and through the gates—which had swung open, apparently by remote control—and was gone.

Roantis and I sat up. We were within view of the house, but its owner had left. I stood up and stretched. Roantis continued to scan the place.

"We could go in if you want," he said casually.

"Nah. I did that already, up in Lowell. I'm still in trouble for it, too."

"Want me to go alone?"

"No. Joe doesn't even know I contacted you. After he struck out on his entrapment plan with the police brass, he thinks nobody's doing anything to get Old Man Critchfield."

"So he let the brass talk him out of it? Listen, inna army, if I'd done that, me and my men would have died right away."

"Yeah. But Joe's in kind of hot water lately with the brass. For instance, somehow they found out he had a conference with one of the North End Wise Guys. They told him to cool it or else. So I'm going after Critchfield myself."

"Why are you?"

"I just . . . I just want to see the record set straight, I guess."

The old ex-mercenary looked up at me and laughed softly.

"I think you're a little bit like me, Doc. You get bored easy. And when you get bored, you get in trouble."

"Speaking of trouble, you're usually in plenty. You still on probation for that bar fight in the Zone?"

"Yeah. Almost over with. Ahhhh, fuck it," he said, rolling over and sweeping the estate with the 7×50 glasses. "I still say we should go in. Hey, how much are you paying me?"

"Nothing."

"Figured. You know a guy could get rich down in there . . . in less than an hour."

"Don't get any ideas." I looked at my watch. It had stopped. My four-hundred-dollar Blackwatch Chronograph Adventurer had broken. It did everything but tell time. I sighed. "In about ten minutes he'll be at the Holiday Inn desk to pick up the envelope. He'll probably open it and look at the prints in the car on the way back here. I just want to watch his reaction if we can."

"And then what? All you've done is made him mad. And making him go *himself*, that's . . . whaddaya call it? Insult and injury. I think he's gonna be mad at you, Doc. And a guy like that is mean, let me tell you." He swept his arm over the estate below. "Hell, anybody got a spread like that, they're *mean*. Look at me. I'm the meanest guy who ever lived and I don't got diddly-shit."

I grinned at him.

"It's 'cause you're not greedy, Liatis . . . and because you spend all your dough on good booze and bad women."

His eyes crinkled up in laughter. They had a slightly Mongol look to them, and his neck was laced with cords and veins. He looked a little like another Lithuanian, Charles Bronson. Only meaner. He flicked his droopy mustache and lit a cigarette.

"How you know the desk clerk dint open the envelope and spill the beans?"

"Not a chance and you know it. Not the way I sealed it, and not with Critchfield's name on it."

So we waited for another twenty-five minutes until the big black car returned. It was going pretty fast, no doubt at the urging of its irritated occupant. It swung around in front of the steps and the old man and his assistant, who still looked vaguely familiar, stalked up the steps and into the house. The old man appeared to be telling the assistant off. They disappeared.

Then nothing happened for almost another half-hour. Suddenly Roantis, who had the binoculars, punched my arm.

"Look who's coming out," he said. I took the binoculars and saw the old man and his assistant come out on the terrace and sit down in wrought-iron chairs around a table. They seemed to be enjoying the sunshine. The old man, who moved with speed and grace for his age, held a cordless telephone which he dialed and talked into.

"He's getting help," said Roantis. "He's looked at your pictures and now he's calling in the heat. You watch."

"I think he's gonna need it. Question is, what do we do now? The note in the envelope said I'd contact him. I'm wondering how and when."

"No time like the present."

"Did you bring a gun?"

"Nope. Judge told me that I can't carry one while on pro. Said it'd be a year in the slammer if I'm caught with one. Too bad, too. This'd be perfect for my streetcleaner."

"What streetcleaner? I don't see any streetcleaner."

"Not *that* kind of streetcleaner."

"Well what?"

"It's a—*shhhhhhhhh!* Hear that?"

"No. I don't hear anything but the wind."

"Well I thought I heard something like bushes breaking. I think maybe it's too bad I dint bring a gun. Too late I guess."

"Well let's go then," I said.

"What's your hurry? Look, number-two man just went inside. Let's hang around and see what happens."

We watched the man walk into the house. The chauffeur

came out the back door and went into the garage again. Then nothing happened for about ten minutes; the old man on the terrace continued to speak into the cordless telephone. Occasionally he got up from the wrought-iron chair and paced the terrace, then sat again. The middle garage door swung up and an enclosed Jeep crept out. It went slowly along the gravel drive and took a fork that led around behind the house, where it disappeared momentarily, then came back in sight, going a bit faster now, and returned to the main drive and left the estate. We watched it till it disappeared, then turned our attention back to the mansion below. After twenty minutes I was getting bored, and said so.

"Yeah, but we've got to wait and watch. Pretty soon now something's gonna happen and—"

Schlick-schlick.

The sound startled us, coming from directly behind. And neither one of us liked the sound. Not a bit. We turned and found ourselves looking down the business end of a shotgun. The guy who was holding it was old Mr. Critchfield's assistant. How he got out of the house and up on the rock behind us I had no idea. Not at first, anyway. And now, twenty feet away from him instead of three hundred, I knew why he had looked so familiar even at a distance. I could now see the thick glasses. And he'd put on the trenchcoat, too.

It was my old friend from the mill who'd smacked Mary down. The guy who'd clobbered me up in Lowell. It was the guy with the heavily starched lapels.

"Move back . . . all the way back," he said, jerking the muzzle at us. We did, until we were right at the cliff's edge and in full view of the house. Without lifting his eyes from us he waved his arm in a high, slow arc. I looked down and saw old Critchfield give a responsive wave, then bring something up to his face. He was watching through binoculars.

"Well, Doctor, I didn't know you had a friend with you. All we could see was *you* from inside . . . and we were careful never to gaze up in your direction when you could see us. Who is he?''

I explained that Mr. Roantis was an old dentist friend of mine. Lapels gave him the once-over and decided he was harmless. Certainly, at five-eight and slightly gray and pudgy, Roantis didn't look like an expert in practically every exotic form of fighting and defense ever devised. That he could kill people with his earlobes usually went unnoticed.

"Please don't point the gun, sir," said Roantis with a pant. "I can't stand it. I'll faint and fall off . . . *please!*"

"Then don't move," said Lapels, approaching me. He held the shotgun cradled in his right hand while he fished in the pocket of his trenchcoat. That coat was a regular bag of tricks. He took out a thin leather sap. It was a spring-loaded sapper with a leather-covered steel ball at either end. He waggled it in his left hand and it flicked back and forth fast on its springy steel shaft. It made a whirring, whistling sound like the wings of a mourning dove. I didn't like it.

"I owe you pain," he whispered, and swung it.

There was a little high whistle and a stab of pain on the point of my elbow. It shot up my arm, up the side of my face to the top of my head. I heard the whistle again and felt the snapper strike my right collarbone. The pain was deep, and traveled through my bones to my chest, my right shoulder, and my lower jaw. The whistle again, and Lapels had reached low and struck my left knee. He hit it hard, and the left leg gave way in a wave of agony. It felt as though my bones were breaking. I sucked air through clenched teeth.

"Please don't! That's enough!" pleaded Roantis, a look of horror on his face.

"Quiet, short stuff, or you'll get it too."

The little truncheon continued to whistle and snap at me like a trained serpent. And Lapels had studied his perverted craft. He knew exactly where to strike so the steel would hit bone and nerve bundles and send the pain into the center of my neural pathways until I was aglow with hurt. He finally tapped me almost delicately on the tip of my jaw, and the world grew fuzzy. Noises were distant, and there was the sound of rolling surf in my poor hurt head.

"That should slow you down, Adams. If I had anything to say about it, I'd kill you here and now. Now let's go, both of you. Mr. Critchfield's waiting."

Lapels walked behind us, the big smoothbore aimed at our kidneys. It would have made me nervous if I hadn't been so woozy already. The sap had taken the tar out of me all right. I could barely walk. Roantis, his pride no doubt injured at having been outfoxed by a common thug, stomped on ahead of me, his hands shoved deep into his Windbreaker's pockets, looking at the ground and saying nothing. We passed my parked Scout, then the Jeep. It was obvious to me now how he'd gotten the drop on us. The chauffeur brought the Jeep around behind the house, out of our line of sight. It had stopped there momentarily for the chauffeur to get out and Lapels, with his smoothbore, to climb in. He'd left the estate, doubled back up the dirt road, then crept up on us. One thing was becoming more and more apparent to me: Old Man Critchfield was smart and tough. And he had help that was utterly loyal and brutal.

After we passed the vehicles we walked down a steep and twisty path, and it was there that Roantis fell down. It happened so fast that I almost stumbled over him. He had tripped over a root and fallen flat on his face. He'd fallen hard because we were going downhill. I regained my balance and leaned over him. He didn't move. He had covered his head with his hands, and was moaning. I noticed one strange thing: his watchband had been turned inside out.

"Get away," said Lapels. I stood ten feet away, swaying back and forth to keep upright. I wasn't faking. Lapels held the shotgun at Roantis and kicked him in the legs. More whimpering from Roantis, whose hands went down under his face for a pillow.

"It's broken," he wailed. "I think I broke my ankle. Please don't kick . . . ."

Lapels listened to his whining and whimpering with a disgusted look. Then Roantis tried to get up several times, but each time he fell back on his stomach.

"Want me to help?" I asked. Lapels told me to shut up and stay where I was. I watched him kick and prod Roantis, finally grow impatient, and reach down and grab the prone man by the back of his jacket collar and heave.

Wrong move.

We walked single file through the gates of the Critchfield estate. Roantis was right behind me, and Lapels followed, holding the gun on both of us as before. The gatekeeper–gardener, a husky chap of Hispanic heritage, watched our little parade closely to make certain nothing was amiss. Lapels nodded at him and he closed and locked the gate behind us.

We were in there now, and couldn't get out. We climbed up the stone terrace steps to the huge oak door. The old black chauffeur opened it and let us in.

"Bring them in here, Lundt!" cried a shrill and imperious voice.

24

"AND SO YOU SEE, DOCTOR ADAMS, WHEN I TOOK LUNDT'S advice on the hiring of DeLucca, I really had no idea of the kind of man he was. I needed someone sufficiently schooled in violence to make the point, you see . . . but I admit I got way more than I had bargained for. I assure you I have fully apprised Mr. Lundt of my displeasure at the choice."

The old man glared across the wide room at his assistant, whose eyes lowered under the withering gaze. He still had the shotgun across his knees, but he seemed intimidated by the old codger nonetheless.

The room was huge, with an ornate plaster ceiling, leaded windows, oak wainscoting, and a gigantic Tabriz rug which extended the entire length of the room underneath the over-stuffed furniture. We could have been in a castle in Scotland instead of a big house on the outskirts of a New England mill town.

I looked steadily at old Critchfield. He was dressed in a wool suit and vest. He looked the part. He was old, no doubt of it. The white hair was almost gone; the flesh had left the beaky face. A big blood vessel stood out like a piece of twine on his high, bony forehead. His chin and neck were bags of saggy wrinkles and liver-splotched skin. And yet there was the look of vitality, of tremendous strength and will in the face and eyes, which twinkled bright blue beneath the bushy white eyebrows. He glared in my direction, a look of self-satisfaction, even hauteur, in his intense eyes. I glared right back at him.

"Your story doesn't impress me one bit," I said. "You say Andrea Santuccio was blackmailing you with the photographs. I frankly find that hard to believe."

"Then believe what you like," he snapped. "I can't stand impertinence. It is true. As I told you, he claimed he wanted to use the money for some rehabilitation project in that North End neighborhood. Likely story. He made some asinine statement that I owed his people some sort of reparation."

"And you don't think you do? You don't feel any guilt at all for helping railroad Sacco and Vanzetti into the electric chair?"

"I didn't railroad anyone. I was an adviser to the prosecution. An able one too, I might add. Many of us who were perhaps less emotionally swayed by the immigrant community's appeals for socialism saw the grave danger that these men, and all like them, posed to capital investment and free enterprise. This ignorant, superstitious, and ill-mannered peasantry! Effluvium of Europe! Flotsam and jetsam washed upon our shores! How *dare* they seek refuge and plenty here, then proceed to denounce the very source of their newfound security and freedom as unjust? How *dare* they? My God, Adams, you're a dunce!"

I was about to rise from my chair and go over and smack him one. I wondered what Mary would have done to him. I shuddered at the thought, and remained seated. I had to remember that we were prisoners in Critchfield's mansion.

"The picture you see before you, which shows Sacco standing in front of the penny ferry in the North End, proves he was innocent. An innocent man was executed. That means nothing to you?"

"It was unfortunate. Many innocent people die every day. It is the nature of the world we live in. It isn't good, but it's all we have. Now Sacco and Vanzetti: two men who dodged the draft and avoided the First World War by fleeing to Mexico, and who at the time of their arrest were armed and carrying literature denouncing the nation that had fed and clothed them far better than their native Italy ever did. Do I feel sorry for them? Not on your life, Doctor. I did not and to this day I *do* not," he shouted, and sat back with a smirk.

"Very well. There then remains a more recent transgression: the murders of John Robinson and Andrea Santuccio. Hear me, Critchfield: I said *murders*. You're the primary accessory before the fact. You're in on it. Up to your wrinkly old ass. And I'll tell you what. I'm going to see you spend your last days not here, in this fancy place, but in a cell six feet by ten, with all those other 'dregs' like Sacco and Vanzetti. How do you like that?"

Well, you should have seen the old buzzard. It was as if I'd hit him between the eyes with a splitting maul. He sat bolt upright on the couch and looked daggers at me with a purple face. He shouted to Lundt to strike me across the face. Lundt remained seated not moving a muscle. Critchfield turned his stare at him. He looked at Lundt, then at the shotgun, then back at Lundt.

"Did you hear me?" he squealed at Lundt.

"Yeah I heard. No."

"Get out. You're *terminated*!"

But still Lundt sat, the shotgun across his knees, and now he glared back at the old man. Then the old man, beside himself with rage, got up off the couch, came over to me, and slapped me. It hurt more than I thought it would. For a guy over ninety, old Critchfield was in good shape.

I stood up slowly and took hold of his right wrist, which I bent back and around in what police call the "come-along" grip, and led him back to his couch. He was a little bent over by the pain, but that didn't stop him from trying to kick me twice. I had to give him one thing: old Critchfield had grit. It was easy for me to see how he'd become so rich and powerful.

I returned to my chair and watched him stare at Lundt. Then he pushed a button on the end table, and almost immediately the black man appeared. He was wearing a white coat.

"I'll have my tea now, Geoffrey," Critchfield growled, never taking his eyes from the man with the shotgun. The chauffeur seemed momentarily to go limp, then recovered. He looked imploringly at his boss.

"Mr. Critchfield, I—"

"*Now*, Geoffrey!"

The man stood motionless for perhaps five seconds before he turned and left. I saw him grab his forehead.

"You want a murderer, Doctor Adams?" said the old man, pointing across the room. "There he sits. DeLucca was *his* friend, not mine. I provided the cash to hire. That is *all*. As I told you, it was not my intention to kill Santuccio . . . just to threaten him and get the film back. I certainly did not wish to kill the other man. *He's* the one you want."

He pointed at Lundt, who sat still. The only person more immobile than the assistant was Roantis, who sat like stone, hands in pockets, looking down at the rug.

"DeLucca and that psychotic associate of his," continued the old man in a tired, gravelly voice. "The one who would get the fits whenever there was a chance to hurt someone. He was the one who performed the unpleasantness on Santuccio. Although I must say he deserved it—trying to extort money from an event fifty years old. Really!"

I watched him with a little pity. No doubt Critchfield gauged everyone and everything by the yardsticks of power and wealth. Accordingly, he showed no compassion, nor did he expect any. He did not believe it existed. It seemed to me that the world of old Joseph Carlton Critchfield was bleak indeed.

"You don't think you should bear any responsibility for—" I began.

"*Don't be an ass, Doctor Adams!* My God, I would hate to entrust my health to the likes of you! Don't tell me what I *should* or *should not* do. Look around you. This property is but one percent of my net worth. I have liquid assets totaling twenty-three million and real property and industrial equities totaling twice that. I have houses all over the globe. I'm rich. I didn't get where I am listening to people telling me what I *should* do, for God's sake.''

Geoffrey entered with a big silver tea tray laden with a tea service for one and a big basket of rolls wrapped in white linen. Critchfield filled his teacup and sipped. Then he drew back the linen and looked at the rolls in the basket. He picked up the basket as if to take one, then set it down again.

"Very good, Geoffrey. That will do."

The chauffeur bowed slightly. I saw the shine of perspiration on his upper lip and forehead. He departed quickly.

"I have my own set of rules, as you shall see," the old man continued. "It may interest you to know that I still work—hard—four hours a day in this room. I swim half a mile a day, and walk four. I work out with dumbbells. I am in better health and shape than most men of fifty. As greedy as you no doubt think me, I do give to charities, and to political funds too."

"That would be the Genghis Khan Memorial Foundation, I presume?"

"I do not find that amusing, Doctor. I think you should show greater awareness of your current predicament as trespassers on my property. I was about to add that I am *clever*. But perhaps even you don't need that explained, seeing that I managed to capture you in your sneak-thievery and have you delivered here."

"You'd have me take the fall wouldn't you?" said Lundt, staring at the old man. "You'd have me take the whole damn rap wouldn't you?"

"Considering my family's immediate plans, it is impossible that these photographs be brought to light just now," Critchfield continued, ignoring his assistant. He picked up a remote-control device and switched on the big television that stood against the far wall. It was hooked up to a VCR video recorder, and showed a tape of a recent debate between Joseph Critchfield III, whose fund-raiser Mary and I had attended, and the incumbent governor. We watched only the last few minutes of the debate, in which it was clear that Critchfield had run rings around the Democrat, who looked increasingly flustered and helpless in the onslaught of Critchfield's well-chosen words, memorable phrases, and awesome grasp of facts and events. The younger Critchfield ended his remarks with these words: "And so, in light of these pressing problems that now seem to engulf our great Commonwealth, I feel a deep and personal conviction that it is time for new leadership in Massachusetts. Accordingly, and in line with the Critchfield family tradition of public service and service to the Commonwealth of Massachusetts, I declare my candidacy and fitness for the gubernatorial office of this great state. Thank you.''

The crowd cheered and carried on, waving signs and placards. The camera switched to a pretty blonde news correspondent, who said: "If this debate has proved anything, it is that forty-six-year-old Joseph Carlton Critchfield III is an astute and able contender. For if there were a winner in this debate, most would agree that the spoils of victory would go to Critchfield, who now faces Democratic challenger George Pappas of Saugus as well as the incumbent. Tonight we'll have a special report on the Critchfield family, an illustrious clan whose wealth and political power have so long held sway over—''

Click.

Old Critchfield sat back and sighed softly.

"God knows they need him. Haven't had a Republican in since Frank Sargent.'' He turned to me and raised his bushy eyebrows. "I'm not sure whether Santuccio knew of my grandson's political plans. There have been rumors for some time. In any event, he certainly picked an opportune time to try and put the squeeze on us. Well, you now see why I absolutely cannot permit the pictures and this distasteful business up in Lowell to become public. I'm sure, Doctor Adams, if you have any sense of public duty, you'll agree.''

"I don't agree. I don't agree at all. That's the same weak

ploy Nixon tried. It didn't work because it *shouldn't* have worked. It won't work now for the same reason. Those negatives will be in the hands of newspapers before the week's out. And you'll be indicted for murder one. Better pack your toothbrush, pal.''

He glared at me again, started to rise, thought better of it, and shrank back onto the couch. The bright eyes glowed bluish-white, like acetylene torches.

"You said you'd make a *deal*,'' he hissed.

"Wrong,'' I said. "The note said I wanted to talk about it. I still do. But the story's coming out. And soon.''

Critchfield turned to Lundt. His mouth turned down in a scowl. He seemed to ignore Roantis, who appeared to be asleep. Then a faint smile played on his lips. He took a roll from the basket on the tea tray, broke it, and set it down on the silver. He turned to me again.

"Thank God I had the cleverness and foresight not to trust you, Adams.'' He chuckled. "In addition to keeping your attention while you were up on the cliffside, my phone conversations on the terrace had another purpose.''

"Aw don't tell us,'' I said, holding up my hand. "We already know, don't we, Liatis? Old Critchfield's hired some more thugs to come burn our feet with cigarettes and stick knives in us so we won't release the photos. Right, Critchfield?''

"Wrong.'' He grinned impishly. "I called my pilot in Lawrence and told him to fuel the Lear jet and stand by for a possible business excursion. The aircraft has a significant range, Doctor Adams. There are several secluded stops I have in mind for you and your friend here. None is in the United States. You will remain there, your whereabouts unknown to your family, until after the election.''

"They'll know who took us,'' I said.

"I don't think so. If approached, I shall deny everything. I know you came here alone because Lundt, in one of his rare moments of mental lucidity, checked the approaches to these grounds carefully before surprising you up there.''

He looked away from me long enough to remove another roll from the basket and break it. He bit at one half quickly, then set it down on the tray with the other one.

"I am a realist, if nothing else," he continued. "I know I haven't long to live, despite my personal regimen. I wouldn't have cared a fig if Santuccio had released those papers if it weren't for Joe and the race. Not a fig. I also don't care if people come nosing around here after you're gone. I don't even care if they lock me up, which they won't. But I will not allow that film to get out."

"It's beyond our control. The *Globe*'s already got it," I lied.

"That's a lie," he said, taking another roll from the basket. "In a few minutes, when my pilot calls back and tells me the Lear jet is ready and at the proper place on the airfield, my staff will escort both of you to my limousine and thence to the Lawrence Municipal Airport, where you will be taken aboard the aircraft."

He looked up at Lundt again while his hands fumbled in the breadbasket. "I don't know if Mr. Lundt feels up to joining you or not—"

"*Not,*" said Lundt, his upper lip curling in a sneer. "You'd try to pin the whole rap on me wouldn't you?"

"And why not? You disobeyed my instructions completely. I did not pay to have anyone murdered. If the law comes here, I'm afraid you'll have to speak for yourself."

"You said *use any means necessary*." Lundt unconsciously raised the gun slightly.

Critchfield stared at him, like a judge passing sentence. He was holding up the edge of the linen that had been wrapped around the rolls. We couldn't see his other hand. I stood up.

"Liatis!"

Roantis was already in the air, leaping toward the old man on the couch. But the ancient, liver-spotted hand was raised, and the small black automatic in it spat flame. Lundt grabbed his chest and jumped up, and the small pocket gun spat again.

In a reflex action Lundt jerked the trigger on the pump gun. It clicked. We knew it would. He shucked the action fast and snapped the trigger again. Empty. Then there was a loud splat as Roantis smacked Critchfield's hand with the sap. The old man sat there on the couch and screamed bloody murder. He held his hurt hand and bawled. Roantis seized the little pistol and emptied it. I examined Lundt, who was now down on the floor. He had taken two slugs. Critchfield sat moaning on the couch like a giant, cadaverous infant. He jabbed at the button on the end table and shouted for Geoffrey, who was nowhere to be seen.

I did what I could for Lundt, who had shoulder and chest wounds. Roantis took a big revolver out of his coat, wiped it off carefully, and handed it to me. It had been Lundt's. He'd taken it when he'd taken the sap. He couldn't be caught with it now. As I walked to the phone at the far end of the huge room I looked out the window and saw the big Caddy glide down the driveway. Geoffrey was at the wheel. He still had his white jacket on. He looked like a dining-car waiter. I heard him call to the Hispanic guard at the gate and motion him over to the car window. The guard stuck his head inside for a second, looked back at the house, then ran around to the passenger side and got in. The big limo spun out of the gate on two wheels.

I picked up the phone.

25

I WAS OUT THERE ON THE PORCH AGAIN, STANDING UNDER the ceiling fan and listening to a Jimmy Rushing tape. A pair of robins were hopping and clucking on the lawn. Joe's unmarked cruiser swung onto the gravel turnaround and he and Sam came up the walk. I went into the kitchen and checked the standing rib roast. I told Mary the guests had started to arrive, poured her some red, and made silver bullets for the three of us. When I came back, old Mr. Five-by-Five was belting out: "Every-day, every-day, every-day, every-day, I *have* the blues—"

"Ain't he a killah?" said Sam, looking up at the speakers.

"How's the new man working out?"

"Doc, he's great, lemme tell you. Big and rough and gentle. He rides my old bike. Oh yeah. And that foxy mama he's got, that Loretta . . . mmmmmmm-*mmmm*."

"Good. Well, you can thank Moe Abramson for both of them."

"*And* me," said Joe.

Brian showed up, and then Moe, who brought ginger beer, tofu, and bean sprouts. We almost threw him out. He was delighted that Loretta was settling in. I was worried about her past and told Mary so. But she'd eyed Amos Railford— the Jamaican recently incarcerated in the Dedham jail, until Joe and Moe sprung him—and said his past wasn't so rosy either. She also took a long look at his body and then said she doubted that he was a virgin, so maybe it didn't matter about what poor Loretta had done in her past.

Roantis showed up toting a strange bundle. He asked to use my workshop for a few minutes and I let him down there. When he didn't show, we all went down and found him standing at my reloading bench, running patches through the ugliest-looking pump gun I'd ever seen. I guess the two cops didn't know Roantis was on probation. I said nothing.

"What the hell is *that*?" asked Brian.

"My streetcleaner. Needs cleaning. Pass the oil."

Schlick, schlick. He worked the action on the old piece with the shortened barrel and black friction tape wrapped around the stock.

"I don't think that's a dove gun, Liatis."

"Nope."

The piece was about as handsome as Godzilla.

"Tell me, Roantis," said Joe, "how'd you ever get the drop on that guy Lundt anyway? All I heard was he crept up behind you on that cliff and surprised you, then marched you down the hill. What happened?"

"I'll tell you," I said. "Roantis tripped and fell flat on his face. I didn't know he had faked it; that's how real it looked. So I went and bent over him until Lundt approached and waved me off. The only strange thing I noticed was that Roantis's watchband was turned inside out. Show them, Liatis.

Roantis flipped his expansion band around so that the back of his watchcase showed. It was stainless steel polished to a mirror finish.

"See that? He'd done that before he fell down. When Lundt came and stood over him with the shotgun, Liatis could see his every move. Then, jerk that he was, Lundt reached down and grabbed Liatis's collar and tried to yank him up to his feet. It was the last move he got in, 'cause our friend here struck like a swamp adder. Before old Lundt even hit the ground for the first time Roantis had taken the shotgun and tossed it to me. From then on I had Lundt covered, as if I needed to. Mr. Roantis here, though he can be uncouth at times, moves with surprising grace and speed, don't you, Liatis? Sort of the Rudolph Nureyev of violence.''

The short man with the droopy mustache grinned and put a dab of Gunslick in the receiver.

''Well, during the next thirty seconds or so Mr. Lundt did not have a very good time. He spent of lot of it airborne, and the landings weren't pleasant. It was over pretty quickly. It was silent too, except for the grunts, cracks, and thumps made by poor Lundt. Liatis put on quite a display—all at Lundt's expense. So when he was softened up sufficiently— Liatis had removed the sap and the pistol early on—we stood him up, brushed him off, and made him carry the emptied shotgun behind us as we went through the gate to Old Man Critchfield's estate. There we went, up those terrace steps and into the huge living room. And all the time Critchfield was convinced Lundt had us covered.''

''Let's get another drink,'' said Roantis, stifling a yawn. We went upstairs. I remembered that just before we stood Lundt back on his feet after Roantis had finished with him, I ran my fingers down the lapels of his trenchcoat. Each one had two pounds of lead shot sewn inside thin leather bags. The old Parisian policeman's trick: buckshot sewn in the cape. Swing the cloth around and you put out people's lights. Roantis had marveled at it, saying it was funny. I had said it was funny all right. A regular riot . . .

Roantis put his streetcleaner back under the rear seat of his old sedan and joined us on the porch. The irony was that he'd become friends with Lundt, who turned out to be another former mercenary. Figured. In fact, Roantis had just come back from visiting Lundt in the hospital. He was going to pull through, thanks mostly to those teeny-weeny slugs. When he'd come to he'd turned on old Critchfield like a cornered bobcat. He'd sung like a bird, and said all kinds of bad things about the old geezer. So the old man hired a superb legal team and railed on and on about treachery, betrayal, socialism, and everything else until he developed a severe headache. An hour later he collapsed, and three hours after that he was dead of a massive "cerebral vascular accident." So time had finally caught up with him, as it does with everyone.

The funeral was very small, although Joseph Carlton Critchfield hadn't planned it that way. Not even the household staff showed up. And nobody ever found a trace of Geoffrey, the Hispanic guard, or the big Caddy. They just went away and never came back. The following day Joe III announced he was withdrawing from the gubernatorial race because of his grandfather's "tragic death." Mary said it was a crock of shit, just like everything else about the family.

I guess I felt a little sorry for Joseph Carlton Critchfield III. He seemed a capable guy, and might have made a decent governor. I doubt if he knew anything about his grandfather's implication in the trial of the 1920s. But he sure paid the price all right; as things stood, he couldn't have won a race for county pencil sharpener.

He declined comment on the Sacco–Vanzetti papers, which had made the front page from coast to coast. Well, he might have declined comment, but the North End went wild. It made the Feast of St. Anthony's celebration look like a warm-up. They danced and sang in the streets for three days and nights, and erected a bronze tablet to Nick and Bart right at the old dock on Eastern Avenue where the penny ferry used to land.

We had a nice meal and a great party afterward, with the two offspring, Jack and Tony, joining in. As the festivities drew to a close I confided to them that I had bought tickets for them too. We were to leave in two days for three weeks abroad.

Later, after everyone had left, Mary and I sat alone on the couch. She was on my lap. Her hair smelled nice. She looked at the Mickey Mouse watch on my wrist. The thugs had stolen the Omega when they beaned me up in Lowell.

"Where's your fancy black watch?" she asked.

"Oh. That damned Blackwatch Chronograph Adventurer broke on me. You believe it? I wore it to the Critchfield house with Roantis so I'd be prepared, and the goddamned thing stopped."

"Serves you right. Gee, it's great the boys will be going with us, Charlie. Wow!" She kissed me and patted my thigh.

"Mary, I have a confession to make. After the past month—what's happened and all, and considering the nature of it—I'm kind of overdosed. You know?"

"What do you mean?"

"Well, when I bought the kids' tickets, I made some, uh, changes in the destination. Hope you don't mind."

"*Changes?* Then where are we going?"

"Norway."

The jumbo 747 jet sat back on its tail and climbed. I saw the JFK runways fall away beneath us as we approached the harbor. Then we would make a buttonhook to the north and head back out over the ocean. We'd come down for the flight the previous day and visited the Tall Ships. Some appeared below us now. We all leaned toward the windows.

A blonde SAS stewardess got up from her safety harness and slowly walked the aisle, checking everybody's seat belts. Mary stared up at her, looking daggers. She has a thing about blondes. She doesn't like them. I think, for some strange reason I cannot understand, she is afraid of them.

"I dunno Charlie. Norway's pretty and all . . . and clean. God knows it's clean. But it's boring. God, how am I going to take three weeks of it? Three weeks of hot cocoa and trolls?"

"I need it, Mary. I need it like the roses need the rain. I need blonde and boring. I need people whose idea of a great meal is hard bread, smoked fish, and turnips. I need people who've never heard of Sacco and Vanzetti or the Cosa Nostra. I need *Lutherans*, Mary. I do. I need people who eat a crumb cake with powdered sugar and think they're sinning."

She sighed and looked down at the harbor.

"But I have another surprise too. If you look at the tickets, you'll see."

"Venice! Oh Charlie, when? The last three days?"

"Yep. I just couldn't stand it. I figure I'll be fully decompressed by then. We're staying at the Paganelli. We've got the same room, Toots, facing the lagoon."

Well, that made it perfect. I knew it would. Just then we banked and began the turn north to head back out over the ocean. And down below us, looking like somebody's doll, was that lady with the book and the torch, standing on her own little piece of turf. Tugs and ferryboats left white wakes all around her. You cannot look at her and not get a lump in your throat.

"Ohhh Charlie . . . she's so beautiful. My dad—"

"I know."

I looked at Mary. Her big brown eyes were very wet. When she finally spoke it was to the statue, and she talked in a heavy whisper I could barely hear.

"Be right back," she said. *"Don't go away!"*

About the Author

RICK BOYER currently lives in Asheville, North Carolina. BILLINGSGATE SHOAL was the winner of the Edgar for the Best Mystery Novel of the Year, 1982. The Doc Adams series continues with THE PENNY FERRY, THE DAISY DUCKS, MOSCOW METAL, and THE WHALE'S FOOTPRINTS.